Dedication

This book is dedicated first and foremost to God, without whom I most definitely would not be here. Thank you for giving me the strength to do this, I never knew that I could.

I also dedicate this book to someone who will only be known as 'S'. This is one of my ways of saying thank you for everything you've done and still continue to do. I know I can be crazy sometimes, annoying sometimes and even downright stubborn, but guess what? At some point, everything you ever told me in order to help me succeed got through. You knew my potential and I guess all the sleepless nights weren't in vain. No matter what happens from here on out, I just wanna let you know that you gave me the power to dream, the vision to think big, the ability to aim high and courage to never accept the word 'defeat' or 'second best'...I hope you're proud of me because I'm so proud of you. You are amazing; the world just doesn't know it yet. That's why you will always be my special friend.

Finally, how could I forget about my girls Lady J and Madame P? The diva train is about to ride out...are you with me ladies? Woot, woot!

Lady Lynxx

Acknowledgments

I would like to say thanks to a lot of people for helping me with this book. I will always say thanks to God first and foremost. My life could have turned out a lot worse than it has and I know that you have been guiding me every step of the way. I would next like to thank my family for being so supportive and putting up with me during this new journey that I have taken. I'm sorry for all those nights I spent on my laptop being very anti-social and engrossed in my book. You all really showed me the true meaning of 'family' and I love each and every one of you dearly! Your support can never be repaid in monetary terms and for that I will forever be grateful.

A huge thank you to the amazing and wonderful ladies of the BHM forums who have been a tremendous source of help and encouragement to be from the beginning of all this writing stuff! Special thanks go out to the Nigerian ladies on the forum who gave me some very useful links about their traditions and customs; they were invaluable! I love you ladies (and the few gents) you are the best virtual cheerleaders a girl could ever have!
Another big thanks goes to all my peeps on thisis50.com for all your comments, helpful publishing links and copyright information, you are a very special group of people indeed.
I really appreciate everybody's support for my writing; it warms my heart every time someone posts a comment, and usually positive ones at that. Without your support, I probably would not have continued to write, talk less of completing a whole novel!

Also, I thank all of my friends who have supported me, even though you hadn't even read anything I written yet. You had faith in me even when I didn't even have that much faith in myself!
A final thank you goes out to all the authors that have provided me endless hours of entertainment over the years. Just look what you have inspired, and I hope you all enjoy my humble efforts.

The Ambassador's Daughter

The Ambassador's daughter

A Lady Lynxx Novel

Chapter 1

Ophelia loved to ride horses. It wasn't a common past-time for most young black girls, but Ophelia wasn't any ordinary black girl. Kemi Ophelia Regina Emeka-Phillips was the only daughter of Nigerian Ambassador to the United States of America, Dr Jonathan Emeka-Phillips. Her love for horses had developed over the years as a result of attending some of the best boarding schools around the world. She had studied in France, England and Switzerland amongst others, and this privilege allowed her to perfect an extravagant pastime such as horse-riding.

Ophelia's passion for riding wasn't as innocent as her parents thought. As an ambassador's daughter, she was followed by security or adult supervision every where she went and frustratingly, even at 18 years of age her daddy still treated her as if she were a baby. Her horses gave her the freedom that she craved so much and once she got into a gallop, she knew nobody could really follow her.
It was around six o'clock in the morning and she had already saddled Lucky up; the beautiful animal was to be her designated horse for the

7

next few weeks. He was a mahogany colored stallion that had been kindly lent to her by the owner of the Texas ranch that her family were vacationing at. The Emeka-Phillips family had been invited there for the Easter holidays as guests one of her father's old friends; not that Ophelia had been given any choice where she was going in the first place.

Upon mounting Lucky, she started a canter down the lane and headed for the woodland up ahead; as they cleared the landscaped grounds, Ophelia skilfully guided the graceful beast into a gallop. The faster they went, the more aroused she was getting and in turn, the vibrations from each gallop pushed her little pussy closer and closer to the point of orgasm. Just as they were coming up to the lake, Lucky leapt over some shrubs and that eventually pushed her over the edge.

When she finally came at last, Ophelia cried out loudly in ecstasy. No one would hear her cry anyway, she was sure that they were very much alone.

Ophelia tied Lucky up to a tree by the lakeside; this way the horse could take a rest and have a drink without her having to worry about him running off. As the day broke, she sat down at the base of an adjacent tree and opened up her legs then gently took off her jodhpurs and panties. The horse ride had got her really horny, so she licked the middle finger of her left hand and began to slide it in and out of her wetness. At her age, she still hadn't tasted a man yet so this was the best she was going to get at moment; *a chance would be a fine thing* she often thought.

After expertly caressing her g-spot with her fingers, she added to her excitement by massaging her cilt with her right hand and then began to synchronize her right hand with the left finger that was inside her; she then threw her head back to savour the moment. Ophelia knew that this technique never failed to give her the most mind-blowing orgasms.

As she continued to touch herself, Ophelia fantasized about her favourite fantasy man *'Greenback'*; he was the hottest gangster rapper of the moment, and she found his body oh so sexy. Her vivid thoughts of him only made her come faster; she could just imagine him on top of her, pushing his dick inside and roughly taking her virgin pussy. Ophelia moaned softly at the thought, and as her imagination ran wild, she reached her second orgasm of that morning; the thought of how the creamy the spunk oozing out of his dick would look like was the most delicious.

Suddenly out of nowhere, somebody spoke;
'Looks like you need some help down there, don'tcha'.
As she looked up, a caramel skinned young man looked down at her; he reminded her of a younger Terrance Howard only stockier and without the green eyes. Ophelia recognized him as Sonny, one of the ranch stable hands; at that very moment she realised that she'd been followed.

'Oh my gosh…what are you doin' here! Just you wait till I tell my daddy!' exclaimed Ophelia like the spoiled little princess that she was;
'I don't think so hun…are you also gonna explain to ya daddy that you were friggin' yourself out here in the open?' Sonny laughed
'Somehow I don't think so'
That seemed to shut her up; as she looked him up and down she noticed that he had something that was long and stiff protruding thru his pants between his legs.
'I see you've been watching me for a while…do you wanna help me out then?' she said brazenly and gestured for him to come down to her level. Ophelia desperately wanted to find out what sex was really like and was fed up of having to watch porn on the internet to get her kicks. After a few split seconds of thought, she decided there and then that Sonny may as well be the one to take her v-card. Inwardly, she knew that he wouldn't tell a soul.

Ophelia put her hand on his crotch and rubbed his hard dick up and down desperately, 'Please Sonny…I wanna see it….I wanna suck it' she begged;

He didn't need telling twice and quickly took his pants down so that his stiffy could break free; Ophelia then sprang forward towards Sonny on her knees and took him into her mouth. She had seen the porn stars online do it a hundred times before so she went at him like a pro; in her attempt to 'deep-throat' him, Ophelia choked and gagged a little. Sonny shuddered and grunted at the feeling; her eager little hands also added to his arousal;

'Yeah baby, I wanna feel the back of your throat…suck me you little cunt…suck my cock!' said Sonny raspily;

Ophelia obliged and sucked him in harder, feeling both powerful and amazing at the same time.

Sonny wasn't the type of guy to come from head alone so after a while, he had to switch up the game a little; he took his cock out of her mouth and pushed her onto her back, simultaneously parting her firm muscular thighs. He then slid a thick finger into her little pink hole; to his delight the pink contrasted sharply with her dark chocolate skin tone and the shape of it was similar to that of a rare Orchid. He became even more excited at the discovery that she was pretty tight; Ophelia winced as he shoved his finger deeper and as he mounted her she realised that he was about to loosen her up a bit

She braced herself for what was about to come…*how the hell is the size of his shaft supposed to fit into me*? she thought. Of course since Sonny wasn't aware that she was a virgin, he pushed into her tiny pussy with out caution. Pain ripped thru her body and a little blood ran down her thigh; upon seeing her face contorted Sonny was concerned and looked down between her legs;

'Damn girl! You could have let a brotha know it was your first time…I woulda been more gentle!'

Feeling guilty Sonny slowed down his stroke and started to kiss her neck gently

'It's okay Sonny, don't worry, I wanted to be fucked so bad that I didn't even care' she protested; at the realization of what she'd just said to him, Ophelia became overcome with embarrassment and looked away shyly;

'Its okay baby, don't feel no shame....everybody wants to feel good
sometimes' said Sonny smiling at her 'you shoulda really told me tho
cos I don't wanna damage you for the next man! I love pussy, but I
don't like to fuck it up or nothing'
Ophelia nodded at his sentiments, then closed her eyes and relaxed
some.

Eventually, she began to feel hornier as he rode on; Ophelia began to
reach down to her clit so that she could make herself come while he
was inside her, when suddenly Sonny grabbed her hand;
'No hands required on this train, ma...just lay back enjoy the ride
and lemme do what I do...I'll take you there' he said softly. Sonny
then changed positions and flipped her legs over her head for
maximum penetration. He expertly balanced himself on top of her
making sure that his rock hard abs rubbed her clit with every thrust.
As he increased speed, Ophelia was getting wetter and wetter. She
could feel herself tightening over his cock and her climax was also
building. What was happening to her was a mind trip to say the least
and the way she was feeling made her inexperienced finger
fumblings of earlier on seem like cheap thrills in comparison;
'Faster Sonny' she cried out 'harder...deeper please...oh please...do
it Sonny'
As she reached her peak, the waves of her orgasm washed over her
body so intensely that she almost passed out from the pleasure; now
she knew what she'd been missing out on all this time.

'Sonny....I'm coming...I can't stop coming....fuck me...fuck me'
Ophelia sang;
her voice was music to his ears; he liked to please a lady, and the fact
that Ophelia was enjoying herself actually satisfied him more than
anything.
Her pussy continued to contract uncontrollably from her orgasm and
finally Sonny couldn't hold back anymore; as her hot moist walls
enveloped him with desire, he just about remembered to pull out at
the last second. As he came and spilled his semen on the grass
below, he squinted his already small eyes tightly and breathed

heavily trying to calm down;
'Oh baby…you be blowin my mind by makin' me explode like that…umm, yeah. That was so good suga'
He then rolled on to the grass with a satisfied look on his face.

Soon after that, Sonny stood up and started to put his pants back on. Similarly, Ophelia put her jodhpurs back on and stopped to look at her watch, it was nearly 7 o'clock and they would soon be looking for her if she didn't start heading back shortly.
'Sonny, do you always ride out this early?' she inquired
'Yeah, every single day and you've given me a great show for the past week...so I thought I'd return the favour today….will I see you tomorrow?' he asked gingerly
Ophelia mounted Lucky and started to ride off before giving him an answer;
'You can count on it Sonny and see you around okay!'
Sonny smiled as he watched her gallop off into the woodland; what a great start to the day…

Chapter 2

Ophelia got back to the inner grounds of Bellevue Ranch at around 7.10 that morning. She had pushed Lucky harder to run faster than a normal gallop in order put him back into the stables quickly. It was imperative that she got ready in time for breakfast so as not to arouse any suspicion.

Bellevue House on the top of the hill didn't look like most other Ranch houses in Texas that Opheila had seen before. This was because the vast compound was actually a cotton plantation in its original incarnation. The owners were mindful of the slavery's shameful past in the South, thus encouraging them to change the name of the property and surrounding grounds, from 'Bellevue Plantation' to 'Bellevue Ranch'.
As she walked up to the kitchen entrance at the side of the house, Ophelia could only imagine the centuries of history contained within it. Soon after quietly sneaking up the stairs, she quickly had a shower and fixed her hair. Breakfast was served every morning at 8 o'clock and lateness was not an option.

Gaylord Edgar Maxwell III was her father Jonathan's old friend and

13

long esteemed sparring partner over the past 25 years. Being an Ambassador had its perks, one of which was being able to rub shoulders with the elite of every respected major profession in the world. Gaylord's track record spoke of such greatness; he was a prolific civil rights attorney in the 1970's, a district attorney in the 1980's and now sat as a member of the Supreme Court. His wife Amanda was also a stalwart of the legal profession who owned her own successful law firm in New York. Bellevue House, which was more of a mansion that a house, was their second home and had been in Gaylord's family for generations.

The Maxwells had two teenage children; the eldest was their daughter Ella-May who was almost Ophelia's age at 17 and son Troy Edgar who was the youngest at 14. Gaylord and Jonathan were firm friends both completely unconcerned with the fact that they were from paradoxically different worlds. His house was their house for as long as they stayed as far as Gaylord was concerned; it warmed his heart so that the Emeka-Phillips family had accepted his invitation for the Easter period and he also looked forward to catching up with Jonathan, who he had fondly nicknamed 'the old goat'

At eight o'clock sharp that morning, both hosts and guests descended upon the main carved walnut staircase that led into the breakfast room. Ophelia had put on a cotton flower print dress that was not at all tight, but revealed her growing womanly curves.

The emerging scene was quite funny to her because put together in one room, they looked like quite an odd bunch; at one end there was the Emeka-Phillips clan's very black and very proud stance and then on the other you had the Maxwell family's WASP, blond haired and blue eyed credentials. The older gentlemen sat the ladies down first; they stood behind their chairs and pushed the seats in for them, after which, they sat down themselves. Keenly following their example, Troy helped Ophelia into her seat and then his sister Ella-May, as was the custom when one had guests.

Ophelia watched quietly as Ella-May laughed at something her father Jonathan had said; Ella's curly blond hair bounced around as she

14

spoke and her blue eyes sparkled; they complimented her pretty face which lit up the room.

The hot breakfast was well received by Ophelia and while she was enjoying their light banter, Gaylord turned his attention to Jonathan and said something that made her blush a little;

'Well it looks like your little girl is all grown up! I haven't seen all of y'all for about two years and she's filled out so much…Johnny you better keep those young boys away from your lil' girl. Why I even remember her naming ceremony!' teased Gaylord mischievously; Ophelia looked down on to her plate shyly; she was so embarrassed!

'Oh don't embarrass the poor child, honey….Ophelia…please ignore my husband' said Amanda 'he is being extremely rude right now!' Amanda playfully shot Gaylord a warning look to which he replied with a raucous and infectious laugh. Ophelia smiled too; after all it wasn't so bad, she guessed that the way her body had filled out in the past two years was quite significant. A late developer indeed, 3 bras sizes and 2 dress sizes bigger in those two years meant she had now 'grown up' in her opinion.

Unfortunately for Ophelia, her own mother Dr Sandra Emeka-Phillips, was about to embarrass her even further;

'Oh Amanda, it's a good thing that Ophelia is no longer a skinny little girl, she wouldn't be attractive to any prospective suitors in Nigeria without some meat on the bone! Besides, in a few years she will be married; her father is already looking for some suitable candidates…aren't you Jonathan?'

Ophelia's cheeks burned at her mother's tactlessness; *doesn't she know that we're in America* she thought. They didn't have arranged marriages in the States, and Ophelia liked to think that she would at least have a choice in choosing her potential life mate.

Amanda politely replied Sandra's outburst;

'Oh honey… there's really no rush for that yet. Ophelia is still young…she should be married after college surely…I know Ella-May isn't even thinking about that yet!'

'Ma! Did you need to bring me out like that' retorted Ella hotly;

15

Parents say just about anything they like these days don't they!
thought Ella.
Thankfully, not long after that, breakfast was finally over and
Ophelia was relieved; at least she had the impending trip to
Chambers department store in town to look forward to.

~~~~

A little later on, the mothers and daughters climbed into the stretch
limo waiting outside the house; they headed into town with the aim
of laying down some serious plastic at the biggest department store
in Houston, Texas.
As Ella-May babbled on about her future purchases, Ophelia
remembered her hot encounter earlier that morning. She had
expected the pain of being de-flowered, but not to actually have an
orgasm. At that point she decided that Sonny would be her lover for
that Easter holiday and also when they returned to Bellevue for the
long summer break. Judging from her first experience with him; she
knew that Sonny would have a lot to teach her.

While Ophelia sat daydreaming, Ella talked to her mother about even
more of her prospective purchases;
'Mama…I totally have to get the new Louis V bag today…I already
asked daddy....'
Amanda nodded and decided to do a little detective work.
'Did he actually say that you could have it? Only your grades haven't
been too hot lately and you know that your performance at school is
more important than anything…'
The trouble with Gaylord is that he let Ella-May wrap him around
her little finger; Amanda always found herself playing the
disciplinarian and she desperately didn't want Sandra to think they
just spoiled their kids just like a stereotypical rich white family.
'Yeah, Daddy said I can have it ma, and I got straight B's in my re-
sits....and Vanessa Bouvier already has it in four different colors!'
exclaimed Ella
'Well the last time I checked …my daughter's name is 'Ella-May
Maxwell' not 'Vanessa Bouvier'! You need to stop comparing

yourself to that little spoiled brat!' snapped her Amanda
'Yes mama' replied Ella; she decided not to press it any further in
case her mother got mad with her and then forbade the purchase of
the coveted *Louis Vuitton* bag.
Being a professional and academic, Ella's mother could never
understand her daughter's need to keep up with the other fashionable
rich girls at her exclusive school.
*Vanessa Bouvier even has her very own Amex card and her father's
accountant settles the bill every month!* thought Ella; in any case, she
couldn't wait to grow up and move into her own place. Her daddy
would always take care of her financially and at least her mama
wouldn't be able to keep tabs on her spending any longer.

Ophelia looked on and couldn't help to feel that white girls were
very fortunate; she herself could never dream of speaking to her
mother so loosely. Ella didn't even bother to ask her mother's
permission to buy the expensive bag; she'd just asked her father prior
to their shopping trip, and just expected Amanda to accept it without
question. Ophelia also found the black stretch limousine a tad too
extravagant for a simple shopping trip; in her mind it was an
unnecessary and blatant show of ostentation. She had no idea that
Ella's mother actually shared the same sentiments; Amanda hated the
pomp and circumstance of riding a limo just to go shopping in
Houston. She could have easily taken her SUV into town, but her
husband insisted on the limo since they had such esteemed guests.
Amanda also knew that Ella-May also liked to be spotted coming out
of the luxurious vehicle by her snotty rich brat friends and this
bothered her. At the very same time Ella was imagining that she
would so be the hot topic amongst her clique once school resumed;
as they finally pulled up to Chambers department store, Ophelia
knew that this would be one a holiday to remember.

Chapter 3

Gaylord decided to take Jonathan out for some fun, but he would have to leave Troy at home. His choice of entertainment was no place to take a fourteen year old boy.
Gaylord was a regular customer of Madame Carlina's high class brothel; he had long since given up hope of his wife being able to satisfy his sexual appetite. In fact Gaylord was lucky if Amanda gave herself to him more than once a month. Even though he loved the fact that she was an intellectual and a success, it seemed as if Amanda was married to her work.

Gaylord's regular prostitute of choice was Tenetria Jones. Tenetria was a pretty young black woman and mother of two small boys; it was quite ironic to him that while she was not much older than Ophelia, their paths in life were dramatically different.
He had been itching to fuck her since the family had landed in Texas for the vacation over eight days ago. What a stroke of luck that the ladies had decided to go shopping; he figured they had at least four

hours and the local golf course was the perfect place to say they'd gone to. Gaylord knew that Amanda wouldn't suspect him and she was the kind of woman that would never dream of calling the golf club to check. He became hard at the thought of Tenetria's tight milk-chocolate body and high bubble butt; anal sex with her was mind-blowing and the extra $100 for that service was peanuts to men such as Gaylord.

When they eventually reached the whore house building, Jonathan felt a little bit sick. He hated the fact that his good friend was forced to visit a brothel. In Africa one simply took another wife or a young housemaid into your home whether your spouse liked it or not. This behaviour was accepted from men of his calibre, and most rich African men almost saw it as a God given right.
While his friend went off into a room with a gorgeous young black girl, Jonathan decided he would only have a blowjob. He didn't ever use condoms but knew it would be folly to fuck a prostitute without protection; at least this way he wouldn't seem like a spoil sport. Jonathan tipped his head back and enjoyed the hot wet mouth that was enveloping his dick. He could only wonder what his friend Gaylord was up to.

Gaylord felt real good right about now; Tenetria was doing a little lap dance for him. She was naked apart from a tiny black lace thong and five inch black stripper heels; he smiled as he thought of Atlanta rapper *Ludacris'* 'pussy poppin' music video. Gaylord figured that the dude knew exactly what he was talking about.
Tenetria herself knew exactly what Mr Maxwell liked; it was the same thing every time and he was one of her most valued customers over the past three years she'd been whoring.
After the lap dance, he was ready for her. Her patron slowly stroked his penis, paying particular attention to the bulbous pink cap. Uncircumcised dicks used to make her sick in the beginning, but by now Tenetria was used to it. She got on her knees and gave him head, slurping and scooping up her saliva just the way he liked it. After a while, she looked up and could see that Gaylord was about to

come; she spilled his spunk onto a tissue and then wiped him down. Afterwards, he laid Tenetria down on the bed and started to nibble on her ample breasts, while finger fucking her at the same time. Just as she was about to come he stopped abruptly and put on a condom. He was already hard again and Tenetria didn't expect him to know or even care that he had interrupted her own throws of orgasm; after all, he was paying for a service. She hated being treated like a piece of meat but felt that this was her only option of work; the hours were good and earned her enough cash to take care of her boys and go to college.

Gaylord turned her on all fours and proceeded to doggie her from behind. The view was spectacular from his end; this was his favourite position to fuck her in, so he fucked her pussyhole with relish.

After sometime, Gaylord lubed up his condom and slotted his dick into Tenetria's anus. The fuck was so exquisite that he was ready to come almost as soon as he'd entered her tightest orifice. Gaylord grabbed her hair upon the point of his climax;

'Shit! Oh my gosh you motherfucker, not the weave!' screamed Tenetria 'Let go of my hair...I just got it done yesterday!'
Gaylord quickly opened his eyes and let go;
'I'm sorry baby, I just got carried away! I know what you black chicks are about your hairdos' he chuckled.

Once they had finished Tenetria had an announcement to make, it was only fair for her to let him know of her plans, as Gaylord's patronage had helped her financial situation immensely over the years;

'Mr Maxwell, this probably the last time you gonna see me...I'm leavin this game after my graduation' said Tenetria 'I just wanted to let you know cos you're one of my most valued customers...the little extras you give me have really helped...I guess what I'm saying is that I really appreciate what you've done for me'
Tenetria looked over at Gaylord for a response.
'Really...wow...well first of all congrats on you finishing college...I'm proud of you Tenetria. But would you consider seeing

20

me again...I mean away from this place?' said Gaylord; he had
grown attached to Tenetria and didn't want to lose her.
'I could get you your own apartment, all expenses paid of course.
You won't need to worry about rent and all that...I'd only ask that
you let me come to see you when I'm in Texas...I'll pay you
too...no questions asked' he pleaded.
Tenetria sighed...*this trick is really hooked on me* she thought. The
sad thing was that she had to make a choice. This wasn't the life she
wanted for herself, and her sons must never find out about this torrid
chapter in her life
'Thanks for the offer sir....but I can't possibly accept. I said that I
wanna leave the game for real. I don't wanna be a hoe for the rest of
my life, and what you're suggesting isn't much different from this.
When it comes to by kids...I am very protective and I don't even
bring men to my home. How would I explain to them you coming
over to visit me at random times?' she said 'Mr Maxwell, you gotta
understand that, I don't wanna owe you nuthin'...I ain't ever owed
anybody nuthin'....look at the end of the day you mustn't get
attached to me. The reality is I'm a hoe and you's a trick...that ain't
gonna change, even if you put me in a fancy apartment with all the
bells and whistles going!'
Tenetria felt bad for being harsh but she could only be real. That was
how she lived; never mixing business with pleasure because that only
complicated things.
After what she'd said, Gaylord had gained a new found respect for
this young woman; 'Ok, I can understand...and I must give you
credit.... you've got self respect in spite of all this' he said gesturing
the room they were in 'and I am happy to have known you Tenetria;
I truly wish you all the best honey'
Soon after he'd said what he had to say, Gaylord got up and began to
get dressed; it was time to go.
'Gaylord, can you do one thing for me? Can you give me a
recommendation, I mean when I start applying for a real job...can I
leave your name as a character reference? That would really help me
if you truly want to help me out that is' she asked
Gaylord smiled as this was the only time she had ever every

addressed him by his first name and it warmed his heart;

'Ok…I can do that for you, it would be my pleasure Tenetria Jones' he said 'I'll give you my office direct line, but if you get through to my secretary Jenny just tell her that it's a 'code red' call and she will make sure that I call you right back'

Tenetria felt extremely grateful for Gaylord's help; if a big name like his could be put down on her résumé, then the sky was the limit in her eyes;

'Thank you sir….and it's really been a pleasure to have known you too' she gave him a kiss on his wrinkled old cheek and laughed happily.

'One for the road?' asked Gaylord taking a brand new condom out of the packet. 'Why not Gaylord? Why the fuck not….' Tenetria replied This time around she made sure that she did come. After he had left her room for the last time, Tenetria counted the money he'd left behind. Even though he had to pay Billy upfront at the front desk before coming through, Gaylord always left her a personal 'tip' for her services. She almost choked on her juice when she counted $1,500 in $100 dollar bills! Surprisingly, it had turned out to be a wonderful day.

~~~~

Troy was happy to be left at home alone by everyone, and the house help had been given the rest of the day off until dinner time. He was supposed to be hooked to his *Playstation*; well that's what he was doing as his father left with Dr Jonathan, but he had other things in mind. Troy crept into Ophelia's room and stole one of her already worn dirty panties. He liked the dirty ones because he could really get the raw scent of her in them. He put the pink lace to his nostrils and inhaled deeply; *damn, the smell of her pussy is so exquisite* he thought to himself.

Troy reckoned that Ophelia was the most beautiful thing he'd ever seen. He figured that since he was only 14, she would never take him seriously stealing her dirty panties was as close as he would ever get

22

to her. He crept onto the top of his made bed and took his pants off; his teenage dick was already hard in anticipation for what he was about to do. Troy wrapped Ophelia's panties around his dick and started to jack off; the visual of her panties on his cock made him want to come quicker.

As he reached his climax, Troy called out her name;
'Ophelia...oh baby....you're makin me come....fuck yeah....oh shit, I want you to suck my cock! I wanna fuck your pussy so bad...Ophelia....Ophelia...let me fuck your black pussy...'
The talk got more breathless and intense as he was about to shoot his load; in the end Troy finally came inside the pink panties.

His head was pounding from the intensity of his orgasm and then he finally came back to reality. *Shit*, thought Troy, he had messed up her panties; what would he do now?
Eventually, after some thought, he decided to keep the panties as a memento of her. Troy was sure that Ophelia wouldn't miss them. She must have millions of panties any how and her daddy was so rich that she must be really spoilt just like his sister Ella-May. After that, Troy didn't give it anymore thought.

~~~~

Later on that night Ophelia could have sworn that she'd left her favourite pink Victoria's secret panties in the corner of the drawer; she'd wanted to wash them that night. Ophelia always preferred wash them herself by hand rather than give to the maids; but the thought of seeing Sonny the next morning made her soon forget about the missing panties.

Sandra came into Ophelia's room to braid her hair for her before bed. This was a kind of Mother Daughter ritual that they had whenever they were together at home.
Ophelia sat by the vanity table and passed her mother a comb; it was a soothing and relaxing end to a hectic day. They had ended up buying so much and her mother even bought her a Louis V bag as

well; nothing as loud as Ella-May's one, but a nice simple Speedy style. Ophelia looked across at the shopping bags on the floor and smiled. She looked forward to wearing all the clothes upon returning back to Europe.

'Oh Opheli, I wish you would perm your hair…it would look so much longer instead of just being this…this afro that you insist on wearing' said Sandra with disgust.
'Mother, I love my hair like this…and besides the relaxer was breaking my hair! That's why I cut it all off in the first place remember...you know my hair can't take any harsh chemicals…'Ophelia replied
'Well you can at least press your hair straight! Combing it is so difficult….have you even started using the skin lightening crème I gave you yet?' said Sandra
Ophelia tried her best not to scowl at her mother's comments; this is what she hated about her. Though she loved her mother dearly, Ophelia felt that she was too fixated on the 'European' look. Everyone Ophelia had ever met loved her clear black skin just the way it was, so why did her mother have a problem with it?
'Mummy…I haven't used it, daddy already said I am not to damage my skin in any way…he doesn't agree with such crèmes' said Ophelia.
'Your father is just being a man, what does he know of beauty? Besides he is looking for a suitable mate for you…making your skin a little lighter may just increase your chances of getting a good catch!' said Sandra.
Ophelia sighed. They were well into the new millennium, so why did her parents still live in the back in the old days, she often wondered. Ophelia herself really wanted to find her own husband but the chances of that happening now were looking pretty slim.
'Mummy, why can't I find my own husband? Isn't it fine as long as you both approve of my choice?' asked Ophelia
'What nonsense are you talking of? You better get that stupid idea out of you head…do you hear me? You are a Nigerian Ambassador's daughter and your husband WILL be chosen for you!' Sandra

exclaimed
'But mummy…people don't really arrange marriages nowadays…I
just don't want daddy to go to all that trouble then I don't agree to…'
Sandra cut Ophelia off before she could finish;
'Is there something wrong with your brain? Is it because you went to
school in Europe? What do you mean 'if I don't agree' said Sandra
mocking Ophelia's voice. 'Your father will pick your future husband
and that is final!'
As a parting shot Sandra threw the afro comb on to the table and
stormed out of Ophelia's bedroom.

Shaken and upset by her mother's rage, Ophelia started crying softly.
She hated it whenever her mother raised her voice or was upset with
her and she couldn't bear to sleep on anger, so after plaiting up her
hair and putting on her silk scarf, Ophelia went to her parent's
bedroom. Her mother was just applying cold cream to her face when
Ophelia knocked lightly on the door
'Come in Ophelia' said Sandra. Ophelia walked in and knelt down
by to her mother's seat.
'Mummy….please don't be annoyed with me. I didn't mean to be
dis-respectful. I'm sorry…I just wanted…' before she could finish
her sentence, Ophelia was so overwhelmed by her emotions that she
started crying all over again;
'That's alright Opheli….don't cry okay...don't cry. I'm not angry
anymore' said Sandra soothingly; she then held her daughter's head
to her ample chest;
'Opheli…I want you to know that your father and I want the very
best for you. This may be the way things are but your father is not
going to pair you with somebody you can't get along with. Trust in
the knowledge that your daddy knows best, okay' said her mother.
'Thank you mummy…I will' Ophelia said obediently.

For a long time, Ophelia had realised that while her life came with
many privileges, it also came with some deep sacrifices. At that point
she decided to make the most of the years before her marriage;
nobody had to know, she just had to be very careful. There would

definitely be more like Sonny; she would make sure of it!

~~~~

The Easter break came and went. Ophelia looked forward to going back to Bellevue that summer and going back to Sonny. The family eventually returned back to the ranch by mid-July; Ophelia had never been so happy to see Bellevue as she was that summer.
Over the weeks her trysts with Sonny became deeper and more intense; she knew exactly how to please him, how to suck him and how to make him squirm. He also knew how to return the favour.

One morning they rode a little farther than usual and found a little abandoned barn. Sonny had always heard about it but had never been there before…he hoped it was empty and figured it would be a great place to fuck. They tied the horses to a nearby fence and went in to investigate the place. Once satisfied that no one was there, they set about entering the pleasure zone. Sonny put his head between Ophelia's legs for the first time; the sweetness of his hot mouth on her pussy was indescribable!
Sonny traced the rim of her pussy lips with the tip of his tongue. He then proceeded to suck her clit with measured force and at the same time he slid two fingers into her waiting wet hole. Her back arched and she drew in her breath sharply; Ophelia gasped so hard that she needed a drink to wet her dry throat. Sonny's fingers thrust like a small dick inside her as he continued to lap her pussy cream like a dog. Once he could tell her orgasm was almost there, he pushed his fat dick into her making her come instantly. The faster he pumped, the more orgasms Ophelia had; Sonny had figured out a while back that she was multi-orgasmic.
They changed positions numerous times until Sonny brought out his dick about to shoot his load onto the straw below; suddenly, Ophelia quickly grabbed his cock let the thick juice flood her entire throat. This was to be their last stand. As Ophelia got dressed, she looked at Sonny's finery for the last time.

'Sonny, we're leaving tomorrow. This is it' said Ophelia with finality

'Can't we keep in touch...can't we email or something? I thought we had a thing going' he replied.

Sonny realised at that very moment that he had fallen for Ophelia; and quite hard.

'No Sonny, it's for the best and I suspect that my father will have me meet my chosen husband to be in the winter' she replied 'what we had has been great....and thank you Sonny...I've learned a lot from you and you've made me feel like a real woman'

Sonny was devasted, so she had been using him all this time? What did he expect anyway he was just a mere stable hand; he'd never stood a chance with her in the first place.

'Ok Ophelia...I see how it is now...good luck with everything aight' he said and then turned to leave the barn.

Ophelia ran out behind him;

'Sonny...I didn't mean to say it like that! I have no choice and being with you made me feel so free...more than I have ever felt in my entire life! Please don't hate me Sonny!' cried Ophelia.

Sonny hated to see a woman shed tears and his heart melted as he looked into her eyes.

'It's ok suga, I ain't mad...I guess I can understand you wanting to have some fun...I'm glad that it was with me...I won't ever forget you Oph' said Sonny

'Thank you Sonny, I couldn't bear it of you were mad at me...I won't forget you too...we better go now' she replied.

As they left the barn on their horses Ophelia caught the sight of something from the corner of her eye. She lagged behind Sonny a little to see who was going into the barn. Ophelia spotted the blond of Ella-May's curls being followed closely by another person. She laughed to herself upon realisation that Ella-May must have been getting her freak on too. *Oh well at least she I'm not the only one,* thought Ophelia. She sped up to catch up with Sonny. It was a beautiful end to a long hot summer and September was just around the corner.

Ophelia could only ponder upon what it would bring...

Chapter 4

September for Ophelia as usually meant going back to school. She wasn't looking forward to the cold English weather, but she did look forward to catching up with all her friends. Since Ophelia was only going back for her graduation ceremony, this would be the last time that she would make the journey. It was strange coming back to the British Isles after spending one year in France and another in Switzerland respectively; her school operated a French school exchange program, which was followed by a compulsory year at a Swiss finishing school. This was the manner in which all pupils ended their schooling career at the prestigious educational institution known as Launceston Academy for Girls.

Situated in the picturesque town of Bath in Somerset, Launceston Academy was founded in 1869 by visionary and literary authority of the time, Dr Cuthbert Fabien. Back then the founding pupils took their classes in a medium sized Victorian era school building. From such humble beginnings, Launceston had eventually stretched to 4 connecting school buildings, one outbuilding (which housed the

28

school swimming pool and showers), a Hockey Field, a La Crosse patch, a Pupil run Farm, Stables and about 80 acres of grounds that surrounded it. The pupils that attended 'The Academy' as the girls often called it; ranged from ages 11 to 18 years. Total pupils in attendance stood at round 332+ girls and the school operated under the religious banner of the Church of England. Dr Emeka-Phillips always maintained that his children would have the best education that money could buy. The best education that money could buy cost Ophelia's father $40,000.00 in school fees per calendar year.

Launceston's pupils came from some of the wealthiest and most privileged parents in the world. The girls in Ophelia's clique were no exception to this; when put together they weren't just born with silver spoons in their mouths, the made up the whole cutlery set. As Ophelia walked into the dorm room; she could see that Minty was already by her bunk. She wondered what her summer had been like; she sure had a lot to tell her best friend...

Ophelia's best friend forever was named Araminta Cassandra Fortescue-Black. Everybody that knew her called her Minty and most of the girls were either titled or had long names, so nicknames were very common at Launceston. Minty's father was also an old friend of Ophelia's daddy, as was also the case with most of her circle of friends. Ophelia was sure that somewhere along the line, or even before they were born, their collective group of daddies had planned this.
As soon as Minty saw her, she ran over to embrace her BFF.
'Hey Phils!!! How the Devil are you hon? I thought the summer would never end...got lots to tell you...I have had a major major summer....oh my gosh Phils, you would not believe...' and as Minty droned on Ophelia started laughing. Minty always spoke too quickly and people only ever understood half of what she said. Ophelia then quickly filled Minty in on the events that had transpired over her own summer, with the details about her liaisons with Sonny included. Minty's eyes soon became as wide as saucers.

Minty was the last born of Lord Alastair Mingus Fortescue-Black and Lady Magnolia 'Maggie' Lauren Fortescue-Black. Minty's father as a hereditary peer, was a member of the House of Lords; the family also conveniently owned half of Knightsbridge in London, a place where one could forget about buying a property unless there was at least £1 million in the bank. Minty was a beautiful English rose type with the kind of noble features that were a direct result of centuries and centuries of selective breeding. She had glossy wavy blond hair and luminous skin that was the colour of the first spring cherry blossoms. Ophelia always told Minty that the *'St Tropez tan'* made her look silly and that she was beautiful just the way God made her. Not surprisingly once Minty actually took up Ophelia's advice, modelling agencies were breaking down the doors to sign her up; unfortunately for them Minty wasn't in the least bit interested in being a clothes horse.

The Fortescue-Blacks also had two sons, Arthur being the oldest and Owen the middle child. Their family home was a huge country pile named Dunraven Manor, and was situated in leafy Cheshire, England. Ophelia had many fond memories of riding through the grounds of Dunraven with Minty. The parents would let the girls go off and 'play' while they had 'big people's talk' in the morning room; they had no idea that the girls didn't play quite as innocently as one would think. In fact Ophelia and Minty's bond was deeper anyone could imagine. Ophelia often wondered how on earth she would survive NYU without her lifelong best friend; but for the time being, she decided to push such thoughts to the back of her mind. She needed to concentrate her energies on her graduation ceremony which was in just two days time.

~~~~

So this is it, thought Ophelia as she put on her evening gown. Whilst looking at her reflection in the mirror, she began to reminisce; she would remember Launceston Academy with fondness, for both the good times and the bad. She thought back to when she'd had her very own 'Britney' moment. Two years prior, just before her sixteenth birthday, Ophelia had had enough. Enough of abrasive chemical relaxers, hot flat irons and constant blow dryers of which, she had endured only in order to keep her hair in the desired straight 'European' style. Over the years, her hair had become brittle and damaged, in a vain and valiant effort to try and maintain the straightness. Even if wanted to get her hair 'done' it wasn't as if she could just go into Bath town center and visit the salon in the same way as her white and Asian counterparts; the local hairdressers just didn't know what to do with her kind of hair. One day in a moment of madness and frustration, Ophelia decided to chop off all of her hair and start all over again. At the end of the cutting frenzy, she was left with a short sharp afro crop.

It wasn't until she'd cut off all her hair that she realised the magnitude of what she'd done. Her parents went mad when they saw her two weeks after the cut; but Ophelia found it amusing that going 'natural' was the most rebellious thing that she had ever done in her whole life. For the most part she was an obedient and responsible young lady.
Coming back to reality, Ophelia was now ready for the ball. As a finishing touch, she combed out her full head of afro hair which complimented her full length turquoise blue gown perfectly. Maybe going natural wasn't so crazy after all. Kemi Ophelia Regina Emeka-Phillips had grown up to become a beautiful black queen.

~~~~

After the Graduation ceremony the atmosphere in the ballroom was electric; it seemed that everyone and their parents had turned up. For once, the teachers actually looked like human beings and appeared to be thoroughly enjoying themselves. Upon taking a quick glance at the floor, Ophelia noticed that there was also a sprinkling of eligible bachelors in attendance for the young ladies of Launceston Academy to look forward to.

After sitting with them throughout the banquet, Ophelia excused herself from her parents table to go and hit the dancefloor.

Minty, Dominique, Issy, Khadijah and Katy were already shimmying and shakin' away; the five girls made up what was Ophelia's little 'clique'. Upon spotting her coming through the crowd, her friends greeted her warmly and enthusiastically.

'Phils, you totally look like a proper African princess' said Issy looking like a Brazilian supermodel herself; Issy was the only person that Ophelia knew that had a longer name than she did. The typically Spanish named Isabella Maria Consuela Amelita Gonzalez Rodrigues-Ruiz was daughter of the Ecuadorian Ambassador to London. Issy was tall, slim and had the kind of beauty would make even supermodel Gisele Bündchen quake in her boots. Issy would sometimes play up to the 'hot sexy Latina' stereotype with guys, but in reality she was actually smart, talented and a deep thinker. Ophelia noted that Issy had 'grown' in the booty area; that culo looked too hot to be the Issy that she once knew.

'Oh my gosh Issy' Ophelia gasped 'you did it! You got the butt implants! When did you do it? It looks hot!' she added.

'Shh phils, don't let the boys hear my secret! My mom actually suggested it, I was gonna ask her before, but she just came out with it first and said like 'mami, you have no ass, we need to hook you up with some' and that was it! Altogether more 'Caliente' don'tcha think?' said Issy giggling and shaking her booty salaciously in their faces. The girls all marvelled at Issy's new derriere. It looked something like J Lo on steroids. *Those surgeons can really make almost anything possible these days* thought Ophelia.

'Wow Issy it really looks real, I wish my mama was that cool' said Dominique. 'Thanks D, I got it done in Sao Paulo, the guy that did it is like the best butt guy in the world. His work is totally flawless, mom also had her boobs re-done' said Issy 'Not that you need a fake butt with that trunk you're carrying' joked Issy, causing Ophelia and the girls to laugh out loud.

It was as if Dominique had stolen her features from Halle Berry and her body from Janet Jackson. Dominique Antoinette Johnston was daughter of the current Jamaican Prime Minister Martin Johnston.

She was the cute 'shortie' at 5 foot nothing in flats but with the voice on her you wouldn't know it; she was pretty, sparkly and fun just like her people back home.

As usual being the life and soul of the party, Dominique had given the DJ some of the mixtapes that she'd picked up while in Jamaica that summer; as the sounds of *Sean Paul* started playing through the speakers, Dominique was glad that she hadn't left the party music to chance. While she moved to the music, the memories of her summer holiday started flooding back; she just couldn't wait to leave England and get back to the sun. That also meant getting back to Devanté; Daddy didn't have to know that the pool boy was so talented. It had been a hot steamy summer…

After she danced to a few tunes Ophelia slowed down to look at her friends' outfits and took in the sight of Khadijah in the beautiful Chanel evening gown that she had on; *trust her to be wearing an original Chanel couture piece* thought Ophelia.

She looked resplendent in the dress; which was not difficult for her seeing that God had blessed her with features that were a beautiful mix of Ashiwarya Rai and Kim Kardashian. She wore a single diamond that seemed to be floating on its necklace and matching earring studs to set off the dress. Being both beautiful and thoughtful, she had presented her five friends with the exact same jewelry set earlier that evening.

As usual, the girls knew that her personal assistant had probably gone and bought them on her behalf. Khadijah's life was too astonishing an existence for most people to fathom, just imagine; an eighteen year old that already had her very own personal assistant.

Crown Princess Khadijah Yasmeena Al Yasin was a rare bird indeed. Most Saudi princesses were already married by the age of 18, let alone being allowed to study in Europe. Khadijah thanked Allah that her father was quite liberal in that respect and wished all of his four daughters to have an education. Crown Prince Sheikh Abdullah Rasheed Al Yasin was a majority shareholder in the biggest bank of the Middle East and also a billionaire. Since he had no sons, his daughters would all be in charge of running the family business with their husbands someday. After leaving Launceston, Khadijah would start to make preparations for her wedding the following year and of course all of her friends were already invited.

By the time that *'My Goodies'* by *Ciara* came on, Katy had already found a posh young man to dance with;
'Hey girls, I've found some one to keep me entertained!' she exclaimed in her charismatic Scottish lilt. As a fiery redhead all the boys loved Katy and she seemed to love them right back; as for her looks, her lily white skin and green eyes wouldn't look out of place in a Ralph Lauren commercial.

Katherine Alice McTaggart was the only child of the Honourable member of Scottish parliament Hamish McTaggart. The family name had its very own pattern of Tartan which was worn on all formal and state events; similarly, their home was a medieval castle named 'McTaggart Hall'. It was situated in the Scottish highlands had been around for over four centuries. Since their home was a castle, its sheer size made the place cost a fortune in upkeep; so as a measure to help the place earn for itself, the McTaggarts rented out the Great Hall of the stately home for celebrity weddings and held paid tours of the castle and grounds during the summer months.
Katy was happy to be flying straight back home after the bash that night, as she was a firm believer of the famous old saying; 'home is where the heart is'.
Katy's charm though, was in the fact that she didn't even know how stunning she was; being down to earth and funny was definitely her strong point.

As the evening wore on, someone got the DJ to change Dominique's mixtape and put on some oldies. As *Disco Inferno* began playing, Ophelia noticed a dashing young McNulty from the *'The Wire'* look-alike staring in their direction. Ophelia also noticed that he was looking directly at her best friend.
'Who is that guy, Minty look…he's checking you out' said Ophelia.

'Oh, him… that's just Dominic, my daddy asked him to be my escort for tonight however he's such a frightful bore... That's why I left him over there' Minty replied.

'Oh don't be mean Minty…he's cute...why don't you dance with him? Ophelia inquired.

'Ophelia, the son of the Marquis of Banbury does not stir my loins in the slightest…yeah he's cute…cute like a puppy dog! Anyway Phils you know the kind of man I like…dark brown skin, muscular, exciting; old Dominic doesn't have a hope in hell with me…' said Minty giggling.

'Ok Minty, I know what you like, but you know seriously, for like 'your official man' you can't really bring a black brother home, Dominic is more like what your parents want to see' replied Ophelia.

'Speaking of Minty's pref, I bet she hasn't told you about her little fling with Kelechi' whispered Issy.

'Issy!' exclaimed Minty quite mortified.

Ophelia was livid. *What on earth does Minty think she's doing,* she thought.

'What my brother Kelechi? You better spill it Minty!' said Ophelia. Then Issy decided to add fuel to the fire;

'Phils you should have seen it, they were all over each other like flies on hot shit!' said Issy, bursting into a fit of wicked giggles.

Since she was now cornered Minty decided to just spill the beans;

'Ok then, since you must know…here goes…while you were off gallivanting in Texas, Kelechi and I got a little more acquainted, we had a few rolls in the hay, I fell for him and then he dumped me at the end of the summer. His excuse was that he thought we were just 'having fun' whatever that is supposed to mean! The End'

Minty sighed at the thought of falling in love with Kelechi over the summer. Even though her parents knew his family well and their fathers were good friends, she knew in her heart that they would never approve of the pairing. Her titled and privileged background meant that she too, just like Ophelia had little choice in the type of man she could bring into the family. Minty knew that Dominic being invited to be her escort at the ball was a small hint from her parents

35

as to what kind of man they felt was suitable for her and for the family image. This was one of the main reasons that she hated the 'posh' world that she was born into.

The thing about black men was that they seemed to give Minty the exciting head rush that she craved so much. She longed for the opportunity to be able to date whomever she wanted to and not give a damn about what society thought. The only problem was that at the same time, Minty loved her family dearly and wouldn't have them gossiped about in any way whatsoever. Lady Magnolia had always explained to her daughter throughout her young life, that duty and honor came before one's desires at all times; Minty had never truly understood the full meaning of her mother's words until the moment that Kelechi broke her heart.

'You know what guys, I'm gonna take a walk outside. I need some fresh air' said Minty. She looked visibly upset as if about to cry; so as she started to walk out towards the garden, Ophelia ran after her. 'Oh gosh, Minty I'm sorry that he was such a dog...please don't cry, shall I walk out with you?' she offered.

'No Phils, it's ok... I just need a few minutes alone. I'm just happy that he couldn't make it to your graduation tonight or I would have been an absolute mess! I'll be back in a few ok hon....and thanks' replied Minty and then walked out towards the garden maze in just past the gazebo.

Ophelia stormed back inside and went over to scold Issy;
'Issy! Maybe you shouldn't have just mentioned it just like that. Minty is like, really upset. I feel so bad cos he is my brother!' said Ophelia

'Oh sorry! Damn, I didn't realise that she was that hooked on him...I thought it was just a little fling thing! Shit, me and my big mouth!' Replied Issy

Just as Issy had finished apologising, Dominic walked over to the two girls looking quite worried.

'Hello there ladies...umm, I'm Dominic, Minty's escort for tonight....she looked a bit upset just now. Is she okay?' he asked.

36

'Hello to you too Dominic' replied Ophelia stretching out to shake his hand 'I'm her best friend Ophelia and this is her other close friend Issy'

As she shook his hand, she quickly thought of an excuse;

'Minty was just a bit sad because this is gonna be our last time together at school. She gets a bit weepy at the thought of it sometimes...'

'Ah, okay then, thanks for that. Maybe I should go out and comfort her...' said Dominic walking off; Ophelia quickly grabbed his arm and pulled him back;

'Oh no, she wants to be alone...so why don't we hit the floor for a while until she gets back?' asked Ophelia.

'Umm...okay...if you say so! I hope she won't get in a tizzle if she sees us dancing together...I mean I'm supposed to be here with her tonight' replied Dominic.

'No don't worry Dominic, trust us' said Issy 'go and dance with Phils and when Minty shows up, I'll tell her where you are ok'.

Dominic shrugged and then being the perfect gentleman that he was, led Ophelia to the dance floor. He was actually not that bad a mover and surprisingly, Ophelia found it quite easy dancing with him.

'So, tell me a bit about Minty Ophelia, you know her better than anyone don't you?' he inquired.

'How did you know?' asked Ophelia.

'Minty always talks about you and she was really looking forward to you coming back from Texas. But tell me...what does she look for in a man? I'm so enchanted by her but she really isn't giving me the time of day' said Dominic

Ophelia pondered upon her answer. Obviously he wasn't stupid, he knew Minty wasn't in to him, but that the same time she couldn't just come out with it and say that Minty preferred the more melanin abundant gentleman.

'I'll say that from what I know she likes someone who can excite her, you know... not boring; a guy who likes to take risks' said Ophelia.

'Oh...so basically I've had the completely wrong approach towards her?' asked Dominic.

'Yep, I guess you could say that!' she replied.

'So what kind of tips do you have for me? How do I sweep her off her feet?'

'Okay I'll give you one and if Minty slaps you in the face for what I'm about to advise you, then you can come back and blame me!' said Ophelia laughing 'but seriously, with Minty, if you really want something from her as a man, you have to just take it. Use your masculinity a lot, she likes a man that can take control of her.....and make her shiver by holding her firmly just like I'm showing you now at the lower part of her waist, I know that she likes that, she really does'

'Okay then Miss Ophelia, I get the idea...and if I don't happen to get assaulted, I will come and find you to give you a big wet kiss!'

'Oh Dominic, that's much more like it!' exclaimed Ophelia excitedly.

Dominic then excused himself from Ophelia and went outside to find Minty.

He found her sitting on a wooden bench just outside the maze. She was crying silently and when she looked up at him with her big blue eyes, his heart just melted.

'Minty, I know those tears aren't just because you're leaving Launceston...is there a young man involved?' he asked.

'Oh Dominic, how did you know? Ophelia didn't...' she began but he cut her off

'No, your friends didn't say anything I just guessed; you'll catch the death of cold out here...let me give you my jacket' he offered.

'No it's okay, I'm not cold...but thanks' Minty replied.

'Look Minty, I came out here to talk to you. I'm sorry about the other guy but I'm afraid that he lost out. You're a beautiful sexy thing and he really didn't deserve you' Dominic gently held her face in his hands and looked into her eyes

'Why don't you let me help you forget him Minty, tonight, right here...let me...' He leaned in to kiss her pink lips and once they touched hers, Minty felt her nipples harden. Wasn't she supposed to only like black guys?

'Oh Dominic…what are you doing?' she asked him dreamily

'Making you feel beautiful again' he replied. Dominic then started to pinch her nipple through her dress between his thumb and forefinger. This was one of her 'spots' and she instantly began to get very wet. He edged his hot tongue into her mouth, exquisitely invading her space and moved on to her neck, giving it light kisses and making her go crazy.

'Dominic, I like it …don't stop…mmm…oh' said Minty.

'I don't intend to stop Minty' he whispered.

After a little while Dominic took her firmly by the hand and led her towards the maze;

'Come with me' he said, in a deep sexy voice and Minty thought she'd just died and gone to heaven. *So Dominic isn't so boring after all* she thought, and then let him lead her away in a haze of wanton lust.

Dominic took Minty further into the maze and when they reached another wooden bench he began to kiss her again.

'I want you now Minty, please, let me in' he demanded quietly

Before she could even reply Dominic began to lift up her flimsy dress and found her panties; he almost ripped them off in a fit of desire and then lifted one of her legs off the floor, propping it up on the bench. When he finally pushed his meat into her with urgency, Minty gasped audibly…she didn't expect him to be so big and as they got wrapped up in each other's sex, Dominic grabbed her hair and held her body up against the wall. He rammed her with his hard cock over and over again, until they were both panting like a pair of horny dogs getting it on in the park. Dominic then freed one of her breasts from the dress and popped the nipple into his mouth, sucking it with measured pressure. All the sucking and fucking soon became too much for her and soon after, she shuddered into a mind blowing open air orgasm.

'Oh Dominic, don't stop…please take it….take my pussy…please…please…oh yes!!' she cried.

At her request, Dominic kept on going and when he finally came, he felt as if his head was about to explode. Just before the creamy fluid came out, he aimed his dick at the ground, but annoyingly, a little of it landed on Minty's beautiful ball gown. Dominic quickly bent to wipe it off

'I wouldn't want you having a Monica Lewinsky moment!' he said cheekily. 'Dominic…trust me…I am never going to wash you off my dress…it will always remind me of the wonderful time we had and thank you…you were wonderful' said Minty blushing.

'Darling, you don't have to thank me at all…it was an honor and if anything I should be thanking you. But I want more of you than this though…can you handle that Minty? Don't worry, I will call you in the morning' said Dominic laughing.

'Yes….I would really like that…let's see more of each other' said Minty.

Dominic then held her hand and looked into her eyes meaningfully 'Minty….I really want us to see more of each other…I even want us to be serious.

I don't mean to scare you but when I saw you in that dress tonight, I thought to myself, "that girl is going to be my wife" so you can see that I'm serious about you and hopefully us, I just want you to know my intentions while I have the chance. Minty…what I'm really trying to say is that you're really the only girl for me….sorry to sound like one of those soppy romantic novels, but that's how I feel about you' said Dominic.

'Well Dominic, what just happened back there wasn't soppy or romantic, believe me! I am extremely flattered by what you just said, in fact I'm floored…if that's what you want from me…then let's just take it from here ok...'

In her mind Minty wanted to be cautious since she was just getting over Kelechi. What he was saying seemed too good to be true, but even though she would take this one day at a time, Minty knew in her heart that she was already falling in love.

As they left the scene, Dominic put his dinner jacket over Minty's shoulders and they walked back into the party. The evening was brought to a close by a speech given by the Headmaster, then everyone started to go home. Ophelia had already cleared out her drawers, closet and locker before the event, so all that she had left to do was load up the car with her things.

As her father's Ambassadorial Rolls Royce pulled away from Launceston, Ophelia turned round to look at the place for the last time. It truly was the end of an Era.

~~~~

That night at the Bath Hilton, Sandra came into Ophelia's room to braid her hair up for bed; she thought back to when her daughter was just a baby and felt a twinge of pride. *Just look at her now, all grown up and soon to go to college in New York City* thought Sandra. The way that time had flown was astounding and what made Sandra even more excited was the thought that in a few years, her only daughter would be married. As she combed out Ophelia's hair, they both quietly thought about what the future would bring.

'So are you looking forward to studying in New York? You haven't really said much about it' said her mother.

'Oh yes mummy, I think I will really enjoy it! Isabella will be going to the same University as me' Opheila replied.

'Oh yes, that's right...actually I was speaking to your auntie recently and she tells me that your cousin Ronke will be attending NYU as well. You girls can really get to know each other then...I know you haven't been able to see much of your cousin over the years...this will give you a chance to catch up with each other...' as Sandra trailed off, Ophelia was livid internally; she had planned to go wild in New York and it was just her luck that her snobbish cousin Ronke would be there too. *That bitch is going to be watching my every move* thought Ophelia.

Ronke was the cousin from hell; pretty, spoilt, sarcastic and also a complete snob. Ophelia would just have to find a way to keep her at bay.

'I'm sure that we'll run into each other and thanks for letting me know that mummy' said Ophelia; then fortunately her mother decided to change the subject

'So Uni means you are one step closer to marriage! Once you finish your degree we'll start making plans. I'm probably boring you, but you'll understand once you're a mother…I still remember when I got married to your dad…I didn't realise what was coming on my wedding night!' Sandra exclaimed; Ophelia gasped audibly, she'd never even heard her mother make any references to sex, let alone with her father!

'Don't be alarmed Opheli, you're old enough for me to discuss such things with you now Even though these days they teach you kids about sexual intercourse at school, it isn't the same as experiencing the real thing. When it's your first time on your wedding night you mustn't be afraid…just let him take the lead, okay'
Sandra squeezed Ophelia's shoulders to comfort her a bit, thinking that the poor girl must be so scared.
In truth' at that very moment, Ophelia was thanking God that there were no visible physical signs that her virginity had already been lost, otherwise she would have been really fucked. The expectations her parents expected her to live by were astounding; they really needed to realize that they were no longer living in the dark ages

'Mummy…you know that nowadays you don't get a lot of women that are virgins on their wedding night…..well apart from women like us that is. What happens if a girl is not a virgin? What can her husband do?' asked Ophelia.
'Well…that night would not be easy for her. Some Muslim families even demand to see the blood stained bed sheet or they will claim that the girl is 'damaged goods' or has been touched by someone else! This will brings unimaginable shame upon her family of course and usually the in-laws will demand for the husband to divorce her on those grounds; even if he loves her he will have to listen to the elders. Long before you were even thought of, women used to be killed if they were not untouched before their husbands. Obviously that is barbaric…but you see the stigma behind it. I'm glad that as my daughter you know it's just not worth it' said her mother.
'Oh I see then, that's a heavy price to pay' said Ophelia.

42

'Indeed it is Opheli...indeed it is' Sandra replied.

As her mother finished off plaiting her hair Opheila made a mental note to get a hymenoplasty operation to reconstruct her once virginal hymen once she was at Uni; there was no way that she could afford that type of shame and of course Issy would probably know a good plastic surgeon once they hit New York City.

Ophelia imagined that University was totally going be a blast and at long last, her very first taste of freedom. It seemed that all the things she'd ever wanted to do, but had thus far been denied by her ever protective parents, were now easily within her reach. Who said that one couldn't have the best of both worlds?

The end of September couldn't come quicker.

Chapter 5

New York City is truly the city that never sleeps; Ophelia found this out first hand during her first few weeks of being at NYU. Even though she had visited New York with her family over the years, she had never actually 'lived' in the city and life on campus was one of the most amazing things that she had ever experienced. It was Ophelia's first real taste of freedom and was sometimes a little overwhelming. For the first time in her life, there were no teachers, parents, bodyguards or chaperones watching over her. If it wasn't for her extremely disciplined upbringing, Ophelia was sure that she would have gone crazy and slept with every single guy that happened to take a shine to her. Fortunately, being an Ambassador's daughter meant that she had a duty to uphold a certain level of restraint.

The students at NYU didn't seem to know what the word sleep meant. There were all night parties, binge drinking and copious amounts of free, uninhibited sex going on all over campus. Since she wasn't much of a drinker Ophelia didn't see the point of drinking

until one lost control of their senses. In her eyes the ugly side of
'freedom' was the sight of young women vomiting on the sidewalk
and talking incoherently because they were so far drunk; Ophelia
was glad that there were other ways to amuse one's self other than
getting wasted. Also, thankfully she had only ever heard about drug
use and never actually seen it; her life so far had been so sheltered
that at first, even the very smell of weed smoke made her feel sick.
Eventually after enough exposure to it, she got used to the smell and
whether she liked it or not, there was no choice but to get used to all
the unsavoury behaviour that was going on around her.
It was a necessity that she adapt to her surroundings just like a grown
up would; thus, university life was an important part of Ophelia's
coming of age.

Both Issy and Ophelia had decided to major in Fashion Design and
Textiles; Ophelia had shown a love for fashion since childhood, so it
wasn't surprising to everyone when she announced her intention to
study it. Even though Sandra would have preferred her daughter to
have studied something more "academic", Jonathan just wanted his
only daughter to be happy. He already had a successful male heir
since Kelechi worked as an accountant for *PriceWaterhouseCoopers*,
so effectively her mother couldn't really protest about it. Ophelia
was also determined to have fun studying what she loved most
because she knew ultimately, that after university she would be
expected to settle down and become a wife.

Apart from Issy, Dominique would be the only other ex-Launceston
alumna to attend NYU with her; Ophelia was glad at this, because if
all else failed, she at least had her two friends to talk to. Amazingly,
her peers and even some of her lecturers were actually intrigued
upon discovering that her father was an Ambassador; to her surprise
this minor detail about her background opened many doors for her,
both socially and academically. Though it was clear to all that
Opheila was from a privileged background, she wasn't stuck up or
snobbish at all and didn't see any point in putting on airs or having
the mindset that she was superior to anybody else. As far as Ophelia

was concerned, as students, they were in the same boat regardless of their many varied backgrounds. Unfortunately, the same could not be said of her cousin Ronke.

Ronke Jamillah Cleopatra Adebayo was the only child of oil rich Nigerian tycoon Samson Adebayo. Incidentally, though Ronke was an extremely ugly individual on the inside, it was completely ironic that in spite of that, aesthetically she was extremely beautiful. God had seen fit to bless her with a luminous light caramel skin tone, which was complemented by hair worn in long dark brown wavy extensions. Her body drove men crazy and she had curves in all the right places; to top it all, her pretty angelic face definitely defied the devil that lurked within. For one who possessed such beauty, it was a shame that she walked through life with her chest high and nose permanently stuck up at the world.

Just before the University year started at NYU, Ophelia thought for a split second that she may have been a little harsh about her cousin's behaviour; unfortunately upon meeting her again, Ophelia discovered that Ronke was far worse than she had originally thought. This girl was stuck so far up her own backside that she wouldn't even bother to acknowledge anyone in passing if she felt they were 'beneath' her. In fact Ronke would often refuse to greet people unless they happened to say hello to her first.

Ophelia couldn't imagine where Ronke's attitude came from. Her parents had always been pleasant and were very charitable people; in a stark contrast to that, their daughter was the complete opposite. She was rude, bossy and condescending when dealing with most people; her warped philosophy in life was that since her father's money ensured that she wanted for nothing; there wasn't any point making an extra effort to be 'nice'

To make matters worse Ronke treated non-African black people with further contempt; she snobbishly looked down on them as the descendants of slaves without any pure bloodline. In her opinion no matter how successful or rich they could dream of becoming, they would never ever reach up to her level of social standing.

To cut a long story short Ronke was a complete bitch.

For the sake of peace, Ophelia tried her very best to avoid her toxic cousin. Whenever she spotted Ronke coming from afar, she would make moves to get away fast; of course this didn't always work and sometimes, there were clashes.
Once lunch time soon after starting their freshman year at NYU, Dominique and Ophelia were in the students lounge deep in conversation when out of nowhere, Ronke came over to crash the party;
'Hi Ophelia' said Ronke sinking into one of the seats at their table
'Oh hello, Ronke….umm there's no need to sit here cos we were just about to leave' Ophelia replied. *Please God let her just go* she thought.
'Oh well, I'm here now so I'll stay. I actually came over because I wanted you to tag along with me to the salon later this afternoon, Bijou couldn't make it, so I thought I might as well take you' said her cousin without batting an eyelid. Ophelia couldn't believe her ears. Ronke didn't even ask nicely, and at the same time referred to her as just a simple afterthought.
'Actually, Ronke I'm busy later and have some important work to do, so I can't come with you' replied Ophelia through gritted teeth.
Remembering her manners, Ophelia decided to be polite and introduce Dominique to Ronke. Even though it was against her better judgement she decided to do the right thing anyway; maybe that would lighten up the mood.
'I haven't even introduced you two, Ronke this is my friend Dominique, we were at Launceston together and D this is my cousin Ronke'
Ophelia nearly sank into the ground with embarrassment at what Ronke did next.
'Hi there Ronke' said Dominique and extended her hand to shake. Ronke looked Dominique up and down slowly then turned away from her with dismissive grunt;
'Anyway Ophelia as I was saying, you need…'
Mortified by her cousin's impoliteness, Ophelia quickly cut her off,

'Excuse me! How dare you be so rude Ronke! You could at least say hello!' she exclaimed.

Dominique held her tongue and looked on in disbelief. Considering the fact that they were only freshmen, she thought better of starting some drama up in the student's lounge. Ronke carried on as if she hadn't heard a word that Ophelia had said.

'Look Ophelia, I don't have time for your' said Ronke and paused to look at Dominique condescendingly once again 'friends', I just need you to come with me to the salon ok. I'm can't just go on my own…I mean, me of all people!' she concluded scornfully.

'I know she did not just look at me like that! Gyal what's your problem?!' exclaimed Dominique. *If that bitch gives me one more, dirty look, I'm gonna swing at her face* she thought; as if she'd read her mind, Opheila tried to diffuse the situation.

'Dominique, I'm so sorry about this, please just ignore her okay…it's not personal that's just how she is' said Opheila to her friend and then faced her cousin.

'Ronke, you must be joking if you think that I'm going to the salon with you. Even if I was gonna think about it, you just blew any chance of that with your stank behaviour, you better find someone else…you're on your own'

At her cousin's comment, Ronke flicked her hair over her shoulder and shot back spitefully;

'Oh come on Ophelia, trust me, you need to go get your own hair done anyway. You are SO not gonna get any hot guys in New York City walking around with that 'fro…I mean what you think this is…a Black Power seminar? Actually…maybe it was a bad idea asking you to come with me in the first place….I wouldn't be caught dead walking next to you anyway…wearing that! Why am I even at this table?'

And with that Ronke got up from her chair, rolled her eyes and kissed her teeth loud and crisp as only African women knew how. She then sauntered off into the crowd with her weave swinging from side to side as she went.

Dominique looked at Ophelia open mouthed in disbelief;
'Phils is she for real? That is your cousin? Like your mom's sister's daughter type of cousin? Sorry to say this cos you're my girl but she is a certified Biatch!' said Dominique.
'Do you think I don't know that? That's why I've been trying so hard to avoid her! I'm so sorry about the way she treated you D, but she's one of those stuck up Nigerians that think they're somehow 'better' than Caribbean or African American people. She's a really nasty piece of work. I can't believe she expected me to ditch my plans to follow her to the hair salon at the drop of a hat! I mean can you imagine?' said Ophelia.
The girls both shook their heads and then headed off back to lectures. As they walked, Ophelia hoped that Ronke wouldn't bother her anymore after this, but knowing her cousin well, the bitch would probably be back again once she needed something.
Oh well, thought Ophelia, *there's always one bad egg in each family*.

~~~~

Later that night in their room, the girls filled Issy in on the 'hair salon' incident with Ronke.
'So that's what happened Issy! What's really making me angry is that I know she's gonna call up my mom with a faked up story and make it seem like I was the one being funny! She doesn't even act that way in front of our parents!' exclaimed Ophelia.
'Wow Phils, if that was me I woulda just slapped her! You need to tell her what's up...I wonder how many enemies she's already made in her lecture group. You're gonna have to point her out to me next time...I really wanna see what this chick looks like' said Issy;
Then Dominique decided to add her own two cents;
'She better watch out if I see her on the street! It's gon be on! I was so mad but I only kept my cool out of respect for you Ophelia' she retorted.
'Thanks D, don't worry about me next time. I know she's my cousin and all that, but she would have deserved it if you smacked her one! You guys should see her best friend Bijou...that was the one that

couldn't make it to the salon with her in the first place' said Ophelia
'Do you mean Bijou Beaudleaux? The model Bijou?' asked
Dominique.
'Yup the very same! They're like birds of the same feather...they
went to high school in Long Island together and they even have
matching *Gucci Bostons*' replied Ophelia
'What's a *Gucci Boston* on its day off?' asked Issy jokingly.
'That's one of *Gucci*'s hottest new bags; it comes in lots of different
colors, but Bijou and Ronke have matching ones. It's sad really
because their lives revolve around money and status. That's why she
said in the end that she wouldn't be seen dead with me, apparently
looking as 'awful' as I do; but you know she was frontin' though or
she wouldn't have come to ask me in the first place! She just wanted
company but she was too proud to admit it...maybe if she would
have asked me nicely...nah, wouldn't have gone with her anyway!'
said Ophelia and laughed loudly.
At that, they all descended into a fit of laughter and then carried on
their gossipy chatter.

~~~~

Eventually after settling in, life at University was proving to be both
eye-opening and entertaining. Ophelia told herself that she would
make the most out of this time in her life, so she worked hard and put
her all into her assignments, thus impressing all of her lecturers.
Ophelia was actually a very talented young designer and dressmaker;
she even took orders from her friends to make clothes for them in
whatever spare time that she had. Issy also did well studying fashion,
however her passion for it would never reach Ophelia's level; the
trouble was that Issy was only at University to make friends, have
fun and pass the time. Studying just happened to be a side effect of
her attendance.

As time went by, word of Ophelia's talent spread around the campus.
Ronke was secretly surprised by this, however being as proud as she
was, it would kill her to ever give her cousin her due credit.
Not to outdone or left out of the fame, she started to find excuses to

hang out wherever her talented cousin was and tried very hard to blend in. Ronke had also developed a habit of casually mentioning, that they were related whenever anybody happened to mention how gifted Ophelia was.

To Ronke's surprise, even her best friend Bijou made her ask Ophelia to design an exclusive dress. She did so grudgingly; however at this request, Ophelia rose to the challenge and simply outdid herself. The garment was so beautifully made, that even Bijou's snotty 'it girl' clique (who just happened to dominate the New York club scene) harangued her into letting them in on who the genius was that made it.

To this end, Ronke was reduced to a level of humility that she had never been to before in her entire life. To make matters worse, after a while her cousin began to be head-hunted for internships at some of the hottest fashion houses in New York.

Needless to say, Ophelia relished every moment of her three year tenure at NYU. They signified her freedom years.

Chapter 6

Washington Square Park just inside the University was the hot spot during the students lunch break. One sunny afternoon, Ophelia was sitting one of the benches within the park sketching away, when she noticed Alizé across the pathway. Alizé Strong was also studying Fashion in the same lecture group as Ophelia, and they had become good friends since being at NYU; she decided to walk over to Alizé with the intention for both of them to eventually go to the next lecture together. Ophelia, Issy and Alizé enjoyed each other's company and often worked in the same teams during class so naturally, they started hanging out together.

Simultaneously, as Ophelia was making her way over to Alizé, a bunch of guys were also headed in the same direction. Alizé's older brother Caspian was going over to pick up the cell phone he'd lent her. Knowing his baby sis, she would eventually claim it as her own if he didn't take it from her as soon as he possibly could. That was the way his sis operated, but he only allowed it because she knew just how to wrap him around her little finger. Such was their relationship, they were very close and Caspian loved his sister very much. He'd already told the guys he wouldn't be long, as they all wanted to hit the local burger joint for lunch.

Caspian Amaru Strong played the position of point guard for the University basketball team. His mother happened to be a huge fan of both *'The Chronicles of Narnia'* books by C.S. Lewis and slain gangster rapper *Tupac Shakur*, hence his unusual name. Needless to say, Alizé was also named after one of her mother's favourite things. Caspian stood tall at 6 feet 5 inches, was light skinned, of a muscular athletic build and devastatingly handsome. At 20 years old he was at his physical peak and was only expected improve over the years; for this reason alone, Caspian often had adoring young girls trailing in his wake. Today was no exception as Ophelia could recognize the two chicks that were walking a little further behind the guys. Ronke and Bijou both considered Caspian a hottie; however Ronke was especially feeling him the most and was on a mission to bag him.

Along with Caspian were, his boys Donnie, Le Quawn and Eddie. Also a sporting jock, Donnie Mollini was on the college football team and held the position of quarterback. He was a white guy, but from the way he spoke one would think he majored in Ebonics. Being into hip hop music and urban culture in general, meant that he often wore the same type of baggy clothes that the other black dudes wore.
With his dark hair cute smile, Donnie also got his fare share of chicks but in truth he had a crush on Ronke on the low. As expected of course, she never even gave him the time of day.

Le Quawn Michaels was also on the basketball team with Caspian. As a center, his position wasn't as coveted as Caspian's, but he played his position so well, that he was already being scouted by the head coach of the *New York Knicks*.
Le Quawn was a typical dark skinned hood type of nigga; he loved gangster rap and sometimes said that he would have gone into the rap

game if he hadn't been so talented at b-ball. Although Le Quawn wasn't nearly as good looking as Caspian or Donnie, he always had a sharp haircut and was meticulously groomed. The mean swagger that he had on him, also ensured that he too wasn't short of attention from the ladies either.

The odd one out of the bunch was Eddie. Edmund Cheng was the only one of the boys who wasn't into sport. He majored in Mathematics and aspired to become an Investment Banker. Eddie was also into hip hop music and regularly supplied his friends with bootleg versions of all the hottest new rap albums and mixtapes. Because he was an Asian of Chinese descent, Eddie felt that he was the least desirable amongst the guys and as a result wasn't very confident with the fairer sex; in truth, many girls on campus actually found Eddie quite cute and his self deprecating manner very attractive. All he had to do was take a few more chances.

As he walked up to his sister, Caspian noticed somebody else coming from the other direction. This poised and elegant vision of lovliness seemed to be gliding towards them on a cloud; Caspian was sure that he'd never seen any woman more beautiful, possibly ever in his whole life. The fact that she was dark skinned and wore her black hair in a natural afro style only added to her appeal. He just couldn't wait to see the view from behind.
'Would you look at that honey…damn she fine…really fine. Do any of y'all know her cos she's coming over here. I sure would love to get into that' said Caspian longingly
'Yeah she's a hottie alright! I can see that booty from the front…ooh wee!' exclaimed Donnie. The guys all laughed in unison. It was just that they all found it funny that a white guy was saying something that you would normally hear coming from a brother.
Alizé decided to put them out of their misery;
'Oh you like her? She's in my tutor group…her daddy's some Ambassador or something…but she don't act like she 'all that' because of it tho'…..can't say the same about her cousin, that Ron-key chick' she said with emphasis on the name.

'Oh word? That Ronke is her cuz? I really hope they ain't nothing like each other…come on Alizé, introduce me to her girl' said Caspian.

'Naw Casp, she ain't no chick that you can just dog out…Ophelia really has some class. I don't think you're used to that kind of chick. Most women throw themselves at ya… but you gonna have to put in work with this one' she replied.

'Okay sis, but you know me already…if you ain't gonna introduce me to her them imma introduce myself' he concluded.

As sure as the statement that he'd just made, Caspian started to make his way over to meet Ophelia and stopped her in her tracks. He stood over her, blocking a little of the sunshine from her view and even though Ophelia was tall for a girl at 5 foot 7 inches, she felt like a dwarf in comparison to him. She looked up at Caspian puzzled and wondered what this tall stranger wanted.

Since he had succeeded in capturing her undivided attention; Caspian tried his tightest 'mack' game on Ophelia by looking into her eyes and staring at her as if she was the only girl in the park.

'Umm…can I help you? Are you ok?' asked Ophelia sounding worried.

'Yeah, I think you can help me…seeing that you made my heart stop from the moment I laid eyes on you. What's your name mama?' asked Caspian.

Ophelia had to quickly stop herself from laughing; it would take her a while to get used to being referred to as somebody's mother. Thankfully, Alizé had previously explained to her that is was actually a term of endearment.

'My name is Ophelia….but I actually came over to see my friend over there' said Ophelia gesturing to where Alizé was. Caspian took her hand in his gently and gave it a light kiss.

'Pleased to meet you lady Ophelia…my name is Caspian….Caspian Strong. I'm Alizé's big brother…when I saw you coming from across the way, I knew that I just had to get to know you. You're so beautiful sugar…' he said in his smoothest deep voice.

Ophelia was both flattered and surprised by his candour; she also noticed that Caspian looked like a heartbreaker. She smiled inwardly as she remembered Ronke's dig at her regarding her afro a few weeks back....if only she was here to see this now.

Ophelia was oblivious to the fact that Ronke was actually watching the whole show from afar fuming. *Ophelia can't get to Caspian before me, she just can't!* thought Ronke. She was almost going mental with jealousy; she'd seen him first and would be damned if Ophelia would get a look in!

'Oh my God Bijou; can you see that, he's talking to that bitch like she's the best thing since lacefront wigs! What does he think he's doing…I fucking hate her...that prim and proper whore'

Apparently, Ronke didn't hold back at all even though she was talking about her cousin; all blood ties were irrelevant when 'her man' was at stake.

In truth Caspian had probably never noticed her very much at all.

'I know, I know *Cherie* I can see zhat' said Bijou in her French drawl. She was a pretty leggy model of mixed parentage and being half and half meant that Bijou had a wild curly mane of hair much like *Mel B* of the *Spice Girls* in her heyday. Her father was famous French author Gilles Beaudleaux and her mother was of Congolese decent, but born in Paris. In typical Gallic fashion, all was fair in love and war as far as Bijou was concerned; if she were in Ronke's position, she would be the one if front of Caspian at that very moment instead of Ophelia. To this end, she decided to give her friend a little advice.

'Look Ronks, if you want him then go and get him. If you are in his face and make all the right moves, then believe me he will forget about her. He is just a man *Cherie*…when it's all said and done; their brains are wired to their dicks' she concluded.

'Okay Beezh, but I don't want it to look so obvious…If I go over right now I am soo gonna look desperate...let's watch. Knowing Ophelia she's gonna be off to a lecture in a minute; once the bitch is gone, I'll move in' replied Ronke.

'Yes Ronks…move in for the kill…ha ha!' joked Bijou. Ronke

giggled back at her friend and then lay in wait; hopefully this
wouldn't take too long.

By the time they had finished talking, Caspian had got exactly what
he wanted from Ophelia; he stored her digits directly into his cell.
'So I'll call you later okay, I'm sure we're gonna have a lot to talk
about' said Caspian.
'Ok then, speak to you later. Alizé and I have got to get to class' said
Ophelia walking off briskly. The girls were working on a project and
Issy would be waiting for them; by now, she was probably hopping
mad with impatience. As Alizé and Ophelia walked off, the guys all
paused to check out Ophelia's back view; thankfully she didn't
disappoint.

'Dayum Casp, you better bag that one cold playa…and I know u got
da digits! Her shit stand like a donkey…and it's so round like a
bubble! Dayum…you always find the hot ones man…' said Donnie.
The boys laughed again at his quip, he sure was right!
'You know what tho? I can't believe Alizé kept that one away from
me for so long! I've met all the other chicks in her class, but not that
one! Look at that switch walk she got on her…she making my dick
hard, na mean?' Caspian retorted.
Eddie shook his head at the comment, in his own mind; he felt that
Caspian might be out of his league with Ophelia
'I don't know Casp, she looks like a tough cookie…you think she'll
even let you tap that? Alizé was right…it's gonna take some
work…maybe even spending some major dough' said Eddie.
'Naw man, Eddie trust me dawg, my game is tight. I'm gonna have
that chick eatin' out the palm of my hands. You gon see it ma nigs!'
replied Caspian.
Eddie wasn't so sure but he kept quiet. One could never tell what
people were like behind closed doors and sometimes, looks could be
deceiving.
'Ay, she hot alright, but I was looking at ya sis' declared Le Quawn
'Alizé is really looking right these days….I know she's ya sis and all
Casp, but a nigga's just being honest'

Caspian looked at Le Quawn with mock anger.

'You better stay away from ma sis. She ain't gonna be another one of ya baby mamas!' said Caspian

Le Quawn laughed at Caspian's comment. They were always teasing him about baby mama drama since his ex Kimera had given him a baby girl a year ago.

Le Quawn and Kimera had already broken up when she found herself pregnant with his child; she imagined that having the baby would bring them closer, but in fact contrary to her high expectations; the arrival of little Sapphira had quite the opposite effect on their relationship. Even though Le Quawn loved his daughter, he could almost not forgive Kimera for making them both young parents. She'd assured him that she was on the pill when she fell pregnant; when in truth she'd actually stopped taking them for a week. He couldn't comprehend why a woman would try and trap a man into a failed relationship at the expense of an innocent child. Le Quawn however, was determined to be a good father to Sapphira Cassidy Michaels; she was the light if his life and main motivation to succeed in his chosen career of professional basketball.

Ronke decided to make her entrance while the guys were deep in conversation. She sneaked up behind Caspian and grabbed his waist from behind, making sure to discreetly graze his crotch area with her hand.

'Guess who it is baby?' she asked.

Caspian was stumped. Who would just come up behind him just like that? Most chicks were intimidated and well as beguiled by him and wouldn't have the guts to do so.

'Umm…I don't know…who is it?' he replied.

'So Caspian you've forgotten me already? We danced at Legends just last week…it's me Ronke'

The fact that he didn't remember her wasn't a good sign.

Damn, why does it have to be this bitch thought Caspian; he'd only danced with her at the club that night, in the hope of getting a quick fuck. She hadn't even given it up even though it was clear that she was drooling. He wondered what kind of game she was trying to play anyway. That night, since he wasn't really interested in her, he'd thrown her digits away. In his mind, she was only a jump-off and in addition, there was something about this girl that he just didn't like. Caspian believed in following his gut feelings and it wasn't often that they steered him wrong. The sooner he could get out of this situation the better; but unfortunately Ronke was behaving like a bitch in heat…

She asked Caspian if they could speak privately as she had something to say that she knew would interest him; a lot. Ronke put on what she believed to be her sexiest voice but in truth, she only sounded slutty. Donnie looked on, hoping that one of these days he would have a chance with her. He bet that he could really turn her out. Once chicks got his boxers off, they found out that his shoe to dick size ratio was on point. Donnie wore a size 13 shoe and extra large Magnums.

'Caspian, I was waiting for your call last week…I gave you my number, but you know what? Never mind that, here it is again' said Ronke and slipped a folded square of paper into his hand.
'I really want us to get a lot more acquainted Caspian. Actually, I feel like going for a drive tonight…do you think that you can pick me up?' she asked.
Caspian looked back at her confused;
'A drive…to go where? I don't even know…' before he could finish his sentence, Ronke quickly cut him off;
'Don't worry, like I said we're gonna get to know each other…just pick me up and we'll go for a drive…who knows what we'll get up too' she said with a wink.
For maximum effect, Ronke ran her finger along his belt buckle seductively
'Maybe I wanna see what's under all this Caspian…maybe I wanna taste something good' she added whilst looking into his eyes for confirmation.
Since Ronke was making it that easy, Caspian decided to pick her up

tonight and smash. After he got the pussy, she would be history anyway; much like his long list of female casualties.

'Ok shortie…I'll pick you up say about ten tonight…I'll beep once I'm outside the block, so just come out when ya hear it aight?' said Caspian.

'Cool, I'll be expecting you Caspian; okay, bye then!' said Ronke and with that she walked off triumphantly with her booty blatantly stuck out, so that he could get a good look.

'Do y'all see that walking off there?...that tonight's pussy…signed, sealed, delivered!' exclaimed Caspian giving Le Quawn a sharp high five.

Eddie looked at Caspian sideways;

'But how you know she gonna give it up? Come on dude, details, details! What'd she say to you anyways' he asked.

'Well my friends…let's just say that she's looking forward to tastin' sum of my cream tonight and I'm looking forward to filling up her mouth with it!' said Caspian with a dirty laugh. As he continued to discuss the specifics of the conversation with the guys; they carried on talking as they headed for the burger bar. In the back of his mind just like Biggie, Caspian hoped that she swallowed.

~~~~

True to his word Caspian showed up at ten sharp that night and he drove off with her in the passenger seat of his shiny new Escalade truck. Ronke was so excited; she knew that after just one night, he wouldn't be able to get his hands off her.

They eventually stopped at a spot just past Union Square; it was a dark corner of the street and Caspian knew that it was unlikely that they'd be disturbed. He'd already been there before with a few other chicks.

They stared to kiss for a while, until Ronke noticed that Caspian was beginning to get hard.

'I hope you're ready for me Baby' she said looking into his eyes. She then proceeded to undo his pants and started feeling round in there

60

for his meat.

'So I see you're a big boy then…let me see if you're gonna fit in my mouth'

Ronke flipped her weave back and descended on to his fat eight inch boner. Caspian flinched and tipped his head back on his headrest as her mouth swallowed up his cock. As she began to put in some work, Ronke listened out for his moans and sped up her stroke as they got louder.

Her jaw was aching but she couldn't stop; she had a job to do and Ophelia was definitely not part of the equation.

She tightened her grip and kept on jerking his dick in conjunction with her oral acrobatics. Caspian was so aroused at this point, that he'd grabbed her hair and started to fuck her mouth slowly, pulling back until he almost popped out of it then ramming the full length of his steel in it again. Usually Ronke would have freaked out if any guy dared to touch her weave, but just for Caspian, she overlooked this minor detail. Her mind started to run wild with freaky things she could do to drive him crazy; for an added visual effect Ronke looked up to let him watch her tongue flicking all over stiff his black cock. As a pièce de résistance she began to dribble hot saliva all over the length of the dick and slurp it back up noisily. *Oh yeah, suck it you hoe, this bitch knows how to give a nigga some good head* thought Caspian hornily.

After about 30 seconds of that performance, Caspian could take no more; he had to bust right about now and preferably all over her face.

'Oh shit, suck it bitch..I'm gonna come. I'm gonna come'

This was Ronke's cue to take him out of her mouth. There was no way that she was going to swallow his semen; so she stroked his orgasm into her scarf that she'd taken off and put on her lap. Ronke looked up at his face while he was coming; for such a handsome guy, she thought that Caspian really had an ugly 'come' face and even worse, he made a horrible gurgling noise as he split into the flimsy fabric. After some more grunting and groaning, Caspian eventually went back to normal. Ronke wiped her mouth, since the deed was now done.

'Damn girl… that was some good head game, where'd you learn to do that….it was awesome' said Caspian.

'Oh thanks babe…it just comes naturally. I like to see a man lose control of himself' she replied.

Judging by the look on Ronke's face, Caspian knew that he couldn't allow what had just happened to become a regular occurrence. If he gave her a chance, Ronke would probably run so far with it that his head would spin. Unfortunately the damage had already been done and just like crack, Caspian was hooked on her head game and past the point of no return.

Eventually they climbed into the back of the car as he wanted to taste her pussy as well. Caspian roughly pulled her panties to one side, then quickly slipped on a rubber and slid his dick in hard. By now, she was already very wet so he was able to enter her quite easily and then fucked his way to oblivion.

After a while she was a little sore from his roughness, but didn't dare complain.

In Ronke's stupid little mind, Caspian would soon be her man and this was only a small price to pay. By the time he dropped her back home at one in the morning she was absolutely exhausted. Ronke slept soundly that night for the first time in months; she was satisfied and calm. The mission had been accomplished.

Chapter 7

By the beginning of the next semester Ophelia and Caspian were intertwined in the throws of an intense relationship. He was her first 'proper' boyfriend, but since she was afraid of her cousin finding out about them, they were really more like secret lovers. Ophelia imagined that just to spite her, Ronke would probably 'casually' mention that she had a boyfriend, and knowing her parents, they would unceremoniously drag her back home on to the first plane to Lagos. Ophelia had fallen for Caspian so hard, that thought of being separated from him was too painful to bear. As a result of this, she made him swear their relationship to secrecy and the only others who knew what was going on were her girls Issy, Alizé and Dominique.

The arrangement actually suited Caspian right down to the ground. He never did get around to dumping Ronke and they were still seeing each other on the low; Caspian was still hooked to her head game. His friends often wondered how he managed to juggle both girls, seeing that they were actually cousins and attended the same university. The guys had nicknamed Caspian a 'platinum certified player' which was actually one of the highest accolades that a young G could get.

Incidentally, just so that he could have his cake and eat it; he had somehow convinced Ronke that while they were 'dealing' he still wasn't sure if he was ready for a committed relationship. This essentially meant that, she was nothing but a booty call. Caspian would call her at random times to hang out, but their meetings almost always resulted in the same final destination. All he wanted from her was sex, sex, sex and more sex; in fact Caspian's appetite for sex with her was insatiable.

Unfortunately and to her detriment, she was a fool in love so Ronke gave herself to him all too easily. In effect, Caspian played her just like a puppet on a string. Even when Ronke eventually realised that he was using her; she was so in love with him that she just couldn't help herself.

To add salt to the wound, he was even bold enough to flaunt other chicks in front of her at the club. He knew she couldn't really protest it since they were not 'official' yet. Luckily for Caspian, Ophelia rarely went to the club, as she was constantly studying hard and had no time for partying.

He knew innately that Ronke's pride wouldn't allow her to announce their relationship unless he declared her as his lady in public; to this end she started to become increasingly aware that the possibility of them becoming an item was becoming slimmer as time went by. As each day passed, she clung on to the hope that he would come around. Ronke was determined not to let all of her hard work be in vain.

Ophelia on the other hand kept Caspian waiting three months before he tasted her pussy. As her first love, he was very special to her and once she'd told her girls the tale of the Sonny affair, they'd schooled her on the rules of the dating game.

The girls motto was to 'make him beg for it and he'll come running' and in all honesty they weren't far wrong; the fact that Ophelia kept

Caspian waiting for sex increased his passion for her even further. Caspian's treatment of Ronke in contrast, was akin to the way that one would use a dirty dish rag.

Incidentally, when Caspian and Ophelia finally embarked upon a sexual relationship, he turned out to be quite a disappointment. Her experience with Sonny had set the bar high for any subsequent lovers and Ophelia had come to expect a man to be creative as well as attentive during the act. Unfortunately for all of his good looks and charm, Caspian was none of the above. He was far too narcissistic and concerned about his own pleasure to care about hers. Even though she was in love with him, Ophelia couldn't help but to feel let down by the fact that he was literally a three minute man. The first time they slept together was an eye opener.
Ophelia thanked God for small mercies that at the very least, she could truly vouch for the fact that all men on Earth weren't like Caspian. At that very same moment, she also made a silent prayer that whoever she would eventually marry would be a much better lover.

Ophelia lay down on the sofa in Caspian's dorm room during their first night together; as they began kissing and fondling, she could feel his erection bulging through his baggy pants. Usually she would have pulled away from him, but this time she was ready for the dick. With an unspoken desire between both of them, Caspian un-fastened his zipper and took out his stiff cock. At the sight if it, Ophelia's eyes widened in anticipation; it was thick and juicy, just the way she liked it. It looked so good that she even wanted to suck on it, but she held back; that would be saved for much later on.
As if in some eerie movie, everything they did from then on was conducted in complete silence. Caspian lifted up Ophelia's cheesecloth floor length skirt that she'd worn with a tank top tee that day, and slipped off her lace shorts underneath.
He then stuck a rough finger inside her and wiggled it around a bit to feel how wet she was, then took it out. Afterwards, Ophelia realised that this was actually Caspian's interpretation of foreplay. Soon after

that, he climbed on top of her missionary style, closed his eyes and started to thrust away at her impatiently. If one were to be brutally honest; it could have been just about anybody underneath him, so long as he had a pussy hole to fuck.

To Ophelia's surprise, after less than four minutes in the saddle, Caspian's face contorted and he fell onto her chest with a grunt; she wondered what in the hell was going on;

'Baby, are you okay?' she asked concerned.

'Yeah I'm good, you made me bust so fast baby. The pussy felt real good' and with that, Caspian took off the used condom and threw it in the trash. Ophelia imagined they would go for second round and waited a while for Caspian to unwrap another rubber, but to her horror he rolled over and fell asleep so fast that she thought it must be a dream.

As she watched him snoring away Ophelia quickly realised that Caspian wasn't the love of her life after all. He didn't even care that she didn't come, talk less of paying attention to her own pleasure. After watching him sleep for a while, Ophelia eventually cleaned up and let herself out of the room; it was blatantly obvious to her that their night together was over.

~~~~

Once she got to her own dorm room, Ophelia decided to check her inbox. To her delight, Minty had sent her a message. She wondered how Minty was doing; she hadn't seen her best friend since the night of the ball all those months ago.

From: Fortescue-Black, Araminta
To: Emeka-Phillips, Ophelia
Subject: MAJOR UPDATE!!!

Hi phils!!

How is it over there in Yankville!! I hear from Issy that you're really doing well with the fashion....you know I've always believed in you

hun!! How are the guys over there? I bet they are 'HOT' as Paris Hilton says! lol!

Anyhoo...just wanted to update u! Since the night of the ball Dominic and I have been seeing each other for about 6 months now and guess what?? He asked me to marry him!! Yes you read right....marry him!! I told him that I need to think..so now that's where you come in....what on earth shall I do?

Before you ask..I love him but I think I'm a bit too young for this..what do you think??

Ok that's it for now! Oh and sorry I haven't called for a while, but you know how it is, your lectures, timezones etc!

LOVE U LOTS

Minty! ☺

Ophelia smiled to herself, but before she could think about a response, she saw another 'received' email flashing in her inbox.

From: Fortescue-Black, Araminta
To: Emeka-Phillips, Ophelia
Subject: MAJOR UPDATE!!! MARK TWO!!

Ok another update! He came over today and formally asked my father for my hand! OMG I was soooo shy to look at every one! Anyhoo, he them gets down on one knee and proposes in front of my family after the luncheon we were having over at Dunraven.

Phils I wish you were here to see it! It was so romantic that I had to say yes!!! I love Dominic so much and I'm soo happy and giddy with delirium!

CAN YOU IMAGINE, THIS TIME NEXT YEAR I'LL BE A MRS!!

I miss you so much Phils, please come over for Easter..we have soo much to catch up on! You're my maid of honor of course!

Bye again ☺

Minty!

Ophelia replied Minty and started typing away furiously; she was happy that things had turned out so well with Dominic. Even though she hadn't expected him to propose so soon, Ophelia remembered that she'd thought he was a nice guy ever since they'd met all those months ago, also the fact that he was titled was a bonus for Minty. Thankfully she would be able to marry the man that she loved without any dreaded 'class' issues coming up. Ophelia thought to herself that in this modern day and age, it was sad that high society still frowned upon the free mixing of social classes and ethnicities. This was the reality of the world that they lived in; wealth and privilege did come at a cost. Often times, it was at the cost of one's true happiness.

As the evening was coming to a close, Ophelia knew in her heart that Caspian would only be a passing phase. His performance that night had put paid to that, and she could never love a man who was selfish to her needs. Ophelia wanted a real man's love more than anything. To truly love and be loved was one of her deepest desires; second best was just not enough. Any man that wanted to be adored by her would need to cater to her needs right back. As she tied her hair in her scarf to get ready for bed Ophelia already knew that Caspian's days were numbered.

Chapter 8

A month after Caspian's disastrous performance, they were still having sex. Not much had changed since then, but at least Ophelia had actually reached orgasm a few times during their sexual encounters; even so, she still couldn't help but to feel that they were just going through the motions. Finally, Ophelia came to the decision to end their relationship. There was no point in flogging a dead horse, and lately Caspian had been behaving erratically; he would tell her he was going to be at a particular location, only for her to be told otherwise by his friends. Sometimes he wouldn't even pick up her calls or return her texts; so inevitably, something had to be done. Ophelia wasn't about to be treated like some side chick anyways.

In the evenings Caspian usually stayed late after practice, to work on his jumpshots at the basketball court. Ophelia figured that this evening would be no exception and he would hopefully be there. The other team mates didn't usually stay behind with him and apart from Le Quawn; none of the others were that dedicated. Ophelia also remembered that Le Quawn usually spent all his spare time with his young daughter Sapphira, so she was sure that Caspian would be alone. She rehearsed over and over again in her mind just how she should tell him it was over; this wouldn't be easy, and the fact that this the first time she'd ever dumped a boyfriend made the task no easier.

Ophelia quietly slipped into the court by the back of the bleacher stands. As she walked through she looked up at the score board and felt somewhat wistful about they way they should have been. Suddenly, a muffled sound came from the other corner of the court. Ophelia's eyes widened at the scene being played out before her;
'Umm, umm, yeah that's it bitch, suck it…swallow that dick. Yeah baby, you know the way I like it'
Caspian was standing on the court as bold as brass with his shorts down by his ankles; he seemed to be commentating every part of the sucking off that he was getting.
This surprised Ophelia, because whenever they had sex, he'd never ever made a sound. She looked down to see who the suckee was, and as she began thinking to herself that the bitch had a wavy dark brown weave, her mind suddenly clicked as she realised that the person pleasuring her boyfriend, was her very own cousin Ronke.
'Oh yes Casp, I know how you like it nigga…watch me lick this *Sizzurp* off ya dick'
She then poured a little of the alcoholic beverage out of its bottle on to Caspian's member and proceeded to slurp it up.
Up until this point, Ophelia was unaware that apart from being a slut, her cousin was also a little freak; she began to storm towards them across the center of the court.

'Caspian, Caspian..what the hell do you think you're doing? What the fuck is this…you're cheating on me…with my cousin? Did you have to go that low Caspian..huh? What you can't hear me now..cat got your tongue?' said Ophelia. Ronke looked up at her and thought that she would set her cousin straight;

'Sorry Ophelia but he can't be cheating on you because he's my man…you must have the wrong idea, doesn't she honey' she replied looking up at him.

'What do you mean your man? Caspian and I have been seeing each other for the past 6 months! So Caspian this means you've been playing us both? I can't even believe what's happening right now….you dirty rotten bastard!' exclaimed Ophelia

Caspian looked on bewildered like a deer caught between headlights;

'Baby, I didn't mean to do this, it's a mistake…please I'm sorry…it's a mistake' and as he spoke, Caspian brushed Ronke away from him and started to walk towards Ophelia, pulling up his boxers at the same time.

Ronke could not believe what she had just heard;

'What did you just say Caspian, a mistake? Everything we've had was a mistake, the way I've given myself to you was a mistake?…nigga you must be crazy if you think…' before she could finish, Caspian cut Ronke off abruptly;

'Ophelia, please don't listen to this trick, for real, it was a mistake…you're the one I love baby…I swear that she was just a jump off' said Caspian visibly adding insult to Ronke's injury.

Ophelia balked at his comments towards her cousin with anger;

This dude is even trying to justify his behaviour! she thought angrily;

Ronke who by now was hurt beyond reason, descended into floods of tears and rounded herself to confront him;

'Caspian, you telling me I was just a jump off, after everything? Do you think I would have been giving it up to you if I knew you only saw me as a muthafuckin' jump off? You said that if I did right you'd make me your woman….you promised me…' Ophelia's mouth opened wide at Ronke's statement.

'Oh come on Ronke, you really thought I'd be serious with you after you sucked my dick and let me hit it on the first night? Bitch please…you even let me fuck you in the ass a week later..' he said with scorn.

Ronke became almost hysterical and screamed like a woman deranged;

'But Caspian, I only did all that because I love you…when I saw you talking to Ophelia that day in Washington Park…I was so jealous that I did whatever I felt I had to do to keep you interested in me…I never thought that you'd be playing us both!'

The coldness in his next reply would make Ophelia thank God that she'd decided to meet him at the court that night, had she not, she would never have realised how wicked Caspian actually was;

'Like I said it was a mistake Ronke…you believed what ya wanted to believe aight….I ain't really got time for your shit so I suggest you leave me and Ophelia alone…Ophelia…baby, please forgive me..I'

The final nail in the coffin turned Ronke into a madwoman; without warning she lunged at his face with her clenched fist;

'You bastard, you muthafuc…' Ronke's words were lost as she lay into Caspian with all her might. He put his arms up to defend his face but she was far too quick, and hit him squarely in the eye; Ophelia could see the blood running down his cheek.

Even though she felt that the bastard deserved everything he got, she didn't see why Ronke should put herself in the position of being expelled on his account.

Ophelia grabbed Ronke by the shoulders and pulled her off him.
'Ronke, leave him alone he's not worth getting expelled over. Let's just leave this place…come on Ronke just leave it…leave it' Ophelia began to drag her cousin away as the poor girl continued to cry inconsolably.

'Caspian, you wait…what you've done to me..someone is gonna do worse to you! Mark my words you bastard…I hate you Caspian Strong…I hate you!!' screamed Ronke. Ophelia had the last word 'I guess I don't need to tell you that it's over…thanks a million Caspian and have a nice life' and with that the girls stormed into the night time air. The fresh cold of the wind stung both of their teary eyes with its sharpness; it seemed that a bond had been forged between them out of tragedy that night and some things would inevitably have to change.

~~~~

As the saying goes, pride comes before a fall. This was never as apparent in reference to Ronke as it was at that point. The shock of betrayal and loss almost sent her spiralling into a nervous breakdown. After that fateful night, she literally became a shadow of her former self and reverted to wearing drab clothes, no make-up .She had also lost weight from neglecting to eat properly. The starkest symbol of her pain where her eyes that had become sunken from sleepless nights of crying and cursing the day that Caspian Strong was born.

Even though she was disliked by many on campus, it was still very sad for everyone to see her broken down like that. Truly a woman scorned, Ronke was bitter yet at the same time completely humbled; she really didn't know what to do with herself as defeat had never been in her vocabulary up until this point. Ronke was used to getting her own way and had never lived any different, daddy had always seen to that.

After what she had been through, Ronke swore to herself that from then on she would never love another man the way that she had loved Caspian. Sadly as a result of the break up, Ronke decided to close her heart to love forever.

Ophelia was fortunate enough to feel differently about the situation. Even though Caspian had betrayed her trust, it wasn't so bad because in her case, since she was just about to dump him anyway. She only wished that poor Ronke had never got involved with such a miserable piece of scum. Over the fallout of the situation, the girls bonded like never before. Ophelia and Ronke had a heart to heart talk about what happened with Caspian and as fate would have it, their relationship slowly developed into a mutually respected friendship. Ophelia expressed to Ronke how much of a bitch she used to be and how badly she had treated people; Ronke in turn told Ophelia of how she was jealous of her and the talent she possessed. Once everything had been brought out into the open to clear the air, it seemed that talking to each other was the best remedy for the varying degrees of pain that they both felt. Thankfully, at least one good thing came out of their dalliance with Caspian Strong. However, even though she had now made peace with her cousin, Ronke was still depressed and knew innately, that she would never be the same again.

Mid-morning on the following Saturday, Ronke went to the hair salon to get her old weave taken out and a new one put in. She was the type of chick who had her hair done every two weeks without fail, so her hair was always on point. Since she visited the salon so often, her stylist Dionne was already waiting for her by the chair. Even though she was a regular client at the salon, Dionne had come to dread Ronke's visits simply because of her bad attitude. The only consolation was that she was a good tipper; when your family was as wealthy as Ronke's, a $50 tip was nothing.

As she began to cut the old weave tracks out of Ronke's hair, Dionne noticed that something was amiss. Normally by now Ronke would have driven her crazy with her incessant moaning and complaining about something or other that she didn't like. Ronke wasn't even talking on her cell phone! Dionne looked at her face through the mirror and could see that Ronke was simply staring into space. At the risk of a curt reply, Dionne decided to ask her what was up
'Hey Ronke, are you ok? You seem a little….well a little bit quiet today. You're not really yourself'
Ronke looked up at Dionne through the mirror and blinked to stop her tears from falling.
'Oh I'm sorry babe, just…well it's nothing that bad…I broke up with my man a last week. I'm just finding it kinda hard to function as normal. Please don't think it's you…I just need a little time'
Even though the words she'd just said were some of the hardest things she'd had to say, it was better for her not to kid herself and face the reality of the matter. Her relationship with Caspian was finished.

Dionne nodded her head and carried on with her work. Looking at Ronke's face, she guessed that the young girl had loved him; maybe

74

he was even her first love.

The first ones are always the hardest to get over thought Dionne.
Ronke then decided to put right another one of the wrongs that she
had committed.

'I believe I owe you a sincere apology Dionne, I'm sure that I've
been one of your most difficult customers, and for that I am deeply
sorry. I hope you can find it in your heart to forgive me…it would
mean so much if you did'

Dionne looked at Ronke in disbelief, was this too good to be true?
'Wow Ronke, I'm still shocked at what you said, that's a big deal
coming from, you. I do forgive you though…I ain't one to hold
grudges….let's just start again on a blank page shall we'

Dionne's kind words melted Ronke's heart.

'Thank you Dionne, I really appreciate that, you don't realise how
much. Thank you again from the bottom of my heart'

After a while, Ronke's hair was washed and conditioned ready for
the next weave to be installed. As Dionne got the extension hair
ready, Ronke felt an overwhelming urge to pass on the weave and
cut her hair short. It was amazing what a break up can do to a woman
and Ronke was feeling much like Angela Bassett's character in the
movie *'Waiting to Exhale'*.

Since wearing weaves for the past three years, her hair had grown
long to mid-back length; she didn't care much for the long hair
though, Ronke just wanted a drastic change from her old self.

'Dionne, I've changed my mind about a weave, can I have a haircut
instead' she asked.

'What you just want me to trim your own hair and do a simple style'
Dionne thought that this was getting weirder by the minute. This was
the lady that would have her weave done every two weeks without
fail for the past three years; Dionne was about to be shocked even
further.

'No Dionne, I'd like a short cut like a Halle Berry cut' said Ronke.
'Are you sure that you wanna cut that drastic? You hair is so long
now, how you gonna throwaway all of that length?' Dionne was
determined to make sure that this was what her patron wanted; she

wasn't about to get sued over cutting some hair off!
Just as Ronke was about to protest Bijou walked into the salon; she'd
said that she would meet Ronke at the salon later on; Dionne had
never been happier to see Bijou, maybe she could talk some sense
into her best friend.

Once she was filled in on the situation, Bijou couldn't believe what
Ronke was suggesting;
'You want to do what to your hair? No no no *Cherie*, I don't think
that you are thinking straight. But that is to be expected considering'
Dionne nodded her head in agreement. I would be a great shame to
cut off such beautiful hair. It was also uncommon for a black woman
to have hair that long, so Ronke would be a fool to cut it all off.
Eventually, Bijou made the call for her.
'Ronke won't have a short cut but she won't be having a weave
either. Maybe it's time to wear your own hair for a while, Ronks.
Dionne can you please give her a roller set blowout and a trim,
thanks'
Ronke looked up Bijou's face. She wanted to tell Bijou that it was
her hair and she would do with it what she wished, but she just
couldn't do it. Ronke knew in her heart if hearts that Bijou was right.
If she did cut off all her hair, she would end up regretting it for years.
After this thought, she leaned back and let Dionne get to working.
This time around; she felt calm for all the right reasons.

After about 2 hours under the hooded dryer, Ronke's hair was
finished and she gave Dionne a bigger tip than usual before leaving
the salon with Bijou. Her hair was styled in a full head of bouncy
dark brown curls and she loved it! Who knew that the hair growing
out of her very own head could look so beautiful?
As she caught glimpses of her reflection through store windows,
Ronke told herself that from then on, she would give the weaves a
miss for a while and enjoy the gorgeous mane that God had given
her.

~~~~

Ophelia couldn't make up her mind on what to do next. Her parents had asked her to come home in December for the annual family end of year/Christmas celebrations. Last year, she was with Caspian so she'd feigned having lots of exams to avoid going back home, however this time she had no excuse. Apart from seeing her mother once in her second year of University so far when she had visited New York for a week, Ophelia had not seen any of her family since leaving Launceston.

She suspected that if she did go to Nigeria, there would be talk of her meeting the suitor that her father had probably already chosen for her. Once she met him, there would only be one year of University left before she had to do the inevitable and get married; she didn't know if she was looking forward to this or not. Earlier that day, she'd emailed Minty to ask what she thought she should do. At times like these, Ophelia knew that her best friend was the only person who understood her enough to give some sound advice. A few hours later, Minty had sent her a reply:

From: Fortescue-Black, Araminta
To: Emeka-Phillips, Ophelia
Subject: RE: To or not to go...that is the question!! Minty, need your help hon!

Hi Phily phils!!!

I guess you're still getting over Caspian right? Or is he already ancient history? I still can't believe that he was doing the dirty on both you and Ronke...I KNOW SHE IS (WAS) A BITCH but no one deserves to be treated like that! And neither do you...at least it was for the best and you caught him in the act! I'm sure that the girl he's with now isn't half as beautiful as you are Phils..he lost a good'n...he really did!

On the going to Africa front....I'm not sure what to say about that! You know that I invited you (in my last email) to Dunraven for the

Christmas period so of course I selfishly want you to come to mine instead..however since I do have the simply divine Dominic to keep me company during the cold cold winter (boo hoo me!) then I'll say that you should go back home.

I think the change of scenery and seeing your family will be good for you. Who knows? Your daddy may have even come up trumps and found you a tall strapping Mandingo for a husband, trust me Caspian won't even enter your thoughts at that point! All I'm saying is go there, see your people and have some fun...maybe you'll come over to me for Easter! I know you'll def be here in summer because of the wedding! Yay!

OK QUICK WEDDING UPDATE:

All the prep is going well but mama is driving me mad with all her fussing! I know that I'm the only daughter but gosh, you'd think that I was Princess Di the way that this mad woman is carrying on! I feel like I should leave her to it and just turn up at the wedding! What do you think...actually never mind..this whole wedding stuff can drive you round the bend! I'm sure you'll be telling me the same thing when you get married in a few years (yes Oph, just a few years!)

That's enough rambling for now, finally FYI things with Dominic are going great! In fact it's fantastic and I can't wait to have this man's babies...I may even get preggers before the wedding! Imagine how that would go down....Great Auntie Maude would choke on her watercress and cream soup! Ha!!

Bye for now... love you lots as always...out of sight is most definitely not out of mind!!

Minty ☺

As usual Minty came through. After some thought, Ophelia called her mother to let her know that she would be coming to Nigeria for the Christmas break. She looked forward to seeing everyone and as an added bonus, her mother had informed her that her older brother Kelechi would be taking leave from work to make it too.

The last time that Ophelia had touched Nigerian soil was at least 5 years back and since then, she had made the inevitable transition from a girl to a young woman. Ophelia decided that the trip would be a good thing for her; it was best to look to the future with positivity and she could only but take a guess at what her life had in store for her next.

Chapter 9

The heat was unbearable once the plane landed on the tarmac. Ophelia looked out of the window and could see the familiar sight of a sun induced mirage at the end of the runway. As the passengers filed off the Virgin Atlantic flight to Lagos, she felt a fresh trail of sweat break and run down the back of her leg. These were the kind of equatorial temperatures that even the plane's air conditioning system had trouble trying to compete with; Ophelia was back in Africa and it sure felt good to be home.

Once she'd got through immigration and customs, she quickly did the long walk to the airport arrivals lounge; as she got closer, she could see him in the distance waving his fabric hat wildly. It was her daddy and boy had he gained some weight! Ophelia picked up her suitcase and broke into a brisk run that ended with a triumphant hug for her father.

'Daddy! It's so good to see you! Where's mummy…and Kelechi? How is everybody?' she exclaimed with excitement.

'Ok, ok, slow down, slow down child. Give an old man a chance to catch his breath!' Jonathan laughed loudly at her impatient talk; *these young ones are always so full of energy* he thought.

Jonathan took her case from her and gave it to the designated driver for the day that, in typically Nigerian fashion was named Sunday.

'Sunday, please take the luggage to the car and we'll meet you outside in a minute' said Jonathan and then turned to Ophelia;

'I'll fill you in on everything once we get to the car, but let me know first, do you want to get a snack here at the airport before we depart? It's just that it's going to be a long journey to the house'

Ophelia wasn't that hungry, but she would however settle for an ice cold drink.

'Daddy can I have a drink instead, I'm not fussed about it, *7up* or *Fanta* is fine'

Ophelia always found it quite disturbing that a country such as Nigeria (with its citizens as resourceful and enterprising as they were) had few of its own major brands of goods. *Coca Cola* more or less monopolized the soft drink industry so locally produced alternatives didn't stand much of a chance. The thought of this always made Ophelia feel angry and disgusted at the wickedness of the western world; this was their so called 'globalization'

~~~~~

Once in the car, they began the hour long journey to their house on the Lagos mainland; the family owned a few properties in Nigeria, but the main family home was a huge mansion in the capital city of, Abuja. The Lagos home was only used for holidays, parties and entertaining. To be quite frank, the Emeka-Phillips yearly family reunion was just another excuse for a big party; not that one needed much of an excuse to have a party in Nigeria. The wonderful thing about having parties back home was that they often spilled onto the streets and neighbours would come over wanting to be fed and also join in on the fun. This was to be expected of course, so one always made sure that there was enough food and drink to feed the whole neighbourhood if possible. Thankfully, Ophelia's mother always made sure that there was a huge spread and as a result of this their annual parties were legendary.

~~~~

The next day, the housekeeper and all the female home help were up at 6 o'clock in the morning; it was normal for people to get up as soon as the sun rose, and there was also the fact that things needed to be prepared for the party later that evening. Ophelia was awoken by the sound of the cockerel in the backyard and the sharp sound of the women's nimble chatter. She could understand some of their words as they mostly spoke in broken English.
A few of the ladies spoke in her mother's tribal language of *Yoruba,* of which Ophelia struggled to understand a few words. Some of the other ladies spoke the *Igbo* language, which was her father's origin and this was even more difficult for her to understand. Unfortunately, since she had travelled so much in her life and spent so much time away from her family; Ophelia had not really been able to grasp any of her parents' mother tongues.

As the day wore on, Ophelia walked to the kitchen and watched the ladies prepare food for a while. She had asked them if she could be of assistance in any way but they had been insistent that she not do any work. It would have been great if they had taught her how to cook a few dishes, but since she was from 'abroad' they treated Ophelia like a celebrity. In the backyard, the ladies were singing as they pounded some yam flour and hot water in a giant mortar and pestle. Someone else was cleaning the fresh peppered beef and goat meat that would later be barbecued for the evening's party. Plantain was being fried inside the kitchen and a popular delicacy made from pureed beans wrapped in palm leaves called *'moi moi'*, was being boiled in a huge cooking pot. What Ophelia looked forward to most was the fried fish that would be served with some deliciously savoury fried mixed vegetable rice. As usual there was also *jollof* rice being prepared for those who preferred plainer tastes on their palette.

Sandra came into the kitchen to see how the preparations were going; she needed to make sure that everything went smoothly, as the party would be the talk of the town. This year a reporter and photographer from *Ovation* magazine (which was Nigeria's answer to *Hello* or *OK!* magazines) would be attending the party. Sandra had also prepared a selection of stunning outfits for both herself and Ophelia to wear on the night; the family also had native costumes made in identical fabrics and they would be worn for some of the formal pictures. Jonathan has seen to it that the family's very own photographer and video guy would be capturing the event as well.

'So what do you think of the menu Ophelia?' Sandra asked her daughter.
'Mummy, it looks absolutely delicious! I want to eat them all now! Can we at least have some of the fish for lunch?'
Her mother laughed to herself and was glad that Ophelia approved of the food.
'It's okay, I'm taking you to a restaurant for lunch. It's just you and me today because I've banned your daddy from attending. I'm sure we have lots of things to catch up on and I want to spend some time having you all to myself' Sandra then gave Ophelia a squeeze and ruffled her hair; she knew that even though her little girl wasn't a baby anymore, she still needed to know that her mother would always love her no matter what. Ophelia herself hugged her mother back and at that moment felt privileged to be loved by her parents; it sure was good to be home.

~~~~

Ophelia could hear the live band striking up a new tune as she descended down the spiral stairs to join the buzzing party. They had opened up the gates at the front compound at around 6.30 that evening, and people quickly started flooding in.
Her parents were already downstairs to greet their guests, but Ophelia was quite nervous and took a little longer to join them. Some of the people down there were her relatives and close family friends who hadn't seen her in so many years; Ophelia was a little shy in

83

anticipation of their inevitable comments that was a 'big girl now' and 'how much she had grown'. She also wished that Kelechi was there to walk her down the stairs and into the party. Unfortunately his plane into Lagos had been delayed; he probably wouldn't get to the party until around 10 o'clock that night.

The scale of the party was pretty impressive. There were white tented canopies spread out over the huge driveway and also scattered out on to the green and the guests were seated at tables underneath the marquee, already enjoying the delicious food and drink. The sound of their voices was almost deafening. As the vibrant conversations and ribald laughter cut through the ambiance into the dusk as the sun went down; the only thing that drowned them out was the band music being blasted out of the massive ground level speakers. Suddenly, the pace of the music changed and sped up, as hot new young musician Femi Ade and his band Fuji Warriors took to the stage. Ophelia guessed that he must have been very popular, because as soon as he got up there, everybody got up and positioned themselves in front of the band to dance; the only exception to this, being a few oldies that stayed seated tapped their feet in time to the beat. The guests swayed vigorously to the hypnotic beat of the drummers, who were already furiously dripping with sweat. Music was an important apart of Nigerian culture and it was not uncommon for people to still be dancing into the early hours of the morning.

Ophelia could see the vibrant colors of the ladies *gelés* (which were large and extravagant traditional head wraps that they wore) and the gentlemen's *agbadas* (that served as the kaftan style traditional male attire) swinging as they danced. She wanted to join in the dancing as she was already feeling the beat; it was now apparent to Ophelia, that while she had lived abroad for most of her life, the Nigerian blood that flowed through her veins was undeniable. Now that she was back home, she felt complete at last.

Ophelia spotted her parents and went up to their table, as she walked along she could feel the eyes of all the men around both young and old staring at her behind. She smiled to herself inwardly; if there was anywhere in the world that a shapely behind would be admired, it would surely be in Africa.

Upon reaching her parents table, Ophelia was presented to some members of her extended family as they filed past. They treated her father as though he were royalty; however, Ophelia knew from experience, that their warm sentiments were only fuelled in the hope of a substantial cash donation from him. Only a chosen few had to good fortune to be rich in Nigeria; if one had to suck up to a rich relative in order to keep their own family fed, then that is what one did. Rather than dwell on such a thought, Ophelia tried to put it at the back of her mind and decided to concentrate on enjoying the celebrations instead. This was one of the things she really loved about her people, they knew how to throw one hell of party. Even when they lived overseas Nigerians loved to party; the basic main ingredients of an excellent get together were good times and good company. Ample food and drink also needed to be added to the mix or the vibe just wouldn't be right.

As the evening wore on, people continued to dance and have fun. For the most part, there were no real trouble makers to spoil things; the only one person that got really drunk was her uncle Saul, but that was normal anyway. He was the family embarrassment and always got drunk after too many bottles of *Guinness* at most parties, however nobody had the heart to stop inviting him to any family functions.

After she'd had some of the coveted fried fish and savoury rice, Ophelia and her parents hit the floor for some serious dancing. Her father led the way and found a prominent spot in front of the band stage. They all stood in a semi circle and were also joined by other members of the family as they started dancing. It was an enchanting sight to see, as the Emeka-Phillips clan were all wearing their matching outfits.

As they danced, the camcorder capturing the event was pushed near Ophelia's face several times. The Photographer almost made her

85

jump when he took a snap of her all of a sudden; the flash from the camera in contrast to the night darkness startled her. Upon noticing her discomfort, Jonathan asked him to take the snaps a little further back, so as not to frighten his daughter like that again.

After dancing for some time, her father pulled out a fat bank roll of $50 bills and began to *spray* Ophelia, her mother and some of the other ladies; this was the Nigerian custom of showering a person with money whilst they were dancing. One of her poorer aunties helped her pick up any money that fell onto the floor and held on to it on to for her; Ophelia's auntie secretly wished that she wouldn't ask for the money back, *what does this spoiled rich girl from abroad know about hardship anyway?* she thought.
The rest of Jonathan's friends and some other well off family members began to *spray* the ladies as well. While it was strange that everyone was *spraying* in US dollar bills rather than the country's highly devalued national currency the Naira, their social circle would never dream of using anything else; Dr Emeka-Phillips and his friends were richer than most of the guests at the party's wildest dreams and as once famously quoted, they had the money to burn.

At around 9.30 her parents decided to go and sit back down. Opheila felt exhilarated by the dancing but she felt a little thirsty and started to walk over to the drinks table to grab a soda; just as she looked over to there she gasped as she spied her other brother Kelechi standing there with a taller friend. They had obviously just arrived at the party and were grabbing a couple of ice cold drinks. Ophelia noticed that Kelechi had also gained some weight, but surprisingly of the muscular type. She was almost running through the crowd to meet him as she had not seen her big bro for over a year. Before she could get to Kelechi, an old friend of her mothers stopped to talk to Ophelia. She chatted to the lady politely but was distracted by the thought of going over to meet her brother. It was then that she could feel someone staring at her.
Ophelia could see a dark and handsome stranger sitting next to her brother looking directly at her. The lady she had been speaking to

86

had moved on by now, so his eyes were impossible to ignore. Ophelia looked away for a moment but when she looked back in his direction, he was still staring at her. This time she decided to be defiant and held his gaze. *Who does this guy think he is?* she thought. Just as she was about to walk over to them, her mother came and took her away to change into her third outfit of the evening.

Back inside the house, one of the maids helped her into a stunning white floor length linen gown; her mother then tied a white embroidered fabric scarf in a headband style around Ophelia's head. The fabric beautifully complimented hair that was styled in long afro twists that fell down her back; the dress had tiny cap sleeves and a scoop neck that revealed her high milk chocolate skinned cleavage. It was also designed to showcase her tiny waist and full round bottom to maximum effect; the bottom and tail of the dress was trimmed with reflective white sequins that sparkled every time Ophelia moved.

As a finishing touch, Sandra brought out her very own diamond bracelets for her to wear. Ophelia was a little puzzled, these were her mother's favourite items of *Cartier* jewelry; she started to wonder what the big occasion was.

'Mummy, thank you but…. how come you're allowing me to wear these? They are so beautiful, I'm afraid that I might even break them' she said laughing.

Sandra smiled as though she could no longer keep a secret;

'Because my dear, tonight is a special night! Don't look so confused darling, you'll soon find out. Now let's get back to the party shall we'

Once they were making their way down the stairs, Ophelia decided she wouldn't worry too much about what her mother was talking about for the time being. As they walked back into the party crowd she noticed that the street was lit up with electric lamps that had been threaded through the trees; the misty sparkle of the light bounced off the sequins on her dress and illuminated her in the most beautiful glow. When she looked up, Ophelia could see that Kelechi was walking over to her and so was the dark stranger. Even though she herself was a beautiful milk chocolate hue, her admirer was so dark that he was near ebony. The depth of his skin color made his complexion almost seem navy blue, she also noticed that his features were so handsome and his teeth so white! He was so beautiful that Ophelia thought to herself that he could easily star in one of those *Calvin Klein* ads just like Djimon Hounsou or Tyson Beckford. Kelechi was just about to introduce his friend when he himself decided to speak;

'Hello there my love, I'm Deji…Deji Olajuwon, you must be the lovely Ophelia'

He bent down to kiss her hand softly; she noticed that he spoke in a posh English accent that had a charm which made her melt inside. Her own accent had been mixed over the years due to travelling so much; he obviously wasn't as easily influenced.

For a few seconds Ophelia couldn't speak, her mind had drawn a blank because she was so mesmerised by him. Kelechi decided to break the awkward silence.

'Actually it's Prince AdeDeji Nasir Yemi Olajuwon, heir to the Ogun state monarchy to be quite exact!' Kelechi then turned to his friend and laughed 'Deji why do you always downplay yourself? Trust me, if I was a prince then everyone would know about it!'

Deji shook his head and turned his face towards Ophelia

'Since your brother has decided to expose me, I am a Prince but I don't like to stand on formality' he said 'besides, I know that ladies much prefer a gentleman that is quietly confident, am I correct Ophelia?'

Without warning Ophelia's voice almost failed her, while quivering with lust, she finally replied;

'Yes, you're quite right' she said in her husky transatlantic twang. Ophelia then felt a firm hand grab her wrist gently; it was her daddy;

'So you've met her already? You kids didn't even wait for me!' said Jonathan half seriously and half chuckling. 'I see that you are both getting on well' and at this Deji, beamed at her father will his full perfect set of gleaming white teeth.

'Dr Phillips, you didn't tell me that your daughter is the long lost

twin of a young Naomi Campbell! Had I have known, I would have
landed in Lagos over 2 days ago' replied Deji jestfully.
Ophelia's brain quickly put two and two together and made five;
Is this to be my chosen fiancé? she thought.

After a few exchanges with herself, Deji and Kelechi, her father
motioned to leave their table;
'I'm going to leave you two to get to know each other better' said
Jonathan and just before leaving, he gently squeezed Ophelia by her
waist and bent to whisper something in her ear;
'I hope that he will do for you my daughter' and with that he walked
off, disappearing into the throngs of the party crowd. After some
time Kelechi also left, tactfully leaving Deji and Ophelia to make
small talk.
As they were going through the usual motions of 'getting to know
each other' talk, Ophelia could feel herself getting wet with every
word that Deji spoke. She had never loved her father more in her
whole life! It was as if he knew exactly what Ophelia would want in
a future husband; smart, considerate, educated, funny, an athletic
body and last but not least, he was extremely attractive. She became
hypnotised by his thick pink lips and tongue as he spoke; she
imagined how those same lips would eventually feel like eating her
pussy out. Ophelia was sure that if he'd laid her down right then and
there she would have gladly opened up her thighs without any
hesitation.
So Minty was right then, she thought, *Caspian who?*

~~~~

By the end of the evening Ophelia was exhausted and the guests
didn't finish departing until 3am; they had thrown one hell of a party
that had all the right ingredients; good food, live music and the
raucous company of family and friends. It certainly ended up being
good night.
Afterwards, Ophelia went up to her room to take off her dress and
her mother was already waiting for her to do the nightly ritual of

plaiting up her hair before bed. As Ophelia sat by the dressing table mirror, her mother carefully put her afro twists into one big braid at the back of her head.

'So what did you think of the Prince? Is he up to your standards?' her mother inquired. Ophelia thought about what her response would be; she didn't want to seem too eager or at the same time un-interested in Deji. She decided to play it cool.
'He is a nice guy…well mannered and well spoken. I like him mother'
Sandra smiled at her daughter's approval.
'Good Ophelia…that is very good! I am happy that you like him; as you may have already guessed, he is to be your husband. Your father has been speaking to Deji's father King Olajuwon about this for over a year now and seeing that they are royalty, you will be marrying very well. It's only appropriate for you my child and for our two families'

Once her hair was wrapped inside her silk bedtime scarf, Ophelia's mother left her to sleep; as she was drifting off, Efua, who was one of the youngest maids in the household, came in to make the last checks on the mosquito nets in her bedroom; soon after this Ophelia let herself float into a blissful sleep.

Chapter 10

It was the morning after the night before and Ophelia rolled out of bed reluctantly. She had wanted to get up just before midday, however her mother had instructed Efua to wake her just before 10 that morning. Ophelia took a bath and moisturized her body with some raw shea butter afterwards that was of local produce; Sandra had long since given up on buying expensive creams like as *Clarins* or *Clear Essence* for her daughter as she would never use them anyway. It seemed that Ophelia much preferred what the 'common' people used; in her eyes, there was nothing wrong with the natural elements that God had provided them growing out of the his green Earth. Sandra guessed there was no harm in that; however she felt that her daughter deserved a lot better.

By the time Ophelia got downstairs, her breakfast was waiting for her. Since everyone else had already eaten, she was left alone at the table. This suited her fine, there was a lot think about as a result of last night and this way she could actually hear own thoughts. Ophelia was glad that she at least found Deji attractive and got on with him;

the prospect of the arranged marriage didn't seem so bleak after all. Even though technically no-one could be forced into an arranged marriage, it would bring immeasurable shame on her family in the community (and even in the country since her father was an ambassador) if she had refused. Deji seemed to be a nice guy and they would at least have a year and a half to get to really know each other before the wedding. Thankfully, Ophelia still had a year and two semesters of University left to go.

Just as she was lost in her thoughts, it seemed that they had a visitor. As soon as she heard his voice Ophelia didn't need two guesses to know who was calling for her. Deji was shown into the breakfast room and offered something to eat; he declined food but asked for some hot tea and sat down opposite her. As his mouth broke into a smile she felt her self melt away all over again.

'Good Morning Princess Ophelia…you know that you're my Princess now right? I think I'll call you that so you get used to it….or do you mind it?' Deji asked her.

'Oh…Good morning to you too Deji…and no I don't mind…it just makes me a little shy, that's all' Ophelia replied.

Deji stirred the tea in his cup without stopping to look down and turned his gaze towards his stunning wife to be. He thought to himself, that she was even lovelier without make up.

'That's okay sweetheart, nothing wrong with being shy. When we met all those years ago, that was my main problem. My shyness is all gone now as you can see! My head has gotten so big now just because I've put on a little bit of weight!' and with that Deji laughed and Ophelia couldn't help but to join in. He made conversation easy and light, never putting the slightest pressure on her. The only thing that Ophelia couldn't figure out was where they had met before.

'Deji, you said that we had met before…sorry but I can't seem to think of where?' asked Ophelia.

'Oh, I don't blame you if you don't remember…we met the last time you were over here. This was around five years back; you must have just turned 15 if I remember correctly. It was at your family's Christmas party…I was the guy that you had a long conversation about rap music with. But back then I was 21, skinny, lanky and wore glasses…ring any bells'

Ophelia let her mind think back to the moment in time that he'd referred to;

'Ahh, I remember now… but wow you've really really changed! You look so different now…so grown up Deji! You look like another person!' she exclaimed.

'I know…about a year after we met, I started going to the gym more regularly and I had *Lasik* surgery to fix my eyes so that I could ditch the glasses. It seems as if that was the best thing I ever did and I suppose as a young man, I was fed up of being a nerd. To be quite honest, I'd been dreaming about you since that very day…' said Deji wistfully, then suddenly switched the pace of the conversation;

'Sorry to change the subject right now, but I must ask…what are you plans for today? It's just that your father has given his permission for me to take you out to lunch and also meet my parents this afternoon….they're simply dying to meet you my dear.'

Ophelia smiled at her father's forwardness and Deji's enthusiasm;

'Well I guess my daddy knows that I don't have any plans for today…but thanks anyway for asking…I hope that you're always this much of a gentleman Deji' she replied cheekily.

His heart warmed at what she'd just said; *at least she has a sense of humor* thought Deji.

'For you my love…I will be a gentleman and thensome'

Deji drove a luxurious *Mercedes E* class air conditioned sedan. As they he led her to the car, the bright sunlight bounced off the shiny black paint; Ophelia guessed that the car was only driven when ever Deji was in town because of its pristine Lagos plates and clean rims. He had given his driver the afternoon off and decided they should have some quality time alone without any interruptions. As they drove off to the restaurant district, Ophelia surreptitiously looked down at his pants and wondered how big he was. Something told her that he would have a lot to offer in that department; he'd already held her by her tiny waist, seeming knowing just the right spot to make her go tingly earlier that day. As if Deji read her mind, he put his hand on her thigh when they stopped at the red light and rubbed it slowly; at this, Ophelia gasped, feigning embarrassment but in truth she was very excited;

'My darling, I want to tell you to something that should put your mind at rest. Even though I'm a red blooded male with physical needs, I promise you that I won't try to touch you intimately before our wedding night. Not only do I love you sweetheart, but I have utmost respect for your body as well…do you understand what I'm trying to say Ophelia? I don't want to spell it out using explicit terms that's all'.
Secretly disappointed, she'd hoped that he would 'touch' her before their wedding night, however her response reflected the quite opposite of her thoughts;
'Thank you Deji, I am touched that you have that much respect for me….it's actually very refreshing to hear a young man speak with such maturity these days' she replied, and then looked away from him as a sign of her modesty and submissiveness.

Deji had booked a table for two at the Sheraton Lagos Hotel restaurant for their lunch. Once inside, they continued their talk.
'Deji, I must be honest with you and do not mean rudeness when I say this but, how can you love me as much as you say you do already? It's just that you don't really know me and…' before she could finish Deji put a finger on her lips to silence her;
'Shh…I guess I should really fill you in on the whole story. Kelechi has actually known this for years now but, I actually fell in love with you all those years ago at the Christmas party. Of course you were too young for me to approach your family since you were only 15, so I waited until now…I prayed each year that you wouldn't meet some other guy that would sweep you off your feet…they just wouldn't know how to treat a lady like you. You are so refined…so regal and destined to be a queen. I could see that in you even when you were only a child Ophelia'

After her horrendous experience with Caspian, what Deji was saying seemed too good to be true. It seemed that a little more investigation was in order;

'Deji, I am so flattered and so touched at what you've just said and I am very grateful that you love me so. At the same time I'm still at a loss because you still wouldn't have known me...I mean the real me, not just a girl you met at a family party...I mean what's so great about me?' asked Ophelia genuinely.

Deji laughed out loud, his wife to be was not only beautiful, but ethically sound too; he couldn't fob her off with flattery and compliments unlike most women he knew.

'Alright Ophelia....since you're twisting my arm, proverbially of course, I'll explain further. Your dear brother Kelechi filled me in on some info about your character, your likes, dislikes etc and I have also spoken to your mother in confidence and she spoke highly of you. Don't be embarrassed but she told me that even though you are living on campus in such a promiscuous place as New York, you have still held on to your chastity. I know that it's not a be all and end all nowadays, but it says a lot to me about you as a woman. Your mother and father also say that you are an obedient and thoughtful daughter. That's basically all the things that I'm looking for in a wife...I hope you don't think me a stalker?' he said looking sexy but worried.

'Oh no, I'm don't think so...I'm actually quite flattered, no one has ever done all that because of me before...so thank you. In that case, please don't think me forward for saying this, but I think I really like you Deji...you make me feel so comfortable...'

As she trailed off, Deji was pleased at her sentiments; maybe in time, she would eventually grow to love him too.

'Oh Ophelia, I don't think you forward at all, in fact you've made me the happiest man on earth!'

He flashed her a bright smile and then they carried on talking and eating, feeling easy and relaxed in each other's company.

~~~~~

At around 3 o'clock that afternoon they reached the Olajuwon compound gates; Ophelia guessed that it was time to 'meet the parents'

'They are so eager to meet you sweetie, and you mustn't be shy with them. My mother in particular always wanted a daughter but was only capable of producing sons, so she is really looking forward to spoiling you rotten'

Deji smiled at Ophelia to reassure her but she only half smiled back, as her nerves had gotten the better part of her. As they drove inside, she could see that the house was a beautiful white neo-classical style building. There were at least 4 stone pillared balconies on the top floor, French slatted windows and 2 stone lions which stood 'guard' at the huge wooden front double doors. Even though her own family home in Abuja was a sizeable mansion, it was nothing compared to the scale of the Olajuwon home; it was big enough to be a medium sized hotel if the owners so wished it to be.

Once they'd parked in the driveway, one of the gatemen took the car keys from Deji and put the *Mercedes* in the garage, which probably was home to an obscene number of vehicles. Ophelia's fiancé offered her his arm, which she linked in hers and then he led her into the house. She wondered if his parents would like her, or if her outfit was appropriate enough for the occasion; once again as if he had read her mind, the ever attentive Deji reassured her;

'Don't worry my, love...you'll be fine. If I am happy to marry you, then I can tell you that my folks will adore you'

Ophelia's heart was still beating a hundred miles per hour at the thought. She hoped that he was right.

If the outside of the house was impressive, then the interior was even more breathtaking; Ophelia thought she'd walked into an episode of MTV Cribs. There were beautiful paintings and sumptuous classical Italian furniture in every corner, and that was just the hallway. She looked up at the ceiling fans and saw that they were made of something that looked like ivory with an intricate cut out design on the blades. The floor was of grey marble with Persian rugs liberally scattered around for good measure. Just before they reached the main reception room, Ophelia caught a glimpse of herself in the full length gilt framed mirror. She supposed she looked fine, well at least she hoped she did.

The King and Queen were seated on one of the huge cream sofas watching *CNN* on the plasma screen; then suddenly, they turned their heads around in unison to see the happy couple. Ophelia did a half curtsey which was a mark of respect when greeting one's elders; 'Good afternoon Sir and good afternoon to you ma'am' she said shyly.

'Oh, so you're here! Welcome, you're welcome my daughter...come and sit down' King Olajuwon ushered Ophelia to sit beside him and the Queen sat on the other side of her.

'We are so happy to meet you dear...welcome to the family and our home is you home. Make yourself comfortable Ophelia...you are very much welcome' the Queen finished off her statement with a big smile to try to reassure the poor thing. Deji sat opposite them looking at Ophelia;

'So mum and dad, what do you think...is Ophelia as lovely as I had described her to be?'

The King laughed at his son and said;

'Deji...she is even lovelier and I'm not sure if you deserve a woman this beautiful! You must be sure to take good care of her and let her want for nothing'

The Queen also spoke;

'Ophelia my dear, whatever you need from my son just ask. Nothing should be too big or small for you to ask him ok....and if he gives you the slightest trouble....then he will have me to answer to!'

They all laughed at his mother's playful threat and Ophelia felt more at ease.

'Thank you sir and thank you ma'am for making me feel so welcomed. I'm honoured to meet you both and must commend you for raising a good son'

The Queen put an arm round Ophelia's shoulders and gave her a loving squeeze 'my daughter, we are happy to meet you too...but you must call us mummy and daddy from now on. No need for formalities now that we have met! Oh before I forget... would you like something to eat or drink? You must be thirsty considering the heat outside'

Ophelia supposed that her throat was a little dry;

'Thank you mummy, may I please have some water?' The Queen stood up and took her by the hand 'Why don't we go to the kitchen together and get some? That way you can see a bit more of the house and we can talk some more too ok?'

Queen Olajuwon led the way as they left for the kitchen.

~~~~

Deji and Ophelia left the house at sometime after 7 that evening. The *Mercedes* was already waiting for them but this time a driver was in the front seat. As the couple sat in the spacious back seat, Ophelia felt a frisson of lust tingle up her spine.

'See, I told you that they would love you! Absolutely nothing to worry about...my parents are very easygoing...just like me. But what did you think of them?' Deji inquired.

'Yes, Deji they're lovely.....very nice people and they made me feel so welcome...I really like them' she replied.

Deji then looked into her eyes and gently stroked her face

'You're so beautiful Ophelia, do you know that? Every time I look at you, I almost lose control of myself....look at what you're doing to me...just look'

She looked down and could see Deji's huge erection poking through his cotton chinos. Ophelia wasn't sure what to do, so she looked away not wanting to seem forward.

'I'm so sorry my darling, you're probably not used to seeing that....I didn't mean to embarrass you...please forgive me Ophelia. I just can't help the way I feel about you'

Her heart almost melted at his puppy dog eyes;

'Its okay Deji, I'm not upset...I just didn't expect that...I guess there would be a problem if I didn't arouse you a little' she replied jokingly.

Deji smiled at her looking relieved.

'Thank you my love and I can promise you this, I once you are my wife, I will make you the happiest woman alive'

When Deji dropped her back to her house, Ophelia felt as though she was walking on air. He escorted her back in and took a few minutes to make some small talk with her parents. After about 15 minutes of talking, he said his goodbyes and began to make his way home, but before he left he gave Ophelia a kiss on the cheek; she decided to walk him back to the car

'So Ophelia, what are your plans tomorrow? Maybe we can go to Lekki Beach? That's if you're not to busy…or am I imposing on you a little?'

It would seem that Deji was very keen on spending time with her

'Oh no…not at all, but I think that mummy wants to take me shopping tomorrow, so how about Tuesday or Wednesday?' she replied

'Okay then, I guess one day without you won't kill me will it? But I'll call you tomorrow evening to confirm anyway. Have a good night my dear, and be sure to dream of me' said Deji with a wicked chuckle.

Ophelia waved him off and as his car drove off into the night, she didn't really know what to make of all his declarations of love and devotion to her.

She had so much to ask about her prospective fiancé that troubled her mind; what was Deji Olajuwon really about? What were his likes and dislikes? Was there ever another significant woman in his life? What were his hopes and dreams, his deepest fears? These were questions that Ophelia guessed would be answered as their relationship progressed. He seemed a little too good to be true, a little too perfect. But just like Caspian, Ophelia guessed that any skeletons would come out of the closet eventually and everything that she needed to know would be revealed in time.

~~~~

The two weeks of her holiday in Nigeria flew by. Deji and Ophelia's parents had set a date in May of the following year to hold the formal family introductions and engagement ceremony. There was a clear change of atmosphere amongst the ladies working in the house once they heard of this. Everyone offered their congratulations and gave Ophelia encouraging pats on the back. She would really miss the ladies of the household; they had made her feel completely at home and waited on her hand and foot. She would surely miss them most once she was back on campus.

The day before she was due to leave, Deji took Ophelia to dinner for the last time. He seemed pre-occupied with something, but Ophelia didn't pry; from what she knew of him so far, he usually said whatever was on his mind anyway. Once they had ordered, Deji brought a small navy velvet box out of his pocket and opened it to reveal a beautiful pair of diamond teardrop dangly earrings. The box had the words *'De Grisogono'* on the interior, in other words they probably cost a small fortune.

'Ophelia I got these for you as a small token of my love for you. I promise you that your engagement ring will be a lot more spectacular, but I didn't want to go overboard on my first present to you'

The light of the chandeliers above the dining room above caught the diamonds causing a brilliant sparkle to emanate from them. They were of a teardrop shape and were elegantly complimented by a very detailed professional pear cut. Upon being tested at the jewellers the earrings could actually cut glass;

'Deji these are beautiful, and so pretty! This isn't what I would call a 'small' token but thank you…I absolutely love them!' said Ophelia;

She put the earrings on and they suited her so, that it seemed as if she had been born with them;

'I'm glad that you like my gift and they look beautiful on you as I thought they would; trust me my darling this is only the tip of the iceberg compared to what I have in store for you'

Deji held her hand and looked down at his napkin on the table as if forlorn;

'I know we've only really had these two weeks together, but I am really going to miss you Ophelia. As you know I work in London at *PriceWaterhouseCoopers* with Kelechi, but I've recently decided to get a transfer to one of the New York offices…isn't that great?' he asked.

Ophelia wasn't sure if it was. What if he would put a dampener on her long sought freedom? Or if he made her feel suffocated? Unfortunately, there was no way she could protest in light of her situation; she hoped that in the end, her fears would be unfounded.

'Yes, it sounds great Deji…..but I won't be able to give you too much of my time because of my studies' she replied cautiously.

'Oh don't worry my love, I wouldn't dream of hindering your studies in any way…I just want to closer be you that's all and of course we'll have some weekends so you can pop over to mine whenever you wish, that's all'. At his reassurance Ophelia felt a little more at ease with things.

After she'd spending most of the Day with Deji, they said their goodbyes and then he took the plunge to give her a full French kiss. He was actually a very good kisser and left her wanting more; maybe the idea of Deji coming to New York could be a good idea in the end.

The next morning Ophelia took her flight back to the States. A lot of things had happened in the short space of two weeks; she had so much to tell the girls at Uni and Minty in London as well. As the plane left the tarmac, Ophelia looked at the photo of Deji that she had taken with her cell phone and wondered if the girls would approve. Something inside told her that he would do just fine.

Chapter 11

The first week back at NYU was crazy, hectic and stressful, just was as Ophelia had expected. The worst thing about coming back from a vacation was the work that one had to do upon getting back. There were exams to prepare for and a lot of catching up to do with the girls. It would seem that in spite of her recent aversions to the male species, Ronke and Donnie had a little thing going after all. They had become friends over the holidays and started to spend their free time together. He didn't put her under any pressure, nor did they mention the name 'Caspian' considering the turbulent break up he had had with Ronke. According to Alizé, it had started off as a friendship at first but by the end of December, Donnie would usually be found not far off from wherever Ronke was. They actually made a cute couple but the difference this time was that Donnie was actually in love with Ronke in comparison to the now infamous Caspian.

Ophelia filled the girls in all the details on about her meeting Deji; the earrings especially went down well.

'Oh my gosh mami! They are huge...*De Grisogono*? Phils I am like
sooooooo jealous of your ass right now...look at the bling guys'
It became increasingly apparent that Issy had got a firm grasp of the
New York street slang, as they girls ummed and aahhed at Ophelia's
gift. Alizé put them in her palm to feel the weight of the stones;
'Ophelia, what kind of head did you give this dude to get him to buy
you these rocks? I mean these are some heavy diamonds babe....my
future husband or baby daddy better cop me summa these
y'all....real talk'
Ophelia laughed at Alizé and replied her;
'Naw...I didn't give him anything...it's basically an arranged
marriage and his family is a lot wealthier than mine. Don't tell
anyone about it though...and I'm not saying this to show off, but
he's a Prince too...check out his pic on my cell...hot or not?'
She held the phone up for them to take a look at.
'What do you mean to tell me that your papa chose you a sexy
brother like him to be your hubby? Dang girl....I think I might just
have to hate on you from now on Phils' said Dominique jestfully;
then each of the girls studied Deji's photograph on Ophelia's cell one
by one.
'Oh he's really a hottie trust me, I know I shouldn't say this because
he's my bro but Caspian ain't got nothing on this one. Mr Olajuwon
is definitely a different breed of nigga altogether' said Alizé drooling
'I mean girl, he's in a whole other league for real, another class than
a regular dude'

Ophelia then told them about the party, how they met, not forgetting
the wonderful two weeks that they spent together. The girls all
agreed that he was 'so romantic' and couldn't wait to meet him.
'So when is he gonna transfer to New York? Anytime soon
Ophelia?' asked Alizé. 'Oh I'm not sure yet, probably by early
spring. This is January so I guess the earliest time will be March'
replied Ophelia.
'You really landed on your feet with that one phils for real! Have
you told Minty yet? You know she would totally drool over his pic'
said Issy in her usual suggestive tone.

'No, not had a chance to send her his pic but we did speak over the phone last week. As you know she is really serious about Dominic and the wedding is like taking up so much of her time these days. She's really in love with Dominic so I don't think that she has eyes for anyone else...' said Ophelia trailing off.

After the girls had finished catching up with each other; the only other update was that of the new relationship du jour between Le Quawn and Alizé. She actually really liked him and it seemed that the feeling was mutual. He was taking things slow with Alizé in light of his failed relationship with Kimera his baby mama and the last thing that he wanted was any more emotional drama in what was going to be his rookie year in professional basketball once he'd finished NYU that summer. Le Quawn just didn't need that kind of stress in his life. Even though Alize hung on to his every word, she also understood the importance of how he felt and respected that.

~~~~

Once she'd left her friends and went to get some snacks, Ophelia thought she'd give her cousin a call. It was just out of caring and considering how Caspian had treated her, Ophelia would have to hear it from the horse's mouth if Ronke was really ready for a new relationship. Donnie might have had the best intentions, but it would only result in heartbreak again if Ronke's heart wasn't in the right place.

As luck would have it they found each other in the hallway just before lunch, Ronke was walking arm in arm with Donnie. They looked quite the happy couple, he was opening the door for her as they walked towards the main set of elevators.
'Hi there guys...so I guess the rumors are true then?' said Ophelia laughing.
The couple looked at each other and laughed too;
'Yeah Ophelia, the gossip is all true, Ronke is my boo and soon to be baby mama...' Donnie was having a wicked joke at Ophleia's

104

expense and her wide eyed look told him that she actually believed the baby mama part;
'Don't listen to him Ophelia…we are not having a kid! He's just being silly, pay him no mind' said Ronke.
'Oh, that's okay then' said Ophelia visibly relieved 'You had me going there for a second!'

After a little idle chatter, Donnie left the two girls to hit practice. It was his final year at NYU and he had to keep himself in top form so as to impress the coaches from prospective NFL teams around the country. Not that he had much impressing to do with the amount of natural ability and skill that he possessed; Donnie's parents were working class and had always taught him that nothing in life was worth having if you didn't work hard for it. He lived by this work ethic and found that it had rarely steered him wrong.

After they picked up a little light lunch, Ophelia and Ronke went into the student lounge to catch up with each other. Once she'd filled her cousin in about Deji and how the trip to Africa went, Ophelia decided to bring up the subject of Donnie;
'Ronke you guys look really happy together, but I'm shocked that you would go for him though. I thought you didn't really go for white guys…is it that serious?' asked Ophelia with concern.
'Well lets just say that he made me forget the 'color' thing. Donnie is a really lovely guy…the complete opposite of Caspian. He treats me like a queen; he actually calls me his 'black queen'. I don't really pay mind to all that though, I think we'll only see each other until I leave Uni and have to get married…by the way did you know that Deji's younger brother Tunji approached my father for my hand? Looks like we're gonna be in the same family!' replied Ronke
'Oh when did you find that out? Only he wasn't around when I was over there' said Ophelia.
'Well my mom called me over the holiday from back home. He is very serious and wants to meet me when you have your engagement party next May. This is Donnie's final year, so I think I might even have to break it off when he leaves in the summer'.

105

Ophelia pondered upon what Ronke was saying, it seemed a little unfair since everyone could see how much Donnie liked her. She wondered if Ronke had even given any thought to how he would take it.

'Ronke is that really wise? Because from what I've gathered, he really is quite fond of you and what you're saying might even break his heart. Have you talked to him about it?' Inquired Ophelia with concern.

Ronke took in what her cousin was saying with a deep sigh;

'I know what you're trying to say....I didn't really think of that. I know he likes me but he hasn't said that he loves me, well not yet anyway. I just figured that since he's a dude, he'd bounce back...but I do see what you're saying Ophelia, thanks. Maybe Donnie and I do need to talk'

Ronke had imagined that just like she did, Donnie only saw their thing as a temporary situation; it was however, becoming clear that his actions were speaking in loud volumes over his words.

~~~~

Deji was transferred to the New York branch of his firm by the end of March as Ophelia had expected. He'd got himself a nice Manhattan apartment on the Upper East Side near the junction of 73rd Street and Park Avenue. The apartment was on the 21st floor of the building and boasted fantastic views of Central Park and the city. Once inside, the property consisted of 2 large bedrooms, a study, 2 bathrooms, a modern kitchen and a huge reception.

Once Deji had moved in, he took Ophelia over to his place so that she could give it her 'stamp of approval', as he put it. Once in the apartment, she felt strange as it was the first time ever that she had been completely alone with him; this potentially meant that just about anything could happen.

He took her on a short tour of the apartment after which, Ophelia declared to him that she loved the place. The decor was very simple and modern; just perfect for a professional young bachelor. There were cream blinds that contrasted with the dark wood window frames, warm beige sofas with tan cowhide cushions that were arranged 'just so', glossy Oakwood flooring with under floor heating throughout and a sophisticated lighting system that could be adjusted to suit one's mood. The master bedroom's main feature was a Mahogany turned wood Baker four-poster king size bed and the floor was scattered with a few creamy lambswool rugs. Both bathrooms were decorated in granite mosaic tiles and Kohler bath suites and last but not least, kitchen was the state of the art.

Just before she was getting ready to leave the apartment, Deji presented Ophelia with a set of keys;

'I thought that you should have these, just in case you ever want to come over sometime. Like I said before, you're free to come over whenever you wish my dear' Ophelia was actually quite touched at this, she imagined that it was his way of telling her that there really wasn't another woman in his life.

'Thanks so much Deji, but don't think I'll just pop in without asking you first. I do respect people's privacy you know' said Ophelia smiling at him.

'Honestly sweetheart, there is no need. You're going to be my wife and I love you dearly. You are my privacy my dear...like I said, come over whenever you wish. I have nothing to hide from you...absolutely nothing' he replied smiling back at her.

'Oh Deji, I am so touched by that....are you sure, really sure about it?'

He picked up her hand and kissed it with his full lips;

'Yes I'm sure ok, I'm not gonna lie to you about that Ophelia. Now let me take you back to campus, didn't you tell me that you had a project to complete? I'll miss you, but you have to study...so let's grab some lunch and I'll drop you back afterwards'

~~~~

Once Ophelia was back in her dorm room that afternoon, she held the key in her hand and thought about what Deji had said to her. She couldn't see herself actually popping in on him unannounced so at that point, Ophelia decided that while he'd given her permission to, it would still be an invasion of his privacy. She would still give him that respect of calling him before going to his apartment and it was only right considering the fact that she was not yet his wife.

~~~~

Late one night about three weeks after Deji had arrived in New York; Ophelia was awoken from her sleep by an urgent knock on her dorm room door. She heard a voice call her name; it was Deji. She quickly put on a robe and ran over to open the door; it was highly unusual for him to call on her this late at night so something must be wrong. With her heart beating nineteen to the dozen, she finally got to the door. Looking worried and bewildered Deji grabbed her and squeezed her tight;

'What's wrong Deji, tell me ...are you ok...is it your family?' asked Ophelia.

'No, I'm fine....it's you I am worried about. I had a dream...a bad dream that something happened to you. When I woke up and you didn't answer the phone, I rushed over immediately'

Ophelia went over to the night stand to check her cell phone and realised that it had been set to 'vibrate' by accident. She'd probably slept through Deji's repeated attempts to get through to her.

'Sorry Deji, I've got 8 missed calls, I must have set the phone to vibrate by accident!' Ophelia then gave him a hug as a gesture of how sorry she was.

'It's okay Ophelia, no harm done, I'm just glad that you're fine, the dream was
really quite vivid and when you didn't pick up the phone I was beside myself with worry. Can I take you to my apartment tonight? I'll sleep in the spare room and you can have the master bed. It's just that I know my mind won't be at rest tonight unless I can see that you're safe....please, I can't bear to think of anything happening to you!'

Deji looked at Ophelia with eyes pleading. He was visibly disturbed so she didn't have the heart to say no.

'Are you sure….should we really be alone together overnight?' she asked

'Ophelia you know that I'd never touch you inappropriately…I just want to have rest of mind that you're safe tonight, that's all my love' Deji held on to her hand as if to lead her out of the dorm room;

'Okay, I need to just take a few things with me and then we'll go' Ophelia quickly threw on a coat and put some clothes, toothbrush, cell phone and other essentials in a back pack and left with Deji. Before leaving she left a note for the girls telling them where she was, and that she would explain the details of the circumstances later.

At the apartment Ophelia made herself comfortable inside the covers of Deji's bed and started to slowly fall asleep; he decided he'd watch her fall asleep, and sat on the mini sofa just opposite the side of the bed .Deji made himself comfortable there and left a dim lamp on; she would probably fall asleep soon, after which he would finally go to sleep in the guest bedroom.

In the dark, Ophelia guessed that Deji couldn't see that her eyes were half open, watching him watching her. A wicked thought came into her mind to find out if his intentions were as innocent as he'd claimed. Ophelia pulled the covers down a little to reveal the shape of her breasts through the thin silky sleep vest that she wore to bed; she then moved the covers off herself as if in deep sleep and unaware of what she was doing. Deji sat watching her and once he caught a glimpse of her hard nipples, he became hard himself. The thought of her lying in his bed just a few yards away from him was almost too much to bear, he knew that he'd promised not to touch her…but she wouldn't know if he touched himself...would she?

He decided to take a chance anyway since she looked as though she was sleeping. *She must be*, he thought with the way her chest was heaving up and down. He wasn't wearing much himself apart from his cotton robe and boxers. After satisfying himself that she was asleep, Deji put his hand down his shorts and started feeling the length of his dick up and down, over and over. He licked his right palm to make it wet before bringing his shaft out and concentrated his stroke on the huge purplish cap, then used his other hand to stroke his balls…as his breathing became faster and more urgent, Ophelia watched wide-eyed in the dark. He bucked in the chair quietly as he got closer and closer to his climax; at that point Ophelia could watch no more, lying still at the sight of his delicious cock was almost unbearable, she had to take it in her mouth.

Deji looked on in shock as he saw his fiancé walk towards him as if in slow motion and get on her knees at his feet. With horror, he realised that she had been watching him commit the shameful act of pleasuring himself all that time; he wanted to put his member away from her eyes but he was so close to coming, that he was powerless to do so. Ophelia bent her head down and opened her hot mouth ready to swallow up his entire dick.

It took all of the willpower and strength that Deji had inside him to push her back; he used one hand and caught her by the shoulder, stopping her in her tracks.
'No baby, I can't allow you to do that to me…please I beg you move back…you shouldn't have seen this. It's all my fault!' he cried;
The pained look on his face told Ophelia that Deji was about to shoot his load. At that moment of weakness, she pushed back against him aiming for his dick, but he ended up cumming on to her lips and the rest of it dribbled on to her chin.

Deji looked at Ophelia shamefaced once the throws of his orgasm were over
'Honey, I'm so sorry that you had to see that…I didn't mean to offend you. Why did you get out of bed…you should have stayed in bed. Oh gosh what must you think of me? It's just that you were lying in bed and you looked so sexy…I wanted to….'
He stopped short of what he wanted to say, he'd already done enough damage.
'Deji, I'm not at all offended and to be honest I'm not a baby either.

When I saw you touching yourself, I was aroused too…so I decided
to find out for myself how you taste…since we are to be married…I
thought it would be fine. I want us to be a lot more intimate now
since we've got to know each other…it that's okay with you'
Deji was quite shocked at her forwardness; however he was glad that
she found him that sexy…maybe they could get more intimate. But
would he be able to control himself and not take her virginity? He
wasn't sure about the answer to that question.
'Ophelia my love, I would love to….but I don't know if I could
control myself if we did. You drive me crazy every time I'm with
you and I don't know if I could hold back from making love to you.
We must not spend the night together again until our wedding night,
or I won't be responsible for my actions!' said Deji with a smile.
Ophelia didn't know what to say to him, but she knew that there was
no arguing with what he said. She would have to take a step back
once again and play the upright stance of a lady.

'Thanks so much once again for having such respect for me…the
more we get to know each other, I find myself liking you more and
more and to be quite honest Deji, I think I'm falling in love with
you…' at that point, Ophelia was almost mad with desire, she
desperately wanted to fuck but frustratingly, she knew she would
have to make do with touching herself instead.
'Really Ophelia…I've been waiting for you to say that for so many
years, I love you too and I want to take you to ecstasy more than you
could ever imagine. Let me give you a little taste tonight….I'll make
you feel so good…. come over here baby' he whispered; and with
that Deji pulled her to him and began to kiss her pushing his salty
tongue down into her mouth while mixing his saliva with hers. He
then lifted her on to the bed in one swoop, pulling down her pyjama
bottoms at the same time.
'Open up your legs for me baby and let me taste you…don't be shy
with me…please'
He then put his lips on her wet pussy and started to eat her out,
gently sucking, then licking first with the tip then graduating to his
whole tongue. Like a master at work, he put Ophelia's clit between

his lips and then let it go again teasing her and making her moan louder than she had ever dared with her other lovers. Deji took his time to work his magic with the main objective being to make her come. He didn't put his finger inside her for fear of breaking her hymen; but to be honest, he didn't need his finger with the way he was working her. Finally, after a deliciously lengthy session of having her pussy ate, Ophelia reached her climax while screaming out the name of her husband-to-be in a haze of orgasmic bliss; 'Yes, yes…Deji! Oh yes…..I love it…I'm…I'm…don't stop!'
Her body moved to an unknown rhythm as the waves of pleasure overcame her, Ophelia had reached a level of orgasm that she had never been to ever before until that night. Deji finished off his work with a satisfied kiss on her lips.
'I'm glad to be of service my dear…but no more until our wedding night. I'm not going to spill the blood of your innocence before the right time…I promise you'

Not too long afterwards, Ophelia got up to clean her self in the en suite bathroom, as she couldn't sleep with her own sticky juice between her thighs.
After she'd cleaned up Deji gave her a few more kisses and then left the room leaving her alone to sleep. Her body was still shuddering from the after shocks, but as a beautiful side effect of her powerful explosion, Ophelia drifted off to sleep almost as soon as her head hit the pillow.

Chapter 12

Back at NYU the next day, Ophelia told the girls what had happened with Deji the night before but for some reason she left out the intimate details. She wasn't sure why she didn't want to tell them everything, but she did know that her relationship with Deji had climbed to the next level. They'd shared a special moment that Ophelia would cherish for the rest of her life.

Issy, who was closest to her after Minty, noticed a slight change in Ophelia's behaviour, but made no mention of it and didn't pry either. It would appear that her friend had fallen in love and Issy was happy for her. She wondered when she too would meet her Prince Charming; only time would tell.

After the spring, the run up to summer seemed to be charging at break-neck speed. Caspian and the boys were due to finish NYU soon; it would be the end of an era for all of them. They all had high hopes for their future careers and typically of young men coming of age, were keen to make their very own special mark in the world. Leaving University would signify their transition from boys into men.

~~~~

Over the course of his final year, Le Quawn's relationship with Alizé had become quite serious. They both loved each other deeply and he wished that she was the one who had given him a daughter rather than Kimera. If that was the case Le Quawn was sure that he would have done the right thing and married her. He'd been thinking of late that if he did have more children, he would do it the right way and marry who ever his special lady would be first. Was that special lady Alizé? He often asked himself. Le Quawn wasn't certain but what he did know was that, since they'd got together he found that he didn't really look at other chicks anymore. One night stands and jump offs just didn't appeal to him anymore they way they used to, simply because Alizé was his boo now.
Even when he went with the boys to their regular club Legends, Le Quawn regularly blew off any would be one night stand chicks. After what Kimera had put him through, he'd learned to see though the fly hair, big booties and sexy bodies, to realise that above all, a woman should be valued for her character first and not the superficial things.

Alizé herself was afraid that Le Quawn would forget about her once he got into the NBA. Caspian had developed a mean streak since his break up with Ophelia and would constantly make snide comments about Le Quawn dumping her once he left NYU. Incidentally, all the girls he'd been with since Ophelia and Ronke only used him for fame or were just straight up hoes. His current chick Courtney was rumoured to be playing him on the side with an older NBA player, however since he had no proof, Caspian couldn't really accuse her of it. In essence he was bitter and jealous of the happiness Alizé had found with his friend, so there was nothing left for him to do but hate on them. Unfortunately for Caspian, Alizé and Le Quawn talked to each other about almost everything.

She decided to get an answer straight from the horse's mouth.
When Le Quawn came over to walk her to her block from Uni, he
took Alizé to eat in a diner on the next street. Once they got inside
and sat down she decided that it was time to face the music
'Baby….we need to talk…..it's about when you leave at the end of
this semester'
 Le Quawn wondered what this was all about, *what could be wrong?*
He thought.
'What do you wanna talk about boo…what's on your mind?' he
asked with concern.
'Well I been thinking about what's gonna happen to us once you
leave NYU; we been going on like everything's perfect, but once
your rookie year starts you won't really have time for all this will
you?' Alizé looked at him as if about to cry.
'Sweetie…where did you get that idea? I told you that I loved you
already; I ain't never said that to any other chick before you Alizé,
no other woman ever. You're special to me suga, so what makes you
think I ain't gonna have time for you?'
Le Quawn wasn't really the romantic type, but with Alizé it was
different; he picked up her small hand and rubbed it reassuringly.
'Well it's just that Casp's been sayin some things to me ya
know…like you're gonna forget about me once you get the draft…I
mean since you're gonna be in the NBA, you'll get hotter chicks than
me chasin' you for sure'
Le Quawn almost raised his voice in anger at her as he replied;
'I don't ever want you to listen to anything that punk says about us
again you hear me? I know he's your brother, but since he got
dumped by Ronke and Ophelia, he's been actin the fool! Forget
whatever he said…don't you know I love you Alizé? I even been
thinking 'bout marrying you some day! Fuck that nigga Caspian,
he's just all about da pussy, that's why be got burned. If it weren't
for the fact that you were his sis, I woulda cut him off for real..
shiiiittt….'

Le Quawn was livid that Caspian had tried to sabotage his
relationship with Alizé out of his own jealously; but Alizé herself

115

was inwardly jumping for joy at what he'd just said. Marriage? That was so much more than she had even hoped for!

'Baby, did you say you thought about marrying me….plain ole me?'
She obviously didn't realise how much he loved her;

'Alizé I love you boo, so you might as well know that now…I wanna marry you and have babies with you someday…maybe soon…so if I asked you mama, would you say yes?'
At this point, Le Quawn knew he was having a special very moment with the love of his life;

'Oh baby, I would say yes in a heartbeat!' she replied happily
'Then let's do it, I already know I'm gonna be playing for the *Knicks* anyway so I'll be able to provide for you and for eventually our children…..I don't want no one else but you honey. So what you say?'
Alizé could hardly believe her ears;

'What you mean now? Today?'
Le Quawn laughed; Alizé's expression was comical as she looked at him in disbelief and surprise;

'Naw boo, not right now. We can have a small wedding at the end of June, just you, me and a few members of our fam. Ya know, just to witness it'
Alizé's heart almost burst at the seams with joy;

'Oh honey, I'm so happy! Are you sure though? You really wanna wife me?'
Le Quawn looked at this sweetheart dead in the eyes; what she failed to realise was that he would give the world for her.

'Yes Alizé Strong, I'm sure. I ain't see no point in messin' around, you're the one and just for the record….I love you'

Alizé cried tears of joy as they walked back to Le Quawn's room to spend the night together. He made love to her with more passion and intensity than ever before; all he wanted was to take her to a plateau of pleasure that she never knew existed. As she began to build up to a climax, Alizé stopped Le Quawn in his tracks, it seemed that something wasn't right;

'Honey….stop a second, I want you to take off the rubber….please take it off, I wanna have your baby Le Quawn…'

It was a delicious dilemma that Le Quawn had set before him. Take off the condom and get the raw feeling of her pussy with the risk of impregnating her or keep it on and be responsible. He already knew what the answer was;

'Alizé, I want you to have my babies too mama, but not this way. It's gotta be the right way for me or not at all. We gotta be married and I love you too much to give you anything less ma so the rubber stays on'

Alizé looked into his eyes; her expression was almost as if she was in pain;

'Ok then baby, I'll wait; I just wanted to feel the whole of you inside of me just for once too…oh Quawn, I want your baby so bad'

Before she allowed the tears of frustration to fall from her eyes, Alizé turned her attention back to the act they were in the middle of; she savoured every position and thrust he engaged her in with relish. The fact that she wanted his baby made Le Quawn even more aroused, he would have to fuck her with even more authority that night and it seemed that she wanted it too; as he pumped away at her, Alizé was almost screaming;

'Fuck me nigga, that's it fuck the shit out of me, yeah baby take that pussy. Take it nigga, it's your pussy, yes…yes…ooh'

She sounded like music to his ears and he stayed hard with the stamina of an athlete that he was. He flipped her over doggie style and slammed his dick in hard;

'Yeah baby, imma give it to you, imma give you that daddy dick…just make sure ya hold on ma'

They carried on into the night until they were completely exhausted and Alizé eventually fell asleep on his chest; Le Quawn stroked her baby hairs while he watched her sleep. *Yes*, he thought, *she really is the one.*

~~~~

Le Quawn and Alizé got married to everyone's surprise, at the end of

June in a small and intimate church ceremony on Long Island. True to his word, the wedding was kept small with only a few immediate family members present, they wanted to share their special day together and not care about the rest of the world for once.

The happy couple took a honeymoon in Cancun, Mexico for two weeks, and of course upon their return Alizé was already in the early stages of pregnancy. She decided she would still attend Uni, start her final year in the winter and finish the rest of her degree once the baby was born; not that she needed to study if she didn't want to.

Since she was now his wife, Le Quawn had assured Alizé that she wouldn't have to work and would want for nothing, but still encouraged her to finish her studies anyway. At times like that, Alizé thanked God for her husband; as fate would have it they were truly a perfect match.

~~~~

Donnie was contemplating on how to break the news to Ronke; he'd got an offer from the *Miami Dolphins* which meant moving down south. He loved her and would much rather have a long distance relationship with her than break off things off; but he couldn't however, tell what Ronke's take on it would be. She had been a little distant of late and wasn't really paying attention to him during their conversations at all. They were sitting down watching some random movie that she'd put on, when Ronke suddenly stopped the DVD.

'Hey girl, why'd you stop the movie? I thought you wanted to watch that?' said Donnie. *What could be wrong with her now?* he thought, sometimes Ronke just blew hot and cold.

'Donnie, I can't do this anymore. I think it's the right time for us to let this go now....it's for the best since you're leaving NYU in a few weeks. I'm sorry to just drop it like this Donnie...'

Ronke couldn't look him in the eyes as she spoke, it was far too obvious that he loved her much more than she did him. It had been great while it lasted, but in her mind and considering her own circumstances, they had to move on.

'What do you mean 'let this go?' how can you just say it like that! Is that all our relationship means to you? Ronke I already told you that I love you, so what's all this about? Just cos I'm leavin' Uni?'
Donnie was shell shocked by Ronke's callousness, it seemed that the old Ronke had never left in the first place.
'Look Donnie, I'm not being mean by saying this, but it's not like we both didn't know the score...remember we had a talk about this, about you leavin. Come on, it's not like I can bring a white guy home to my parents....and you can't tell your folks that you're gonna be serious with a black girl! Besides, I told you about the arranged marriage thing...I'm even due to meet my husband to be when I go back home at the end of the month....'
She felt bad for taking the stance that she had done, but what other choice did she have? Clearly Donnie had other ideas;
'Ronke you telling me that now? Now that I love you so much baby? You think it was easy for me to tell my parents that I was seeing you....I go through flak everytime I go home, my daddy be sayin to me, 'why don't you get yourself a nice blond girl' huh? All because I love you Ronke! I can't believe you're doing this to me!'
Donnie looked as if he was going to cry but he didn't at that point. There was still too much between them that had to be said

'Donnie, I do love you...it's just that....come on, you've gotta see the sense in what I'm saying'
He turned and faced her like a man gone mad;
'Love? You think you know about love? Well let me tell you about love sweetheart.... Love is me watching Caspian dog you out and not being able to do anything about it! I had to watch while that muthafucker slept with both you and your cousin behind your back! Love is seeing you drool all over him like some kind of hoe and you know what? I still loved you even then! Love is stopping you to make small talk, just to get your attention, even when you treated me like an outright bitch....love is telling my Pop that he could go to hell if he didn't like the fact that my girlfriend is a black girl, so Ronke! You don't know anything about love...'
As he trailed off from his tirade, Donnie could see the tears run down

her face and at that point, he felt like a complete bastard for making her cry;

'Oh Donnie, I'm so sorry I put you through all that. I've even tried to hold back my feelings for you only cos I know the inevitable must happen. I have to go through with this arranged marriage; I have no choice in the matter or I'll bring shame upon myself and my family. Please baby, try to understand......I'm sorry but I'd rather break your heart now than later and I know that Miami want to sign you up so that means that you'll at least be able make a fresh start after us...I'm so sorry Donnie...please forgive me'

Defeated and forlorn, Ronke descended into a flood of inconsolable tears;

'Please don't cry baby...I love you and I'm sorry for what I just said too....I know you're right but....we don't have to end it now. Maybe we can still see each other... maybe I can come to New York when I'm free, there's always that chance....'

This was going to be more difficult to do than Ronke had originally thought. She did love Donnie very much and she supposed that allowing him to come to see her every now and again wouldn't hurt. He probably couldn't make it to New York from Miami that often anyway, but in the end, Ronke knew that she couldn't refuse him. The way he was starting to kiss her neck gave her the answer that she was looking for

'Yes Donnie, let's take that chance....oh my God...oh shit...I want you baby...I wanna feel your big cock inside me right now'

Never one to mince her words, Ronke took off her jeans and panties for Donnie to enter her. Luckily he always kept some condoms in his backpack or his pant pockets; he could never tell whenever his lady would want to fuck and that was one of the things he loved most about her. She was wild, wanton and spontaneous whenever she wanted the dick, and that suited him just fine.

Donnie didn't know for sure if she would eventually cut him off once he moved to Miami, but one thing he did know for sure was that, he would cherish every moment they spent together until he left NYU in the next two weeks. That night, he fucked Ronke until she had no pussy juice left and had lost the ability to speak; as they came to the end of their session, Donnie ended up on top and was fucking her slowly, maintaining a long, deep and luxurious thrust. Sweat dripped off their bodies and Ronke felt as though she could hardly breathe; she'd come so many times that there was actually dried pussy juice flaking off between her thighs. Her lover had satisfied her completely as he always did; to this end, Ronke didn't even know if she was capable of eventually letting him go. As that thought went through her mind, he started to speed up towards his own final climax; at last, Donnie drew back and splashed his creamy juice all over her flat tummy simultaneously letting out a triumphant roar. Not knowing if this would be one of their last times together, he looked wistfully into the eyes of his love and shed a painful tear.

From that point forward, no matter what happened to them in the future, or wherever she ended up in life, as far as Donnie was concerned, Ronke would forever be his woman.

~~~~~

Caspian couldn't wait to leave New York City in light of the recent developments. His sister was all lovey dovey with Le Quawn, Donnie was hooked up with Ronke and Eddie was still in love with his steady girlfriend Leilani, and was looking forward to starting his summer internship at Merrill Lynch. They were all happy in their lives and disturbingly, Caspian was no longer the center of attention like he used to be anymore. He didn't like that at all, he didn't like it one bit. Unfortunately, because Caspian was his mother's favourite, she had spoiled him rotten so he was used to being treated like a king. To make matters even worse, his latest girlfriend Courtney Smalls had dumped him for Dwaine Williams, who just happened to be winner of the previous year's prestigious NBA 'Rookie of the Year' award.

Caspian had been warned by Eddie that Courtney was a notorious social climber, but being typically arrogant, he didn't even stop to listen to his friend. She was a beautiful Tracey Edmonds look alike and the quintessential type of arm candy chick, that most popular basketball and football players, wanted hanging off their arm. Courtney's café au lait skin color was commonly described as 'high yellow' and she wore her hair in unbelievably long Beyonce style curly extensions. In a complete contrast to the beautiful exterior, her beginnings were very humble; nobody would have guessed that her mother was a hard edged an ex-stripper and alcoholic. Courtney's father had long gone and left them to fend for themselves, thus subjecting her to a torrid and difficult upbringing. As result of this, her main objective was to get married to a rich husband and amass as much wealth and status as she possibly could without actually doing much work at all.

In the end, Courtney began to treat Caspian as if he were just a nobody once she started to concentrate her energies on bagging Dwaine. Caspian was devastated, he was actually beginning to really like Courtney, and she was the type of chick that he eventually wanted to wife.

After contemplating on his future, Caspian thanked God for small mercies; thankfully the head Coach at the *Washington Wizards* had picked him to join the team. If not for that, he would have had to stay in New York City walking around with egg on his face.

As he walked to the NYU b-ball court for the last time before he left the campus, Caspian realised that Ronke's words had begun to haunt him after all.

Chapter 13

Once the girls left Uni for the summer, things started to get a lot more interesting; incidentally, Ophelia had her engagement ceremony to go back home with Deji for the end of June. The original May date had been moved forward, to allow her enough time to complete her end of second year exams. Literally the day after she'd finished the last exam, Deji whisked her away to Lagos by private jet, usually she would take Virgin Atlantic's first class flight, however her husband-to-be was starting to make a frequent habit of upgrading her. Upon realisation that Ronke was also going so she could meet Tunji for the first time, he insisted that she tag along with them as well.

The three of them left for the JFK private charter air strip together to take a *Gulfstream IV* jet back home to Nigeria.

Kelechi was due to be there for the ceremony as well, but he was flying in to Lagos from London instead. He'd decided not to make the move to New York with Deji in order to pursue his own private

123

investments. Kelechi had no intention of relying on his father's money, and had the drive and ambition to build his very own empire. He was looking forward to filling his dad in on how his business ventures were going; to this end, Kelechi was certain that his father would be very proud of him.

During the flight, Ophelia wondered what Tunji's character was like in comparison to his older brother's. She hoped that Ronke would get on with Tunji as well as she did with Deji, however, Ronke was a notoriously strong willed and determined young woman. Whatever man she did eventually end up with would need to be firm and masterful enough to be able to tame the proverbial shrew.

Once they'd landed in Lagos and got into the city, Deji dropped both of the ladies at their respective homes, before finally reaching the Olajuwon mansion himself. Ophelia was eagerly looking forward to seeing everyone again. This time, the housekeeper and the rest of the maids no longer saw a small girl, but a young woman the first flushes of true love; Ophelia was glowing from the inside out and it showed. Even though Deji had kept his promise not to touch her intimately until their wedding night, he made her feel as though she was the center of his world, and she found that kind of love intoxicating.

Sandra also noticed that her daughter was had blossomed and remarked upon it exuberantly;
'Well Ophelia, it looks as if Deji is treating you well my dear, you look positively radiant! Oh yes...he really is a good boy!' she exclaimed;
Just as she'd finished talking, her husband Jonathan came up behind her and put his arm adoringly around her shoulder. It would appear that Ophelia wasn't the only one in love. She had never seen her parents show public displays of affection before and they were smiling at each other much like a shy young couple; Ophelia wanted comment on it, but she decided err on the side of caution and just watch what was going on for a while. Maybe she would ask her mother about it later on that night.

Jonathan's heart was filled with pride as he looked at his only daughter, now all grown up and doing so well;

'Ophelia, I must agree with your mother, you're looking even more beautiful than usual, and that means that Deji is really doing you good my daughter'

Ophelia smiled shyly and as she thanked her parents for their compliments, Jonathan was pleased that the match between his daughter and Deji was a successful one; he would found it unbearable if she was unhappy about the pairing and there certainly wouldn't be any wedding going ahead if that was the case. Ophelia's happiness and contentment meant more to her father than she could ever imagine. If he had got wind of any objections that she may have had to an arranged marriage, then Jonathan would have been happy with her own choice.

As fate would have it her mother was not as liberal. Ophelia was blissfully unaware that it was Sandra, and not her father who had aggressively pushed for her to have an arranged marriage. Secretly obsessed with wealth and status, it was Sandra's aim to have the Emeka-Phillips family pushed up to the highest social echelons in Nigeria.

If that meant Ophelia must marry Deji Olajuwon, then that measure would have to be undertaken. On the other hand, Sandra was relieved that her daughter actually liked the boy, or there would have surely been a lot more protest. Her own mother and Ophelia's grandmother Lysandra had drummed the notion of marrying well into Sandra's head since her childhood. It was no mistake that she'd ended up with the eminent Dr Jonathan Emeka-Phillips as her husband. Her own situation did not start with an arranged marriage, it was a calculated one. Sandra effectively stole Jonathan away from his then fiancé, and married him within the year once she fell pregnant with Kelechi out of wedlock. Only her own mother and some of the older family folk knew of the story; Kelechi and Ophelia had no idea.

As she contemplated the forthcoming event, Sandra was beside herself with glee. The ceremony was due to commence in a few days time and all the arrangements had already been made. She'd had been planning for this moment ever since the day that Ophelia was born and nothing, absolutely nothing was going to ruin it. The engagement however, would be nothing compared to the actual wedding that would be staged in the following year. It would be the wedding to end all weddings and she'd already flown the event planner in from Italy twice, to look at the venue and figure out logistical implications of the undertaking. Ophelia was a good girl and left her mother to do all the planning; all she wanted to do for herself was choose her wedding dress. Sandra grudgingly allowed her that; deep down, she supposed it was Ophelia's marriage that was being planned and not her own.

~~~~

After the traditional engagement ceremony and family introduction, all of the guests were led into the big reception room for the engagement party. As they walked in, there was a huge banner over head with the words *'Congratulations on your engagement, Deji and Ophelia'* emblazoned across it and there were waiters at each table ready to serve food and wine to them all. The happy couple were seated at the head table in the center of the room with both sets of parents, siblings and their respective partners. Ronke and Tunji were put next to each other as were Kelechi and his supermodel girl friend Adora Abiola.

Richard Kelechi Emeka-Phillips had finally brought a lady home to meet his parents after being a confirmed bachelor for the majority of his twenties. At 28 years old, he felt he was still too young to settle down, but at least having Adora in his arsenal would shut his mother up. He knew that Sandra might not approve of his choice of woman, but as a man he wasn't about to have his mother run his life. Kelechi felt sorry for Ophelia who in his opinion had the misfortune of being born female.
If it wasn't for that, their mother would surely have not been unable to control the poor girl's life in the way she always did. It was never

done in an overt way, because Sandra was always subtle about it, so
much so that even her own husband could never accuse her of being
overbearing. She played the perpetual role of the good mother who
only wanted the 'very best' for her two children.

~~~~~

Adora felt as though her relationship with Kelechi was finally getting
somewhere at last. Even though he was notoriously vague about their
future and where they were going, in her mind, meeting his parents
was a significant milestone. Adora Chinela Abiola was former Miss
Nigeria and had also previously won the third runner up place in the
Miss World beauty pageant. She had recently given up runway
modelling, and was currently a spokesmodel for *'Bailene's Boudoir'*
which was the hottest lingerie company to come out of Brazil. Adora
was certainly born for modelling standing tall at 5' 10" and
possessing a knockout combination of an athletic build, pretty
cherubic features and light caramel skin that was scattered with the
cutest freckles. Adora was frequently mistaken by people as being of
mixed race, but in truth she was actually a pure blooded Nigerian.
Pure blood however, was questionable at times due to the centuries
of British colonialism and slavery that was a part of her native
country's history.

True to her name, the rare beauty that Adora possessed made it quite
possible for her to have any man on Earth that she so desired and not
surprisingly, dozens of highly successful rich men broke down doors
just to try and get to her. In spite of this, Adora fell in love quite hard
for the very plain looking Kelechi; whatever he lacked aesthetically,
he compensated for with bags of charm and dry humor. Even when
his behaviour was erratic and aloof towards her at times, her love for
him in contrast, was solid.
Her previous lifestyle had made it quite difficult for her to meet any
men that were suitable enough for her wants and needs; but since
becoming Kelechi's woman, she quickly realised that in order to
fulfil her real ambitions of being a wife and mother, she had to quit

runway modelling. Becoming a spokes-model for *Bailene's Boudoir* had made it easier for Adora to cater to her man; she only hoped that sacrificing her career wouldn't be in vain and Kelechi would end up being the man of her dreams. She was already financially independent, so all she really wanted was a steady and reliable man as her partner. Adora would never be satisfied with a man who only wanted her to be his trophy piece and thankfully, Kelechi had no use for trophies either.

Adora almost died of happiness, when Ophelia confirmed it to her that Kelechi had never brought any other woman home to meet the family; to this end she figured that her chance to become a wife may be approaching faster than she'd expected.
Even though she was four years younger than Kelechi at 24, Adora had an aching need to settle down, get married and pro-create. Of her 4 sisters, was the only one that was yet to have any children; this predicament had long since left her with a dull ache inside that ate away at her on a daily basis and ultimately, Adora knew that without the blessing of a child, she would never be complete.

~~~~

Ronke didn't really know what to make of Tunji Olajuwon at all. Prince Tunji Emmanuel Rafiq Olajuwon's package wasn't quite as spectacular as his older brother's, but he was still reasonably handsome and considered quite a catch for most Nigerian young ladies.
He was tall at just over 6 feet and had a stockier build to Deji's athletic one. His skin was of a bold terracotta shade and his face cute enough, yet slightly diminished by his small, shifty and piercing light brown eyes. At any rate, he came across as being a little too flashy and immature for her liking.

When they'd officially been introduced to each other via their respective families three days prior, he'd insisted on making her view his vast collection of fast cars and expensive watches in a

128

feeble attempt to dazzle her with a display of his wealth; when Ronke didn't fall all over him the way other girls usually did, Tunji really didn't know what to do with himself. Since then, they had grudgingly exchanged words through polite yet awkward conversation; Ronke supposed that she could have done a whole lot worse and at the very least he wasn't poor; on the other hand judging by the reckless way that he spent money she wouldn't be surprised if he was broke by the age of 30. Once they were married, Ronke decided she would nip that in the bud in the first instance. Incidentally she was finding it quite hard to read him, so in the interests of caution, Ronke played down her usual wilful temperament. It would seem that patience was the name of the game this case; she would have to just wait and see.

~~~~~

When her father Jonathan got up to make a little speech about the engagement, Ophelia was so shy that looking down at her ring was the only thing that made her feel a little more at ease. That evening, Deji had presented her with a twenty carat platinum set princess cut diamond ring. It was almost the highest grade of stone one could buy on the open market as a rare 'D' coloured internally flawless piece. The spectacular ring had been hand crafted by *Graff* jewellers in Geneva and shipped to the Madison Avenue store in New York in time for Deji to take with him to Nigeria for the engagement ceremony. Kelechi had remarked that the ring must have cost close to a million dollars and even though she had grown up with wealth, a million dollars on her slender finger was still a lot for Ophelia to take in. She'd cried when Deji had presented if to her; did he really think she was worth that much? Ophelia wasn't sure, but she wasn't about to take the ring off ever!

~~~~~

The engagement party has been a resounding success. All of Sandra's hard work had paid off and the guests had been commending her all night on a job well done. Ophelia herself, was

both relieved and exhausted that the proceedings were over. After
some rational thought, she decided against wearing her engagement
ring in New York. She would put it in her safety deposit box instead
for safe keeping; there was no way she could wear that huge rock on
campus, without some asshole attempting to jack it off her hand.

When the ladies finally retired upstairs for the night, Jonathan,
Kelechi and Deji stayed downstairs talking. Tunji decided to leave
with his parents instead, he wasn't interested in doing anything else
'family' related for the night and would much rather be in bed.
Jonathan opened a vintage bottle of *Cognac Hennessy* for the
purposes of a celebratory drink. The men weren't really hard
drinkers, however this was deemed a special occasion; Jonathan saw
the evening as the start of Deji being accepted as a member of his
family. He liked the young man very much; he also liked the fact that
when Deji wanted something, he was extremely determined to get it.
Jonathan maintained that determination and perseverance was one of
the best qualities that a man could have. His thoughts then turned to
his son Kelechi, had he just introduced them to his future wife?

'So Kelechi is the lovely Adora your proposed wife to be? I know
you only introduced her to us as your girlfriend but since you have
never brought a girl home before, I was just wondering if she is the
one…' said Jonathan teasingly.
Kelechi laughed a little nervously before answering, but as usual was
very honest with his beloved father;
'Daddy to be quite honest, I think she is but I don't know for sure
100%. Adora has shown in not so many words that she would love to
be my wife, however I don't know if she can truly leave the life of
modelling and glamour behind. It's not that I don't want her to have
a career, but when my children are born I want a wife who will be
there for them…well during the first five years of their lives at the
very least. I don't want my kids to be dragged around from photo
shoot to photo shoot, you know?'
The men all nodded their heads in agreement with Kelechi, but Deji
decided to give his friend a little advice;

130

'Kelechi, I do think you should cut Adora a little slack though, she already stopped the runway modelling for just magazines and catalogue work so as to give more time to your relationship. I also concur from speaking to her that she is aching to be a mother, as you know that all of her sisters already have at least one child and she feels a little left out. All I'm saying is talk to her about it…you may be surprised'

Kelechi felt somewhat sheepish at that point, *how did Deji know all that*? he thought. He probably needed to pay a little more attention whenever Adora spoke; Kelechi admitted to himself that he didn't always listen carefully when his lady was speaking,; along as he got the point of what she was saying, then that was all that really mattered in his eyes.

'Deji, I must admit that I feel a little ashamed right now, I didn't realise that Adora felt that way. When she gave up the runway modelling, she did say that it was because of our relationship but I didn't really pay attention to the rest of it…I guess I've taken her for granted a little haven't I?'

Since Kelechi didn't know what else to say, he guessed that he would have to have a heart to heart with Adora sometime the next day or at least before they left Africa.

'Kelechi, if you really want a successful marriage, then you need to listen to your woman. Even if you don't agree with her and end up going against her words anyway, at least you will have the whole story and not half' said Jonathan, he then put a thick hand down on Kelechi's shoulder 'my son, from what I saw tonight, that girl is head over heels in love with you. At the same time a heart can only be left dangling for so long before someone else captures it away. She is an astoundingly beautiful woman as she is gracious and well mannered. I suggest that you put a ring on her finger as soon as possible without a moments' hesitation!'

Kelechi drained the Cognac out of his glass, what his father was suggesting would mean that his life would be changed forever, was he sure that ready for all that? Only time would tell;

'Thank you very much daddy and also Deji, for your sound advice. I will talk to Adora about this tomorrow. Who knows, another

engagement might be announced before the end of the week!' he said laughing at his own suggestion and the other men joined in.
They continued talking until quite late about the state of business in general and the global economy before finally retiring to bed. Deji was invited to stay the night and he gladly accepted; as he fell asleep that night, he knew that he couldn't have wished for a better set of in-laws.

~~~~

Sandra went to sleep soon after going upstairs, thus leaving the young ladies to have a little chat; Ronke decided to stay the night as well, and stayed up to talk in Ophelia's room with Adora. In all of her years of existence, this was the closest that Ronke would ever get to having a slumber party. During her period of being a stuck up bitch, she had always felt that practices such as slumber parties and the like as being 'common' and beneath her. Ronke now realised that once gone, it was too late to reclaim the fun she'd allowed herself to miss during the years of her adolescence.
She decided that it was time to live for the moment from now on; she wasn't too sure however, if Tunji would fit in to her newly found philosophy.

As the ladies entered the bedroom, Ophelia sat on her bed while Ronke and Adora made themselves comfortable on rattan three seater sofa by the window. After some small talk about the wonderful evening they'd had, the subject turned to the men in each of their lives; Adora looked longingly at Ophelia's huge engagement bauble and wished earnestly for her very own one;
'Ophelia you're so lucky to get a man like Deji, look at the rock he gave you! It's stunning, absolutely stunning! My poor finger is still bare…just look at it. I wish Kelechi would make it official between us' said Adora wistfully.
How much do I have to give up to be worthy enough to be his wife? she often thought. Only God knew the answer to that.
'Adora don't worry about Kells, he'll soon do the right thing. Trust me, you being brought all the way to Nigeria to be with him at my

132

engagement party says a hell of a lot. I wasn't lying when I told you before that he's never brought a woman to meet our parents. Just give him a little more time Adora, I'm sure that he won't let such a beautiful girl like you go….in that case he would be a fool'

Ophelia made a mental note to have a private word with Kelechi when she had the chance; poor Adora had the right to know if she would be a permanent fixture in his life or not and such a woman did not deserve to be kept in limbo.

'Thank you so much Ophelia, you've been so nice to me, so welcoming! Everyone has been really nice to me, it seems too good to be true you know….' Adora trailed off and as she spoke Ronke was studying her. She reminded her of her best friend Bijou however, in stark contrast to her; Adora seemed to have a very kind heart and not a trace of a mean streak. One could tell that with Adora, her beauty was secondary and she cared much more for the simple things in life. Even though Ronke was very beautiful herself, even she was in awe of Adora's incomparable physical perfection, why on Earth was Kelechi dragging his feet with this one she wondered? Her thoughts then turned to Tunji and what the ladies first impression of him was;

'What do you guys think of Tunji? I don't really know what to make of him since we've met and Ophelia, as I'm sure you've gathered that he is nothing like Deji! I myself find him quite immature'

'Well to be honest, I didn't talk to him much….he seemed okay to talk to I suppose. Maybe you need to get to know him a little bit more before you can make a sound judgement' said Ophelia, being the voice of reason as usual.

'I agree with Ophelia, I didn't talk to him much as well, I will say however that he seemed a little distracted tonight. Like he'd rather be somewhere else…but I guess that an engagement party isn't the most exciting thing for a young guy to do!' said Adora laughing at her own sentiments; she imagined Tunji was probably bored out of his skull all evening, so it was no wonder that he went home so quickly.

'Okay then, I guess we don't really know each other well enough.

Maybe we just got off on the wrong foot....Ophelia did I tell you that the day after we met he took me to their family home and showed me all his fancy cars and expensive bling? I wasn't very impressed by that, it was like he wasn't interested in knowing me at all and just talked about himself all afternoon!'

Ophelia was shocked at Ronke's admission; she was right, that was quite immature;

'Woah, Ronke you didn't tell me that part, wow! I sure hope he grows up, and quickly! You must have been so disappointed....shall I have a word with Deji about it?'

Maybe Deji could talk some sense into his brother, well at least Ophelia hoped that he could.

'Thanks Ophelia, but I think I should deal with this one...maybe once we get to know each other, things will be better' said Ronke.

In the end Ronke decided to hope for the best, it would be a complete disaster if she ended up rejecting Tunji's proposal and she actually did want to have 'Princess' as a title, just as Ophelia was going to get by marrying Deji. Unfortunately, her compatibility with Tunji was a situation that even her daddy couldn't fix and Ronke was beginning to realise that there were a few things in life that came at a high moral price. She would need to decide swiftly whether or not she was prepared to make those sacrifices in order to achieve them.

Chapter 14

Almost as soon as they had landed back in New York from Nigeria, Deji and Ophelia had to fly to over England to attend Dominic and Minty's wedding. Ophelia had last seen Minty during the Easter break when they had met in London for her maid of honour's dress fitting. She was quite nervous to see everyone again considering the fact that she was now part of a couple and no longer plain old Ophelia. There was also the fact that her old Launceston school mates would in attendance, some of whom she hadn't seen since the night of the leaver's ball two years prior. She couldn't help but wonder if any of them had changed much, if at all.

The wedding ceremony was due to be held at The Cathedral Church of Christ in Cheshire, then the guests would be driven on to Dunraven Manor for the reception. The Cathedral was a beautiful sight to behold with its bell tower and intricate stained glass windows. The pews were decorated with pink roses and white peonies to fall in line with the 'English rose' theme that had been

135

picked for the wedding. The theme was a most fitting homage to Minty's looks, which were often described as such. Fortunately, everything was perfect on the day, from the venue of the cathedral to the sunny weather, which was typical of mid-July in England.

Minty had been up since the crack of dawn and she couldn't sleep so she went to Ophelia's room to see if she was awake. Her best friend had arrived the previous day quite late and missed Minty's hen night; Ophelia had gone straight to bed almost as soon as she'd reached Dunraven exhausted from jet-lag. Since they were still unmarried, Deji had checked in to a small but luxurious hotel nearby.
When Minty got to her room, surprisingly Ophelia was also awake; she was sat up in her bed reading a book.
'Phils, how come you're up hun....I thought that you'd be asleep for sure.' Ophelia laughed at her;
'Me...you're asking me how come I'm awake...what are you doing up? Pre-wedding nerves?'
Minty sighed and looked unsure of herself as she answered.
'You could say that...I'm sure of marrying Dominic, it's just that since we've been together, everything has been perfect. Am I ungrateful for thinking that once he's got me down the aisle, he's gonna change somehow? Oh Phils, am I just being silly?'
Who knew? thought Ophelia, but what else could she say but to re-assure her friend?
'Oh Minty, don't worry so much...I'm sure you will be fine. Dominic's a really great guy and he loves you too much to make you unhappy' Ophelia got up and hugged Minty reassuringly 'honestly girl, just concentrate on looking your best for the wedding today....let's go down and get an early breakfast shall we?'
The girls then went downstairs to eat and things were looking a lot more optimistic once Minty had got some food inside her.

Later on that day Araminta Cassandra Fortescue-Black emerged from the cathedral as Mrs Dominic Christopher Parker-Graves, wife to the heir of the Marquis of Banbury. The newly married Lady Parker-Graves wore a beautiful *Elie Saab* silk satin strapless ivory bridal gown that was hand embroidered in an intricate mother of pearl and crystal beaded design. The dress was beautifully complimented by a crystal beaded veil and 18 foot long train. Minty looked ethereal, almost like something out of a fairytale and as a finishing touch her hair was pinned up in a chignon decorated with pink and white roses at the back; she held a matching bouquet of pink and white roses that had been freshly cut that morning.

Dominic almost cried once he took in the sight of his beautiful bride and as she walked towards him down the church aisle, their tryst in the garden maze seemed like just yesterday. Now she was going to be his wife; he then looked across at Ophelia with a heart full of gratitude, if it wasn't for her timely advice who knows if he would be standing in a cathedral marrying the woman of his dreams? Ophelia herself stood next to the reverend father looking very much the beautiful maid of honor; she was dressed in a pale pink cap sleeved empire line dress and she wore a pretty pink corsage on her wrist to accent the outfit. She felt that the wedding itself was beautiful and romantic; the entire event was well planned and executed in the most impeccable taste.

After the church ceremony, the wedding party filed outside the cathedral for formal photographs that would mark the occasion. Minty and Dominic were the picture of a happy couple and Lady Fortescue-Black could be seen discreetly trying to dry the tears from the corner of her eyes with her hanky; it really did turn out to be the perfect wedding.

The Fortescue-Blacks had hired a few luxury mini vans to ferry some of the guests from the cathedral to Dunraven Manor for the reception. The rest of them that came in their own stately cars made their own way to the venue and the newly married couple were thrown into a luxurious Rolls Royce Phantom. Minty looked across at her husband as they made their first journey together as man and wife. She didn't even realise she was crying tears of joy until Dominic reached over and wiped a tear from her eyes; he then pulled

his bride close to him and kissed her intensely on her soft lips. At
that very moment, Dominic told himself that it couldn't get any
better than this.

~~~~

Upon reaching Dunraven for the reception, it seemed that the party
had already started. If they hadn't already everybody let their hair
down and after a few drinks, the revellers started to get on the dance
floor. Ophelia used the opportunity to get down to the business of
catching up with the rest of the Launceston girls, but not without
introducing them to Deji first. Issy and Khadijah also had 'significant
others' to introduce and this only added to the excitement of it all.
While Minty was having her customary first dance with her father,
Deji was introduced to Katy and Khadijah. He'd already met Issy
and Dominique in New York and had met Minty the night before.
After Deji was introduced, Issy introduced her own new main
squeeze; thus far, none of her friends had any idea that the
relationship with Eduardo was so serious; *she's obviously been
keeping this one under wraps* thought Ophelia.
Eduardo Angel Leon, just happened to be the eldest son of Latin
America recording artist and proverbial 'sex on legs' Ricardo Leon.
He had naturally followed his father's footsteps into the music
industry however, he wasn't fortunate enough to inherit daddy's
golden voice. He'd decided that he wanted to work at a record label
instead, so through some family connections, Eduardo eventually got
an internship with a New York based rap record label named
Dangerous Records. This essentially meant that Eduardo had access
to tickets to most bands that were playing in New York at any given
time and in some cases, even backstage passes. Incidentally, he also
had a little side hustle of promoting popular night clubs just to keep
him amused on the weekend; Eduardo hated being bored and hoped
that the wedding reception would get interesting as the day
progressed. Maybe he could sneak Issy off somewhere private for a
quickie later on. She was definitely a keeper in his book; he only had
to take one look at that culo to make his dick hard.

Eduardo came sharply back to reality, as he was introduced to all of Issy's posh, rich bitch friends; he couldn't help to think of how spoiled the all must be. Even though he himself had a rich father, throughout his child-hood Eduardo had never seen any of that so called 'money'. Ricardo Leon was a mean and tight-fisted bastard who believed that once he had planted his seed to make a baby, his work was done. He had never supported Eduardo's mother financially nor any of other three women who had between them, bore his five illegitimate children. The only kids that he spent any kind of money on were the three that were born by his long suffering legal wife Maria-Carla. So as a result his own harsh upbringing, Eduardo concluded that Issy and her friends didn't realise how lucky they were and knew innately that each of their lives so far had been a relatively easy ride. The best thing about his character however, was his determination to make it in life with or without his father's millions.

The next introduction of the day was to Khadijah's new husband Sheikh Hassan Abdul Rashid al Khalid. Unfortunately, Ophelia had missed their wedding due to exams and her own engagement celebrations in Nigeria; it was wonderful to finally meet the Sheikh at last. Khadijah's husband was a major shareholder in numerous technology stocks worldwide; even though his family being Saudi royals were oil rich, he had made his own fortune from some wise and calculated investments in tech stocks during the late 90's. The foresight in his investments came from a growing concern of his that someday, all of the oil would dry up.

Hassan was a moderate Muslim, had impeccable manners and treated Khadijah like a queen; the only blight on his character was his debilitating addiction to gambling. His wife was yet to discover this addiction, but he knew that she would eventually find out at some point. The lowest point of his existence was the day that he'd gambled away a £10 million London property on one crazy night in an upscale member's only casino in Las Vegas.
The Sheikh knew that he had to get help, but would he be able to

give up the rush of gambling unspeakable amounts of money?
Hassan didn't know the answer to that for sure, but he hoped that
getting married would provide him the love and stability that he had
been searching for his whole life. Ultimately, he earnestly wished
that he would eventually leave all of his ugly behaviour in the past.

Both being business minded, Deji and Hassan of hit it off almost
immediately, much to the delight of their respective partners; who
knew that a wedding could also double as a networking event? As
they exchanged numbers, Minty finally came over to the group and
began to compare engagement rings with Khadijah and Ophelia.
Minty showed off the beautiful square shaped ring made by *Tiffany*
and its matching wedding band. It was quite a sparkler though not a
huge rock in contrast to Ophelia's one, which was closely followed
by Khadijah's custom designed *Cartier* ring.
Once again Ophelia's spectacular engagement ring was a hot topic.
Khadijah remarked upon the clarity and brilliance of the stone;
incidentally, her opinion was the most valued amongst the girls. This
was mainly because as a Saudi princess, Khadijah had been exposed
to rare and precious stones for almost as long as she could remember.
She eventually turned her attention to Deji and quizzed him about the
stone;
'Who found this magnificent Diamond for you? Ophelia already told
me that it's a *Graff* piece, but do you know the actual dealer that
produced it? It's so rare to get a diamond this big and this flawless,
well commercially available that is! Ophelia's ring makes mine look
tiny in comparison' concluded Khadijah, laughing at her own
insecurity.
'Oh come on Khadijah, that thing on your finger is definitely not
tiny! If you really must, I can give you the direct line of the
gentleman who attended to me at *Graff*.
If you mention my name then he should be able to sort it out for
you...or shall I give it to Hassan instead? I'm sure that he can
arrange for you to have your heart's desire when it comes to big
stones...' said Deji trailing off
'Oh yes please give me the details Deji! At least I'm getting a year's

140

head start on our first wedding anniversary present this time next year and who knows? If we have had a little one by then, then the rocks will be even bigger!'

They all laughed out loud at Hassan's comment. He was a natural comic but it wasn't really what he said, but the way he said it that added to Sheikh Al Khalid's infectious charm.

Deji was pleased by Khadijah's expert assessment of the much admired ring; he intended to spend a whole lot more on his gorgeous Ophelia, that much was certain. 'Thank you so much Khadijah for your expert opinion and believe me this is only the tip of the iceberg compared to what I am yet to do for my beautiful princess. For her love, even the world is not enough' he then put his arm around her and planted a loving kiss on her forehead. Ophelia was so overcome with emotion that she would have started crying at that very moment if it wasn't for Katy chiming in with a funny remark;

'Well Deji, since that's the case, I was just wondering if you have any spare brothers? I don't mind relocating to Africa if a rock that big is what's to be expected, and there's also the added bonus of having a year round permanent tan!'

Everyone on the table laughed at Katy's retort; she was being the clown as usual and for the most part, Ophelia felt safe in the knowledge that her friends hadn't really changed.

As they continued their conversations during the reception Ophelia gathered that, Katy was currently at Glasgow University studying a degree in law. She didn't have a steady boyfriend at the moment, however knowing her friend Ophelia was sure that she wasn't short of any male attention. She decided to get to the bottom of that later; Katy would surely have some racy stories to share with the girls, but unfortunately it wasn't the time or place for it.

Sometime later after their small talk and just before the bride and groom were due to leave for their honeymoon, Dominic brought his parents over to meet the group.

'Guys I wanted to introduce you all to my parents....mum,

dad…these are some friends of mine and Minty's. You know her school mates from Launceston?' said Dominic.

'Oh yes, that's right! Good day to you kids and what a pleasure it is to meet you all' replied his father.

'Hello' said everyone in reply almost in unison and then Dominic proceeded to introduce each one of them to his folks one by one, Ophelia couldn't help but to be in awe of the stark contrast between Dominic's clean cut look and that of his parents.

The Marquis and Marchioness of Banbury may have been rich and titled, but they were completely down to earth. Darius and Tilly Parker-Graves looked like a pair of old hippies who didn't seem to have left the 1960's.

Dominic's father still sported rose tinted round specs a la *Ozzy Ozbourne* and wore his hair long, greasy and wild even inspite of his ever receding hairline. Dominic's mother was much the same with ropes and ropes of amber beads on her neck, regulation waist length bleached blond hippy style hair. Her look was finished off with an exotically beaded bohemian style gypsy skirt that was perfectly complimented by her golden gladiator sandals.

Ophelia didn't know what she had expected of Dominic's parents, but she didn't expect them to be so far removed in appearance to their son. She did however, think that their eccentricities suited them well and also added to their appeal. Dominic finally got to Ophelia and introduced her to them personally;

'Mum and dad this is Ophelia, Minty's best friend and also the lady responsible for getting Minty and I together. I do believe that if it wasn't for her sound advice, we probably wouldn't be here celebrating my wedding!' said Dominic proudly.

The Marchioness embraced Ophelia, much to her surprise;

'So you are the mastermind of all this sweetheart? Thank you so much for helping to make my son so happy! This means that he'll be leaving home at last and we'll have some peace!'

Dominic shook his head and they all burst out laughing at his mother's comment. The Marquis decided to add his own dig;

'Trust me Ophelia dear, we've been trying to get rid of this one since

142

he's left University so it's a sincere thank you from us for helping to have him taken off our hands. Now I can use my razor in the morning safe in the knowledge that it won't have been used! Our Dominic has a little habit of leaving hairs behind on the blade, I actually think he does that to wind me up!'

There was more laughter all around and Minty gave Dominic a mock quizzical look;

'Darling, you do know that there will be none of that 'leaving hairs behind' business, or you might just have to move back with your parents!'

Dominic laughed heartily at his wife's sentiments;

'But sweetheart, I thought that you loved me for me! Left behind hairs and all…or did you only marry me for my body?' he asked salaciously.

'Well…I don't really think I can discuss that in front of your parents now can I! Let's save it for tonight shall we?' replied Minty with equal suggestiveness. Ophelia was cracking up with laughter at this funny exchange of words, and wondered what they would say next. The Marchioness delivered the next punchline which sounded even funnier than a regular person would in her posh English voice;

'Minty dear heart, you can say anything about Dominic in front of us! We don't 'do' embarrassment and believe me, I've seen it all before. Darius, do you remember that night we left our dear son at home and we came home earlier than expected and we caught him…' Dominic abruptly cut her off before she could finish;

'Ok mummy dearest, that's quite enough about my teenage exploits…maybe it wasn't such a good idea to introduce my parents to you all. Let's go before you two try to cause anymore defamation to my character shall we?'

He then proceeded to drag Darius and Tilly away from them with an expression of mock exasperation on his face.

Dominic ignored his parents protests as he led them back to their table; everyone agreed that it was great that they had a sense of humor and were so easy going. Just before he left, Dominic winked at Ophelia and gave her a smile of deep gratitude as he walked away from everyone. Soon, he would be leaving for his honeymoon in

Mustique with his new wife and couldn't be a happier man. Ophelia could never imagine the impact that a few kind words of advice she had given him now had on his life; and at that very moment, Dominic knew innately that he would consider Ophelia a friend for life.

Once the bouquet had been thrown, all the wine been drunk and the happy couple waved off on to their honeymoon, some of the guests had started to leave Dunraven Manor to try and get back to their respective homes for an early night. Ophelia and Deji headed off to Heathrow Airport immediately to catch the late flight back to New York. Deji wanted to be rested enough from the flight and be refreshed once he was back at work two days later. Ophelia herself was happy to not have University to go back to and she decided that once back in New York, she would try to visit Alizé and see how her pregnancy was getting on. She hadn't seen Alizé since before she got married to Le Quawn and she wondered how her friend enjoying life as Mrs Michaels; Ophelia fell asleep on the plane pondering upon that very thought.

~~~~

Once they arrived on the island of Mustique, Minty felt as though she had reached paradise on Earth. It was the most beautiful picturesque island with stunning views that looked like they came straight out of a postcard. They would be staying at *The Cotton House* resort for two blissfully long weeks in the Caribbean sun. It was originally an 18th century coral warehouse and sugar mill, so the place was steeped in centuries of history. Some of the original features and furnishings of the house had been carefully restored by the late renowned British interior designer *Oliver Messel. The Cotton House* was so exclusive, that celebrities and royals alike considered it their very own private retreat; the place was very intimate indeed with only 20 guest deluxe rooms available on the main hotel premises. There were also private suites and cottages if a guest happened to prefer even more privacy. As one would expect, the amenities included spas, personal massage, a world renowned pool

144

and suit case unpacking service upon arrival amongst others.

Minty and Dominic had booked a private suite which had wrap a around veranda that gave them direct access to the white sandy beach. Since they had reached the island late in the afternoon, they would be having dinner quite soon and then retire early for the night. As dusk fell, the couple waited in anticipation for what would be their honeymoon night. Minty wanted to rip Dominic's clothes off as soon as the maid had finished unpacking their luggage but she held back; it would be worth the wait for it to be one of the most explosive nights that they would ever spend together.

Following a light evening meal, the couple retired to their honeymoon suite for the night and symbolically left the rest of the world behind. Once their fingers touched, it was almost as if they were magnetic; Minty began to peel off Dominic's clothes, clawing away at him like a wild cat and he obliged by ripping the flimsy strap of her linen dress and pulling her it off. As they staggered to the cotton draped colonial style four poster bed, Mrs Parker-Graves was almost completely naked apart from a thin *La Perla* thong. Dominic slammed his wife onto the bed and sank his hot mouth on to her neck, liking and sucking just the way he knew that she liked it. Minty's back arched with pleasure and she gasped loudly in conjunction with parting her legs underneath him. He then paid attention to her lips and kissed her for what seemed like a lifetime, his tongue brushed against her own both doing an imaginary dance with each other; she was already very wet by now, but there was more foreplay to come.

Her nipples seemed to be on fire as Dominic gave each breast dedicated attention in quick succession making her squirm even more; he was determined not to enter her until she literally begged for the dick.
Her husband showed no mercy as he tantalisingly moved his head down between Minty's legs making her spine tingle; Dominic was a master of eating the snatch and he savoured every part of the task he

was undertaking with passion. Minty wished she could figure out how he knew exactly which buttons to press that would always send her over the edge; his technique had never failed to make her come thus far.

Using almost the complete surface area of his tongue, Dominic licked her pussy lips over and over like a hungry dog; the faster his tongue flicked, the more of the sticky clear come juice Minty leaked; he let the wetness envelop his whole mouth and the rest of it seeped down on to his chin. When he could feel her body moving uncontrollably as she drew nearer to orgasm, he sank both of his hands under her ass and pulled her pussy sharply on to his face. This manoeuvre was his 'special move' that turned his wife into a mad woman and as he buried his mouth on to her clit, Minty climaxed triumphantly. The orgasm was so intense, that she felt that she would pass out at any second; Dominic didn't give her body the time to contemplate such a notion before he entered her powerfully, his thrusts were deep and urgent from all the time he had held back while pleasuring her. Now, it was his turn to lose control.

Minty arched her back in ecstasy as each stroke of his dick hit her g-spot, sending her into waves of tiny orgasms. He fitted her like a glove as he swelled up to full capacity inside her and sooner rather than later the feeling of her wet pussy walls was more than he could bear. Dominic could feel the semen building up in his nut sack, and looked forward to the prospect of finally being able to come inside his beloved, without the usual barrier of latex; Minty looked up at the expression on his face and knew exactly what was coming next 'Baby, let me take it in my mouth…pour it down my throat' she said lustily.

'No honey, not today, I want to come inside you for the first time…it feels so good Minty…oh yes' he whispered and at that very second, Dominic closed his eyes tightly as he pumped his hot come into her. He sincerely hoped that those magical few seconds would result in the creation of their first child; nothing would please him more than for Minty to be the mother of his yet unborn children.

Once he had come back down to earth after his explosive orgasm,

Minty looked into her husband's eyes lovingly and spoke to him without words. From that moment on, she knew for sure that their hearts would belong to each other forever.

Chapter 15

Ophelia was having a fabulous summer with Deji; since they'd got back from Minty's wedding in London, he had pulled out all the stops to keep her amused.

There were shopping sprees on Fifth Avenue, meals at the swankiest New York eateries, even more jewellery and he was even contemplating buying Ophelia her own car. She had balked at this idea, mainly because apart from the fact that she hadn't yet learned how drive, New York was a walking city so where on Earth would she drive it? Deji finally gave in to her protests and agreed with her usual sound reasoning; any kind of vehicle he could ever dream of buying for Ophelia would probably end up sitting in a garage somewhere, collecting dust.

Some weeks passed, and Ophelia decided she would go and see Alizé; they'd spoken over the phone a few times within the past few weeks, but since then Deji had been seriously monopolizing her time so she hadn't been able to see her friend up until that point. It would have been great if Dominique & Issy could have come too, but they had both travelled back home for the summer to Jamaica and

Ecuador respectively.

Ophelia and Alizé arranged to meet at a time when Le Quawn had gone out with the boys so as to indulge in some good old fashioned girl talk. They decided to meet each other at a downtown Starbucks on Broadway not too far from the *Century 21* department store on a bright Sunday morning.

At 11.15 that Sunday, Alizé walked in to find Ophelia already sitting at a table waiting; they were actually due to meet at 11am but as per usual, Mrs Michaels was late.

'Hey Ophelia girl! I'm so sorry that I'm late; you know how the Subway be on the weekends. I had to get a bus into Manhattan because the trains weren't making local stops from Brooklyn....so how are you girlfriend?' said Alizé chirpily

'Oh I'm great Alizé! And don't you worry about being late! I'm so happy to see you hon...shall we order?'

'Yep, let's go ahead and do that'

Once they had bought their beverages, the ladies sat down at a table for two by the window.

'So tell me Alizé, how is married life? I still can't get my head around how quickly you two got hitched' said Ophelia excitedly.

'I feel so lucky Oph, he just loves me so much you know? I even thought he would dump me once he got into the NBA but you know what? That was just Caspian filling my head with lies. He was so jealous that Le Quawn and I have such a good relationship, that he started to really hate on me and get this...since y'all dumped his ass, all the other chicks he's had after that have either been hoes or golddiggers. Actually you know what? Let's forget about Caspian for now, I am just too happy being in love to think about him!' Alizé replied.

'Woah, I didn't know that he would stoop that low and try to jeopardize your thing with Le Quawn...he's even jealous of his own sisters' happiness...'

'Yup, you betta believe it!'

'Just because his love life is a disaster area, that doesn't mean that

149

everybody else's should be' said Ophelia with a frown.

'Don't I know it, I'm just glad that he's taken his ass to Washington to play b-ball or he'd be driving me mad if he was over here. Caspian's problem is that our mama spoiled him and treated him like a little prince. He's her favourite out of the two of us. Mama even used to tell me that I was a 'mistake' while I was growing up; apparently she didn't plan to have anymore kids after Caspian. Her golden boy was more than enough for her so you can imagine what it was like living around that? I think if one day I'd just not come back home, then my mama would have been happy' said Alizé visibly saddened.

'Oh Alizé you poor thing! I'm sure that your mom still loves you in her own way....but I thought that you and Caspian were pretty tight though?'

'Yeah we were, until I decided to keep you as a friend after your falling out with him. Caspian's take is that since we're family, I should be on his side. That's what our mama said too, but I just think that's just childish. He was the one cheating on you, not me, so why should I lose a friend?'

Ophelia nodded in agreement; sometimes people needed to realise that blood wasn't thicker than water.

'You know what Alizé? I'm so glad that Le Quawn is a good man and he didn't let Caspian come between the two of you. I mean no wonder your brother is jealous. You're happily married and have a baby on the way....maybe he wanted that too. Anyhoo, moving on from that how is the pregnancy going? Are you still being sick in the mornings? And how is Le Quawn feeling about the baby?' asked Ophelia

'Oh gosh Le Quawn can't wait Ophelia! I've only got morning sickness on some days, so it's not too bad. It's still a long way to go until the baby is born though, look at my jeans. I'm not really showing yet'

Alizé then got up to show Ophelia her jeans. Since she was only two months gone one couldn't see much tummy at all.

As they continued talking Alizé looked down and noticed Ophelia's huge engagement ring.

'Oh my gosh how the hell did I miss that enormous rock! Did Deji get that for you….is that your engagement ring?' asked Alizé.

'Yes babe, it's my engagement ring, I'm only wearing it for now but once we get back to Uni, I'll lock it away in my safety deposit box. So does this mean that you approve of it?'

'Approve? Approve? It's da bomb sweetie! That is some serious bling baby! Lemme take a pic of that to let Le Quawn know what he needs to be working with from now on!'

Alizé then proceeded to take a quick snap of the ring with her *Nokia* cell phone. 'There it is! Now I can look at it whenever I want and dream until I get my own. Honestly babe, it's gorgeous'

'Aww thanks Alizé, I'm so happy that you like it. I can't believe that he got me this…I think I'm falling in love with him you know. While we were back home he confessed to me that he's been in love with me since we met all those years ago, you know the time when I was 15 and he was 21…that was like over five years ago now! He looked like such a nerd back then' said Ophelia and laughed at the memory of a dorky looking teenage Deji.

'But boy did he grow up to be a stunna? He's the perfect guy for you Ophelia, for sure'

The ladies carried on talking light-heartedly for a little while then suddenly, Alizé's tone became serious;

'There's something that I've been wanting to talk to you about for a while now. If you don't want to answer what I'm about to ask you right now then I'll understand completely…..But I wanted to ask you Ophelia, will you be my baby's Godmother?'

At first Ophelia was stunned, she hadn't expected this at all; then the feeling of surprise became a feeling of being deeply touched. No one had ever asked her to be a Godmother before, but Ophelia supposed there was a first time for everything.

'Oh Alizé, I'm so honoured and flattered that you would even ask me that! Of course I'll be the baby's God mother, I gladly accept!'

Ophelia and Alizé then hugged each other, and that sealed the deal;

'Fantastic Oph, and thanks for saying yes; real talk though, I don't know what I would have done if you'd said no!

They both laughed to each other and then after some time, finally left the Starbucks. Alizé decided that she wanted to visit Century 21, so after doing a little shopping for a few hours the girls parted ways; but not before promising to keep in contact until University resumed in October.

~~~~

Time seemed to fly by like the wind and before they knew it, it was already time to go back to NYU.

By all accounts everyone had had a good summer; Alizé was nearly five months pregnant and showing, Dominique had dumped the pool boy Devanté, and was now dating Bobby Lee (who was a young actor that was currently starring in a Broadway play) and finally, Issy's relationship with Eduardo had become stronger. Ophelia herself had grown to love her fiancé immensely over the past few months, but it was now time to turn her concentration to her studies. This was their final year and make or break as regards to the qualifications they would all gain at the end of the three years. At least this year, there was no Caspian to distract her from work and hopefully Ophelia would be able to reach her full potential as a young fashion designer.

Everybody worked hard and really got stuck in to their respective final year projects including the heavily pregnant Alizé who worked liked a trouper even inspite of her ever increasing tummy. The following March, once Easter had came and went, Alizé finally left University around one month before her baby was due.

The girls threw her a small baby shower and made sure that she had a good send off before her approaching motherhood. Alizé was a little scared but she had confidence in the birthing plan that her midwife had drawn up for her, and her mama would also be on hand to give her some experienced help and advice.

One evening in mid-April of that year, Alizé's waters broke while she was in the kitchen making herself a peanut butter sandwich.

Once Le Quawn knew what had just happened he swung into action, calling the appropriate medical personnel to let them know her labour had started and making sure that she had enough stuff packed that she would need for her stay at hospital. Alizé, like a good patient, was taking steady deep breaths once the contractions became more frequent. When the time came, Le Quawn drove like a fiend to get his young wife to hospital.

On Tuesday April 16th at 3am in the morning, Alizé gave birth to her first child Shalimar Mahalia Michaels. The name Shalimar was chosen because that was the name of Alizé's late grandmother's favourite fragrance and Mahalia because Le Quawn's grandma's favourite gospel singer was the late, great and incomparable Mahalia Jackson. The little girl was a little bit on the small side at a 6lbs 3oz birth weight, but she sure ate like a little soldier to make up for it. The prettiest thing was that Shalimar was born with a full head of glossy black curly hair.
Le Quawn fell in love with his child all over again the same way that he had fallen in love with little Sapphira when she was born just three years ago now and once she herself first set her eyes upon her newborn daughter, Alizé's heart filled up with the most indescribable and overwhelming feeling of love for her. What made her even happier was the fact that they were finally complete as a family at last with the arrival of their beautiful baby girl.

~~~~

As the old wives tales go, babies grow quickly and before they knew it, it was time for Shalimar's christening. Ophelia revelled in the role of Godmother to her and she made sure that she prepared herself for over a month in advance of the ceremony.
Just so that they wouldn't feel left out, Alizé had nominated Issy, Dominique and another one of her other close girlfriends Dawn to be honorary Godmothers and proverbial 'Guardian Angels' to her daughter; Le Quawn was assigned the task of choosing the baby's Godfather, which was only fair considering.

As expected the ladies had made a big deal of little Shalimar's christening outfit, each buying her a little something to wear on her special day. Alizé literally didn't have to buy anything at all because her daughter's Godmothers had brought Shalimar so many beautiful gifts; Issy had bought her a *Tiffany* baby's bangle engraved with her name and birth date on it; Dominique offered a cute pair of cream silk *Chloé* booties, Dawn found Shalimar some adorable tiny diamond stud earrings and Ophelia pulled out all the stops with a beautiful lace trimmed christening gown that had been flown in all the way from the *Petit Trésor* boutique in LA. She didn't intend on such an extravagant gift as she wasn't trying to upstage Alizé's other friends and family, but Deji had insisted upon it. Once he knew that Ophelia was going to be Shalimar's Godmother, his take was that since they were now effectively a couple, such gifts would represent the both of them and it wasn't his style to do 'simple' gifts. Incidentally, after all that fuss, Deji was unable to make the christening in the end because he had to leave at the last minute on some important business.

Once the ceremony was underway, Shalimar looked like a little princess in her outfit. Alizé held the baby in her arms proudly and was still in awe of this little person that had completely changed her life. Afterwards everybody remarked on how much of a good girl Shalimar had been and how well behaved; she didn't even cry when the Reverend Father poured holy water on her tiny little head. Funnily enough, Shalimar's maternal grandmother now had a new baby to dote on and was making such a fuss of her new granddaughter that Caspian was effectively left to the side. He had actually come up from Washington for the christening and had not been to see Shalimar since the day she was born. This was to be the first time that Caspian would see his baby niece and he already almost hated the poor child; when he had arrived he expected his mama to make a fuss of him as usual but this time to his surprise, she barely had time for him. Needless to say it was shock to the system for her golden boy and as far as Caspian was concerned all he could hear her saying was 'Shalimar this', 'Shalimar that', Shalimar, Shalimar, Shalimar; it was almost too much to bear that he had been replaced in his mother's heart by the new baby and during the past few days he had silently seethed inside with jealousy. Hopefully the christening would be all over soon and he could go back to Washington, not to return to New York City for a very long time.

Ophelia didn't get to see Caspian properly until the christening party after the church. She was hoping that they didn't have to cross paths and decided to keep a wide berth from him. As far as she was concerned, they had nothing left to say to each other. She wished that Deji was with her to keep Caspian at bay, however in spite of his absence she took comfort in the fact that at the very least she had her engagement ring on her finger. Upon spotting Caspian walk over to Le Quawn and Donnie, Ophelia thanked God at that very moment for small mercies.

Tense wasn't the word to describe the vibe once Caspian came over to gatecrash Le Quawn and Donnie's conversation. Donnie was filling Le Quawn in on how life was in Miami, when Caspian interrupted their flow of conversation in his usual brash undertone. 'So how is the proud father doin? I'll bet you be feelin real jiggy now that you got Alizé as your second baby mama. I guess you got what you always wanted' said Caspian cynically.
Le Quawn was beginning to think that haters would do what they did best. Hate. He wanted to smack that sarcastic smile off Caspian's face, but this was his daughter's christening and he wasn't about to let things get ugly.
'Well Casp, it's good that you finally came you see your niece at last seeing that she's been born for the past two months. Mighty good of you to turn up eventually' replied Le Quawn with equal cynicism 'so how can I help you now Caspian? It's just that Donnie and I were having a really important convo ya know?'
Donnie looked at Caspian and stuck out his hand to slap palms with him
'Yeah we was. How'd it do bro?'

155

'I'm aight Donnie, I'm good. I actually came over to have a little man to man talk with Le Quawn. Unfortunately it's a little family business so imma have to ask you to excuse us for a minute aight?' What else could Donnie do but leave them to talk? He felt a little left out but he supposed Le Quawn and Caspian were in-laws now, whether they liked it or not.

'Aight Casp, no sweat. Quawn just come and find me when you guys are done'
Donnie bounced off to find Alizé with Shalimar and her older half-sister Sapphira. Kimera didn't want to attend the christening but she agreed to let Sapphira be there as long as Le Quawn would pay for her outfit for the occasion. Donnie wondered what the guys were talking about as he picked up Sapphira and bounced her on his lap playfully. Donnie loved kids and looked forward to having his own someday; in his opinion, Le Quawn didn't just know how damn lucky he was.

Caspian was starting to become an extremely spiteful individual indeed. He intended to burst Le Quawn's little bubble with what he was about to say to him next. Le Quawn wondered what on Earth Caspian wanted now. He had a self-satisfied look on his face and Le Quawn just couldn't read what was coming.
'Look dawg, say what you gotta say already' said Le Quawn impatiently
'I just wanted to give you a lil' advice, well seeing as we's family and all now…..and I know that Alizé's ma sis but the bottom line is she's still a female' said Caspian
Le Quawn looked on puzzled.
'So watchu tryin' to say, cos I'm not catching ya drift rite now'
'Well just a word of man to man advice, I hope you got a DNA test when Shalimar was born, cos I know for sure that in Sapphira's case….you ain't the only nigga that's in the runnin' for that kid. Let's just say that Kimera was letting niggas hit it like the shit was Christmas. Believe me bro…I should know' said Caspian with a sardonic laugh.

It took almost every ounce of will-power and self control that Le Quawn possessed inside him not to break Caspian's jaw open at that very second. Almost past boiling point, he just couldn't comprehend why this fool had just said such an awful thing about his own blood sister and what made Le Quawn even madder, was that Caspian was implying that the light of his life Sapphira wasn't his own daughter; 'Can you hear what you just said about your own fam Casp? Are you frickin crazy nigga? And if you thought Sapphira ain't mine why ain't you say it all this time…or you just tryin to stir up some shit, not that I'd be surprised!'

'Well who was I to say anything? It ain't my fault you wanted to be the 'responsible father'….oh come on don't tell me you believed that you and Kimera were exclusive man, gimme a break Le Quawn…if you don't believe me then go ask the bitch' said Caspian scornfully

'Look Caspian….you can say what you want about Kimera, I ain't even cool with her no more, but don't you ever, ever imply anything like that again about Alizé do you hear me nigga? You and I both know that if this was another time and place I woulda knocked you out on the floor by now for talking reckless about her like that. You ain't even got no shame bra, that's your own sis you're talking about! Anyway I don't have anymore time for your ish'

Le Quawn got up to leave before Caspian said something else that would push him over the edge and in turn, Caspian drained his glass of champagne before delivering his parting shot;

'Aight Quawn, whatever. I'm just trying to help a brotha out ya know. I'm just sayin, you wouldn't wanna spend all your money on a kid until its 18 only to find out that it ain't yours. Just find out….just so you know fa sho'

As he watched Le Quawn walk off, Caspian laughed to himself and was actually a little bit drunk. He slumped back into his seat feeling triumphant about the wicked seed of doubt he'd just cast in Le Quawn's mind. *That'll take the bastard off his high horse*, thought Caspian.

In the case of Kimera, he had mercilessly pursued her until she finally relented and given him what he wanted. The feeling of fucking his own best friend's woman has been both intoxicating and powerful at the time; Caspian didn't give a damn about the consequences either, was it his fault that Kimera was such a hoe? When she fell pregnant Caspian thanked his stars that he'd used his last rubber that night; at least he knew he wasn't one of the contenders for Kimera's little brat. Caspian's thoughts then turned to what he had implied about Alizé, and he felt a tiny pang of shame. In his heart of hearts, he knew that his sister was straight as a die but his jealousy of her happiness and seemingly everybody else's, had spread through his blood like the AIDS virus. He also wasn't looking as good as he used to due to his inner hatred of every one else's good fortune consuming him. This wasn't helped by a newly found drinking habit, coupled with the occasional penchant for a line or two of smack.

For the first time in his life Caspian Strong wasn't the center of attention anymore and quite frankly he just couldn't handle it; unfortunately for him, his mother's love had rendered him an emotional cripple and as shallow as a sidewalk puddle. Even his first love of basketball was neglecting him now and he was struggling to be noticed at the *Wizards* due to the simple fact that he was now playing in a team of excellent athletes; his own talent ultimately seemed mediocre in comparison.

What mama failed to notice, was that her little Prince was headed down the lonely road to self-destruction; as he spiralled head first into depression, Caspian only just about made it through his rookie year.

Le Quawn was fuming as he met up with Alizé in the main party area; it seemed that Caspian had stuck the proverbial knife in deep. Could Sapphira really be someone else's child? For the past four years had put almost every dime he earned into providing for his beloved daughter, it would almost break him if he found out she wasn't his. The only good piece of advice that Caspian gave him was to make sure that he found out for himself. Le Quawn would ask Kimera what the deal was once he dropped Sapphira back to her mother the following day. As he approached his wife, his face was

158

black and thunderous; Alizé sensed a problem straight away.

'Honey…honey talk to me papi…what's the matter? What's made you so mad baby?' she inquired looking concerned.

'Hey suga, I can't really talk about it here so, I'll tell you later aight. Let's get back to celebratin. Imma be aight, just give me a minute' he replied.

Alizé wasn't so sure, but since she knew he would let her know when the time was right. Even though the closest thing she'd ever had to a 'father figure' was her older brother, once she got to know Le Quawn back when they'd first started dating, there was something about him made her trust him implicitly. He was one of those rare people that was as good as his word. If he said he would do something then there was a 99% chance that he would do it. In this case she decided not to probe further about his black mood.

'Okay then, I guess we'll talk later. Have you got yourself a plate yet? Aren't you hungry? Maybe some soul food will cheer you up a little, huh?' she asked him tenderly.

Alizé stroked her husband's hand in an attempt to soothe what ever was up with him; as she looked into his deep ebony eyes searching for an answer, Le Quawn's heart melted. He decided that he would put Caspian's ugly lies at the back of his mind for now; his baby shouldn't have to suffer because of them.

'Ok mama, I'll get myself something to eat…while I'm there shall I get you anything suga?'

'You know what? Shalimar is with her grandmama and Donnie is distracting Sapphira at the moment…you sit down and I'll bring you your meal. You've already made me so happy a million times over, so let me cater to you this time ok?' she replied

Alizé waved off Le Quawn's protests and walked off to get him a hot plate of food. She knew that she could trust her man but at the same time Alizé was also aware that if she didn't treat him like a king, many other chicks would kill to be in her position. She took a glance at her wedding band and made a silent prayer of thanks to God. At least her daughter would grow up having a real father instead of watching her mama hook up with a new man every year. It would appear that being a wife and mother was one of the best feelings in the world.

~~~

Later that evening once the children were in bed, Le Quawn filled Alizé in on what Caspian had said earlier in the day.

'Yup, so that's about it! I swear I was gonna knock the sense out of his head but I just held back cos of the christening and everything. Back in the day I woulda…'

'No honey, I'm glad that ya didn't. It takes a real man to have that much self control like you did, ya know? And thanks for trusting me Quawn, it really means a lot to me. You know I would never, eva cheat on you baby. I just can't even imagine it…I can't imagine wanting somebody else..'

Alizé shuddered at the thought; she had never been loose and didn't intend to start to be anytime soon.

'Oh, it's aight….Caspian obviously doesn't know you very much at all for him to say that or maybe he's just so jealous that he can't think straight. The worst thing is, I'm gonna have to confront Kimera when I drop Sapphira off tomorrow…lawd knows what she's gonna say to me. I really don't know what to think. With her you never really know where you stand. I just know that she deliberately had Sapphira just to trap me; I mean what kind of woman uses a baby as a pawn?'

'Trust me honey, there are a lot of them walking around town. Anyway don't think about it too much, just ask her for a straight answer tomorrow. Do you need me to come wit you? I could just wait in the car….I don't need to come in her crib or anything'

'That's fine suga, but thanks for offering. I know I can always count on you'

Le Quawn kissed his wife and as usual, a deep desire stirred within his loins, Alizé could feel him getting harder and as they locked lips like they had a million times before; she guessed they might be making another baby that night.

He flipped her over the sofa arm and pulled up her robe to reveal the round brown ass that was underneath; he then sank his dick into her from behind making her gasp from the size of him. That was one thing Alizé would never get used to and normally he would make her very wet before even attempting to enter her; but for some inexplicable reason tonight was different and as he took her roughly doggie style, Alizé became even more turned on by his insatiable desire for her. He grabbed her hair and pulled her head to the side, then buried his face in her neck, licking and sucking it with the intent to drive her insane. Alizé was becoming increasingly wetter by the minute and before she knew it, she fell into a rapturous orgasm that seemed to last forever. Why on earth would she ever cheat on this man in her life? The sex only got better and better as time went by and no woman on earth could ever ask for more.

Chapter 16

Le Quawn took a deep breath as he walked Sapphira to her mama's door. He looked down at his daughter in her cute dress and pretty afro puffs. He felt the poor child deserved to know who her real father was whatever the case may be. He pressed the door bell with a heavy heart and shortly after Kimera let him in. Once in, he sat on the couch in the living room and waited for his daughter to greet her mother and be made a fuss of. After a while, Kimera got with the programme and put Sapphira to bed.

Le Quawn wanted to talk to her about something and Kimera was instantly worried, *what in the hell could he want?* she thought. Times like these called for some alcoholic assistance, so she poured herself a stiff drink in the kitchen to toughen herself up, before going in to the living room to hear what he had to say.

'Look Kimera, I'll make this real quick aight. Someone was telling me yesterday that it's possible that I may not be Sapphira's biological father. I decided not to jump to any conclusions and ask you for myself…is this true?' asked Le Quawn

'What…who said that Le Quawn? Is it that Alizé making up shit about me…that bitch betta…'

'Aye, don't be calling nobody a bitch aight Kimera? It wasn't her anyways and she wouldn't say such a thing; Alizé has got class. Why are you defensive all of a sudden anyway K? Have you got something to hide?...I asked you a simple question…so can you just answer please…'

Kimera sighed and thought about her answer. If she lied to him now, he would probably get a DNA test anyway just to be sure and then she would later be found out; it was far better to spill the beans now and come clean. Her tone dropped from its usual high pitch, as she confessed to Le Quawn what was probably the greatest sin that she had ever committed in her life thus far.

'Le Quawn, I ain't gonna lie to you. I don't know if Sapphira is yours 100%, maybe 90% sure but, I can't say that she's yours no doubt. Now before you go off on one and call me a hoe, I know I was wrong to not tell you but I just wanted my baby to have a good father and you was the most responsible nigga that I know. I gotta tell you that imma regret this 'til the day I die...it was around when you broke it off with me for the last time. I was so desperate to get you back, so I thought that if I fucked around with a few guys, word would get round to you and you'd be jealous and want me back...' as she trailed off, Kimera stared to sob heart-wrenching tears of loneliness and shame. Where the hell had all that crap got her? She was now reduced to being a single mom living alone with her young daughter; most men didn't want to get involved with her anymore after the tales of what she had put Le Quawn through hit the neighbourhood.

'So you mean to tell me that you woulda let me to raise a child that might not have been mine? You know how hard I worked while I was in NYU...I nearly worked myself to death for that baby Kimera! What the fuck was you thinking? Why the fuck would you think that sleepin with other niggas would bring me back to you...things between us had broken down to the point that I didn't even wanna see you on the street, talk less of giving a damn who you wanted to open your legs for! I didn't even hear anything about this until Shalimar's christening yesterday. I even thought Caspian was just

talking smack...I guess everybody knew the truth apart from me!' he
thundered.
By now, Le Quawn's voice was now loud and booming; Sapphira
had woken up and toddled in to see what was going on. Upon
hearing her daddy's angry voice, she was afraid and started to cry.
He picked her up and walked her back to her little bed.

'Don't cry baby, daddy's not angry with you' Le Quawn rubbed her
little head and soothed her back into bed 'come on princess, go back
to sleep. Yeah that's right...sweet dreams honey and daddy will come
pick you up next weekend okay'
Sapphira eventually settled down and dozed off; as he gave her a
loving kiss on her forehead, Kimera stood by the door watching the
scene and crying silently. Couldn't it have been different between
them? And was she really that bad?
Kimera already knew the answer to that question. That was the
reason Le Quawn had to be in her apartment having it out with her
that evening.

Then a hair-brained idea began to form in her mind. Maybe if she
offered him the prospect of some regular pussy, he wouldn't fuss
about the issue. It was clear that he already loved Sapphira no matter
what the outcome of the DNA test would be; so Kimera decided to
do with her womanhood what she did best, use it as a bargaining
chip. As Le Quawn walked towards the door, she started to unzip her
jeans and looked at him desperately. He knew from her expression
exactly what that meant.
'Quawn please, I'm real sorry for what I did to you but I can make it
better...and I've been so lonely, I need a real man to do it to me' her
voice then lowered to barely a whisper 'you can have me whenever
you want baby, ain't nobody have to know. Whenever you drop
Sapphira off we can do a lil somethin somethin...ya know...please Le
Quawn. Ain't no other man ever filled up my pussy like you have
nigga.....' as she trailed off, he shook his head pitifully; obviously
Kimera Hamilton hadn't changed one bit. Is this what she had
reduced herself to? Using sex as a way of fixing her problems? He

guessed that she hadn't really learned from the situation she had now found herself in; Le Quawn thought back to when they had first met just after he left high school. He was attracted to her beauty and self-confidence. She was a complete contrast to him being a redbone with long hair, and she made no apologies for that. Kimera even used to joke with him that all the darker skinned chicks were just jealous of her cos she was 'light and pretty' and she labelled all of them ashy, busted looking hoes. They used to laugh about it back then, but over time Le Quawn quickly realised that she was actually very shallow and callous. If he didn't spend enough money on her, pick her up from college or pay for her to get her hair done at any point, there was a problem. The younger Kimera was the typical round the way hottie, so she expected men to spend their money and lavish attention on her as if it was her God given right. It was tragic to see how her star had faded into a pathetic shadow of her former self.

'Hey Kimera, stop right there okay. Zip your pants up and let's get back to this conversation we were having. Oh and for the record, I'm taken now...I'm married to Alizé and she knows why I'm here and what we're talking about so don't try any slick moves. I will get to the bottom of this, so say whatever else you have to say about it before I leave here. The next time I'll contact you will be to let you know where to show up to get the DNA test done.'
Le Quawn sat back down in his designated seat and looked at her squarely; if she thought it would be on tonight, then she was very much mistaken. A part of him felt very sorry for her, she had chosen this lonely road all by herself; Kimera visibly wilted in front of him like a broken flower.
'Oh...I see then. I'm sorry for doing that Quawn...what the hell was I thinking. Umm...okay then I don't think there's anything more for me to say. I'd just be repeating myself anyways...did you say that Caspian told you about all this?' she inquired
'Yeah he did yesterday...what about it?'
'Well I think I might have to let him know that the night we did it...'
'Who did what...you and Ca...'
'Umm, yeah...me and Caspian slept together...oh Le Quawn this isn't

165

easy for me either ya know. I can't say how sorry and stupid I feel...'

'Ok whatever, just carry on already'

'Alright...when we slept together, I noticed that the condom had broken but I didn't think anything of it...I was still on the pill that week. Well at least most of the days anyway, but I think that he should be part of the DNA testing...along with the two other guys that could be Sapphira's daddy'

Le Quawn couldn't believe what he was hearing; his beautiful innocent daughter could possibly be the biological child of four different men. He knew at that moment that he had to leave Kimera's home before he exploded with rage; *how the hell could she have been so irresponsible!* he thought

'Kimera, I've heard enough now okay...enough! I've gotta go and I'll call you to let you know when the time comes. Goodnight'

Le Quawn stormed off towards the front door and Kimera followed in his wake crying hysterically.

'Le Quawn, please don't leave me like this...I'm really sorry...so very sorry for all this. I even hate myself more and more each day. Please don't hate me too!'

Her words fell on deaf ears as he'd already shut the door behind him. As he drove off back to his home, Le Quawn was crying inside. When he could take no more he finally stopped in a lay-by to cry alone. He kept asking himself how on earth a woman could be so wicked, twisted and mean, but the cold of the evening air could not offer him a logical answer. Sapphira deserved more than Kimera as a mother and in his opinion, some people just didn't deserve the right to bear children.

~~~~

The day of decision arrived and Le Quawn left with Alizé for the family planning center. Shalimar had been left in the capable hands of her grandmama for the afternoon much to Alizé's protest. This was the first time since her birth that Shalimar had been left in the care of someone else apart from herself, and she was finding it

166

difficult to let go. As they drove off, Alizé figured she should stop being so paranoid and thank God that her daughter was with her grandmother and not some random stranger. After they had been on the road a little while, she turned her thoughts to the impending meeting instead and wondered what the outcome would be.

They didn't have to wait too long to hear the results of the DNA test. Alizé stayed in the waiting room with Sapphira while Kimera, Le Quawn and another dude named Smithy that they knew from around the way, went into the doctor's room. Caspian was going to make a call into the meeting and the last absent contender was a local small time drug dealer that went by the name of 'Kamikaze'. He had left his DNA sample for the purposes of the test the week before, but didn't want to hear back from Kimera unless the kid was his.
Le Quawn's heart was beating nineteen to the dozen as the doctor opened the envelope that contained the results, he looked over to Kimera and he could see tiny beads of sweat forming on her forehead; it was finally time for her to face the music.

'Okay are you all ready for this...I know it isn't easy but I'm glad you're all here to do the right thing' said the doctor sympathetically. They all nodded in agreement, however Caspian who was on the speaker phone chimed in with his usual brash talk;
'Aight doc, just tell us already. Some of us have things to do ya know'
'Thank you Mr Strong, I'm just about taking the results out of the envelope now..I won't keep you too long'
Le Quawn thought he'd stepped on to the set of an episode of Maury when the doctor next spoke.
'In the case of Sapphira Cassidy, this DNA test determines that Jonathan Turner is her biological father'
'Oh shit it ain't me? Cool, I'm gone then' and with that, Caspian cut himself off from the phone call abruptly.
Kimera subsequently collapsed and fainted on the floor in shock, *thank God we're in a doctor's office* thought Le Quawn. When she finally came around she was dazed and confused to say the least;

then the realization eventually came that the father of her child, was no other than that no good hustler Kamikaze. Jonathan Turner was his government name, but everybody knew him as Kamikaze in the hood simply because he went through women like a hurricane and also when he decided to waste someone, he would come through the spot spraying bullets everywhere.

Kimera couldn't even figure out why the hell she had even fucked with a guy like him; he was just bad news. She thought back to the night they'd met in the club soon after she had broken up with Le Quawn and remembered that they were both drunk. Kimera couldn't recall whether or not they had used protection, just that they'd gone into the back of his truck in the parking lot and had a quick fuck. She now had a bitter price to pay for a measly yet reckless five minutes of her life.

Smithy felt awkward and relieved at the same time. He felt sad to be witnessing somebody else's human tragedy but equally felt as if he was intruding on Kimera's privacy. After all it wasn't as if he really knew her, they'd only had sex once when he came to her apartment to fix the boiler. Plumbing was his profession by trade so he usually made regular house visits to many of single moms living alone around the way. Some of them used to come on to him and he would usually brush them off since he already had a steady chick; but when Kimera did so, it was different.

She was the girl that all of the guys had jerked off over in their teens and most of them would have killed to get a chance to bone her. He thought all his Christmases had come at once when she'd walked into her kitchen wearing nothing by a flimsy short negligee and heels. She cocked her leg up on a chair to reveal her pretty shaved pussy and mesmerized him when she'd egged him on brazenly with her freaky talk; his mind flashed back to her teasing;

'So, what are you waitin for nigga...this pussy ain't gonna wait all day you know...'

While thinking back, he realised that he'd jumped on to her so fast that he forgot that he didn't have a condom. She'd said that she was on the pill, so in the heat of the moment, Smithy put the notion of protection at the back of his mind. He knew better now though, sometimes these pretty chicks were the grimiest of hoes. Eventually, Smithy said his goodbyes and left. Inwardly triumphantly thanked his stars that he wasn't the kid's father; *what kind of a mother did she call herself anyways* he thought and then walked out of the office.

Le Quawn felt as though part of his world had just collapsed...whatever would happen to his little Sapphira now that Kamikaze was her daddy? he wondered. When he'd left Kimera in the doctors' room, she was crying as if somebody had died. Actually, a part of her had just died in there once she found out that Le Quawn wasn't her baby daddy; she would have had the strength to kill herself if it wasn't for the fact that her child would be left without a mother; in a moment of utter despair, Kimera asked herself angrily when the fuck it all went wrong for her.
Kamikaze already had three other baby mamas that were notorious for trying and snatch each other's weaves out whenever they crossed paths in the street and there was no way on earth she could stand to be seen as one of those hood-rats.
In the end, Kimera made a hard decision within herself that day. She would leave Brooklyn and move uptown to Harlem where her cousin Samantha lived. That way, at least once she'd notified Kamikaze of the situation, she wouldn't have to see him around the way and it was highly unlikely that he would come all the way up to Manhattan to drop round and see her very often. As Kimera took Sapphira in her arms and was about to leave the building, she didn't dare look Le Quawn in the face out of her abject shame.

'Kimera please don't leave yet...I just wanted to say that regardless of what's happened, I still love Sapphira as my daughter and if it's okay, Alizé and I would still like to see her on the weekends...if that's okay with you that is'
Le Quawn fought back the tears of sorrow for his poor little girl and continued on;
'I set up a trust fund in her name when she was born, so when she's

169

21 she'll be paid a lump sum check from it and then yearly payments until she is 35 years old. Also if you need anything for her, clothes, food nappies anything, you got my number so just holler at me, aight Kimera. I know this is a bad situation but you can make the best of it...Sapphira don't have to suffer if you play it right...na mean?' he then cleared his throat in an attempt to stop his voice from wavering into a painful wail.

'Thanks Le Quawn...thank you for everything you just said. I'll remember that and I'll always be grateful. You're right that I gotta make the best of this situation and I'm gonna try my best. A lot of things have to change about the way I live my life too so I guess...I guess, I got exactly what I deserved' she replied, and with that Kimera broke down again, which naturally caused Sapphira to start crying too. Alizé quickly consoled the child while Le Quawn and Kimera hugged each other tightly; he let a tear roll down his face at last. The love he had for Sapphira seemed as if it was choking him, as the realisation of the fact that he had never been her real father in the first place almost killed him. Just before they left, Le Quawn took Sapphira from Alizé and gave her a kiss on her head as he always did; when she looked at him with concern and said 'Daddy, don't cry' in her little voice, it almost tore him apart.

After a little while, Kimera took Sapphira from him and left the building; a forlorn Le Quawn cried heart-wrenchingly as he pondered upon the fate of the little one with a father like Kamikaze. As Alizé consoled him he was thankful that at the very least he had Shalimar; but deep down, Le Quawn knew that he would never be the same again.

Chapter 17

The end of Ophelia's final year at NYU had approached and she couldn't believe that it gone so fast. Wasn't it just yesterday that she was a wide eyed teen that couldn't get enough of New York City? Now the flashing lights of Times Square or the millions of yellow taxis no longer filled her eyes with awe. Ophelia still loved the city, but nothing could beat the feeling of discovering New York for the first time; of all the many places she had travelled to in the world, nothing else compared to the dynamic buzz of this much fabled city. It would forever be her second home.

Ophelia and Issy worked on their final project like a pair of crack heads on the pipe. Between them they had drawn 500 rough sketches, and out of those chosen 60 final designs, then narrowed those down to 25 core outfits and cut out a mountain of patterns until Issy had wrist cramp. The theme that the students had been given for their graduate fashion show was 'Empire of the Sun'. It was up to them to translate that phrase in the most effective way on to the catwalk. This year the student fashion show would be held at the

Metropolitan Museum of Art, and rumor had it that some big wigs in the rag trade would be showing up including Diana La Tour who just happened to be the editor of the worlds most famous fashion magazine *'La Mode'.* The word on the grapevine was that Madam La Tour, as every one called her, had got wind of the fact that Ophelia and Issy had bagged Bijou along with some of her other top model friends for their final show. They had all offered their services for free once Bijou had told them who the show was for, so it was only a matter of time for *'Transatlantic'* to become the hot new label du jour. Both Issy and Ophelia agreed that name was perfect for them as it reflected the kind of lives that they'd lived thus far.

The girls felt that things weren't the same without Alizé so they invited her to come and work with them whenever she wanted. If by a fabulous stroke of luck they were able to get a big time fashion house to sponsor their fledgling label, they assured their friend that she would have a job with them as a designer whenever she wished. Alizé herself was enjoying life as a new mother far too much too go work, but she would be sure to go back and complete her final semester of University in the New Year. Then and only then, could the prospect of beginning a career in the fashion industry be contemplated.

Shalimar was doing great and Kimera had eventually agreed to still let Sapphira stay with Le Quawn on the weekends. When Alizé filled the girls in on the 'Kimera' saga, they were all shocked beyond words. It was almost unbelievable to them that Kimera had exposed herself to the possibility of H.I.V and unplanned pregnancy by recklessly having unprotected sex with so many men. Thankfully, the worst that had come out of the situation was a beautiful little girl being brought into the world.

There was the most amazing buzz backstage on the night of the fashion show. Each group had 15 minutes of catwalk time and had to show 25 outfits in total. Alizé left Shalimar with Le Quawn for the night to come through and help the girls out. Dominique also lent her hand by helping the models get into the outfits and Ronke only turned up because Bijou would be there too. Eventually somebody threw a dress into her hands thinking that she was one of the helpers, so in the end she decided to make herself useful. Deji was in the front row of the audience after being banished from the backstage area by Ophelia. She shooed him away by telling him that there was no way she could concentrate on her work with his hotness lurking around. Eduardo had also suffered the same fate, so the two men kept each other company. He remarked that the girls had better 'lay the smackdown' with the show after leaving them in the wilderness of the notoriously crazy fashion audience, but Deji felt assured him that they would do just fine.

Ophelia's palms went cold as the DJ played *Chaka Khan's* classic 80's song
'I feel for you' on the speakers as the opening track for their fifteen minute show. The girls could see the catwalk on the plasma screens backstage and even though the models had to make some quick changes, they could still snatch glances of how the outfits looked under the stage lights. It was a culmination of their three years of hardwork and experience being displayed out there and Issy hoped to God that none of the clothes flunked. In truth, the very opposite was underway as photographers furiously took snaps of Bijou et al, in some of the most fabulously cut, flowing, sparkly, bright and sexy clothes to ever grace the museum. The fash pack knew a hit when they saw one, and even Madam La Tour couldn't keep her eyes off the stage. The show finally ended with Bijou to close and she sashayed out of the catwalk to *Britney Spears'* infamous hit 'Gimme More' with a fierce swagger that almost set the runway alight.
It was 'Gimme More' alright when the models walked back on with Ophelia and Issy. The girls were completely taken aback to receive a raucous standing ovation; it was simply as the famous saying went, 'a fashion moment'.

~~~~

Over a week later Issy and Ophelia were still in shock from the fallout of their triumphant fashion show. *Transatlantic* had already been offered numerous sponsorship deals to get the label off the ground and *La Mode* magazine had promised that they would get a small article about the show featured in the next month's issue. Ophelia was so giddy from the intoxicating feeling of success that she felt as though she was walking on a cloud. Deji took her out to *Cipriani* for the umpteenth time to celebrate, and all of the waiters stopped by to congratulate her on a job well done.

At the realisation that her beloved husband to be had let all the staff at the restaurant in on the good news, Ophelia's heart was warmed by the fact that he was so proud of her success. Could this man do no wrong?

A few days later it seemed that he could, when he announced that he'd have to go away on business again for a week. Ophelia was looking forward to spending the whole summer with him alone, so when Deji told her of his impending business trip, he was met with her disappointment and sadness.

'Oh honey, please don't give me that look...you know that I don't want to leave you now, but it's work so I have to' he said tenderly.

'Deji, I don't mean to complain but it's just that I've been looking forward to finally leaving Uni so we can spend more time together...can't I come with you?'

'No my love, I'm afraid I would be seen to be very professional bringing my beautiful fiancée with me to work would I?'

'Ahh...that's true. I didn't think of that. I'll miss you terribly Deji...'

Ophelia started crying as she realised that she was head over heels in love with this man. In the year and a half that they had known each other Deji had personified exactly what Ophelia had envisioned her true love would be like and then some. He didn't pressure her, he was understanding, considerate and so much more; she knew that everyday she didn't see him would be like being without a part of herself. Deji had really come to represent her other half and the sooner they were married the better. She only had until September to wait and then they would finally be husband and wife.

~~~~

Issy knew that Ophelia was pining over the absence of her boo so she decided to cheer her up a bit. Eduardo had managed to bag some spare tickets and backstage passes to a Greenback concert that weekend. It was a fabulous stroke of luck that Eduardo worked on the same record label that had Greenback on their artist roster. Issy had become quite a little 'fixer-upper' in recent times due to her boyfriend's associations and she could usually get her close friends into the hottest clubs and gigs in town.

Since Greenback had been Ophelia's favourite rapper for the past five years, there was no was that she would pass up an opportunity to see him perform. Along side him would be his band of 'brothers' that made up the other rappers within his crew that collectively called themselves 'The Click'.

Ophelia thought back to her days in Launceston when Greenback had first exploded on to the music industry with his debut album entitled *'A millionaire state of mind'*. Playing music with such aggressive and blatantly sexual content as Greenback's was banned at school, so Ophelia and Minty would sneak off and play his album in their secret hiding places. Both girls as young teenagers had a huge crush on the rapper and would listen to his entire album while exchanging sexual fantasies of what they would do if the ever met him and debated on how big his manhood was. Greenback was lusted after by both males and females alike due to his rugged muscular physique and upper body which was covered in tattoos. The moniker 'Greenback' was simply a metaphor for dollar bills, but most of his fans referred to him simply as 'Green' and as a testament to the amount money that he lavished on an extravagant lifestyle, the haters liked to call him 'Niggarachi'.

His meteoric rise to fame was an inspiring and harrowing one. Green was almost killed in a gang drive by where he was shot 11 times and amazingly survived. The story of his attempted 'assassination' became ghetto folklore and before he knew it Greenback and The

Unit were clearing over 50,000 copies a month in mixtape sales. The music industry sat up and took notice of the young hard edged rapper from the mean streets of Queens and the rest as they say, was history. Since then he had sold over 70 million records worldwide and earned over $100 million a year due his lucrative sponsorship deals and his unparalleled business acumen. Estimates of his wealth by Forbes magazine were just speculations, but both Greenback and his team of accountants knew that he was well on his way to earning his first billon dollars.

Ophelia used to follow Greenback's career religiously back in the day, but now that she had Deji, there was no room to give another man that kind of time. Since her fiancé was out of town, it would be the only chance she would have to go to that kind of concert for a long time. Ophelia knew that Deji would not approve of her listening to gangsta rap music, especially considering some of the very suggestive lyrics that Greenback frequently peppered his songs with. One of her most favourite of his hit records was the salaciously titled 'Candy Bar'. The lyrics never failed to set Ophelia's imagination alight:

Come girl, taste my Candy Bar
Just touch it, it's hard so hard
Come on girl don't be shy
Lick da cream and suck it dry...

Incidentally, Issy had given her two tickets to the show, so Ophelia asked Ronke if she wanted to tag along. Though rap music wasn't really her thing, she decided she would go with Ophelia anyway to see for herself what all the fuss was about this Greenback character. Since Donnie had left for Miami a year ago, it wasn't as if she had any other plans on a Saturday night. Ronke still hadn't moved on to dating other guys since their separation and whenever he could, Donnie would still visit her in New York where they would carry on from wherever they left off.

Chapter 18

Surprisingly on the night of the concert, Ronke actually quite
enjoyed herself. Greenback had an amazing stage presence and
seemingly boundless energy. He moved up and down on the platform
engaging the whole crowd from on end to the other. Ophelia herself,
felt as if she was in another world as she re-lived the music of her
teens through every song that Greenback performed. She wished that
Minty was here with her see him on stage in all his tattooed glory,
but as fate would have it that was not to be. After the show Ophelia
remembered that Eduardo had also got them backstage passes and
she soon found herself been ushered with Issy and the girls into the
side exit led down to the artist's area. As they walked into the main
dressing room, she could her Green laughing heartily with his friends
over a joke that one of the boys had just made. Eduardo then walked
up to him and gave him a high five and a brotherly hug; who knew
that Eduardo and Green knew each other all this time?
Ophelia felt as if she'd entered a dreamlike state when she was
introduced to Greenback as well as some of the boys from The Click.

After a little small talk, the entourage decided that they wanted to hit the clubs to round off the night so Issy and Eduardo decided they would tag along with them. Unfortunately, probably from all the excitement, Ophelia had a slight headache and would much rather go home. As she contemplated what she would do next, Greenback announced that he wouldn't join them either and intended go back to his hotel room instead to work on some new mixtape tracks. This was not unusual for him to do as he was completely uninterested in the whole clubs, girls and drinking scene that the entertainment industry was notorious for. Green was all about the money and forever kept his eye on the next move. In the back of his mind though he knew that his intentions for that night weren't so innocent. The ladies that Eduardo had just introduced him to were both beautiful as well as articulate women. He wasn't interested in hoodrats, groupies or hoochie mamas and was always on the lookout for something a lot more refined. Ronke and Ophelia seemed to fit the bill and Green didn't care which one he got tonight as long as he was able to smash.

When the Tyra Banks look-alike with the hair first came around the corner with Eduardo and his girlfriend, Green's dick instantly became stiff; to top that, right behind her was a chocolate beauty who would give Naomi Campbell a run for her money. Surreptitiously, he checked out the backview and was satisfied that they both met his qualification range for booty. The lighter-skinned one seemed to be flirting with him as they chatted about this and that; he wasn't really listening to her words but rather looking at her thick glossy lips…maybe a small hint would get her to follow him back to the hotel.

'So how are y'all ladies spending the rest of the night? Off to the club too or do you want to chill with me at the hotel….I guess we could just talk and don't worry about getting home late. That what the concierge is for, I can arrange a car to take y'all home…'
Green's trick was to make his intentions sound as innocent as possible. Even if they did have the intention of fucking him that

night, most females wouldn't want it to look blatantly obvious that they were going off with him for that reason. Ronke licked her lips at the prospect of his hard ghetto dick inside her and though she had never paid much attention to this guy and his music in the past, since meeting him in person Ronke admitted to herself that he was very sexy and had the most amazing animalistic magnetism. He seemed to be like a beast, maybe she'd be able to find out for herself just how much of an animal he really was.

'Oh Green, that sounds like a wonderful idea! Of course I'd love to stay up and chat with you' said Ronke with a twinkle in her eye 'Ophelia, do you want to hop in a cab home… you said that you had a headache earlier'
Being her responsible self as usual, Ophelia thought it wrong to leave her cousin alone with Green. At the same time she wondered what he would have to talk about and how he interacted with regular people without all the 'industry' guys around him. Ophelia also didn't want to go home alone so late, Deji usually escorted her right her front door just to make sure that she got in safely.

'No…that's fine Ronke. I can't leave you all by yourself, I'll just tag along with you guys. At least I'll have some company and I don't feel much like being alone tonight' she then turned to face her newly appointed host for the rest of the evening to express her gratitude; 'Green, thank you so much for inviting us over, I really appreciate it' said Ophelia.
Green smiled at Ophelia and nodded his acknowledgement however completely unbeknownst to her; he had taken her statement to mean something quite far removed from what she had actually said. As far as Green was concerned he was probably going to hit both pussies at some point later that evening and he didn't mind which one he got to taste first.
'Alright ladies, shall we go then?' he ushered them to walk in front and seemingly being the gentleman said, 'please sweetie, go ahead ladies first'.

The band of three arrived outside the Hammerstein Ballroom where the concert had been held and filed into the gigantic black SUV that was waiting for them with the engine already running. It was instantly spacious inside the vehicle and the seats were luxuriously upholstered in the most sumptuous premium soft black leather. Once Green reached into the chilled cabinet and brought of a bottle of *Dom Perignon* along with a pair of crystal champagne flutes, Ronke was mildly impressed. This was more along the lines of what she was accustomed to, and this guy seemed to know exactly what a lady wanted; she hoped that he was equally as attentive in the sack. While Ronke gladly accepted the offer of champagne, Ophelia declined gracefully. Alcohol wasn't really her thing so she wouldn't force it upon herself just because a celebrity happened to offer her some. She noted that Green himself neglected to take a drink. So was this the secret to his success? It would appear that the rapper was completely teetotal.

During the short car journey as Ophelia looked out the window, she was oblivious to the suggestive looks that Ronke was giving Greenback while she was sitting right next to her. There was a strange carnal attraction that Ronke was feeling towards Green; he wasn't her type at all and essentially a ghetto gang banger nigga with none of the refinement that she usually looked for in a man. The one thing that he did possess though was an intoxicating air of money, power and success that she just could not resist.
She seriously needed a fuck that night and it had been at least three months since she had last seen Donnie; it was beginning to feel as if there had been a drought between her legs. As the golden liquid flowed down her throat rapidly, Ronke could feel her libido building up exponentially. It seemed to be a wonderful idea at the time to sexily slide her middle finger in and out of her mouth repeatedly as he watched her. Green who was sitting directly opposite Ronke, smiled salaciously and put a hand on the crotch area of his baggy jeans attempting to hold himself down. He was as hard as a brick now from all of Ronke's teasing and began discreetly rub himself that area in anticipation for what was coming next.

Once they all got into the hotel elevator Green pressed the button headed for the top floor; as they glided upwards, Ophelia began to feel tiredness overcome her. She didn't usually stay out that late and it was soon approaching one in the morning. She figured that once they reached his hotel suite, she could maybe take a quick nap on a couch or something.

The presidential suite was everything that its title promised with icing on top.
At $4000 a night, it was the kind of place where absolutely anything that one requested could be provided by the room service facility or even the concierge. It was aptly decorated in the finest furnishings and boasted pieces from *Ralph Lauren Home, Armani Casa* and a *Kohler* fitted bathroom amongst others. Green casually threw his suite entry card on the coffee table and took off his Timberland boots.
'Ladies, please make yourselves comfortable, mi casa es su casa!' he said with an infectious smile.

Ronke and Ophelia both sat down on a squashy cream sofa that could have comfortably held about four people; as they started making small talk Ophelia felt so relaxed in her spot that she fell asleep in within minutes of sitting down. Ronke looked over at Green and smiled. Once their eyes met, they both knew what was about to down, but since she had been wearing her jeans all evening, Ronke needed to freshen up first.
'Hey Green, I need to use the bathroom…which way is it?'
'Walk straight down the hall and then make a left at the end….come find me in the master bedroom once you're done aight'
'No Green…you come and find me. Give me five minutes'
Ronke walked to the bathroom pleased in the knowledge that she had taken control of the situation; he would just have to learn who the boss in this equation was.

Once in the bathroom she washed herself between her legs and put her panties in her bag. After that, she took her clothes off and threw on one of the luxurious towelling bathrobes that were hung up on the side. Green did as he was told and turned up exactly five minutes later to find Ronke tying the bathrobe belt around her waist.

'Oh I see that you made it then, I hope you don't mind me borrowing your robe…I didn't think I'd need my clothes at the moment' said Ronke laughing as she gestured to her pile of clothes on the bathroom floor. Green walked right up to her face to face and untied the robe;

'Looks like you won't be needing this either' he replied.

Inevitably, he looked down at her naked body and found that Ronke's pale caramel skin was a beautiful sight to behold. Her breasts were a firm medium size with hard dark brown nipples and she had her pubic hair waxed with a Brazilian strip in the middle; to top it all, her waist was nipped in just so. When Green cupped one breast in his hand and brought his head down to lick her nipple, Ronke gasped in response throwing her head back. His tongue felt so good on her titty that she returned the gesture by grabbing on his belt and pulling his pants down. Before he let his pants touch the ground, Green took a fresh pack of Magnums out of his pocket and slipped one condom over his dick; clearly, safe sex was the only kind of sex he would allow himself to partake in.

'I was just about to ask if you had protection…I'm glad you came prepared' said Ronke.

'Yup…gots to be' he replied. The words ended there for the moment, it was time for some action from then on.

He gently pushed her down to the floor on all fours across the cream shag pile carpet and started to seriously fuck her doggie style. This was his favourite position and from the sounds that she was making it seemed to be one of Ronke's too. After the long drought from any kind of phallic activity, the feeling of a big fat black cock inside her was an exquisite physical trip. She instinctively buried her head down on the floor and pushed her fat ass up in the air; she arched her back as Green began to pump at her behind even faster. He relished in the tightness and wetness of her pussy, it was so sweet that he could feel his nuts firming up ready to release his first orgasm of the night; Ronke added to his excitement by repeatedly clenching her hot snatch over his meat.

'Damn baby…your pussy is so tight….oh yeah…ooh. You making a nigga wanna bust a nut on this fine ass' he said breathlessly.

'No…not yet Green, I'm loving your dick inside me so fuck me harder…harder please, that's it! Don't you dare stop fucking me you black muthafucker…yeah that's it nigga…. fuck me'

Ronke flicked her hair over her shoulder and looked up at him with the lustful eyes of a cheap slut.

'Ooh I like that dirty talk baby…keep talking like that and imma lose my shit right now' said Green teasingly, but in truth he was enjoying her pussy far too much, he'd have to stay in this saddle a bit longer than he had anticipated.

After a little while longer in the bathroom, he decided on a change of scenery.

They moved to the huge bed in the master bedroom to continue their filthy liaison. Upon reaching the there, Ronke realised that she had lost the notion of being in control of the situation from the moment that Green had laid a finger on her. It was as if he was the ringmaster cracking the whip and she was powerless to do anything but dance to his tune. Green was used to 'breaking bitches' on the regular and even the most hardened strong willed feminist types became putty in his hands once he got started; Ronke was a light-weight in comparison to some of the females he had broken down in his time. As he prepared to fuck her anus he thought back to one particular sexual encounter when he had slept with one young lady and hit her pussy with such force, that she had to visit the emergency ward the following morning. Green maintained that it wasn't his fault that she got injured, when she'd begged him to fuck her harder he was only doing what the lady had asked for.

'Baby have you ever been taken in the ass? Cos I'm about to…' he trailed off and reached over to night stand to bring out a gigantic tube of Superlube.

183

'Yeah…I have. Fill my ass up already'
Green felt a wave of satisfaction come over him at her delightful
words, this bitch was exactly the kind of woman he liked to fuck; she
was nothing but dirty a freak.

Ronke looked up at the clock, and from what she could tell they had
been at it for little over an hour now; his porn star stamina was
beginning to tire her out, but she was yet unaware that Green wasn't
even close to finishing it. As sweat dripped off their bodies onto the
450 thread count *Frette* sheets, Ronke could feel an orgasm building
up as Green fingered her pussy in conjunction with giving her some
mean anal. Forever a multi-tasker, he drove her even crazier by
pinching one of her nipples with his other free hand. He wasn't a
small dude by anybody's standards but when it came to the pussy,
Green could balance his body weight over a woman with the delicate
grace of a prima ballerina. After a few intense minutes of the triple
stimulation, Ronke whimpered into a spectacular multiple orgasm
that rendered her stomach weak and turned her legs to jelly. Soon she
had come till she could come no more. She begged Green to take his
penis out of her to take a breather; unfortunately, he had no intention
of doing so.

'Please baby, please, no-more! I can't take it daddy…ahh' she
protested feebly.
He smacked her butt and flipped her over on to her back with
authority.
'It not about what you can't take it's what you will take bitch, now
quit whining and take this nigga dick like a real woman' he replied.
Ronke was so turned on by his masterful display of masculinity that
she had yet another orgasm; this time he was hitting it missionary
style with one of her legs flipped up over her head for deeper
penetration.
'Ow please daddy, please time out!' she screamed.
Her pussy was now swollen from all the abuse and in an involuntary
motion her walls gripped on to his cock as he sped up to his own
long awaited climax.

Ophelia woke up wondering what time it was, then heard the noises coming from the master bedroom. She listened closely to make sure that she was hearing what she thought she was hearing. Ophelia crept up to the door that was slightly ajar, from the small crack she could see Green's tattooed back bobbing up and down and then a female's leg cocked up in the air. She watched wide eyed as he pumped away at her cousin and then she heard Ronke's unmistakable voice;
'Oh shit….I can't stop coming! I beg you daddy I can't take no more!'
Ophelia was getting very aroused as she listened to the sexy commentary unfolding before her. It was as if she was watching a porno flick, but with the added bonus of the irresistible smell of sweat, dick and pussy all rolled into one.

As Ophelia continued to watch them, Ronke's senses were overwhelmed by all the stimulation that she had been receiving. As the ecstasy of her umpteenth orgasm consumed her, Ronke cried tears of joy. This was shaping up to be the best sex that she had ever had in her life. This was the point that Green was aiming for before he would stop, once he was done with her the bitch would probably fall straight to sleep. Suddenly out of the corner of his eyes, he caught a little peeping Tom watching from behind the bedroom door.
'Oh so you been watching all this time you little pervert…' said Green. He then took his dick out of her cousin and started to walk over to the door.
'Come on then mama, you wanna get you some of this dick too?'
Ophelia's throat went dry and she couldn't speak. Her pussy was already wet and it had been almost two years since she had last got some dick. Even though she was madly in love with Deji, this would probably be the only opportunity she would ever get to have a threesome in her life. That instant, the decision was made and she would let that night would be her proverbial 'one for the road' before her planned hymen reconstruction op.

As if she was in a dream, Ophelia met Green in the middle of the

bedroom and dropped down to her knees in front of him.
Automatically and without thought, she popped his juicy dick into
her insatiable mouth.

'Damn shorty, are you trying to break a nigga's dick off in ya
mouth….mmm... I like that stroke, that's it bitch. Grip that
motherfucker hard'

Green was actually very impressed with her head game. As she
jerked his cock in one hand, she also didn't neglect to caress his balls
in the other. After holding back for over an hour, he was ready to
shoot his load in Ophelia's mouth but all of a sudden she stopped
sucking him off and pulled her skirt down. It looked like she wanted
to change the game;

'Green, I want you to fuck me…now'

Ophelia bent over and touched her toes so as to give him a full view
of her hot wet snatch. She then reached her hand back between her
legs and slowly slid her finger into herself, leaving a trail of clear
come juice on the back of her thigh; Green thought he would bust
right then and there from her apparent brazenness.

He went over to her and stuck a thick calloused finger into her pussy,
jamming it inside her hard like a miniature dick. The penetration was
both painful and sweet; as Green finger fucked Ophelia, she released
her creamy juice on to his ample hand.

'Oh…umm…Green…you're gonna make me come. Harder
baby…faster…oh, Green' said Ophelia in a seductive whisper.

'So you like it like that huh…just wait until you get tha dick baby.
Now gimme the cream out this lil pussy bitch' he replied.

Green was within his element now, two bitches were always better
than one in his opinion, especially when it came to sex; his finger
kept her deliriously on the edge of an orgasm but when she couldn't
quite get her there, Ophelia guessed it was time to go for the main
event.

'Baby, let me ride you. I wanna be on top' she said pushing his hand
away.

Green obliged and in an instant, Ophelia was riding him like a well
seasoned cowgirl. Soon, she was about to come all over his

186

humongous cock and unleash all her sexual frustrations on him.
Green himself was holding back from busting with all his might. He
would need to squirt soon, but he eagerly wanted to see how intense
Ophelia's orgasm was going to be. From the way that she was
grabbing his balls and the sweetness of her pussy twitching away
vigorously, Green was anticipating a quite beautiful work of art.
'Come on baby, I can feel you pussy about to come; give it to me
now…pour dat juice on my dick bitch…'
'Yeah…I'm coming, oh baby…yes, yes, ooh! I'm…aah!'
Ophelia's body convulsed from her crotch upwards and the ferocity
of her orgasm exquisitely blew her brains out. When she finally
expended the peak of her climax, she collapsed in a heap on Green's
expansive muscular chest. He himself was now ready to release, so
he pushed her aside gently and stood up at the side of the bed to
prepare for a spectacular money shot. As he started to jerk the come
out of his dick, Ophelia jumped back up on her knees to suck him.
Not to be outdone, Ronke finally stirred from her position and
scooted underneath to lick his balls.
'Oh shit, both of you want this…it's coming out…get ready for
me…' and as the words left his lips, Green's jizz sprayed out on to
both of their faces. He spread the come out over the two of them, but
as a finishing touch Ophelia grabbed his dick and sucked dry every
single drop of semen left.

As Green recovered from the explosion that had just occurred, the
girls both looked at each other knowingly. The details of what has
transpired that night, would forever be locked the presidential suite.

~~~~

Just before he was about to leave the following morning for his daily
workout, Green woke the girls up to let them know of his plans.
'Hey..sorry to wake y'all up. I just wanted to let you know that I'm
just off to workout and I got a busy day ahead so I probably won't
see y'all when I get back. Don't worry about the door, just shut it
when you leave. It's on automatic lock'

'Thanks Green and oh before you go…let's just keep what happened last night between us okay. I know you talk with Eduardo and all…so I'm just sayin' said Ronke 'and by the way, you were magnificent last night. I had the time of my life Green….'
'You're welcome mama, and don't worry, I don't kiss and tell okay. We had a blast that kind of shit comes like once in a lifetime and it's never repeated again. I'm just glad that we seized the moment'
Green bent down to give them both a peck on the cheek as a final goodbye.
'See y'all around and take care. Oh do you need a ride home? Just take a limo and the hotel will put it on my tab…no problem'
'Bye Green…and thank you' said Ophelia
He just about caught the words as he ran down the hall to get to the gym; routine and discipline was paramount to Green and the reason he was so successful. After such a fantastic night, it was time to get back to the grind.

Ronke and Ophelia quickly washed and got dressed. They didn't want to be in the hotel once Green got back, it would somehow only seem desperate and embarrassing if they did so.
By 9.30 am they hit the streets and took the subway home. They decided not to take a limo on his tab since they didn't have far to go; also if any one of their friends saw them in a limo at 9.30 in the morning they would be sure to wonder where the two were coming from.
'Ronke, you know that whatever happens we must never reveal to anyone what happened last night. Not even to our best friends. If Deji ever found out what I did he would probably kill me. I know he's sweet and all that but I don't know how he would react'
Ophelia thought of Deji finding out about her ménage a trois and shuddered inwardly;
'Don't worry. This secret will be sealed with me to my grave. If Tunji ever found out, I can forget about being princess of anything! I ain't telling nobody what went down..not even Bijou' replied Ronke
'Good then. I won't even tell Minty'

Thankfully, when they next met Issy she assumed that they had both gone back home that night. She herself had gotten drunk and eventually couldn't remember the finer details of the evening anyway.

~~~~

Later on that month, Ophelia had a secret hymenoplasty to repair her broken hymen membrane. She also asked the surgeon to tighten up her pussy at Issy's insistence; this essentially meant that when Deji finally tasted her, she would feel the full sensation of being a virgin all over again. Ophelia thanked God for giving humans the ability to perform this wonderful feat of technology. It gave her the chance to sow her wild oats while at the same time, sparing her from the shame of not being a virgin on her wedding night; in Ophelia's humble opinion, from here on out, things could only get better!

Chapter 19

Efua checked her calendar again. It was definitely three whole months since she had last seen her monthly visitor and it was time to face up to the reality that she was with child. At the tender age of fourteen, she had managed to get herself pregnant.

Efua Chikwe was the eldest out of her five siblings and was thus considered old enough when she was twelve, to be taken from the village and sent to the city to work for the Emeka-Phillips household. Efua's mother was relieved at the prospect of having one less hungry mouth to feed; after all it wasn't so bad to send her daughter off to be a maid, it happened all the time. At the very least, the child would be certain to have three square meals a day, clothing and shelter, maybe even a semblance of an education if she played her cards right.

Unfortunately, for all her good intentions Efua's mother could not have imagined what would actually happen to her daughter in the rich man's household.

From the moment Dr Emeka-Phillips laid his eyes on her small but developed figure, he knew that in a few years he would have to have her and once she turned fourteen, Efua noticed that her employer's behaviour towards her started to turn. On occasion she would catch him staring at her bottom in her threadbare cotton dress and keeping his eyes there for much longer than was comfortable.

One fateful day, around two weeks after her fourteenth birthday, Dr Phillips summoned her to his office; the Madam happened to be abroad in Italy at the time to purchase even more items for her precious daughter's wedding.

At first Efua was happy to be called to her boss' office; she imagined that maybe he had decided that she should attend some schooling or even give her a little pay raise. Efua walked in slowly not knowing what to expect. Those innocent thoughts were soon wiped from her mind once she'd realised the reality of his intentions.

'Efua, come in, come in and sit down here'

Jonathan pointed to the chair in front of his expansive Oakwood desk. She sat down as she was told, being careful not to disturb anything else in the room.

'How old are you now Efua, about fourteen?' he asked

'Yes *Saa*' she replied

'Okay, that's good. So tell me, what do you know of boys or even men? Have you had any boys asking after you….after all you're a fine young girl' said Jonathan.

He licked his lips much like a hunting wolf upon noticing her nipples poking through her dress; he bet they would be firm and juicy like a ripe mango fruit.

'Emm…no *saa*. I no dey talk to boys-o. Madam say if them dey catch me talking to boys, she go send me back to de village again' said Efua, with her voice quivering in response.

Which kind trap be dis? she thought. Efua surely didn't talk to any boys much, only the gatemen and the driver. They had all tried to feel her up at some point, but she always smacked their hands away and had even reported them to Octavia the housekeeper to keep them at bay.

'Okay…that's good Efua. Do you know what this is?'

191

Dr Emeka-Phillips stood up and walked round to her. He seemed to have something sticking out from under his pants. Efua instantly knew what it was and nearly choked when he let his penis out from his zipper.

'Have you seen a man before Efua, like this? Do you know what it is?'

He was getting even more aroused as Efua's expression was frozen there transfixed; the poor girl had probably never seen one that big before.

'No *saa*, I don't know! Please mek I go back to my cleaning-o! I don't know this one!'

Efua was now very afraid. The *Oga* had just shown her his thing and she had an idea what he wanted to do next. It was probably what her mother had warned her not to do with boys or she would get pregnant. Her whole body became tense with fear and a bead of sweat broke free, and ran down the length of her back.

Efua essentially knew that Dr Phillips could do anything he wanted with her and as a poor housemaid; she was basically powerless to stop him. She was also mindful of the fact that she couldn't afford to lose the money she was getting paid from her job, for it was her family's sole income. Every Sunday Efua took her pay back to her mother in the village and there was no way she could go back home and tell her mother that she'd quit her job. Whatever he wanted to do to her, she knew there was absolutely no choice but to comply with. Upon the realisation of her miserable fate, Efua began to cry.

'Don't be such a baby! Are you telling me that you haven't seen this before eh? Open your mouth girl' he commanded.

Jonathan was already at the point that he desperately needed to release himself. He grabbed her by her plaited head and forced his penis into her open mouth. Efua almost vomited but she held herself back, they would definitely send her back if she was sick all over her boss' clothes. As he stimulated sex with her mouth, Efua shut her eyes tightly and let the tears flow down her face. Everything from the smell of his genitals to the roughness of his hands holding her head

192

still were completely foreign to her.

Jonathan moaned rhythmically as he fucked her face, he would even have been able to deep throat her if it wasn't for all her involuntary gagging.

Efua prayed to God it would be all over soon, maybe if she cried hard enough he would think she was still a little girl and leave her alone.

'Yes baby…your mouth is so sweet' said Jonathan

Dr Phillips sickened her to the stomach with his talk; she wondered why he was doing this. Then all of a sudden, he made a kind of shrieking noise and Efua instinctively knew that something was coming. To her horror, Jonathan came in her mouth exuberantly and jerked her head so hard, that he almost twisted her neck off. When he eventually took himself out of her mouth, Efua sat there frozen in shock, and the tears kept on flowing all by themselves.

When she finally came to her senses, she spat the thick white fluid into the waste bin.

'Efua, that's alright now' he wiped himself then patted her on the back as if to soothe her down. 'Don't cry okay? I will give you a little extra money every week to take your mummy. But you must never tell anybody of this, not even Octavia and especially not Madam. I like you Efua, that's why I did that. And next time, don't you dare spit my seed in the bin. You must swallow it all, do you understand?'

Efua nodded and wiped her mouth with her hand, her dress was soaked to the skin with sweat and her only other dress was still outside on the washing line drying. What on Earth could she tell Octavia had happened once she came back from the market with the rest of the girls?

'Emm…please *saa*, my dress dey wet now. I dey sweat. Wha I go say for Octavia. She go ask me wha happen *sha*' asked Efua

'Just tell her that I asked you to make me some tea and you spilled some water on yourself' he replied dismissively

'But she go beat me *saa*!' she protested

'Then tell her that I forbid her to lay a finger on you. Now go back to

work and take this with you'
Jonathan pressed about 500 Naira into her palm which probably only equated to a measly $4.00; later that night she would have to work a lot harder to get paid some more.

Once she left his office and closed the door, Efua ran all the way to the maid's quarters. Upon reaching the room, she threw herself down on the mattress, sobbing inconsolably, she cried for her virginity that would inevitably be lost to the *Oga* and also cried for the way he had treated her like a cheap prostitute.
Efua wondered how a whore could possibly live with herself, but after some deep moments of thought she came to realise that the only thing that kept prostitutes going was the money. From then on, that was all she would allow herself to think about.
For the sake of her family's bellies, this would be her ultimate sacrifice.

~~~~

Two days after the office incident, it very late at night and Efua had the duty of checking that all the mosquito nets were intact before she was allowed to go to bed. She dreaded going into the *Oga's* room, so she left going into his room until last.
For the past two days she had feigned period pains to avoid going to his room and Octavia had ended up having to send one of the other maids to do the net checking on her behalf. Tonight however, she had run out of excuses and none of the other maids; who were all more senior to her; wanted to do that menial job.
Just after midnight, Efua crept into his room, hoping to God that he was asleep. It was to her misfortune that her boss was wide awake sitting in his bed bare-chested; she noticed that he didn't have his pyjamas on. She scurried in and tried to quickly pull down the mosquito nets around his bed, but before she could reach them Jonathan pulled her firmly by her slim wrist.
'So you have been running from me eh? I told Octavia to make sure that you are sent up tonight. I can't believe you kept me waiting two whole days you little tease' he then pulled her down to the bed,

194

forcing Efua to sit down at the edge; he then began to stroke her smooth young cheek.

'Don't be afraid Efua….I told you that I liked you eh? Do you think that I would hurt you? There are just some things that I need from you and I will reward you well if you are a good girl. Do you understand?'

Efua looked at him and nodded; what else could she do and who would save her from him?

'Please *saa*, I beg. I no like am wey you dey touch me. I beg *saa*' said Efua. She was trying to plead with him not to violate her body in the only way she knew how.

'Come on Efua…all your friends must have told you about this. Sometimes a man has needs that he must satisfy' he said to her softly.

'But *Oga*, what about Madam?' replied Efua innocently

'Well I don't see Madam anywhere, do you?'

'But *Oga*, I'm a small girl. I dey small for you. You no go like me'

'No Efua, you're just ripe for the picking and I'm going to turn you into a woman tonight. You're still a virgin isn't it?'

'Yes *saa*, na true *saa*'

'Okay, well that's it then. Take off your dress and get inside the bed with me. Don't argue with me just do it now…and don't try to fight me. It will be better for you…'

Her heart started to beat faster at his menacing tone, it would seem that playtime was over. The fear of what he was about to do the her made Efua almost pee herself as she took off her flimsy dress. She was wearing no bra and only some faded old pink panties.

'Take that off too' he demanded in a deep dark voice

'Please *saa*, I no want do am'

'I said take it off, Now!' he barked

She took them off gingerly and stood stock still like a statue.

'Come in here then' he pulled the covers open for her to enter the bed; he was buck naked underneath the sheets.

'Just relax Efua. It's better if you don't struggle.'

Jonathan parted her legs to look at the treasure inside, her pussy smelled a little musty but she was still clean. He then sucked on her little breasts and used his finger to gently loosen her up a bit, just so he wouldn't have to rip her open.

'Do you like it….look at you getting wet. I know you do'

If seemed so wrong yet Efua liked the feeling of his finger inside her, she tried to keep quiet but could not help but to whimper.

Shortly after that, Jonathan took her completely unawares. He got on top of her and pushed his way in. The pain ripped through her body like a blade, so much so that she had to cry out;

'It dey pain me *saa*, I beg!'

She wriggled like snake underneath him to try and stop the pain.

'Shut up and relax. It's not that bad…you are such a baby Efua'

Jonathan just ignored her protests and continued.

By the time he had finished with her that night, her body was sore and raw from the damage, but the physiological scars had cut far deeper than the physical ones. As she dragged her body from the bed, the gravity of what had just occurred hit her with full force.

'Stop crying Efua….stop it I said! And you better get used to it; Madam is going to be in Italy for another week so nothing will keep me away from you. Come here dear'

It was amazing that Jonathan expected her to just accept what he'd just done. Sadly, it wasn't the first or the last time that he would take advantage of one of the young maids. It really wasn't such a big deal in his eyes, in fact he felt that she should feel privileged.

'It's paining me *saa*!'

'Let me make it a little bit better hmm?'

'No…no…please'

'Don't worry, just lie down'

Since she was crying so much, he would try to make her feel better about the whole thing. Jonathan loved to eat pussy, but it was something that his wife had ever allowed him to do. Was it any wonder that he was forced to resort to impressionable young things? The thought soon left his consciousness as he wiped away the remnants of the blood between her legs, then buried his head down there licking and sucking gently.

196

'Just relax Efua, you will soon like it'

Even though she was still raw, his tongue was making her feel a lot better. Efua found herself liking this thing he was doing and when he put a finger in again, she couldn't help but to softly moan. Whatever he was doing was easier and made her feel relaxed again, he kept on going until eventually Efua almost reached the point of orgasm.
She still couldn't help but to feel that what they were doing was wrong. There were so many feelings and new sensations that were overwhelming her, how could it be right for a man that was surely old enough to be her grandfather to be doing what he was doing between her legs?
That thought soon escaped her mind as she approached a climax; after a steady build up of pleasure, Efua reached an ecstasy that she had never known in her entire life. Before that moment, she didn't even know what an orgasm was and as Jonathan took her there, tears of joy escaped from the corners of her eyes.

And so the abuse of Efua's body continued. Eventually, she came to enjoy the sex, sometimes she would even make excuses to go to his office or his room for some trivial reason just so that they could be alone. Even when Madam came back from Italy, they would try to steal secret moments together when nobody was looking.
This carried on for 6 months until Efua discovered her pregnancy. Partly due to her ignorance and somewhat out of shame, Efua had neglected to tell Jonathan that she had recently started seeing her periods. Incidentally, one of main reasons that Dr Phillips preferred young girls was that if they had not yet started menstruation, he could spill his seed inside them to his heart's content; there was also a significantly was lower risk of them passing him H.I.V.

Once Efua realised that she was probably pregnant, she knew that it was high time that she informed the *Oga*. She decided to let him know when she was next sent his office by Octavia to pick up his dirty tea cup. When she walked into his office that afternoon, Jonathan noticed that Efua didn't have her usual happy face on. His

197

mind instantly panicked and his imagination ran wild with questions. Had someone discovered them? Had she come to tell him that one of the maids had seen them together? What on Earth could be the matter…

'Why the long face Efua? What's wrong with you…come on, you can tell your daddy' said Jonathan smoothly.

Efua gulped as she broke the news.

'Dr, I think I'm pregnant'

'What preg…but you haven't started seeing your periods yet!'

'Umm…yes *saa*. I dey start my period since five months now'

'You stupid girl! Why didn't you tell me eh? Is that why you used to avoid me on some days? I should have known…I hope you're not trying to trap me!'

'No, no *saa*. I no know dat I go reach pregnancy. I tink say I be too small to take in' she protested.

Efua looked at Jonathan's face and shuddered with fear at the next prospect; he was probably going to try and make her have an abortion. This was one of the dangers of getting one's self pregnant out of wedlock; Efua thought back to the horror stories that her own mother had told her. Some of the young girls in her village that had attempted abortions, had actually died shortly after the shoddily conducted operations. What ever happened, Efua made a vow to herself that she was going to have the baby; even if her job was on the line it wasn't worth risking her life for.

Jonathan had to think about what they were going to do and think fast. He knew that his wife must never find out about his little liaison with the young maid; Sandra could put up with most of his indiscretions, but a baby as part of the equation might push her over the edge. To make matters worse, his wife had been unable to carry another child to full term since giving birth to Ophelia. After three subsequent miscarriages, their obstetrician diagnosed that Sandra's womb was too weak to hold another baby, so they stopped trying for more children after that. In spite of her condition, Jonathan refused to take another wife; he actually loved Sandra and could not bear to put another woman on the same pedestal as her. He would have to come up with a solution to his current problem fast;

'Efua, what do you want to do…do you want to have the baby?'

'I don't know *saa*, but I no want abortion. I no want die saa, I beg'

'No, I'm not going to force you to have an abortion, don't worry. But you know that you cannot stay here while you are pregnant. Also we'll have to tell Madam and everybody else a story about how you came to be with child. They wouldn't understand about us'

Efua nodded in agreement, but she could stop the tears flowing from her eyes.

'Come on Efua, don't cry now. It will be okay'

Jonathan suddenly felt a deep burden of guilt at what he had done. He had put this poor young girl in such a desolate predicament; it was unfortunate for her, as getting her pregnant was the last thing he'd wanted to do.

'Efua don't worry okay. This is what we're going to do. When Madam or Octavia asks you who the baby's father is, just say it's one of the local boys; so that way you don't implicate me. Then you will stay here until your belly starts showing, after that you will go back to your mother in the village until the baby is born. Once you give birth then you can leave the baby with her and come back to work. Don't worry, I will make sure that both you and your mother are given money. You won't be short of that I can assure you'

Jonathan rubbed her shoulder as if to reassure her, but in her heart Efua didn't trust a word that the *Oga* said. He had already violated her and taken away her innocence, it really couldn't get much worse in her opinion. Efua also dreaded telling her mother what they had done; she could lie to everyone about who was responsible for the pregnancy but never her mother.

Eventually, all parties would have to come to terms with the situation and whether they liked it or not, the wicked deed had been done. During the course of the next six months of her pregnancy, Efua Chikwe felt as though she had aged six years.

~~~~~

199

Efua's baby boy was born in the humid month of August one month before Jonathan's daughter was due to be married. Almost exactly fifteen years to the day after she herself had made her entrance into the world, Efua gave birth to her son Emmanuel Alexander Chikwe. She took the liberty of putting the name of the child's father on the birth record, but decided everybody's life would be easier if Emmanuel used her surname.

In a complete contrast to the bleak circumstances of his conception, he was a happy and contented baby. Efua loved him so much that she wondered how she could have endured life before his arrival; her mother was also enchanted by her new grandson and she herself spoiled the little one with what ever limited resources they had. Jonathan of course didn't once go to visit Emmanuel, and as long as he gave sufficient funds for the child's up keep, that was all that mattered to him. He wouldn't however, give Efua a free ride just because she had given birth to his a child. Just over six weeks after giving birth Efua was forced back to work in his household. Jonathan still continued his abuse of her on occasion, but this time took great precautions to prevent her from falling pregnant again.

Far from becoming a destitute case, Efua's attitude actually changed remarkably in the face of such adversity. She decided to keep some of the money that Jonathan gave her for Emmanuel aside to pay for a local retired teacher to give her some basic schooling; the birth of her son convinced Efua that she was not going to spend the rest of her life as somebody's maid.

She was determined to empower herself with knowledge and get a better job and maybe even be able to create a brighter future for both herself and her son.

Efua could foresee that the longer she lived in the Emeka-Phillips household, the more that Jonathan would mistreat her; who knew whether or not he would even get her pregnant again?

To that end, from the day that Emmanuel was born, Efua made a promise to herself to have left Dr Emeka-Phillips' household before such had the opportunity to happen again.

Chapter 20

September finally arrived and it was time for Ophelia to get married; upon landing in Nigeria, she was greeted with the mild heat of the autumn sun. Deji was by her side, swelled up with a feeling of immense pride that he was soon to marry the girl of his dreams. They had arrived a week before the wedding ceremony and were looking forward to their friends and family flying in from around the world in a few days time.

Ophelia anticipated it to be a blast; Minty, Dominic, Issy, Eduardo, Dominique and even Alizé and Le Quawn whom she had only known for a few years, would be coming over to Africa for the wedding ceremony. Khadijah and Sheikh Hassan would be making their own way to Nigeria from Dubai, but would only be attending the Church wedding on the Saturday.

Sandra and the wedding planner had pulled out all the stops for the wedding guests, and had also arranged their accommodation with their utmost comfort in mind. The event was billed to be the most talked about weddings of the year; there were to be at least 500 guests invited most of whom Ophelia had never even met. That was neither here nor there in Sandra's eyes; the main thing was that her daughter's wedding would be talked about in the legions of high society for many years to come.

Deji himself wanted the whole thing to be over and done with as quickly as possible; once the pomp and circumstance of the wedding was over, the he could finally do what he had been anticipating for the past six years now; the moment that he would finally make love to his beloved and much idolised Opheila. As they rode in the back of the air-conditioned car from the airport to the Emeka-Phillips residence, Deji thanked God for the privilege of possessing a beautiful untouched bride. That made her even more precious to him and no other woman apart from his own mother could ever take her in his heart; so much so that he could almost bet his life on it. Ophelia looked over at Deji staring at her as if in a dream; he'd been doing that a lot recently, she wondered was on his mind.

'Sweetie, why are you staring at me like that? Do you like this new make up I'm trying out or something? Come on Deji, talk!' said Ophelia playfully
'I was just thinking about how much I love you…and how lucky I am to have the privilege of marrying a lady like you. Beautiful, educated, smart, sassy and last but not least, untouched by any other man' Deji picked her hand up from her lap and kissed it gently; 'my love, do you know what a rare pearl you are? And how hard it is to find a woman that is completely pure?'
Ophelia could only smile sweetly at his sentiments; the truth of the matter would probably break his heart. That was the story of her life, always being presumed to be much more innocent than she actually was; in the case of being Deji's woman, this was a clearly marked advantage. Ophelia laughed inwardly at the hypocrisy; it was fine for men to run around sleeping with every chick in town, but her own fiancé expected her to be pure as a snow white lily. She wondered if

her engagement ring would have been as big if Deji found out that he wasn't her first one.

Incidentally, the surgeon had done a fabulous job of reconstructing her hymen and she knew innately that on their wedding night, he would be none the wiser.

Ophelia wondered if Ronke had taken similar precautions or was she planning to fob Tunji off on her wedding night and pretend she was still 'tight'. *Who knew?* thought Opheila, but she made a mental note to speak to Ronke about it once they saw each other in a few days.

Ophelia's mother had planned the traditional Yoruba wedding to take place on Friday and the church ceremony a day after on the Saturday; apart from friends and family travelling in from around the world to attend the wedding, many distant relatives on both sides of had already arrived a week prior to help Sandra prepare and show support for the soon to be wed couple. It was a prerequisite of a traditional Nigerian wedding for all family members to show as much support as they could for the impending union. If a relative arrived alone and without any people, they were seen as being quite unsupportive; a good interpretation of how this was reflected in the culture was demonstrated in an old Yoruba saying that went *'â eniyan la soâ'*. This roughly translated in English as *'without people to support you, you are naked'*

Once they finally arrived at the Emeka-Phillips compound, Ophelia was a little overwhelmed by all the attention they were getting, there was a marked buzz in the atmosphere in comparison to the way she was usually received whenever she came home. The housekeeper and the maids all ran out to greet the happy couple, with Sandra and Jonathan following closely behind to welcome their daughter and her fiancé. Ophelia's heart melted at the display of affection and how happy everyone was to see them; had her wedding day almost arrived already? As if she was in a dream, the last three years seemed to have passed within the blink of an eye. Before she had time to slip further in to her thoughts, Jonathan greeted the couple heartily and reached out to embrace his little girl.

'Hello to you my daughter and of course you too my son! So it is finally here! We hope you are as excited as we are!' said Jonathan 'your mother has planned an extravagant occasion on your behalf and everybody here has been looking forward to it for months now' he added.

'Yes sir, we are very excited and equally delighted to see you all. Dear mother, thank you so much for arranging what looks like a magnificent undertaking. I hope that you haven't mistaken our wedding for a State event?' replied Deji laughing out loud at his own comment; by the look of things at the Emeka-Phillips residence, one would think that the President's own daughter was getting married.

'Well my son, I only have one daughter, and it's not everyday that she gets married so I think I'm allowed to go a little bit overboard on this occasion!' replied Sandra

They all laughed at the jokey banter, and soon after the group went into the house to escape the heat of the mid-day sun.

As they walked through the front door the scene inside the house looked like chaos; there were a multitude of relatives around, most of which Ophelia had never met before in her life. When Sandra finally showed them into the huge back garden, Deji and Ophelia were astounded by the size of the Marquee tents that had been put up to cover the guests' tables; there was also a stage area that no doubt would be for the band that would be playing at the wedding reception. Ophelia didn't even want to think of how much this was costing her father; left to her she would have opted for a small but intimate wedding ceremony. Unfortunately for Ophelia such decisions had already been taken out of her hands by her mother since the day she was born.

Deji stayed for a few hours before de-camping to go home to the Olajuwon mansion; Ophelia walked him to his car and kissed him goodbye before waving him off.

This would be the last time they would see each other until the traditional ceremony on Friday and only five whole days before she would finally become Mrs Olajuwon.

~~~~

Two days later on Thursday, Ophelia's friends landed in Lagos just a day before the traditional wedding ceremony was due to take place. Deji had chartered a private jet to ferry them all over from New York; they only made one stop in London to re-fuel and pick up Adora and Kelechi before reaching their final destination of Murtala Mohammed International airport in Lagos. The party were met at the airport by Ophelia, her father and a fleet of SUVs to take them to the Sheraton Hotel in Lagos. Once they had all checked in and got settled down, they got back into the cars and made the brisk journey over to Ophelia's home for a hearty lunch.

Forever the gracious hostess, Sandra made a fuss of the guests and cajoled them all into eating far much more than their fill; she was determined to make sure that Ophelia's guests would want for nothing during their short stay in Lagos. It pleased Sandra immensely that they had arrived, as their presence at her daughter's wedding would only add more prestige and affluence to the proceedings. Ophelia herself was happy that her friends had finally arrived; it was nice to have people that she was familiar with around her at last amongst the tens of clingy relatives that she'd had no choice but to put up with during the past few days. Ophelia felt bad for feeling that way, but it was all too exhaustive having to deal with them as they expected her to give them her attention all the time. All she wanted at the end of the day was a moment's peace. The only person that wasn't babbling on about how lucky she was to be marrying a Prince and how grand the wedding was going to be, was Efua her assigned maid. Efua had a seemingly innate ability to know when to stop talking and didn't ask much questions; she was simply calm, efficient and polite.

Ophelia's heart went out to the poor girl; since she had recently given birth, she had been forced to leave her baby in the village with her mother in order for her to come back to work. Apparently, she was unfortunate enough to have fallen pregnant for one of the local thugs who had subsequently run off, never to be heard of or seen again. Maybe if her father would allow it, Ophelia would ask Efua to come and work for her once she moved in to the Olajuwon home; she was sure that her soon to be in-laws had adequate home help, but it would put her mind at ease if there was someone that she knew personally accompanying her into the household. Ophelia decided that if Efua was released to her, then she would encourage the girl to bring her baby with her too; after all a child rightfully deserved to be with its mother.

~~~~

After an almost agonising wait, the day of Ophelia's wedding finally arrived. According to Yoruba custom they were already married since conducting the traditional ceremony a day prior, however their union would not be formalized in the eyes of the government until they had taken their vows in a church and signed the registry.

The previous day's traditional wedding ceremony had been both exciting and enriching to Ophelia's soul. In Yoruba culture, all the various rituals and preparations that are included in the wedding process contributed to Ophelia's transition from girlhood to womanhood. She had been woken up at the crack of dawn on the Friday by her mother and a collection of elder female relatives who were referred to as *iyawo iles,* which roughly translated as 'the ladies of the house', to be taken to the fattening room. This ritual was symbolic of the age old practice of a woman being encouraged to eat and become plumper prior to her wedding, so as to make herself more attractive to her husband. In the old days, a young lady's health and affluence was judged by her size and thin was most definitely not in; some villages would even confine a woman to the fattening room for up to 2 weeks prior to the wedding in order to ensure ample weight gain. In modern times the fattening room was only used a few hours before the actual ceremony in order to observe the tradition.

The women then changed into *'aso-ebi'* which were the matching native outfits that the bride's family had chosen for the occasion so that they could be clearly identified. When they arrived later on to start the festivities, the groom's family would also be in their own distinctive matching dress. As Ophelia's girls, Minty, Issy, Dominique, Khadijah and Issy were all excited to also be wearing *aso-ebi* along with the members of the Emeka-Phillips clan. The girls marvelled at the white satin embroidered *Iro* and *Buba* which were a loose scoop neck top and floor length wrap respectively; the wrap was the 'skirt' of the outfit. The ladies topped of the look with matching silver *gelé* headwraps; they also accessorised their outfits with expensive jewellery, colourful bags and flamboyant shoes. Ophelia and her friends looked quite a pretty picture in the native dress; but to Dominique and Alizé being a part of this traditional African ceremony meant much more. This was their first opportunity to experience the customs and traditions of their ancestors that had been scattered across the globe as a result of the miserable scourge that was the slave trade. Ophelia was delighted that her friends were so enthusiastic to wear the traditional costumes as she considered them to be a part of her family as well.

Since she was the bride, Ophelia was being made a big fuss of by the women and most of all her mother. They were making a huge production of tying her *gelé* just so; apparently the angles had to be just right and they also wanted it to showcase her beautiful hair. Ophelia's thick afro hair had been pressed straight for the occasion and over the years she had grown it to almost waist-length. While they were tying her elaborate head wrap, her great-auntie Amaka said some thing in Yoruba that Ophelia didn't understand. The old woman seemed to be marvelling at her pretty tresses and Sandra's chest puffed up with pride at her sentiments.

'Mummy, I don't understand what Granny is saying…what is she saying?' inquired Ophelia
'She is saying that you look like a little angel with your hair…she also said that you have the best kind of beauty, a natural one' said

Sandra

'Oh how lovely! I'm so flattered too, Mummy can you please tell her that I'm saying thank you? Or can she understand me?'

'Yes Opheli, I'll tell her what you said'

Sandra translated what Ophelia had said, and then the old lady gave a wrinkly smile and gestured for her to come over.

'Go on Opheli, kneel down in front of her, she wants to make a prayer for you'

Ophelia obeyed her mother and she knelt in front of her great-auntie; as a mark of respect, the whole room hushed down to hear the old woman's prayer. She put a hand on Ophelia's forehead and made a heartfelt prayer for a good marriage and many children for the young woman. Amaka eyes filled with tears as she made the appeal to God to grant her grand-niece a successful marriage. She thought back to her own wedding over 60 years ago, the elders back then had also made similar prayers for her as it was a sign of good luck to have the oldest members of your family endorse your marriage; her dear husband was dead and gone now but Amaka thanked God for the happy years she had spent with him. As in her own case, she sincerely hoped that her earnest prayers of prosperity would be granted for Ophelia too.

~~~~

Sometime after midday, the Olajuwon clan arrived to start the wedding process. Seats had been arranged in the great room of the house with the bride's family sitting on one side and the groom's family directly opposite of the other side. The *iyawo iles* of Deji's family came in with great fanfare, along with the rest of the Olajuwon clan, in order to present the wedding gift box to the bride. 'The box' consisted of a selection of gifts which would be requested by the bride's family prior to the wedding. It was mandatory for the groom's family to present a box of clothing to the bride, so Ophelia was given five sets of *Iro* and *Buba* in different colourful expensive fabrics, matching head –ties, bags with matching shoes, a selection of pure Arabian perfumes, a Bible and an assortment of fine jewelry.

The next part of the ceremony was the recitation of prayers that were focused on the fertility and success of the marriage. Again the groom's family had brought offerings for the prayer and each item brought had a particular significance in accordance with Yoruba traditions. Amongst the items were kola nuts which were a symbol of longevity of the union, a jar of honey for sweetness of the marriage and then alligator pepper to represent fertility. After the prayers, Deji's family presented a sum of money that would serve as the 'dowry' to Ophelia's family for her hand. This was only a mandatory symbolic offering from the groom's family to observe the culture; the families had already decided to give the money to charity afterwards, as the Yoruba believed that no amount of money can equal the worth of a child.

After the prayers, Deji and Ophelia finally took their vows. The couple were sat on two separate 'thrones' next to each other and one of the elders conducted the recitation of the marriage rites, after which Ophelia was asked if she wanted to marry Deji and acknowledge him as her husband. Once the two had recognized each other as husband and wife, a veil was placed over Ophelia's head which would be taken off upon entering her husband's home. After the veiling, the final prayers were made to bless the union; Ophelia was encouraged by her own family elders to be a good ambassador of her original family and raise good, disciplined children. As they gave their admonitions of love and support for her, it was all too much and Ophelia was brought to tears. She was moved by the prayers of goodwill that were been offered by her relatives and even though she didn't understand most of the words which were being recited in Yoruba, it was the fact that they all vehemently wished such good to come out of her marriage that touched her the most.

Eventually the feasting and partying began which meant Ophelia would be leaving shortly to be received at her new husband's home; Sandra took her off to change into yet another beautiful native outfit that matched Deji's own; now that they were married, both husband and wife had to look 'together' as a unit during such family events.

The guests all filed out into the marquee outside to get to grips with some long awaited food and drink, music was already playing loudly as the crowd prepared for a long night of partying and celebration that would continue well into the morning of the following day. Once Ophelia had been taken into Deji's home, there would be a similar parting going on at the same time in the Olajuwon residence as it was customary for both sides of the family to express fulfilment at having witnessed their children reach such an important milestone.

Sandra finished off dressing Ophelia and put the veil back on her head, the time had now come for her to hand her daughter over to her new family; choked up with emotion she held back the tears. Her dream had come true and her daughter was finally a Princess.
'Opheli, I guess it's time for you to leave for your husband's house now…are you ready?' Sandra held her daughter's hand at first and then gave her a warm hug.
'Yes mummy, I'm ready! Please don't cry…I'm coming back tomorrow anyway for the Church ceremony. I'll be ok and I know that Deji will take care of me, I would have thought you would be happy right now…' Ophelia replied
'Oh I am happy sweetheart; please forgive your old mother. I'm just crying because you're all grown up now….I can't really baby you anymore'
'Don't worry mummy, I'll still be your baby no matter what!'
Minty walked in on mother and daughter but waited a while before speaking so as not to intrude on such a tender moment.
'Oh gosh, both of you better stop all that now or you'll have me crying too! You know I'm five months pregnant so the waterworks can just start at random times' said Minty with a chuckle.
'Sorry babe! Mummy's just a bit emotional right now cos she thinks I'm not her baby anymore!' Ophelia replied cheekily
Sandra wiped her eyes with a hanky as crying in front of people just wasn't her style
'Don't be so silly girls, go ahead with you! I'm sure the Olajuwon ladies are waiting to take you over. You know that Deji won't be there at first? They have to bring you into the house and then he will

210

meet you about an hour later. That is what's customary' said Sandra
'Yes mummy I know, we've been through this how many times?'
replied Ophelia
'Don't be smart with me now just because you're married! Off you
go now!' Sandra ushered Ophelia off with a playful smack on her
little bottom. Minty and Ophelia both laughed and walked out of the
room to meet the rest of the girls. Ophelia was permitted by tradition
to take some of her friends and relatives with her for moral support
for the first time entering her husband's home so all of her girls,
along with Ronke and Adora would be accompanying her to the
house. Eduardo, Hassan and Kelechi would arrive at the Olajuwon
residence later on with Deji.

The *iyawo iles* on the Olajuwon side were waiting for Ophelia once
she got to the cars so they immediately got in and embarked on the
journey to Deji's home.
Upon reaching the house, cold water was poured on Ophelia's feet as
this was symbolic of her entering her husband's home in peace.
Afterward, she was unveiled and received by the rest of the *iyawo
iles* in the house which were the wives of the other Olajuwon men,
namely Deji's cousins, uncles and the like. Finally King Olajuwon as
the oldest male in the family, made prayers blessing the marriage and
once all those formalities were over, the celebrations began.
Deji arrived with the rest of the guys about an hour later to meet his
new bride, upon seeing her he greeted her with such a welcoming
embrace that her insides melted. He then kissed her deeply as if she
was one of his most prized possessions. Similarly, Ophelia was quite
looking forward to giving him all her body on the first night of their
honeymoon;
'Oh Ophelia, I can't believe this day has come and we're actually
married.....you do know that I love you more that anything don't you
my love?' said Deji lovingly, he then bent to whisper in her ear
seductively, 'when I take you, you're going to feel so good that
you'll wonder where I've been your whole life. I'm not playing with
you Ophelia, you just wait and see'
As soon as he'd started speaking, her panties were already wet with

211

anticipation at his talk. What turned Ophelia on the most, was the fact that he didn't need to use any profane words to get his point across; she knew exactly what he meant. She giggled girlishly at his comment as if she were shy;

'Oh Deji, you'll have to be gentle with me…and I already know you're one hundred percent man underneath all this' she replied teasingly

'Ophelia you delicious little minx, I do believe that you're teasing me. I like it but hold that thought…here comes my father'

After King Olajuwon had said what he wanted to say and left them alone, Deji and Ophelia had a little meal then partied on into the night. It was a wonderful feeling to have their friends and family celebrating such an important event in their lives; eventually Ophelia had to make her way back to her parents home to get a good nights rest for the church wedding the next day. It had been quite a long yet fulfilling day. She drifted off to sleep safe in the knowledge that she was now officially Deji's wife, Princess Ophelia Olajuwon.

Chapter 21

Ophelia and Deji held their Church wedding at the First Anglican Church of Lagos and emerged from the church to a huge spectacle. They stepped out of the building to meet a vast crowd of people, most of whom had been unable to watch the ceremony from inside the Church as it was already filled to capacity. The wedding planner had actually anticipated this and had arranged some plasma screens set up outside so that the people could see what was going on inside the church. The fact that it was a Royal wedding filled many of the people in the neighbourhood with excitement; there was a certain pride in knowing that someone who lived on the same stretch of road as you was marrying a Prince. On the other hand, such an occasion meant that the whole street would invite themselves to the wedding reception party at the Emeka –Phillips compound and that meant a guaranteed meal to some of the more poorer neighbours. Sandra had also taken the liberty of ordering some wedding goodie bags that contained a little slice of wedding cake and '*Deji and Ophelia's Wedding*' monogrammed pens and crockery for the guests to take home with them as a mementos of the joyous occasion.

Ophelia looked exceptionally beautiful on her wedding day; she wore a gorgeous strapless *Vera Wang* number that had a full ball size skirt that was embroidered with tiny little diamonds throughout. The dress seemed to light itself up as she walked out of the Church with Deji into the afternoon sun. Issy and Alizé had helped her make her decision about the choice of dress, but at the last minute they sent it to a specialist atelier in Paris for the inclusion of the diamond 'beads'. The whole effect was an act of fabulousity in motion and the photographers could not stop snapping.

Minty wore a similar dress as maid of honor but in a beautiful deep purple which was the color of dress chosen for the bridesmaids; she filed out behind the happy couple with Alizé, Issy and Dominique who were observing bridesmaid duties for Ophelia along with Adora and Ronke. Khadijah was not permitted to be a bridesmaid due to her Islamic faith, so she sat in the very front pew so as to could get a full view of all the proceedings. The ladies were accessorised with fresh African Violets in their hair and the best man and ushers wore charcoal grey Armani suits with purple ties; they wore the same violets in their lapels. Deji himself looked majestic in a pure white suit and ivory damask waistcoat. The outfit was complimented with diamond and platinum cuff links with matching tie pin to flatter the sparkle of Ophelia's dress.

As per usual, Deji couldn't resist an extravagant touch by wearing a snappy pair of blinging white alligator skin loafers.

He squeezed his Bride's hand as they stepped into the luxurious white stretch limo that would take them from the Church to the wedding reception at the Emeka-Phillips home. As the limo pulled away, a bunch of children ran behind the vehicle as if to catch a little bit of magic before the couple's car left the street.

Once inside the car, Deji took Ophelia into his arms and engaged her in a sumptuous French kiss; he then started to claw away at her strapless bodice as if he was a wild animal; now that Ophelia was completely his, Deji's would not stop until he possessed her entirely.

214

'Oh God Ophelia, I don't know if I can wait until tonight. I want you now....'

He somehow got his hand up her extensive skirting and found her pussy, but instead of putting a finger inside her Deji began to lightly rub her clit instead.

'Yes Deji I like that, it feels so good.....'

'I know sweetie, just sit back and enjoy the ride cos I'm gonna make you come soon...'

After a few minutes of gentle fingering he got on his knees in front of her and proceeded to devour Ophelia's snatch as if it was a gourmet meal; needless to say an orgasm was inevitable. Deji had to muffle her mouth a little so as to minimize the noise she was making, but the driver probably had an idea of what was going on in the back of the car anyway. Once she had gotten over her climax, Ophelia decided to return the favour. Deji was shocked to say the least that his beautiful virgin wife possessed the ability to deliver some of the most mind-blowing head he'd ever received.

'Ophelia, stop a minute. Where did you learn to do that? I mean it's fantastic and all but I know you've never been with a man like this...' said Deji worryingly; Ophelia had to quickly think fast.

'Oh, that's just from too many nights watching *Porntube,* I wanted to learn a few tricks before we got married and I practiced on a cucumber'

'Ha! I can't believe it, but I like your forward thinking. Don't let me stop you from licking the cucumber then' he replied

They both laughed at the smuttiness of his quip and Ophelia finished off her work by sending her dear husband into a sea of orgasmic bliss.

This was only a prelude to what physical pleasures they would share together and the best was yet to come.

~~~~

After an amazing reception party and a tear-inducing speech from the father of the bride, Deji and Ophelia were waved off to their honeymoon by an overjoyed crowd. They left Nigeria for a relaxing two week vacation in Hawaii; Deji had booked the presidential suite at the *Hyatt Regency Resort and Spa* in Maui which was situated just off the main touristy areas but close enough to the miles of beautiful sandy beaches. Ophelia had never been anywhere more picturesque apart from when she had been to visit Dominique in Jamaica a few years back; the destination had just the right level of peace and tranquillity that Mr and Mrs Olajuwon needed to embark upon the beginning of what would hopefully be a successful marriage.

Ophelia's nerves started to peak by the time dusk fell; it was almost time for the moment of truth, the moment they had both been waiting for since the past two long years. Deji took the lead and when he started to walk over to her side of the room Ophelia knew that it was Showtime.

'Sweetheart, shall we turn in and get an early night? Since we've landed I've been going crazy with anticipation…come over here and let me help relieve you of those annoying clothes'

He pulled her close to him and unzipped her skirt at the back, and then he managed to slip off her halter-neck top and bra without her noticing as he buried his head into her slim neck. As he continued to kiss her, he touched her in all the right places with intuitive skill of a violinist who knew exactly which sequences of notes would turn the ladies' insides to mush.

Ophelia moaned softly at first, but began to increase in volume as Deji's fingers explored her body. He laid her on her back and capably pulled her skirt off; she was a little shy for him to see her in her nakedness and she wondered what he was thinking; was she everything he had dreamed of?

Whilst Ophelia was lost in those thoughts, Deji undressed to reveal the magnificent specimen of manhood that was his body; his physique was built from years of intense physical workouts and it showed. Even his six pack abdominals looked as though they had been carved by the hands of the hands of the great master sculptors themselves; Ophelia was indeed a lucky girl.

'Deji your body, it's so beautiful, so toned and your abs are something else' she said excitedly

'Oh my darling, I'm so glad that I meet your standards, but my dear your body has rendered me speechless. I guess I'll have to show you how much your sexy body is turning me on...'

He balanced himself on top of her and parted her legs sharply, he had waited long enough to taste her pussy and wasn't about to delay a moment longer.

'I'm sorry if this hurts a little my sweet, I promise you that it will get better after tonight. Just relax and let me inside of you'

Opheila supposed she should play along and be the 'virgin', this was going to be fun;

'Deji...I'm scared, please be gentle with me. I don't know how that big thing of yours is going to fit into my little hole'

'Like I said just relax babe, it will fit in'

Ophelia tipped her head back as Deji embarked on conquering her seemingly virginal pussy; she winced as she felt the pain of being de-flowered all over again. He started with short shallow thrusts to wet her up a little, then he snapped her thighs further apart so as to ram her all the way to the hilt with his ginormous cock. Ophelia had hit the jackpot with this one, his was the biggest dick she had ever had a nearly 10+ inches; she would need a minute to get used to it.

The strange thing was that even though they both shared a deep love for each other, unlike what she had expected their sex was pure lust and without an ounce of any idealistic 'love-making'. Deji fucked her pussy like a man deranged, he seemed to have forgotten that she was a virgin and Ophelia expected to be very sore in the morning.

He changed positions and lay behind her on his side spoons style but made a variation on it by cocking one of her legs up with the knee bent for even deeper penetration, needless to say Mrs Olajuwon could feel an orgasm building up; she wanted this Mandingo to fuck the shit out of her literally. As the pounding increased in its intensity, Ophelia felt the need to empty her bladder.

'Oh shit! Oh Deji...yes, yes! It's so good...fuck me! Damn, I think I'm going to wet myself...' she cried;

Deji grunted a muffled reply and kept on riding; his sinews dripped with the fresh sweat of hot sex. It would seem that he didn't enjoy the act unless it was rough and filthy; Deji sincerely hoped that beloved Ophelia would soon get used to it.

This was only a starter to the evening's proceedings and he was already looking forward to the main course. As Deji glided inside her tight walls, he could feel the tip of his penis touch her cervix with every thrust; she squeezed his meat as a reflex action to his satisfying stroke.

'Deji, you better stop for a minute! I think I'm going to piss myself…please, please stop'

'Well my darling, you've turned out to have quite a dirty little mouth haven't you? I'm not stopping anytime soon so if you're going to wet the bed, then let it flow you horny slut!' he replied;

Ophelia gasped at his tone as he had never spoken to her like that before; was this an ugly side to him? She didn't know whether to complain or be flattered.

As Deji continued to ride her, Ophelia found her way to three earth-shattering orgasms and he kept pumping away until something amazing happened; as she reached her fourth orgasm, Ophelia's pussy squirted a stream of clear come that hit him in the face as he sprayed the hot fluid with his free hand.

'I'm sorry Deji I can't help it! It feels so good…..my pussy is…oh shit'

'Ophelia it's okay, it's not pee. You're squirting baby, it's amazing that you've reached this level of orgasm on your first time… looks like you are a naturally good fuck girly. That shit is wonderful and you're only making me wanna fuck your hot snatch even more!' he declared.

They continued to fuck for hours and hours until they reached the end of their marathon session with Ophelia on all fours doggie style. Amazingly he had stayed hard for the duration of the session and was now ready to bust a nut.

'I'm about to come in your tight pussy you little whore…it's making my cock juice rise to the top. I'm gonna come, oh yes baby. Let your pussy suck it up…ahh…ahh…yes!'

Deji's desire peaked and he collapsed and rolled over in a heap onto his back. As she looked over at him lying next to her, Ophelia was still in awe of what had just happened; he had now succeeded in owning her totally and no other man would ever compare.

Chapter 22

Not too long after the newly wed couple had gotten back to New York and back to normal life, it was time to travel again as Ronke's marriage to Tunji was imminent; they were eventually married three months after Deji and Ophelia in December of the same year. Ophelia had been worried about the pairing since her own wedding; the interaction between Ronke and her intended wasn't fantastic to say the least. They seemed to be just tolerating each other and Ophelia also knew for a fact that Ronke's father Samson would never force his daughter into an unwanted matrimony, so why were they going ahead?

Ronke herself took her approaching nuptials with Tunji as a power move; since meeting her future husband, she knew that he was quite pliable and it would be easy to wrap him around her little finger to pander to her every whim.

Unfortunately for Ronke, the monster bubbling away under the surface was expertly hidden; life for her was about to change in a way that she would never have forecasted in a million years. The

220

wedding that eventually took place was almost as big an event as
Ophelia's but much to Sandra's delight, it didn't quite make it to the
same level of grandeur. The weird thing was that Ronke seemed
worried about something but Ophelia couldn't quite put her finger on
it. She asked her cousin repeatedly before the wedding if something
was wrong, but Ronke denied it; what could she do in that instance?
Ophelia decided to leave it alone for the moment.

In truth, Ronke was panicking internally over her missed period;
maybe she shouldn't worry, it may have been delayed by anything. It
might even have been the stress of the wedding that was making it
late. She racked her brains and thought back to her final tryst with
Donnie. Ronke had travelled to Miami a month before her nuptials to
have one last steamy liaison with him; she was sure that the condom
they used was intact…or was it? If she was pregnant it would be
disastrous and there was no excuse that she could have to leave
Nigeria to go and arrange to have a secret abortion; he would ask her
too many questions also it was too much of a risk to just up and leave
without his permission.
They were soon due to move in to Tunji's brand new Victoria Island
home in one of the most upscale neighbourhoods in Nigeria. Rather
than continue to live at the Olajuwon home as Deji planned to do,
Tunji wanted to make his own life away from his parents and away
from Lagos. Eventually, Ronke decided to just enjoy the wedding
and worry about that later; she would find a way to fix things no
matter what the case was.

Incidentally, their wedding night was a complete shambles; Tunji
had insisted that they wouldn't take a honeymoon until he had
completed some important business in Nigeria. This meant that
Ronke spent her first night as a wife in the vast 10 bedroom, 6
bathroom mansion that was now her home. Rather than being treated
to a night of passion, Tunji feebly crashed into bed and fell asleep
within seconds. He didn't even wait until Ronke had got into the
sheets and as a result she felt completed rejected but decided to give
him a chance; maybe the poor guy was really tired and it had nothing

to do with her. She imagined that he would probably want some pussy by daybreak.

To her surprise, seven days passed and Tunji didn't even so much as kiss her let alone reference sex; *what the hell is wrong with him* she thought. Wasn't she good enough? Ronke hated the way he was making her feel, it took her back to the days of Caspian and how he played to her insecurities making her feel worthless.

Eventually, she spoke to her mother over the phone to express concern at this but her mother assured her that he would come around; maybe she wasn't being seductive enough. Her mother suggested that she dress up in some sexy lingerie and wait up for Tunji in bed, she told her daughter that she was convinced that it would work.

That night Ronke took her mother's advice, and when Tunji came into the bedroom she was waiting for him in a sexy black lace *La Perla* bra and pantie set. She finished off the look with fishnet hold-ups and five inch *Manolo Blahnik* heels.

'Baby, I've been waiting for you. I know you've been working hard and I thought I could help you unwind…' she breathed sexily
Tunji looked at her as if she was crazy; he didn't have time for any of this crap at all;
'Ahh! What's all this rubbish? I this what they taught you in America all these years? I told you that I am busy with work and when I get home I just want to eat and sleep! I don't have time for you Ronke…sex will just have to be at the bottom of the list!'
'But, Tunji, we haven't even had our wedding night! I am a woman and I have needs too…you can't just leave me in this house alone without showing me any affection. I'm not a blasted stone you know!'
'Hey…you better stop right there! Don't you dare take that tone with me woman! Get changed into some decent clothes and stop parading yourself around like some cheap whore!'
With that, Tunji walked out of the bedroom slamming the door;
Ronke fell to her knees on the spot. *Why does he have to treat me like some kind of ornament?* she thought pitifully. It was as if he had

married her to just sit in the house for the sake of saying that he had a wife. She suspected that there was another woman involved, but she was probably someone from a lower class that Tunji could not be seen to marry into. Anger rose within her at the prospect of being used as a pawn; she would have to see to it that she got her own little bit on the side as well and he would be sorry in the end. On the other hand, her period still hadn't come; so Ronke decided to send the housekeeper Esmeralda to purchase a home pregnancy test for her from the pharmacy. Ronke didn't think to tell the woman not to mention anything to her husband.

Late the next morning, Esmeralda brought her back a pregnancy test and five minutes after she peed in on it, the two blue lines that showed up on the testing device confirmed her worst fears; Ronke was pregnant with Donnie's child. In anger and confusion, she threw the used test in the bathroom trash and without a second thought stormed off to get some fresh air and think. Once she had left the room Esmeralda's nosiness got the better part of her and she checked the discarded test. So she was right! The madam and the *Oga* could not wait until their wedding night and had sex before their marriage; how exciting! She couldn't wait to tease her boss as soon as he arrived home from work. Esmeralda had virtually raised Tunji since he was a boy at the big Olajuwon compound in Lagos, so she was able to speak to him almost like a mother. Even though Queen Olajuwon was Tunji's birth mother, she wasn't he one who tended to his cut knees or blew his runny nose as a boy and as a childless woman at the age of forty-five, he was closest that Esmeralda would ever get to having a child.

She thought about jokingly confronting Madam Ronke about the pregnancy as well, but thought better of it, that one wasn't the most accommodating person in the world and at times the spoiled wench behaved as if she was just too good for Nigeria. Esmerelda wondered why the *Oga* didn't just marry a nice local girl that had been raised to have good manners and could at least boil a pot of water! Following that thought, she went back to work and set about delegating the more tedious chores to the junior maids; maybe later on she would stop to have a sweet cup of tea and a cookie; if it was good enough for Madam Ronke, then it was good enough for her too.

About four o'clock that afternoon, Tunji returned home from work. He was ravenously hungry and ready to eat almost anything that was put on the dinner table in front of him; maybe a bite to eat would soothe his foul mood. The $20 million dollar government construction contract that his company had been working to complete for the past two weeks, had fallen through. Regrettably, the contact that he had within the government office whom he had bribed with one million Naira, had been approached by a rival company who subsequently offered the man a substantially bigger bribe of three million Naira. Tunji was livid at losing the contract and the greedy bastard had the nerve to tell him that he had been cheap to only offer him one million; that was an unspeakable insult, seeing that the double-crosser was now sitting pretty on top of a cool four million Naira. Why was Tunji even surprised? That was the way a lot of people did their business in Nigeria and he was just stupid enough to get burned. He made a mental note to never again transfer funds into any idiot's bank account, until his end of the transaction had been confirmed and was binding. Tunji was determined to move on with other business ventures in spite of this set back and as the famous saying went, he had to live and learn.

He was just about to take the first bite of his food when Esmeralda came in to the dining room grinning, *what on earth is she so giddy about*? he thought. She was starting to work his dammed nerves. 'Esme, what is it? What's so deliriously funny because I'm not in the mood for any kind of rubbish today' he said irritably
'Oh, no good afternoon? Its okay…now you are a grown man you think you can just have mouth eh? Anyway, I know your little secret…you have been a naughty boy haven't you?' she said mischievously
'What are you prattling on about?'
'Don't be smart with me; I knew that you couldn't wait until your wedding night! Madam asked me to buy her a pregnancy test today

and it was positive;
Congratulations my dear!'
She went over to embrace Tunji, but his body went stiff. He put the
mouthful of food he was just about to eat back on to the plate and
judging by his expression, Esmeralda knew that she had just put her
foot in her mouth.
'What do you mean pregnant? Where is the test....give it to me
now!'
His raised voice made her jump; *why is he so angry* she thought.
Maybe he wasn't he ready for a child yet, maybe that was what it
was, she would have to try and soothe him down a little.
She took the test stick out of her pocket and placed it down on a
napkin.
'Here it is *saa*, its positive. Tunji you should be happy right now,
come on....I know it's happened quite soon, but that's not so bad'
'Shut up Esme. Just shut up. I have been too busy with this damned
contract to even think about sex. The last time I even kissed Ronke
was the day we got married; our marriage has not even been
consummated yet! Are you completely sure that Ronke used this
pregnancy test?'
'Yes *saa*...she even asked me to go to the pharmacy to buy it early
this morning. Please Tunji maybe there is some mistake; don't be
angry with her. Maybe this test is wrong... I beg of you, take it easy'
Esmeralda's mind was filled with panic; what had she done! Why the
hell had she opened her big mouth; she knew how bad Tunji's
temper could be and she hoped to God that this was some mistake
and Ronke had an explanation or he might just kill her in this house.
Esmeralda for one, wasn't about to have blood on her hands!
'Take this food away Esme and leave me for now. When the Madam
gets back, send her to me. I will be in the living room and apart from
that, I do not wish to be disturbed'
As Tunji got up from the dining table and walked out; her heart was
beating in her mouth as she dreaded the inevitable consequences of
her actions. Esmerelda prayed to God that this was all a big mistake.

Ronke arrived home about an hour after Tunji did; she didn't really mean to get home that late, but she had spent the afternoon visiting a few clinics to find out if she could have her little problem discreetly removed. She didn't really trust the Nigerian Doctors, but there was no real choice in the matter; it was imperative that she terminate the pregnancy before any symptoms such as morning sickness or sudden weight again began. As she walked into the house Ronke noticed that it was very quiet; no one had come to greet her or even attempt to take her bags up to her room. There was something wrong but she couldn't quite put her finger on it; was the house being robbed? She stopped to listen for a moment as her senses peaked, then all of a sudden Esmerelda approached her; it seemed that the old dear had been crying.

'Esme, what's the matter? Are you alright? And where is Tunji?' inquired Ronke

'Madam, the *Oga* wants to see you in the living room. He said that you must see him immediately before you do anything'

'But what's wrong with you? You've been crying!'

'Don't worry about me Madam, please just go. He insists that you see him right away'

Esmerelda took Ronke's shopping bags from her and turned tail; she would have liked to warn the Madam, but what difference would it make? They would all just have to wait and see how it panned out. Ronke felt confused by her housekeeper's behaviour and she intended to get to the bottom of this. She walked into the living room to find Tunji standing up by the French doors, looking out of the window.

'Tunji, what's going on…why Esmerelda is looking so miserable?' she asked worriedly

'Hello Ronke, so you decided to show up then? Sit down over there' Tunji gestured to the armchair opposite the three seater couch.

'Tunji I just asked you a question! I will not sit down until you let me know what's going on!'

'You want to know what's going on? Okay I'll tell you…. when did you intend to inform me that you let some bastard fuck you and get you pregnant before you married me? And when were you going to reveal that you are not a virgin as you have masqueraded yourself to be?' as Tunji's voice began to get louder with each sentence; Esmerelda and some of the rest of the house staff who were listening from behind the door knew that it was about to go down.

'Tunji...what the...' Ronke was rendered speechless, how the hell could he have known! She didn't tell a soul and Esmerelda was the only one that she had asked to get her a pregnancy test. *Oh shit! Is that why her face looked like death a minute ago* thought Ronke. To her abject horror, Tunji threw the used pregnancy test stick down on the coffee table.

'Are you still going to lie Ronke? There's the proof! Would you believe that Esmerelda brought this to me in excitement because she thought that I was the father? Like I would even touch your miserable corpse! What's wrong Ronke? Cat got your tongue.. .'

'I...I...I can explain Tunji. This was a mistake!'

'A mistake Ronke? A mistake? I'LL SHOW YOU A FUCKING MISTAKE YOU BITCH! By the time I'm done with you'll wish you were dead!'

Tunji lunged at Ronke and punched her squarely in the face with the full momentum of his 200 pound body weight; for one who had never being beaten ever before in her life, the pain felt as if she had just been hit by a bus. The skin just above her brow line burst upon impact and when Ronke saw blood pour down into her eye, she began to scream;

'Please Tunji, please I beg you...stop!'

'Shut up you whore,.... I said shut up!'

He dragged her up by her hair and threw her on the glass coffee table shattering it into a thousand pieces; by then her arms, neck and face were badly gashed and bleeding. Ronke felt as though he was going to kill her so she began to beg for her life.

'I beg you Tunji STOP! Please don't kill me...I beg of you! Somebody please help!'

It seemed as if nobody heard her cry; if she died right there, none of the miserable house staff would come to her rescue anyway, the only thing for it was to fight back.

He was now kicking her belly like a football and when she tried to shield her face he started to target that instead. Ronke desperately wanted to defend herself, but Tunji was far too strong; he straddled over her and held her arms flat on the ground with his knees then began to pound her face with heavy roundhouse punches like a man unhinged.

'So you're trying to save you're trying to save your pretty face eh? So that you can carry on whoring after I'm finished right? By the time I'm finished with you, your own mother won't even recognize your pathetic face'

Tunji then spat on her and continued his barrage of slaps, kicks and punches to Ronke's head. The final straw was the blood curdling scream that rang out when her head hit the corner of the marble bottomed lamp; every thing went black and she finally passed out. At this late point in the game, one of the gatemen and the driver ran in to beg Tunji; he was doing too much and they didn't want him to kill her even inspite of her apparent infidelity.

'I beg *saa*, no kill am for Madam! I beg saa make you dey stop beating am!' said one of the gatemen. When they eventually pulled Tunji off Ronke's body; he was still giving her body blows in a fit of rage even though she had clearly passed out. Tunji finally stopped and got up off the floor satisfied that had given her the beating of her life. *That will teach her the bitch* he thought.

He then straightened up his tie and spat on her once more before walking out of the house; Tunji grabbed the keys to his *Ferrari Enzo* and drove off to God knows where.

When Esmerelda walked in and saw Ronke's state, her legs failed her and she burst into tears at her Mistress's feet. Ronke was unrecognizable, her hair was caked with dried blood and her head had swollen up like a football. *What have I caused in this house!* she thought.

They needed to get Ronke to the hospital and fast; while they put her in a car to take her to the doctor, Esmerelda took the liberty of calling Ophelia. She knew that the other Mrs Olajuwon was very level headed and could deal with this situation calmly. Ronke's mother would have just been hysterical and make the already desperate situation much worse.

~~~

By the time that Ophelia got to the emergency ward, Ronke was hooked up to breathing apparatus and a drip. From what she had gathered, Ronke was lucky to be alive; there was also a chance that she would be brain damaged for life and she was also deaf in one ear. Tunji had succeeded in dislocating her jaw, fracturing her skull, breaking three of her ribs, rupturing her ear drum and finally breaking two her fingers, one of which had her engagement and weddings ring on it. The finger had swelled so badly that the nurses had to saw the rings off or they would have cut off her blood supply. When Ophelia walked into to see her cousin, her insides did a back flip from the extent of Ronke's injuries; Ronke gave her a tiny smile and whispered her name in a deathly quiet voice.

'Oh Ophelia….thank you for coming…'
'It's okay sweetheart, don't try to speak okay. Esmerelda called me and just explained everything. That bastard is going to pay for this! I'm calling the police; they should be at your house to arrest that scum by the time he gets home. Just relax and let me take care of this, Deji is away in New York right now or he would have come with me too; God knows what he will do to Tunji when he gets back!'
'No Ophelia, please. No police, this is my fault and he is my husband. I can't let you'
'But Ronke what are you saying! He almost killed you…the doctor said that you should be dead by now…I know that you don't love him and only married him for that title! No title is worth this Ronke, please don't be hard headed, I love you!' Ophelia pleaded
'Ok Ophelia, call the police and then what? A divorce? You know that I can't do that to my family, it would mean social death! Even the poorest village people in Nigeria never divorce….I'll just have to learn to handle myself but please Ophelia I insist on no police. Have

229

you forgotten that I am pregnant with another man's child? Yes, Donnie's baby survived the attack. If that ever gets out then I'll be the laughing stock walking around with egg on my face'

'Oh my God Ronke, what a predicament! You and Donnie should have been more cautious...but you didn't deserve to be beaten up like an animal!'

The gravity of the situation finally hit Ophelia with full force; she had tried to be strong since reaching the hospital but Ronke's admission caused painful tears to flow from her eyes.

'Please Ophelia, I know you mean well but this is the way I want it. Don't cry okay, I'll get better and it will work itself out. I think he's seeing someone else on the side anyway so maybe he'll move her in to the house after this and then I can demand to be moved to my own home. Can you believe that he hasn't even touched me since we kissed in the Church on our wedding day? I haven't even seen him naked let alone have sex with him...but at the end of the day, we both knew our reasons for this marriage even though they were never voiced aloud. Tunji wanted a trophy wife and I wanted a title; I just never imagined that he would be violent...'

After sometime Ophelia left Ronke to sleep and she now had the agonizing task of letting Ronke's parents know what had happened. Before that however she decided to pay Tunji Olajuwon a visit; someone had to let him know that he couldn't just beat up on women like that and get away with it and may as well be her. Ophelia, Esmeralda and the rest of the house staff that also came to the hospital left for Tunji's house.

The red Enzo had been parked haphazardly in the driveway so they knew he was already home; when Ophelia stormed into the study, Tunji had his feet up and was drinking a large glass of brandy.

'Tunji, you have a fucking nerve sitting there like that as if nothing's happened! You nearly killed her; what did she do to deserve that! I swear, once Deji gets back you'll have hell to pay!'

'Oh please do shut it Ophelia! Deji won't do a thing. You of all people know that in Yoruba culture, once married, my wife becomes my property so I can do what I wish to her. Don't interfere because it's none of your business; you just keep your nose of out people's affairs ok!'

'Let me tell you something Tunji Olajuwon, Ronke is my family; yes my flesh and blood, so when you try to kill her with your bare hands it is my business! If you ever, ever lay a finger on her again you'll be fucking sorry you pathetic lowlife scumbag!'

Tunji rolled his eyes and turned the news on with the remote control as if to drown her out; *who the hell does she think she's speaking to anyway?* he thought.

'Yeah Ophelia, whatever. Just shut the door on your way out'

His nonchalant attitude filled Ophelia with rage and she grabbed the glass of brandy out of his hand and threw the brown liquid in his face.

'I'll give you whatever! I'm not Ronke, and I will die before I let you batter me the way you did her!'

Tunji bounced out of his seat and raised his hand as if to slap her but she stood firm; *he wouldn't dare touch me, he just wouldn't!* she thought.

'Tunji, if you dare harm a hair on my head I guarantee you that if I don't kill you then Deji will. He is the kind of man that will defend his woman to the death, so don't you even fucking try it do you hear me! Be careful Tunji, just be careful…'

And with that, Ophelia stormed out of the God forsaken place and left for her home. She decided to let Ronke's parents know what had happened the next day on a level head.

Once home, Ophelia called her husband to explain the events that had transpired and Deji assured her that he would be on the next flight back to Lagos. It had been a long night so when she finally hit the sack, Ophelia descended into a fitful and restless slumber.

Chapter 23

Three weeks after the beating, Tunji called a family meeting between both sets of parents, himself, Ronke, Ophelia and Deji. He needed to clear the air with everyone and by the time he had finished his story hopefully the majority would be on his side.

Once Deji landed in Lagos, he had stormed off to find Tunji and the two brothers ended up in a bloody fight; the last time they had fought was all they way back in their early teens over a Super Nintendo game console. Back then, their father had beaten them both for fighting and told Tunji off for disrespecting his older brother. Now they were older, the game had changed and they were both adult men in their own right. This time around, Deji won the fight outright, and Tunji had to fall back in defeat like a coward; it didn't matter though, because by this point Ronke was already a broken woman. The shame that hung over her head made her feel as if she deserved to be treated the way that Tunji treated her. He was careful now though to never hit her in the face, instead he might punch her in the stomach occasionally just to let her know who the boss was. Anything went as

232

long as it wasn't an area that was visible to the naked eye and so the abuse continued in secret. Heartbreakingly, Tunji knew innately that Ronke wouldn't tell a soul.

During the meeting, Tunji stated his case of why he had beaten his wife and also took the opportunity to apologize to her parents for her current state. His excuse for such depravity being that he felt she had cheated him by being impure and had he known such information prior to their wedding, then he wouldn't have gone ahead. Ronke also apologized to Tunji's parents for her infidelity and also to her own parents for the disgrace. Finally the meeting concluded with both families agreeing to keep what had happened a secret, however the elders told Tunji off about his temper and Ronke was admonished even more so about the illegitimate pregnancy. In an attempt to get things back to normal, it would be arranged for Ronke to fly to New York and get her face reconstructed by a plastic surgeon, after which her baby would be terminated.

It took all of the strength that Ophelia had inside her to stop herself from walking out of the room; Tunji had essentially been given a slap on the wrist for attempted murder and she hoped to God that the bastard wouldn't end up killing her cousin the next time. Little did she know that the abuse had never stopped in the first place; once Ronke was back from hospital after the beating, Tunji decided that it was time to consummate their marriage.

At first Ronke found it strange that Tunji didn't want to fuck her pussy, he was only interested in penetrating her anus instead. The first time they had sex, he fucked her in the ass so violently that it bled. After that, he would make her satisfy his sexual needs at any given time without any consideration for her own plans or even returning the favour. On other occasions he would even demand oral sex in communal areas of their home, even though he knew full well that members of the household staff could walk in at any moment. Before long, Ronke concluded that he meant to humiliate her and break her will down to a tooth pick; that sad thing was that it was working. The beautiful Victoria Island mansion that she lived in became her fortress and the title of Princess was a prison; to this end Tunji made sure that Ronke was accompanied everywhere she went so essentially, there was no escape. Even when she travelled to New York for the surgery, he insisted that Ophelia go with her. Ophelia didn't mind going and wanted to do so anyway, but she didn't take kindly to Tunji giving her orders; in the end she would only be there for her cousin. It ripped her heart the way that Ronke cried for her aborted foetus and when Bijou laid eyes on her best friend's disfigured features, she begged in tears for her to leave the monster that she called her husband. Ronke stood firm; she maintained that it was her life and she would have to live with the mistakes she had made. The honour of her family was paramount and that reason alone gave her the strength to bear the pain. Incidentally, the plastic surgeon had actually done a great job; by the time her face had fully healed, there were only a few small scars by her cheekbone and brow-line, however those who knew the old Ronke could tell immediately that something inside was terribly wrong; the end result being that Tunji Olajuwon had succeeded in breaking down her spirit.

~~~~

A few months on, Ronke tried calling Donnie in secret several times to let him know of what had happened. The final blow to her despair was to find out that he had already moved on; she had called him at his Miami home only to meet the answer phone. Against her better judgement, she left a message on the answering machine only to be rudely interrupted;

'Hello Donnie…it's me Ronke. I've been calling you and well….I have something to talk to you about. I really need you baby, please call me…'
'Who the fuck is this? And why do you keep callin my man?' said an arrogant female voice 'look he's with me now and your ass is ancient history!'
'Excuse me? Look girl, whoever you are, you don't have to be rude to me! Just let me speak to Donnie please!' Ronke heard Donnie's

voice enter the room in the background; maybe if she spoke loud enough he would hear her voice

'Donnie! Donnie…it's me Ronke'

'Baby who's on the line?' he inquired

'Nobody baby, it ain't nobody important!' said the female, she was about to cut the line off when Donnie grabbed the handset;

'Hello? Who is this…?'

'It's me Donnie, it's Ronke. I wanted to talk to you; I hoped you would be alone'

'Oh…well how are you doin girl?'

'Not too bad, but that's what I wanted to talk to you about. Sorry about the bad line, I'm calling you from Africa'

'Oh word? You in Nigeria? That's what's up…what's on your mind?'

Ronke could hear the female in the background becoming impatient at the other end

'Donnie who is that bitch? I told you that I won't stand for this mess ok….get her off the damn line!'

'Patience, could you just wait a second, jeez! I'll get to you in a minute…daddy is gonna take care of you in a minute ok boo?...Sorry about that Ronke, as you can see somebody is breaking ma balls right now…carry on then'

'Who is she Donnie? Another Nigerian chick…my replacement?'

'Oh come on Ronke don't be like that; you're the one that left me remember? Anyway Patience is my lady now, I can tell you that much'

'It didn't take you long did it Donnie…it's only been five months since we last…since we last….'

Her lips couldn't let the words escape as the love of her life had now moved on and she was trapped in an amazingly paradoxical existence. How tragic must she sound to him right now?

'Ronke, I don't know what to tell ya…I did love, you but since you left me I realised there was more to life than running to New York every so often to see you, for what usually only amounted to a few hours of ya time. You didn't expect me to stay in limbo did you?'

'Well no, that's not what I'm saying; it wouldn't be fair on you. I just didn't expect someone else to have taken my place so quickly that's all. Well never mind about what I had to say...I can only wish good things for your life Donnie; maybe I shouldn't call you anymore, now that I know the score...'

'Thank you Ronke and yes maybe it would be for the best if you didn't call, I mean considering my situation and everything...no hard feelings?'

Ronke paused a while before answering him; she was on the verge of losing him forever and closing the door on this chapter of her life.

'Don't worry Donnie babe, no hard feelings. Take care and goodbye...I love you'

Before Donnie had the chance to reply, Ronke cut the phone line and then proceeded to erase his number from her phone and his email address from her contacts list; he'd already moved on in life now and so must she.

She cried herself to sleep that night, as the pain of her double loss was almost too much to bear. Thankfully, Tunji now slept in a spare room and left her alone for the most part; this meant that she could come to terms with her silent grief in peace. Ronke had never felt so alone in her entire life.

~~~~

A couple of weeks later, Tunji announced that they needed a vacation; Ronke wasn't sure what had gotten into him...was it a trap?, she wondered.

He'd decided they would go to Marrakesh for a week and at the last moment, Tunji's best friend Innocent decided to tag along.

Apparently the two men had a new business venture to work on, so they would be setting the wheels in motion for the project while on vacation since they were still contactable on their *Blackberries*.

Ronke thought that this was great; whenever Tunji and Innocent hung out together, they could be gone for hours and hours. She also knew that they liked to gamble away thousands of dollars at a time and were partial to the occasional line of smack; once they left her at the hotel she was going to be relatively free to go and do her own thing.

236

Going to Morocco for the first time was something else; from the architecture of the buildings to the terracotta of the landscape and then the hustle bustle of the bazaar; Ronke felt as though she'd stepped on to the set of an Indiana Jones movie. Tunji had booked one of the Pavilion suites at the luxurious five star *Amenjena* Resort Hotel in the Medina district of Marrakesh. According to the description on the Hotel's dedicated webpage, *Amenjena* meant 'peaceful paradise' and was honest and faithful to the ethos of Morocco. Its palms and African skies reflected a tranquil theme that was echoed throughout the Moorish oasis.

 The Resort was set within the back drop of the picturesque snow-capped Atlas Mountains and was not too far from a local bazaar. The décor inside the suite was quite impressive and included high domed ceilings, a king-size platform bed and an open fireplace; the suite also had its own private courtyard along with a pillared gazebo and a 25 foot pool at the back. Their bedroom was furnished in a selection of sumptuous red and orange Moorish upholstery with golden trim set against the back drop of muted peachy cream walls. Ronke walked into the bathroom to find it featured a columned tub decorated with green marble highlights, double vanities, soaring mirrors, twin dressing areas and a separate shower. The Brass lanterns and Berber carpets that were scattered liberally around the suite discreetly reinforced the Moroccan theme. In addition to all of this, the concierge also took the time to mention all of the high class facilities that the resort had to offer including a world renowned spa, gym and racket sports facilities, an 18 hole golf course, hair and nail salon, *Crème de la Mer* facials and other beauty treatments, designer boutiques and a complimentary butler service.

In spite of everything she had been through thus far; as soon as they'd arrived there, Ronke had a feeling that her stay at the *Amenjena* would be a memorable one…

Once she'd had enough of the Hotel's luxurious facilities, Ronke decided to explore the local bazaar market. She arrived at the market just after midday and the place was as busy as hell; she had seen similar markets in Nigeria but due to her privileged upbringing, she had never set foot in one of them before. This experience was definitely an eye opener for Princess Olajuwon; she was cheated out of her change on the first few transactions, overcharged on the next and then the final insult was a little street kid running off with her favourite orange *Hermes Birkin* bag. Ronke was stupid enough to leave it on the side while she looked through some Persian style rugs that cost a fraction of what she would expect to pay in New York; even though it looked like a fruitless exercise, Ronke gave chase. Her cell phone and hotel key were in that bag, not to mention her wallet.

'Hey you! Thief!' she screamed 'Give me my bag back! Please…STOP…I need my bag; I'll even pay you more than what's in there! Please give it back!'
The stall owners in the bazaar all shook their heads as she ran past; this is what happened everyday and usually at the same time. Foreigners were just too careless with their belongings; anyone with any common sense should know that thieves and pick pockets were everywhere, especially in a packed market. Ronke continued to run until suddenly, a tall stockily built, butter skinned looking man who was dressed head to toe in white robes, jumped out at her; she was about to scream in fear until she noticed that he had her bag in one hand and the little thief in the other. At last somebody had come to her rescue;
'Here is your bag madam and sorry about my nephew; I had no idea that he had become a petty criminal! He's supposed to be at school!' said the Moroccan stranger. He seemed to be admonishing the kid and the boy looked visibly afraid; eventually the stranger finally let him go, but not before he apologised to Ronke.
'I am sorry Madam…please very sorry' said the thief
Ronke didn't really know what to say at that point; she was still in shock from having to chase him down the market street. She looked around her and realised that she didn't even know where they were, so to add insult to injury, she was also lost.
'It's okay kid but just don't do that again! Look if it's money you

need I have some cash in here; let me find it' as Ronke started to
check inside her bag for a few notes the tall stranger motioned for
her to stop;

'No madam, it's not right and it's not as if he is starving! He is just
going to spend that money buying cigarettes with his wayward
friends or one of the bigger kids will take it from him! Please I insist
that you do not give him any money!'

'But…are you sure? What about his parents if you don't mind me
asking? Can't they use the money?' she asked with concern.

'No madam, for sure his mother is fine. His father, who is my
brother, passed away a year ago so that's why he is able to just skip
school unchecked. It is unfortunate, but when he lost his father, it
just went downhill from there; Qasim used to be such a good boy!'
the stranger then turned to Qasim who was now crying. Ronke felt so
sorry for the poor little thing.

'It's okay Qasim, you can go now, but no more of all this rubbish!
Your mother will be disappointed with you and you know that your
father would not have wanted you to end up doing something like
this; think about that ok and go back to school immediately'

The boy ran off and left them both standing there; finally Ronke
regrouped and realised that she was still lost, it was turning out to be
quite a day and she owed this dusky stranger a debt of gratitude.

'Thank you so much umm…I just realised that I don't know your
name. My name is Ronke, may I ask yours?' she inquired

'Of course you can my fair lady; my name is Syed and I own some
of the stalls around the market. I was just on my way to pick up some
outstanding rent from one of the stall holders when I saw him
running with your bag. I'm really sorry about him, I know this is no
excuse but losing his father hit him quite hard. I think that rebelling
is his way of handling it at the moment'

'It's okay, that's fine Syed; I guess God said we were supposed to
meet each other. The only thing is that I'm lost and I was trying to
get a good price on a carpet but I guess it's probably been sold by
now. Somebody else was interested in buying it as well'

Syed laughed to himself; the market used underhanded tactics to gently nudge the tourists into buying things. If someone else wanted to buy the same item you had been eyeing up, wouldn't it instantly become a hundred times more attractive?

'What's so funny?' asked Ronke smiling

'I'll tell you in a minute; let me ask you, did this other customer happen to have shocking red hair and wear a cheap looking Rolex?'

'Well I didn't look at her watch, but the hair sounds about right. Why do you ask?'

'Because that is just Miriam trying to keep you interested in the item; you see her job is to pretend that she really wants that carpet and that she wants it at all costs. Hopefully you being the foreigner will think that that particular one is the best thing since sliced bread and you will both bargain with the stall holder until you eventually buy it. Normally, you will end up buying the same carpet for twice the price of what you originally would have if you were bargaining alone. I'm afraid it's just another way to fleece you of your hard earned cash... but that is the way of the market!'

Ronke shook her head; these innocent looking people could be really dubious! She would need to be a lot more vigilant from now on.

'Thanks so much for explaining that Syed; I feel like such a fool! This is actually the first time that I have ever been to a market in my life and I must say that it is highly exhilarating! I think I've had enough excitement for one afternoon though and I need to get back to my hotel for some lunch. Do you know the *Amenjena*?'

'The *Amenjena*? Of course I know it; it's one of the most expensive hotels in Medina! But before I take you back there, may I take you to lunch nearby instead? When you're in a foreign country it's nice to eat where the locals do and you'll find, that is normally where the best cuisine is...please Ronke, it would be my pleasure'

Before responding to him, Ronke thought about it for a second; should she really go off with a stranger in a foreign country? Was it safe? Maybe she should pretend to call her husband so that Syed wouldn't get any funny ideas;

'Ok Syed I would love to go; but please let me call my husband first. Just so that he will not be worried if we take a while. Please just give me a second ok'

As she walked into a corner to make the pretend call; Syed took in the sight of her. How could any man in his right mind let a beautiful woman like Ronke walk the streets of Marrakesh by herself? She looked like she had just stepped off the pages of one of those western fashion magazines that his wife sometimes looked at; Ronke's Jade green floor length maxi dress complimented her shape beautifully. It didn't show too much skin, but it revealed just enough to make Syed go hard under his flowing white robes.

As she walked back to him, he licked his lips at the thought of tasting her black pussy that would almost certainly be pink inside; Syed knew that he had to have her and sooner rather than later was his preferred option.

Ronke was enchanted to find that Syed was the perfect gentleman and while they had lunch, she found herself flirting with him; maybe it was because she was desperate for any kind of attention since her husband never gave her any. At the same time she knew that she had to be cautious; there could not be a repeat of her abortion ordeal and if Tunji had a reason to beat her senseless ever again he would probably kill her. Syed looked at her face and wondered what she was so worried about;

'Are you okay Princess? You seem worried about something; I hope you're not itching to leave already?' he asked

'Oh no Syed, I was just lost in my thoughts. I'm so sorry'

'So that means that I'm boring you?'

'No Syed, heavens no! I'm quite enjoying your company!'

'Then if that's the case, may I ask if I can see you again? I mean before you leave Marrakesh. I would really love to take you to dinner' he picked up her hand and kissed it gently 'I know that you are married but it seems that your husband doesn't even know your worth. How could he bear to leave you roaming the streets of Morocco alone and un-chaperoned? I know that if you were mine then I would never let you go anywhere alone!'

Ronke's heart melted as his sentiments; no man had ever treated her that kindly talk less of kiss her hand. They would have to be careful, but she decided that she would definitely see him again.

'That is so sweet of you to say Syed and yes I would love to see you again. The only thing is that I have to be very careful because if my husband gets an inkling that I am seeing another man then he will probably kill me. He doesn't really love me at all but at the same time he sees me as one of his possessions. If he found out that someone else is capable of making me remotely happy then he will lose it'

Syed wiped the tears of desperation that began to fall from Ronke's eyes; a beautiful woman such as herself should be uplifted by her husband, and not downtrodden; in his opinion, that was tantamount to committing a mortal crime.

'Ronke my dear, please don't cry anymore; I promise you that I will show you happiness for as long as you will allow me to while you are here. That's the thing about life, sometimes you have to take your happiness wherever you can find it, otherwise risk losing it forever'

He walked her back to the top of the market and from there Ronke made her way back to the hotel; they had arranged to meet at noon the next day for lunch again and who knew what else…

The following day, Syed took her to another place for lunch. It was a private room and they were seated on floor cushions which was traditional for Moroccan décor; she expected to see other people up there but they seemed to be every much alone.

'Syed, where is everybody?' asked Ronke after they had eaten

'They have left us alone' he replied

'But why would they do that?'

'Because I asked them to; that's the great thing about private dining rooms, they are private!'

Ronke laughed at his candour; *where is he headed with this?* she thought.

'Syed…did you intend for us to umm…'

'Make love?'

'No, did you intend for us to fuck…I don't really do the 'making love' thing'

'Well I think it's time for me to introduce you to it; making love is

far better than you give it credit for…come with me Princess'
Syed led her into a secret bedroom behind a curtain covered door; the
room had a huge wrought iron four poster bed inside it and a small
en suite bathroom at the back.
' I hope this will do…it's not as nice as your five star resort, but I
can promise you that you will feel a lot more luxurious in here than
you do all alone in your cold bed'
Ronke smiled at him and the proceeded to slip off her linen dress, as
it fell to the ground she gave him an answer;
'I know…'

~~~~

After kissing her for what seemed like a life time, Syed began to
nibble on Ronke's breasts; she almost came as his warm lips
enveloped her nipples, her body had not been ravished like that for
an achingly long time. Ronke wanted to return the favour so she
started to reach down to put his dick in her mouth, but to her surprise
Syed stopped her in her tracks;
'All in good time my sweet Princess, I said that I want to make love
to you and that is exactly what I'm going to do'
In one quick motion, he lifted her up from under her thighs so that
her pussy was suspended in mid-air then sank his face into her
wetness, causing Ronke to twitch and squirm. The heat of his tongue
inside her most private cavity was exquisite and combined with the
agony she felt from balancing the rest of her body weight on just two
elbows, she felt the most beautiful sweet pain. She figured that he
would stop soon, as he had been down there for a good fifteen
minutes. Ronke herself had only ever reached orgasm through oral
sex alone once before; she figured that she should let him know so he
didn't waste his time trying.
'Syed…it's okay if you want to stop that and try something else; I
don't usually come from oral sex anyway so it's not your fault…trust
me, I'm still enjoying it'
'What makes you think that I want to stop?...Ronke, can I ask you to
do something for me?'
'Yes what's that?'

243

'I want you to trust me and let go; let yourself go and try to forget everything. All the heartbreak, all the pain….just let it go'

'But Syed I don't know if I can do that…I don't even know how'

'Princess can you try for me? Just imagine that we're floating and that we have all the time in the world…'

With that he continued to lick her out, but this time he lowered her hips back on to the bed. Ronke did as she was told and decided to live in the moment; after this week she would be going back to a life of misery anyway so she may as well enjoy this.

He began to pull each pussy lip between his teeth and let each go in quick succession; at the same time he started to rub her clit rhythmically and increased in speed as her moans intensified. After a little while Ronke came at last and amazingly, tears escaped from her eyes as the delicate climax rocked her to the depths of her emotions.

'Oh Syed, that was so beautiful…so wonderful…oh my God! I can't believe my body can feel this good…I don't want this to end…please…'

Ronke began to sob deeply as all the feelings of hurt and pain she felt overwhelmed her at that very moment and came crashing down; *Why can't we stay locked in this moment forever* she thought between her tears, *why does life have to be so cruel?*

'Princess please don't cry so, just enjoy these few days that we will spend together and cherish them for the rest of your life…'

He then put on a condom and entered her sweet little opening causing her to arch her back with pleasure. As he thrust away gently and looked into her eyes, the tears didn't stop flowing. He wished that he could stop the pain that she felt and kissed her passionately on her full lips as if to tell her as such. They carried on for an eternity until he finally came quietly, after which they both felt completely at peace.

Ronke was exhausted so she fell asleep soon after; he allowed her to sleep, but after a few hours she woke up with a start. What time was it? She looked up the clock hanging on the wall, it was past six in the evening and she had to get back to the hotel! Time had flown and she had been with Syed for a whole six hours. Syed quickly got her a taxi and she was able to reach the hotel by half past six; she quickly thought of what she could say to Tunji as to why she was late. Maybe she could say that she was held up at the bazaar.

When Ronke entered the suite, it looked exactly the same as she had left it earlier in the day. Upon quick investigation, she realised that she was alone then out of the corner of her eye she spotted a note on the coffee table:

Ronke,

Just to let you know, will be out all night so don't bother waiting up.

Tunji

She scrunched up the note and threw it in the bin, if she known that she wouldn't have bothered to rush back so quickly. His vague note confirmed what she had known all along; there was another woman other than her in their marriage.

~~~~

Syed and Ronke continued their steamy liaisons until the end of the seven days; during that time she only saw Tunji three times and Innocent once. They seemed to have left her to her own devices and that suited her just fine. On the last day she shared a fabulous four hours of pure sex with Syed and then they had to say their goodbyes. They exchanged email addresses as they had come to the conclusion that it was safer to communicate through that medium to avoid Tunji discovering their affair. After the long walk back to the hotel, Syed kissed her for the last time; they had fallen in love under seemingly insurmountable circumstances and now it was time to embark upon the painful task of saying goodbye.

'My Princess, my Queen…please don't be heartbroken. If we are

245

meant to be together, then it will be; just always cherish the moments
that we have spent here and please don't forget me' said Syed
'I won't Syed; I will never forget you as long as I live! I love you so
much and thank you for making me feel like a woman again'
Finally, they embraced and she ran off into the hotel complex; it was
better to have loved and lost than not at all.

Once back in the hotel room, Tunji was no where to be found as
usual but strangely his cell phone was on the bed. After a while it
started ringing and Ronke grabbed the phone and ran to find him,
maybe it was an important business call and she didn't want him to
get violent if he missed it. She figured he would be with Innocent in
the suite next door so she walked through the back courtyard that
linked all the suites and their individual pools. As she walked round
to Innocent's suite, she could hear a distinct moaning coming from
inside his suite. That meant that Tunji couldn't be there if Innocent
was with a woman; or wasn't he?
Suddenly she heard Tunji's voice, he was the one moaning! Was he
arrogant enough to cheat on her while she was just next door? She
stormed in to investigate when suddenly, reflected in the floor length
mirror she caught the reflection of Innocent fucking her husband in
the ass; Ronke nearly screamed out loud but quickly caught herself.
At that very moment, the old Ronke was woken up. As she plotted
her revenge, she quickly set the cell phone to silent mode and used
the internal camera to make a video clip of the scene. Once she had
at least five minutes of footage she crept away silently and went back
to their room. Upon reaching there, she quickly sent the footage to
her own cell by Bluetooth and then uploaded the clip to her private
hotmail account. She had a good mind to post it on Youtube but she
had to hold back in order to implement her plan. The final part of the
retribution was to delete the clip from Tunji's cell phone memory;
she threw it back on the bed when she was done. He wouldn't even
know that she had touched the phone.

Tunji came back about an hour later in good spirits; he was now
satisfied and ready to go to the airport. As usual he expected Ronke

to have packed his bags not forgetting to put his *Hugo Boss* linen suit in its special *Louis Vuitton* suit carrier.

'Ronke...Ronke! Where are you woman...I'm ready to go now! Have you finished packing?'

She walked into the living room area carrying the last piece of hand luggage that needed to be taken down.

'Yes Tunji we're all packed for the airport; the cases are in the car, they're just waiting for Innocent to load his own and then we can go' As she headed for the door, Tunji picked up his cell phone and noticed that there was a missed call; *why didn't she pick it up?* he thought.

'Come back here Ronke. Why is there a missed call on my phone? Couldn't you have just taken a message, eh? Are you that stupid woman?'

'But Tunji...I'

Before she could speak he punched her in the stomach, causing her to double over in pain; as she fell to the ground, Innocent walked in on them.

'Come on Tunji, there's no need for that now! Just leave her and let's go to the airport; I'm sure whom ever it is will call you back'

'Whatever' barked Tunji and stormed out of the room.

Tears began to run down Ronke's face at her humiliation; but this time they were tears laced with determination. *He will pay dearly for this* she thought, *by God the bastard will pay*.

Strangely, it was the same person that had invaded her marriage that took pity on her and helped her off the floor;

'Ronke, let's go honey. Sorry about what he did...he can be a monster sometimes can't he? You'll be ok sweetie, I promise' said Innocent in his Californian twang.

She then stood up dignified and defiant; safe in the knowledge that her day in court was soon approaching.

'Thank you Innocent and you're quite right. I'll be fine'

Innocent watched Ronke as she left him in the room and made her way downstairs; something had changed in that woman just now and it didn't seem quite right. He couldn't quite put his finger on it; but it was a distinct feeling. In the end he decided for forget about it and dismissed it as being nothing.

As the plane took off from Marrakesh early that evening, Ronke was absolutely calm for the first time in a long time; she was now in complete control and boy did it feel good.

Chapter 24

Ophelia woke up on a cold New York December morning and looked to her left; the bed was empty so she knew that Deji had already left for work. When she realised the time was 8.15, she jumped out of bed and ran to the bathroom; she was due to be at work in her studio within the next 45 minutes.

Issy, Ophelia and Alizé were on the verge of launching the *Transatlantic* ready to wear collection; they had been successful in finding a high-end clothing manufacturer that would be able to distribute their range throughout the 52 states and the eventually worldwide. It had been quite a hectic year for them all with Ophelia getting married, Alizé dealing with being a new mom and Issy planning her own nuptials with Eduardo. He had popped the question a few months back when the couple had gone through a pregnancy scare. It turned out that Issy wasn't pregnant, but from that moment on Eduardo knew that he could see them being very capable parents. He also loved Issy very much and wanted to give whatever children they would have together the stability in their upbringing that he himself was deprived of. At first, Issy's parents were apprehensive seeing that Eduardo was the son of a well known philanderer, but once they got to know him, they soon realised that he only had eyes for their beautiful and stunning daughter.

Ophelia was having a pregnancy scare of her own; she had now been married little over a year but was yet to get knocked up. Ophelia and Deji had both gone for medical check ups at his insistence, but the docs had assured them both that they were very healthy and fertile and that sometimes these things took time. That was all very well and good, but Ophelia couldn't stop being stressed about it; she would love nothing more than to give her beloved Deji a child. His love for her was a rare one indeed and she loved him even more with each passing day to the extent that she felt dizzy sometimes; all that love needed to be distributed to more than one person!
Once in the bathroom, she picked up the pregnancy test on the sink stand and emptied her bladder on to it. She then jumped into the shower, she figured it would probably read negative anyway as she'd been doing the same test every two weeks for the past six months. Upon leaving the shower Ophelia ran to get changed and forgot all about it.
It wasn't until she reached home that evening and met Deji that the thought of the test even came up.
When she walked into the apartment her beloved kissed her for longer and deeper than normal; *what's gotten into him today* she thought. Maybe he'd just had a good day at work.
'Honey what's up? And what are you so happy about today? Not that I'm complaining!' said Ophelia
'Well don't you have something to tell me?' asked Deji
'Umm…not….really. There's nothing really new to report, you know that the launch is on schedule and all of that. So no I don't'
'Erm anything to do with two little blue lines?' he enquired.
'Baby…you've lost me. Two blue lines….'
As Ophelia trailed off, it finally dawned on her that she had forgotten the test on the toilet cistern that morning; Deji had probably found it

and discovered the fantastic news that she was finally with child! She jumped on him with happiness.

'Oh my gosh Deji, I completely forgot! Are you sure? Are you quite sure?'

'Well the test don't lie sweetie; let's just arrange a check up with the Doc just to confirm. Oh and you know that we shouldn't mention anything to anybody until the end of the first trimester'

'I know, I know but I don't know if I can contain myself; my girls will be so happy and so will our parents!'

'I know honey' said Deji, he then cupped her face in his hands they way he always did and looked into her eyes 'I love you so much that it hurts me sometimes, do you know that? If there is anything in the world that you want, anything that you need; all you need do is ask and I'll do everything within my power to make it happen for you'

Ophelia's eyes were locked in his gaze; she wished that they could remain in that moment forever as she replied him;

'Oh Deji my sweet darling; you already have'

Their next kiss was a prelude to a long night of beautiful love-making; they had now passed the stages of initial lust, so when they shared their bodies that night, there was so much more of a deeper meaning.

Deji himself wouldn't have wanted it any other way; one night stands were fine for a quick fix but there was nothing like being with someone who knew your body so well. One who knew when to tease you and when to stop, who knew exactly how firmly to grip your shaft to take you just over the edge; then knew how to bring you exquisitely back into the sex, by using yet another skilful move or technique.

Ophelia knew his body like a map and she held him back from orgasm with the delicacy and precision of a master craftsman. When he eventually came, the quality of his climax was astounding. Before that night, Deji had never screamed out loud at the point of orgasm; his body shook uncontrollably and his eyes started to water as he unloaded his prime stock into her. After that, sex would never be the same again. His body now belonged to his wife exclusively and all the other secret extra-curricular chicks that he had would need to fall back. It wasn't surprising to Deji at all when he deleted most of the numbers in his cell the next morning.

~~~~

At the end of the month, Deji and Ophelia travelled to Lagos for the Emeka-Phillips Christmas bash for the second time as husband and wife; Nigeria still hadn't changed much but at very least they had changed for the better. The couple had mutually decided to announce their good news during the family reunion, so at that point their parents were still in the dark about their happy news; Ophelia was glad to have baby news, because Sandra had been driving her mad calling her every few weeks to ask if she was pregnant yet; at least now she could shut the old dear up.

Queen Olajuwon on the other hand was the epitome of patience; she'd actually confided in Ophelia that she herself took over two years to become with child for the first time and reassured her daughter-in-law that she shouldn't worry.

Ophelia was looking forward to seeing how Ronke was doing and when they eventually met, there was a marked improvement in her temperament; it was a welcome relief and Ophelia figured maybe Tunji had changed for the better.

'Hey sweetie!' said Ophelia embracing her cousin 'you look well, it seems that your little excursion in Morocco did you the power of good. Come on then, tell me all about it! Has Tunji decided to do right after all?'

Ronke laughed out loud at this concept; it would have been fantastic if that was the case, but unfortunately for Tunji the actual truth was dramatically different.

'Ophelia, it's great to see you too! Morocco was great, in fact it was fantastic; but I can assure you that Tunji had absolutely nothing to do with it. Let's just say that I made a very good friend' said Ronke cheekily

She then explained about her little liaison with Syed, how they'd met, and how they eventually fell in love with each other. Ronke also

252

told Ophelia of how Tunji sometimes used her body for sexual gratification, but had never actually included her own enjoyment to the exercise.

'What! You're kidding right? Actually knowing you Ronke , you're probably not! Not that I blame you honey; a woman can only endure so much pain up to a certain level. I guess you're entitled to a little good loving too'

The two women took a walk into the backyard where the tables had already been set up for the following night's party. They sat down on some wire framed chairs and continued to talk. Ronke then poured her heart out to her cousin;

'Ophelia, I've been through so much with this man that it's even unreal. The good news is that I was right; there was someone else in our marriage all along. Hopefully my suffering will be over soon and I will eventually go and live somewhere else by myself'

'Woah! Really? There's another woman….oh my gosh, can you imagine! But how can you prove it?'

'Trust me, I have lots of proof. Like I said, there was a third person in this marriage. I plan to confront Tunji in front of our parents on the Sunday night after the party when we all have dinner. It should be every interesting and I'd love to see if he will deny it; but I beg of you Ophelia, don't breathe a word to Deji. Not that I think that he will blab, but I need to maintain the element of surprise, also the timing is everything in this case'

'Ok Ronke, just for you I promise'

Ophelia then hugged her cousin and squeezed her hand to show some moral support

'Good luck Ronke and God knows that you're going to need it!'

~~~~~

On the fateful Sunday night, just before Ronke was about to drop her bombshell, Deji and Ophelia broke their happy news. It was wonderful to see everybody's faces light up and offer their congratulations to the couple. Apart from Deji and Ophelia's two sets of parents, Ronke's parents, Kelechi, Adora, Ronke and Tunji were also in attendance at the dinner table. They had all had a satisfying meal and on top of it all some good news that had been very well received; eventually they all moved on to the family room and settled down on the couches that were just in front of the huge fifty inch wide plasma screen.

At 9.45 that evening, Ronke decided to exact her revenge. She stood up in front of everyone and cleared her throat before she eventually spoke;

'Erm…sorry everybody, but I too have an important announcement to make…'

Just as she began to take the DVD out of her bag and make a small speech, Tunji's cell phone went off; it was Innocent on the line so he ran outside to take the call.

'Excuse me but, I just have to take this call. Its business…' he declared and with that, made his exit. Once he was outside the house, he continued the conversation with his lover;

'Yes baby, don't worry I'll see you tonight. I'll find a way to keep that bitch distracted or hell, I might even tell her that I'm going to a club'

'Come on Tunji! We've discussed this before, there's no need to go there and call your wife a bitch. If anything you should be grateful to her; she's covering up your whole lifestyle and isn't really complaining that much' said Innocent

'Whatever Innocent! Your parents are dead and gone so you don't have to bother putting up with a woman in your house; can you imagine what it's like to walk into your bathroom and catch a whiff of that 'pussy' smell? Exactly!'

Tunji lost himself in conversation, and before he knew it ten minutes had passed; he didn't realise they had been talking for so long. He also remembered that when he'd left the room, Ronke was about to say something important so he quickly ended the call and ran back inside.

When Tunji walked back into the family room, he didn't notice himself up on the TV screen at first. Once he recognized himself and

254

Innocent being broadcasted for his whole family to see, a strangled cry escaped from his throat.

He was frozen to the spot and one by one, everybody turned around from their seats to look at him; Tunji was open mouthed in shock. He noticed that his father's face was like thunder and his mother was shedding heavy tears; all of a sudden, Ronke's mother Angelina broke the silence.

'So is this why you have made my daughter suffer so bitterly, ehn? Because you like to engage in this….this type of abomination! Is that why you nearly killed her for me? Ahh! I will kill you this night Tunji Olajuwon, so help me God!'

She then lunged at him, slapping his face sharply in the process; they both fell to the ground and Tunji like the coward that he was, started trying to hit his mother-in-law back. A fight ensued and when Deji jumped in to try and pull Tunji off Angelina, Ronke's father Samson took over the attack on Tunji. Eventually, King Olajuwon, Jonathan and Kelechi all had to get involved in trying to break up the brawl. Amid all the confusion, Tunji managed to break free from the mêlée and ran away; once he got outside, he jumped into his Ferrari and sped off as fast as he could.

His mind was spiralling out of control so he headed for a beach that was just a few miles away. He needed somewhere to think, but after everything that had just been revealed, how could he ever go back home?

After three long hours of deep thought, Tunji called Innocent for the last time; his last words to any living soul were both painful and poignant;

'Hey, it was great while it lasted wasn't it babe… whatever happens after this Innocent, always remember that I love you'

Tunji cut off the call, then walked over to the trunk of his car and took out his glock handgun and looked at it for a while. He cried for the life he was about to leave behind and for not being able to say goodbye to his perpetually well-meaning parents. Tunji only hoped that Ronke would get everything that she truly deserved; marrying that woman had effectively ruined his life.

The past twenty-six years of his life flashed past as he sat on the bonnet of his red Ferrari and put the muzzle of his gun into his mouth; the last tear drop just about reached the crease of his nose as he pulled the trigger. When they found his body the next morning, there was a tiny picture of Innocent still cocooned inside the palm of his left hand.

Tragically, about two weeks after Tunji's suicide; Innocent ended his own life. It was almost unbearable for him to have a to maintain a marginal level of existence with all the finger pointing and name calling that he had to endure. Some people had even sent him death threats in the mail. It could have been that, this was the straw that effectively broke the camel's back. Moving back to California was an option, but Innocent wasn't about to fool himself; life would never be the same without Tunji and his own extended family had already dis-owned him a million times. It was apparent that there were some cases in life, when life was just not worth living.

~~~~

After a few months, Ronke left Nigeria for London in search of a fresh start. The fallout from the tragic circumstances of Tunji's death had affected her life in more ways than one.

The Olajuwon family all but stopped speaking to her as a result of their abject grief; she had meant to humiliate him as he had done her, but never in a million years did Ronke expect Tunji to commit suicide. The burden of guilt would forever be on her shoulders and she came to regret marrying him in the first place; sadly, apart from her own parents, only Deji and Ophelia understood her side of the story.

Deji himself reassured her that Tunji only ended his life because he was a coward and quite frankly he was ashamed to refer to him as his brother. Ronke prayed the God would have mercy on the poor bastard's soul.

Incidentally, Tunji had actually written her into his will and given her a 25% share of his assets but he had also sealed the final nail in the coffin by bequeathing 50% of what was left to Innocent. The last 25% was to be distributed between any children they may have had and his parents. During the will reading, it was agreed that Ronke would be given 30% of his assets and the remainder left to Tunji's grieving parents.

Ronke wasn't aware how much wealth Tunji had amassed through shrewd business deals until then; at the age of 26 his estate was worth a cool 50 million dollars.

Even though her parents weren't short of a dollar or two, Ronke had never personally been that rich in her life. All the money she had ever had was that which she had been given, not to mention the fact that she had never worked a day in her life. It was quite strange being seemingly independent; in fact Ronke found it a little scary.

Eventually, upon the sound advice of her mother she bought a small two bedroom apartment in the upscale Chelsea district of London. Accompanied by just two suitcases, Ronke Olajuwon got on a plane headed for England and left the past firmly behind her.

Chapter 25

Deji and Ophelia stayed in Nigeria a while following the death of Tunji. The heat of the African sun wasn't the most comfortable place to be pregnant, but considering the recent tragic events, Ophelia soldiered on. *Transatlantic* had been launched just before Christmas and was as expected, a runway hit. She was grateful that Issy and Alizé were capable enough to run things in her absence but Ophelia missed the companionship of her friends as well as her cousin. Kelechi and Adora had to go back to London not long after the tragedy so she was alone in trying to help Queen Olajuwon deal with the grief of losing her last born son. The home was no longer a place of happiness and light as it used to be and quite frankly it became a drain on Ophelia's karma.

The Queen became a shadow of her former self as she mourned the loss of Tunji; even though he had disgraced them all by his shameful secret, she still loved her son. What was even more difficult was the fact that the King didn't want Tunji's name mentioned in his presence; in his mind he only had one son and that son was Deji. It was as if Tunji had never existed. Ophelia felt as though she was walking on egg shells. Instead of looking forward to her approaching motherhood, she was busy playing homemaker, counsellor, shoulder to cry on and the supportive good wife.

Consequently, when her father finally agreed to release Efua from his house into the Olajuwon household, Ophelia was beside herself with delight; it was great to have someone she could really pour her heart out to at last. Deji was fine to talk to sometimes but after a while she could sense that he didn't really want to elaborate on the subject of Tunji. This was understandable and often when she wanted to talk about it, Ophelia would just leave it alone. Talking to Efua made things easier and at the very least she was someone who wasn't a strain of Ophelia's emotional resources. As the two got to know each other, she was surprised to discover that Efua was quite the little student.

She had learned quite a lot over the past year from her tutor and was thirsty for more knowledge; unfortunately his resources were now quite limited and Efua simply couldn't afford to buy any more books. When she explained her situation to her mistress, Ophelia wondered how the poor girl managed to cram it all in; it wasn't easy being a maid and one had to be up at the crack of dawn to commence the various chores of the day. There were also her weekend visits to her son Emmanuel to consider; Ophelia hadn't yet asked Efua if she would like him to come and live with them in light of the current circumstances.

Efua would often give Ophelia regular updates on how the child was doing and even brought pictures in to show her Mistress how big her little boy was getting. It was almost heartbreaking for Efua that she was unable to tell Ophelia that the very child that she doted over was her own baby brother.

Incidentally, when Ophelia was going to throw out her old laptop, she thought of Efua and then presented her with it the next day; to Ophelia giving away her old laptop was no big deal, but to somebody such as Efua the value of it was immeasurable. Her introduction to the world of computers and the internet was one of the most significant contributions to Efua's education; she would forever be loyal to Ophelia for that act of kindness.

About a month after Efua had started to use the laptop, Ophelia approached her with a proposition; if she accepted, then she could possibly fulfil her dream of achieving an academic qualification. While Efua tidied away the laundry into the closet, Ophelia asked her question;

'Efua, there's something that I wanted to ask of you, I've already spoken to Deji about it and he thinks that it's a good idea; what do you think of coming to work for Deji and I as our au pair in New York?'

'Emm…madam, you mean America? And please what is 'oh pear'?'

'Oh sorry Efua, I should have explained. An au pair is like a live in nanny, only you are not legally licensed to look after children. You would be living with us and helping to run our home and take care of the baby when I start working again. Also, I think that it would be a good idea your you to bring Emmanuel with us …that is if you would like to'

Efua looked at her Mistress for a few seconds; *is she serious?* she thought.

'Madam Ophelia….are you sure? You want me and Emmanuel to come with you and the *Oga*?'

Efua seemed dumbfounded with shock and Ophelia couldn't help but to laugh;

'Yes you Efua, I've thought about it for a while and even though it would be a big adjustment for you I'm sure that you'll like New York….you can even do some studying in a proper school in your spare time if you like'

'Madam, you would allow me to? And bring my baby as well! Thank you, thank you Madam Ophelia…I am so happy! I can't wait to tell my mama…she will pray for you-o! She will do a very strong, strong prayer for you and your family for this opportunity. I will be the first person in my family to go abroad! Thank you…I am so grateful ma!'

'Oh don't worry Efua, you're very welcome! I can't think of anyone else I'd like to look after my baby once I get back to work. I mean we've known each other for years…also I know that you have a son yourself so you understand how to care for children. I'm just happy that you said yes!'

'You're happy? Ahh, how could I even say no to you? You gave me a computer...do you even know how much that meant to me?'

At that point, Efua's deep gratitude for Ophelia's generosity brought her to tears; how could she be so good to her and her father be such a monster? Efua's whole life had been one hardship after the other so far and now somebody, a most unlikely somebody, was willing to give her a break in life. There was no way that Efua would squander this opportunity, but she was at a loss for the words to express herself the way that she really wanted to. Saying thank you to Ophelia could never cover it all.

'Efua don't cry...please. I know that you've had to struggle for so much, but I can assure you that while you are with me I will treat you with the respect and decency that you richly deserve. Now don't worry about putting away the rest of that laundry; take tonight off and give yourself a minute for it to all sink in. New York is a million miles away from the type of life that you live here so you have a lot to think about'

'Madam, thank you very much. I'm nearly finished with the laundry...please let me finish it then I will go'

'Efua, honestly, leave it and go, go on now'

Ophelia ignored her protests and ushered her out of the room. That girl worked much too hard and needed a break anyway she thought. The place was always spotless when Efua was around so a little bit of unfolded laundry wouldn't make a difference. Ophelia rubbed on her growing belly and contemplated on what the future would bring; Tunji's revelation had already taught her that anything could happen and never to rule anything out. Only God knew what was behind the next corner.

~~~~

Deji had Efua and Emmanuel's passports and visas prepared with amazing speed and before Ophelia knew it, they were getting ready to leave for New York. She was now six months pregnant and was anxious to start preparing the nursery for the new arrival. Even though she wanted to be supportive to the family in light of Tunji's passing, it was a welcome relief to finally be going back to normalcy. The Queen was still grieving only three months after her son passed and Ophelia wondered how King Olajuwon would cope in such a gloomy house.

How could any of them tell Deji's mother that she was destroying her relationship with her own husband over a son who after all, was now dead and gone. Deji himself was hurting because his mother had become obsessed with the tragic memory of Tunji; he tried to understand her all of those months, but didn't she realise that she also had a living son who needed her love?

It was only a matter of time and Ophelia began to lose weight under the burden of all the stress; she couldn't bring herself to eat when there was so much sadness around.

It was upon noticing what the atmosphere was doing to his wife that Deji made arrangements for them to leave Nigeria quickly; they had a baby on the way and the poor unborn child shouldn't have to suffer because of it.

~~~~

Just two weeks before they were due to leave for New York, another devastating tragedy befell the Olajuwon household; as she was been driven back from the hair salon, the Queen's car was rear-ended on the expressway at 90 miles per hour. The sturdy *Mercedes* she was travelling in was concertinaed on impact and she was killed instantly; Queen Angelica Remi Olajuwon had died at only forty-seven years of age.

King Olajuwon, Deji and Ophelia were just about to sit down to lunch when they got a call with the news. It seemed like fate had dealt the family a cruel blow, but in her heart Ophelia felt that God knew what he was doing. She knew that the Queen was lost without her beloved son and maybe it was for the best. When Tunji died, a part of the Queen died with him and she would probably have never been the same again.

Deji and his father were beside themselves with grief, so the rest of the family as well as Ophelia's and Ronke's families rallied round to help support them through the unbelievable tragedy. Ophelia even over extended herself to the point that the family doctor prescribed her with bed-rest for the next few weeks, it was upon this news that the King knew that he had to act. After his dear wife was buried and the mourners had left the home; he called Deji to have a talk. It was time for them to leave Nigeria. They had endured enough sorrow and he was not about to compromise the safety of his first grandchild.

'Deji, my son....I know this isn't an easy time for you and obviously you can only imagine what this whole ordeal has been like for me, but I think it's time for you and Ophelia to go back to New York now. You've done more than enough and have been a wonderful son to me; I could not wish for a better son Deji and I mean that. Even before I knew about Tunji's disgraceful acts, you have always been like this; very thoughtful and considerate and I as a father appreciate that, but son....it's time for you to go'
'But dad, you need me here. You've just lost mum only two weeks ago now....I can't leave you here alone...how will you cope?'
'Ahh Deji....I know you mean well but I will be fine, don't forget that I brought you into this world so I must have been able to cope by myself at some point mustn't I? To be honest with you...I am really thinking of dear Ophelia, she has been invaluable and tried her very best to keep the house running smoothly even though she has had to also deal with the burden of her pregnancy at the same time. If you won't leave for me, at least do it for her. Just because I've lost my wife, it doesn't mean that yours has to be neglected by her husband. Deji, I have watched you and in your grief you have stopped being attentive to that poor girl. I mean you didn't even notice that she was depressed until she lost all that weight; but it was what the doctor said about bed-rest made me realise what I had to do...'
'I know dad and I feel so ashamed about that and that's why I was making fast moves towards us leaving as you know, then mum had the accident. I know that you're right but I feel awful to leave you alone. I suppose it's for the best and I'd like to thank you for your foresight in this matter; you have only made me feel even more proud to call myself your son'

At that point, Deji, who had been trying to stay strong since the beginning of the series of tragic events, broke down. He loved his father, but was torn between his duty to him and to that of his own wife; thankfully the wisdom that came with age ushered the King into making Deji to do the right thing. Ophelia walked into the room to find her husband sitting down sobbing with his head in his hands. Seeing him cry sent alarm through her and she quickly went to embrace him;

'Hey Deji what's wrong…tell me' she looked up at her father in law for an answer;

'Daddy, what's wrong with Deji? Why is he crying…is it' she stopped short of what she was going to say; the mention of the poor Queen's death was almost too much to bear.

'My dear daughter, please don't ask. You probably have an idea anyway, just comfort him for me. That is what he needs right now' Ophelia nodded as she understood what he was trying to say and with that, the King walked out of the room leaving the couple alone. She rubbed Deji's back soothingly as he cried tears of sorrow; Ophelia would give anything to ease the pain. She could only imagine what he was going through.

~~~~

Landing at JFK for the first time was an amazing event for Efua; alternatively Emmanuel of course, was still a baby and didn't really know what was going on. The poor thing had cried throughout the flight and the stewardesses had to reassure Efua that he wasn't sick and that it was perfectly normal for small children to cry during flights.

Deji and Ophelia had travelled in the first class cabin and left Efua in business class with Emmanuel; Ophelia had wanted them to travel in first class too, but Deji disagreed with her. He maintained that there needed to be a barrier between a boss and employees and that line should never be crossed; while he realised that Ophelia and Efua got on well with each other, Ophelia needed to understand that they would never be conventional 'friends'

After they cleared the notoriously long line for the immigration desks at JFK, the group picked up their luggage and got in to the waiting limo that would take them to the Manhattan apartment that was their home.

Efua's eyes widened in awe as she looked out of the car window while they drove along. The place had so many tall buildings, the people spoke too fast and the air was a little to thick for her due to the smog from the car exhaust fumes. All of that was forgotten however; from the moment that she saw the famous Manhattan skyline for the first time. As the car came out of the Queens Midtown tunnel and sped into the heart of the city, it was impossible to take everything in. She wished that Emmanuel could understand what was happening to them. After everything she had been through and when all Efua had to look forward to was a life of hard ship and struggle to raise her son, she had finally fallen on her feet and been given a chance. All her life, Efua always felt that the concept of 'God' was only a luxury for the privileged few but now for the first time ever, she knew that he had been with her all along.

Once they got into the apartment, Ophelia showed her the room that she would be sharing with Emmanuel; Efua gasped audibly as she walked in it.

Ten members of her family could have comfortably slept in that room and there was even a small two-seater couch by the window that she decided would be Emmanuel's bed. The closet was equally spacious, all of her meagre belongings were able to fit on just one shelf and she didn't own any clothing that needed hanging.

After she had seen her room, Ophelia took Efua on a tour of the house and showed her how to use some of the hi-tech electrical appliances; she also explained to Efua what tasks she needed to do on a daily basis so that their home would be run smoothly.

Efua tried her best to take it all in, but in truth it would take her a few weeks to learn everything; she still couldn't get over the fact that plates could be put into a machine and washed automatically!

Ophelia decided that they would order some take-out for the night since they were all quite jet lagged and it would be unfair to expect Efua to know how to cook them a decent meal.

The next morning, Ophelia took Efua and Emmanuel out to do some shopping. She had realised when Efua unpacked her clothes the night before that most of the poor girl's things were threadbare and the other kids would only laugh at her when Efua walked out on the street. She decided that they should go down to 34th street in Midtown Manhattan to shop. They hit Macy's first, where they found out that Efua was only a tiny size two and even then some of the clothes still hung on her. Eventually, by the time they had finished at Macy's, checked out the rest of the stores on the street and visited the Manhattan Mall, they had bought quite a few things and Efua couldn't stop smiling. Until then, she had never had a stitch of brand new clothing in her life and when they got back to the apartment, she spent a few minutes taking in the aroma of that 'new clothes smell' Efua only wished that her mother was there with her to see it all; she decided that she would try to send back some pictures every couple of months, just so her mummy could see how well her daughter was doing.

Incidentally Ophelia came through on her promise and soon enough Efua was studying online for some basic education certificates and making regular trips to the local library. After being deprived of a decent education all her life, Efua took to learning like a duck to water; she soaked in all the knowledge that she was able to read like a sponge. There was so much to learn and she was wanted to catch up with it all; to this end Efua was often found asleep at night with a book in her hand. She was determined to make the most of this hand that God had dealt her and in a short space of time, the future already looked a whole lot brighter.

~~~~

Not too many months after Efua and Emmanuel were brought over to New York, Ophelia gave birth to a healthy 8 pound baby girl. Angelica Elizabeth Olajuwon was born on a humid August afternoon after her mother had spent an agonizing 16 hours in labour. Ophelia had a difficult time trying to push the baby though the birth canal due to her narrow hips. It was a trait of the women on her mother's side of the family, all the ass was at the back and they had no hips on the sides. It was both an amazing and terrifying experience for Deji. He felt helpless that he couldn't do anything to help his wife; she had to do this all by herself and bear the pain. In the end, just before the doctor was about to prepare her for a c-section, Angelica decided to show her face and stormed out into a brave new world. She was a serene and gorgeous baby who seemed to have inherited the beautiful spirit of her late grandmother and so she was named after her. As an after thought, Deji and Ophelia decided to give Elizabeth as her middle name after Sandra's just so that she wouldn't feel left out. Of course Sandra wasted no time in proudly announcing the birth of her first grandchild to the world; the news of Angelica's arrival delighted family and friends. Until then Ophelia hadn't realised just how many people she knew across the globe. Thankfully she had Efua to help her go through all her emails and bring her attention to the important ones only. The others were sent a generic reply with thanks for the warm wishes of congratulations.

Even though Efua was happy to do this for her mistress, she couldn't help but to feel a pang of jealousy for all the well wishes and gifts that the Olajuwons were receiving. She thought back to the shame of her own pregnancy and remembered that Jonathan had not even so much as bought Emmanuel some nappies let alone give him a present.

Efua swore that she would work her hardest to give her son all the things that she had been deprived of in life thus far, all she needed was a little education, some time and she would get there. As she changed Angelica's nappy for what seemed like the hundredth time since she was born, Efua could swear that the baby smiled at her…maybe the little angel had read her mind.

Chapter 26

It seemed that Minty hadn't seen Ophelia in an age; now that both of them were busy mothers and Ophelia was becoming quite a famous fashion designer, there was almost no time for them to talk or email each other anymore.

At the beginning of October, Dominic had managed to wrangle a few weeks off work so they went off the New York for a short break with the kids and there they would visit Deji and Ophelia.

Since they had been married they hadn't wasted time in making babies and already had two children; their son Zachary was two years old and their little girl Charlotte was fast approaching her first birthday. Being a mother was the most wonderful thing that Minty had ever done in her life; not only did the children represent the love that she shared with Dominic, but they also filled her days with endless joy. She was blissfully happy with her husband and had not even thought about another man since they had been together; Dominic himself could not have been prouder of his wife and kids. In his eyes Minty was just another extension of himself just like an arm or a leg and he couldn't imagine life without her.

Upon reaching New York City, the family checked into the Waldorf
Astoria on New York's east side and soon after, Minty dragged
Dominic along to Bloomingdales for some serious retail therapy. The
next day the family paid the Olajuwons a visit at their beautiful
apartment that overlooked Central Park. Minty was beside herself
with excitement as this was the first time that she would see little
Angelica, she was sure that the baby was as beautiful as her mother
was. Once she finally laid eyes on the child Minty knew that she
wasn't far wrong; she greeted her friend Ophelia with a warm hug, it
had been far too long.
'Phils, oh my gosh, I've missed you so much! I can't believe it's
almost been a year since we last saw each other! But sweetheart how
have you been?'
'Oh Minty, I've been fine, just fine. Angelica is great; she's sleeping
through the night now and doesn't give us much trouble. I'm so
happy that she's here; I just love her so much Minty' said Ophelia
excitedly
'I'm sure you do hun, she's just beautiful' Minty replied
Dominic and Deji came in to meet them trailed behind by Zac and
Lottie
'Oh yes she is quite a lovely baby Ophelia, you should be proud' said
Dominic, he then greeted Ophelia with a kiss on the cheek
'Dominic sweetie, how the devil are you? You've been keeping
Minty away from me all this time you naughty boy!' said Ophelia
teasingly
'Huh me? Don't blame me! Now we have the kids I even have to
schedule myself in just to get some quality time with her' Dominic
replied
Deji shook his head and patted Dominic on the back;
'Mate, I know just how you feel. Once the babies come we are just
relegated to an after thought...until they want another one that is!'
They all burst out laughing at his comment, Deji was being cheeky
as usual and he knew it. Suddenly Zac started crying about
something or other so Deji bent down to pick him up trying to soothe
him a little bit;

'What's wrong with you old boy; why you cry?' said Deji in a comical voice

'He's probably just hungry, it's past noon and he usually has his lunch now' said Minty

'Okay then let's feed these kids. Let me go and ask Efua to make us some lunch' replied Ophelia

'Efua?' asked Minty

'Oh yes, I forgot to tell you. I have an au pair so that I could concentrate on *Transatlantic* once Angelica was born. She used to work in my father's house in Nigeria as a maid, but since we got on so well I asked her to come with me to New York to help us with the baby. By the way, she also has son, a two year old named Emmanuel. I'll introduce you to him later as he's probably having a little nap right now' said Opheila

'Oh, okay let's meet Efua then!' said Minty excitedly

Shortly after that, Efua was formally introduced to Dominic, Minty and family and they took to each other instantly; even though she wasn't used to having white people around the home, Efua found the couple very easy going and their children equally as enchanting. After a few days into their stay, Efua was even confident enough to watch all of the kids while both couples went out to see a Broadway play. The children had all fallen asleep by 9pm and Efua virtually had the place all to herself. Ophelia et al wouldn't be back until at least eleven so she did something that she had never done before in her life; she gave her newly made friend Leon Taylor-Grant a call. At 19 years of age, Leon was studying film making at University and would often be seen in the library researching until closing time almost everyday of the working week. They'd met a few weeks back in the central library and Efua found it surprising that he didn't seem to be bothered by her African accent. In fact on the contrary, he was quite mesmerised by it. He'd been watching Efua since she had been visiting the library for a while, until one day he decided to go over and speak to her; Leon was uncontrollably drawn to her and he thought her to be as beautiful as a delicate little flower. She reminded him of a pretty young Jada Pinkett-Smith with her short afro crop and tiny frame; there was also something about her that made him want to protect her from all the horrible things that the world had lurking within it.

In spite of all the flattery and attention he showered on her, Efua was sceptical of why he was interested in her and what he ultimately wanted from their friendship. Since already being burnt by her experience with Jonathan, she was aware of how some men operated and had first hand knowledge of their wicked ways. To this end, Efua was determined to get to know Leon first and find out what his intentions were before they got in too deep. She revealed to him that she had a two year old son at the age of 16 from the beginning, but again that didn't worry him in the slightest and after a little small talk, Efua took Leon's phone number. She dared not give him her own, but she explained to him that her employers were very nice people and she didn't want to take advantage of their hospitality by having random guys call up the apartment. In the end, Leon waited a week for Efua's call and by the time he picked up the phone, he didn't really expect her to be on the other end of the line.

'Hello...hello, can I speak to Leon please?' asked Efua
'Who is this?'
'My name is Efua, I am the girl from the library...do you remember me?'
'Of course I remember you' said Leon teasingly 'I'm just playing wit you girl. But to what to I owe the honor of this call?'
'Oh Leon, hello...I just took the opportunity to call you because my boss has gone out to the theatre; she probably won't be back until around eleven and the kids are already asleep, so I thought that we could just....you know just talk'
'Aight Efua, that's wassup! Trust me I can see us talking all nite long if you'll let it...'

From then on, Efua would find ways of calling Leon every couple of days to talk, even if it was only for a few minutes and over time they slowly built up a relationship. Soon enough Ophelia had an idea that

Efua had got herself a little boyfriend. At this point, she knew that they had to have 'that' talk; not long after Minty and Dominic had left New York for London, she decided to bring up the subject;
'Efua, sit down…we need to talk' said Ophelia
'Yes Ophelia….what's wrong?' replied Efua
'Is there somebody that I should know about? A little friend of yours perhaps? Because I've noticed a phone number that I don't recognize come up on the phone bill quite a lot. Don't worry, the calls are local so they don't cost that much, I am just curious to know who it is'
Efua's heart began to beat like a proverbial drum; what would she say? She decided that since she and Leon were only talking innocently, she would tell Ophelia the truth.
'Opheila, I'm sorry that I didn't tell you but…I met someone in the library; his name is Leon and we're now friends. I didn't want you to think that I was disrespecting you by having a man call the house that's why I've been calling him instead.. I'm sorry if I made you angry by doing so….I didn't really mean to'
Ophelia shook her head; there was nothing wrong with having friends, after all it was healthy for her. She just had to be careful about the young man's main objective.
'Efua sweetheart; I know that he's your friend but I just want you to be careful. What are his intentions with you…does he mean to make you his girlfriend?' asked Ophelia
Efua laughed shyly at this concept; secretly she would love to be Leon's girl but she was too afraid to allow him to even talk about such a subject
'Erm, we haven't talked about that yet, we're still friends'
'But does he like you that way?'
'Umm….I think so Ophelia and I really do enjoy talking to him, but I'm afraid of being with another guy after going through what I did with Emmanuel's father; I just want to get to know Leon before I decide anything'
'Oh Efua, that's very sensible; but then again you were always wiser than your age…does he know that you have a son?'
'Yes, he knows about that; he's been someone I can just talk to about that issue and he hasn't judged me so far'

272

'Well he sounds like a nice guy from what you're saying...tell me how old is Leon and what does he do?'

'He's nineteen and is studying Film making at University; I think he also works at that big shop Saks on the weekend'

'Okay then, Efua...can I ask you to do something for me please? I'd like you to bring Leon here to visit; I want to meet him for myself. You can be friends with whoever you want to be, but since I am still responsible for you; I need to know that you are associating yourself with decent people; maybe Deji can also be there too'

'Yes Ophelia, I will ask him to come by on Friday evening; I think he will be free then'

'Right then, Friday night it is! I look forward to meeting him...'

~~~~

That Friday, Deji and Ophelia met Leon for the first time and found him to be quite a polite yet intelligent young man; he seemed to care for Efua a great deal and for her son too. After meeting him they both felt inclined to give their blessing to the friendship as well as anything else that it may develop into. They maintained that it was far better to be supportive of the relationship as Efua was no longer a child and there was no sense in pretending otherwise. After the father of her first son had ran off leaving her destitute, it was nice to see her with a better guy who would actually be there for her. As time passed, Leon became a very permanent fixture in their lives. Efua herself found that she had fallen in love for the first time, but out fear she stopped short of allowing Leon to consummate their relationship. There were still too many issues left that had not been dealt with and so much more that she held back from him. Maybe someday she would have the courage to tell Leon about her ordeal with Jonathan, but at present it just wasn't the right time.

~~~~

After they had arrived back to London from New York, Minty and Dominic wasted no time in planning their next holiday; they wanted to take a skiing trip without the kids at Klosters in Switzerland for a week. Lady Fortescue-Black had agreed that she would love to take the kids off Minty's hands for a while; due to the fact that they lived in London and Minty's parents in Cheshire, she never did get to see enough of her grandchildren. This would be an opportunity for her to spoil them to her hearts content.

The skiing resort in Kolsters was a favourite of Royals, celebrities and the stinking rich; Prince Charles was known to visit there for his skiing trip at least once a year and when she was alive, there was always a paparazzi frenzy whenever Princess Diana visited along with her two sons Prince William and Prince Harry.
Dominic and Minty booked themselves a luxurious chalet that sat on the top of the mountain side and gave them spectacular views of the ski slopes and surrounding valley. They were both accomplished skiers and during their stay they often raced each other on some of the steepest and most challenging slopes; the only track that Dominic insisted that Minty not veer on to was known as 'the black run.
This infamous stretch on the mountain was unbelievably steep and only the most confident of life time skiers, snowboarders and athletes ever attempted the dangerous run; Dominic had attempted it once before and had ended up with a broken foot for his trouble. Apart from that, the rest of the resort was relatively safe.

It was wonderful to have a few days to themselves again and be able to make love the way they used to before the kids, but Minty still missed her babies terribly. Dominic was good enough company but now that she had children, she didn't feel complete until she could snuggle their little bodies and kiss them goodnight. As she lay down to sleep on the third night of their five day break, Dominic rubbed on her arm to soothe her as if he had read her mind; he then began to make love to her using only the light of the Alpine sky as a guide. They moved on to the thick fur rug in front of the open fire and as Dominic mounted her, the thought of the children were deliciously pushed to the back of Minty's mind. After he had pleasured her for the duration of a seemingly endless orgasm, she got down on her knees while he sat on the leather armchair and proceeded to give him some of the most mind-blowing head she had ever given him before. Minty was the type of woman that believed in being a complete slut for her husband so there was almost nothing that Dominic could watch in a porn flick that she wouldn't do. She knew that he liked her to drown his dick in saliva, so she made it wet and clamped her jaw tightly around it in conjunction with pumping the shaft with firmly with her fist. Dominic stroked her lush blond hair as she serviced him; his beautiful wife could do it just a well as the pros and that's why he could never ever dream of leaving her. Before long they were both exhausted and after her husband came in her mouth; Minty crashed into bed and fell into a blissful sexed out slumber.

The next morning after breakfast, Dominic decided to break some difficult news; since they had enjoyed a wonderful week so far, he thought it best to strike while Minty was in a good mood.
'Sweetheart, I have a little confession to make; now before you fly off the handle please hear me out first. I've been put forward to be assistant partner to the head of European Operations at the firm…and I accepted'
'But that's wonderful! Why would I fly off the handle at that…its great news!'
'Well, it means that I'll have to re-locate to the Munich office indefinitely…I know that you won't want to move to another country, neither is it fair on you hun so I've been able to negotiate an apartment over in Germany, but I will be home with you and the kids on the weekend….Minty?'
Minty sat there fuming silently; she couldn't believe that he had made such an important decision without her, weren't they supposed to be a team?
'Dominic…you didn't even say a word to me? How could you do that….we are supposed to discuss things together first! I tell you everything even down to changing the brand of nappies I buy for the kids. What, do you expect me to just accept that like the 'good little wife' now?'
'Well Minty, I'd hardly compare this to nappies…and I knew that if I

told you that, you'd just be against it. It wasn't an easy decision but I made it for the good of the family and my career. Come on Minty, it's really not so bad…you hardly see me anyway because of work; please sweetheart, try to see the sense in it. I'll be made partner within the next two years if I make this sacrifice now, that's my plan'
He went to rub her hand but she pulled away sharply;
'Well what can I say since you've already made up your mind?'
Minty threw down her napkin and left the breakfast table;
'I'm off to hit the slopes, I just need to think Dominic so don't come to find me, I'll meet you back at the chalet later on'
With that, she stormed off on to the ski lift leaving Dominic trailing in her wake; before he had the chance to follow her, Minty sped off down the slopes on her skis.
In her anger she missed the warning sign that signalled the beginning of the black run, and as fate would have it, that was the last time Dominic would see Minty alive.

By dusk, Minty still wasn't back and the mountain patrol raised the alarm to look for her; Dominic didn't for one second think that she would attempt the black run; he'd already told her that it was much too dangerous. It was only by chance that one of the other skiers found her body splayed out on the rocky mountain terrain below. By then Minty had long since left the land of the living. In her last moments, Minty had struggled to manoeuvre in the harsh terrain and tried to get back to the safer side of the mountain; sadly, once one hit the black run the only way was down. As she tried to jump down on to the next slope, one of her skis got caught on an icy precipice and snapped causing Minty to fall an agonising 200 feet to her death. The official autopsy report declared death by mis-adventure; they had found that when she landed from her drop, the sheer gravity of the fall broke her neck on impact and the surrounding shattered bone fragments severed her spinal cord which caused irreversible damage to her brain. Tragically, it was also revealed that she was in the early stages of pregnancy for her third child; Dominic was still in shock and was trying to take in the enormity of what had happened as he flew back to London with Minty's body in the cargo hold. The guilt that he felt was indescribable. As he walked back on to British soil once the plane had touched down, Dominic emerged from it a broken man; he blamed Minty's death on himself solely as a result of his foolish male pride.

The following funeral for the young Lady Araminta Parker-Graves was an unspeakably heartbreaking affair; the calm silence of the church was broken by the sound of Dominic's wrenching sobs. He had lost the love of his life forever and she had not long turned 23 years of age; he looked across at his young children, Zac and Lottie and more tears rained down onto his face. They sat with their grandmother, not really knowing what was going on; only Zac was old enough to know that he wanted his mummy but she never came back.

Ophelia and Deji had flown over immediately from New York to pay their respects as had Sandra and Jonathan; the rest of the Launceston girls were also in attendance still bewildered and grief-stricken by the sudden nature of the tragedy. Ronke, who now lived in London, accompanied Ophelia to the funeral for moral support. Minty had been Ophelia's best friend for as long as Ronke could remember and she could only imagine how devastated her cousin must be; there was also the fate of the two small children that Minty had left behind to consider. Ronke wondered what would happen to them and how on earth Dominic would be able to cope. As they left the church, she found Dominic standing alone by Minty's grave as if he was rooted to the spot; she decided to go over and lend him a few words of comfort;

'Dominic, I just wanted to tell you how sorry I am for your loss. I myself just lost my husband last year so I kind of know what you're going through. Please, if you need someone to talk to don't hesitate to call me' said Ronke and slipped him her contact details on a business card 'you don't have to speak right now…just don't forget that you have a friend'

Ronke started to walk away but then Dominic gestured for her to stay;

'No don't go away, thanks so much for this…umm aren't you Ophelia's cousin?'

'Yes I am…I'm Ronke Olajuwon. I've actually just moved to London recently to make a fresh start after my late husband committed suicide in Nigeria'

'…I think I know the story…he used to beat you up right? And was he gay?'

'Yes, that's right exactly. I still blame myself for his death though…I decided to expose the fact that he was gay on DVD in front of our parents. It seemed like a good idea for revenge at the time, but I didn't mean for him to kill himself. I just wanted him to leave me alone and stop abusing me…that was all'

'Ronke don't blame yourself….I keep blaming myself because if I didn't take my stupid promotion then my wife would probably still be alive today. What you did was only in the spirit of survival…'

They walked on and continued to talk about each of their experiences. Eventually, since they were both united in grief Ronke and Dominic struck up a great friendship. He desperately needed a shoulder to cry on and somebody to just listen; it came to be that Ronke was just that.

In time, they began to have coffee together just to talk or sometimes spend lazy Sundays together watching Zac and Lottie play in Hyde Park. Theirs was an easy friendship; neither expected anything from the other, but the tragic nature of their circumstances made the growing bond between them become even stronger.

It wasn't until Ronke announced to him that she was going to spend some time with Bijou in Milan that Dominic realised that he had fallen for her. Similarly, while she was in Italy Ronke felt as if a part of her was missing with each passing day that she was away from him; as testament to this, she sent him daily emails and they spent the evenings talking endlessly over the phone.

Once she got back to London, Ronke couldn't believe who was waiting for her at the terminal Dominic was standing there with a bunch of a dozen red roses and a car to take her home. He'd decided that he'd lied to himself for too long about loving her and that life was for living; Minty certainly wouldn't have wanted him to be moping over her death forever and his children also desperately needed a mother.

As she approached him, Dominic met Ronke with a warm embrace; 'Ronke, I've missed you so much…I thought you'd like these' said Dominic passing the flowers over to her.

'Dominic, they are beautiful! Do you know what?'

'What sweetheart'

'No man has ever bought me flowers…so that means that you have the honor of being my first'

'Really? I wouldn't believe you if I didn't already know that you wouldn't lie to me. But let me just cut to the chase; I think I'm in love with you…can you handle that?'

'Well only if you can handle the fact that I'm in love with you too…or shall I say lust? Honestly Dominic, it's been so long since I've last been with a man and I'm ready for you to fuck my brains out'

'Well… it would be very un-gentlemanly of me to refuse such a beautiful lady that request; just say the word and I will happily oblige'

'…Dominic, I just did!'

After putting the kids to bed later that evening Dominic and Ronke did what had been long coming; as they made love passionately, nothing else needed to be said. Dominic cried for the pain of losing his dear Minty. He never dreamed for one second that someone else would take her place, but somehow in her passing he found that love had shined upon once again in his lifetime when he met Ronke. She kind of sensed why he was crying and kissed him even harder in an attempt to ease the pain; before she'd known him, Ronke didn't realise that she could fall in love so hard.

He made it so easy to love him and was everything she'd been searching for in a man all her life, only she didn't know it until then. She knew from that moment that she would be there for Dominic for as long as he needed her to be and to her surprise his children were also beloved to her as they were in essence, another beautiful part of him. Incidentally, Ronke didn't really want to have any children of her own children anyway so luckily, she had landed on her feet in this situation by gaining a ready made family.

Once they had finished and were getting ready for bed, Dominic realised that he didn't want Ronke to ever go back home again; he had already lost his wife and he would do everything to make sure that he didn't lose her as well;

'Ronke, I know that this is sudden but from everything that has happened I want to hold on to whatever little piece of happiness that I can…sweetheart will you marry me?'

Ronke sighed a deep sigh and looked into her lovers eyes; she would love nothing more in the world but to marry him but it was much too soon.

'Dominic…I….I don't know what to say! I want to say yes…but baby, it's too soon. Minty hasn't even been gone a year yet and you want to get married again…it wouldn't be right hun…not to her memory. Also don't forget about her family; they might feel a way about it. I'm saying a provisional yes to you but not now…let's wait, but at least you'll be safe in the knowledge that I'm your wife in everything apart from name. I mean I literally live here now!'

'I know Ronke…but I don't want to wait. I love so much you can't you see that?'

'Dominic please…this is tough for me too. Please respect my wishes and let's just wait…baby you know that I'm making sense. Don't make me feel even worse than I already do about this…'

'Ok madam….whatever you say! But I won't let you go back home…you're staying here with us!'

And with that, he kissed her again and made love to her but this time with a new found intensity. After going on until it was almost daybreak, they finally fell asleep in each others arms.

Chapter 27

Ophelia woke up to the intoxicating sound of the Muezzin calling people to prayer from the nearby mosque. Dubai was an amazing paradox; it was a stifling mix of piety and sin. On one side there was the devout Islamic community who observed the five times daily prayers and walked around in elegant black or white robes and on the other was the influx of overindulged westerners that consisted mainly of Americans and the British. The place had become a boom town, and had changed so much since Ophelia had last visited on an Ambassadorial visit with her father over ten years back.

Incidentally, Khadijah had invited Ophelia and Deji over to her palace for a few weeks because she was terribly lonely. Since marrying Hassan just over three years prior; Khadijah was still struggling to adjust to life as an Arabian wife.

There were certain freedoms that she took for granted while she lived with her father in Saudi Arabia. There was also the fact that she had spent most of her upbringing in overseas countries, namely England, the States and Switzerland which in turn made her accustomed to a

281

very different way of life. It wasn't that her husband restricted her in anyway; it was a lot to do with the society's expectations of her in general and the fact that she had a dragon for a mother-in-law didn't help.

Hassan's mother had been living with them since his father had passed two years prior and she was the ultimate Arab alpha mom from hell. If there was anything that Queen Rabia could interfere in, she would get stuck into it nose deep; this situation was made worse by the fact that Khadijah was still yet to produce a child.

Hassan himself had the patience of a saint and continued to reassure Khadijah that she would become with child when Allah deemed it fit; in spite of his mother's incessant rants, he loved her too much and thus had no intention of taking a second wife. Still, Khadijah could not help but to think that his position would only last for an appointed time.

Ophelia's heart went out to her friend; she herself knew what it was like to have trouble conceiving, but from what she had observed in the palace, Khadijah was under an extreme amount of stress. On the first few days of their visit, she accompanied Khadijah on her daily shopping trips and discovered that her friend would just buy lots of useless junk much like a crack addict that just needed a fix. As a result of this, Ophelia concluded that Khadijah was binge shopping in order to mask the pain of a more deep seated problem.

Ophelia walked into the luxurious black Sicilian marble decorated en suite bathroom to clean her teeth and take a shower; she could see that no expense had been spared in furnishing the palace. She was still yet to test out the massive Jacuzzi bath that was showcased on a higher platform and had three steps up before one could get in it; the bath was also made out of black marble and had 24 carat gold taps to compliment the look. Somebody had thought that pristine white towels with black and gold monograms would look good against the black marble and Ophelia was inclined to agree with them. To get an idea of how big the bathroom and the surrounding palace was; Deji and Ophelia's bedroom suite was situated on the west wing of the house so it was a 15 minute walk if she wanted to visit Khadijah in her own bedroom over in the east wing. To this end, they made arrangements to meet in the central breakfast room every morning and then plan their day from there.

Deji was already soaping himself down inside the huge shower closet; the place could have easily catered for the bathing needs of at least ten people. After brushing her teeth, Ophelia joined her husband in the shower smiling at him lustily; watching him slide the soap suds across his hard body made her go crazy every single time. Once he'd washed his face, Deji realised that she was in there staring at him and laughed; two could play that that game.

'Why are you just staring at me like that baby? I feel as vulnerable as a stripper right now...' said Deji jokingly

'Oh do stop Deji, and I'm not just saying this because you're my hubby, but you are a very sexy man...with an equally sexy body! I'll never get fed up of telling you that'

Ophelia walked up to him and when they were skin to skin she whispered in his ear for maximum effect 'and it's not just the water in here that's making me wet right now' she then stretched up to kiss him and at the same time started to stroke his dick with her slippery hand. Her excitement peaked when she realised that he was already hard as a rock, Ophelia wanted him to ram his steel into her pussy that instant;

'Deji, I.. .' before she could finish he slid two fingers into her open mouth;

'Shh...I know exactly what you want, so why don't you shut the fuck up and let me give it to you'

Ophelia gasped audibly as he flipped her legs up on to his hips and pressed her up against the mosaic tiled shower wall; the feeling of the water raining down on them as he thrusted away made her feel even more aroused. She also loved the fact that Deji was so strong that when he pulled away from the wall, he was able to bounce her up and down on his dick in mid-air; as she moaned loudly with pleasure Deji didn't dare stop, he knew his wife well enough to know that she would be coming soon.

They eventually ended up on the wet floor and after Ophelia had climaxed until her pussy ached, Deji finally allowed himself to release his cream into her; little did they know that he had just planted the seed that would result in the making of their second child.

Later on that day, Khadijah and Ophelia left the men behind to go and get some serious beauty therapy on; they both got a leg and bikini wax, *Jurlique* facials, deep tissue massage, eyebrow threading and then finally a luxuriously time consuming manicure and pedicure. As the nail technicians worked their magic on them, the two ladies had a heartfelt talk;

'Khadijah today has been great…I feel so pampered but I totally wouldn't have the time to do this every week like you do! You're quite the spoiled princess hun and I like it' exclaimed Ophelia

'Oh Phils, it's only because I have nothing to do all day, it's better than staying in the house with that witch! Trust me…if you were me you'd be out every single day! I would love to have a job, but all that is frowned upon over here…people would think badly of my husband and just gossip about us all day…I can just imagine them saying 'why does she have to work' and 'what a disgrace, my husband would never allow me to work' blah, blah, blah! You get the picture…and the last time I checked Phils, you were a Princess too…'

'Yeah I know but…I'm not as spoiled as you…not that there is anything wrong with being spoiled. Hassan really loves you doesn't he?'

'Yes he does but I'm scared that if I don't get pregnant soon then he'll start looking for a second wife…oh Ophelia I just couldn't handle it if he did!'

'Is that why you keep shopping like a madwoman? Khadijah…I do believe that you're a shopaholic! But just to drop in my two cents, I think you two should take a vacation away from here…it might help you relax because you seem really stressed right now'

'Really? Is it that obvious?'

'Honey as obvious as the nose on your face'

'Ok, there's no need to be that blunt! But where would you suggest that we go then?'

'Umm...*the Cotton House* in the Maldives is great...it's secluded and comfortable. Minty and Dominic actually had their honeymoon there and Deji and I have visited a couple of times....gosh, I'm still getting over the fact that dear Minty is gone'

'I know...me too; she was gone too soon you know. Just talking about it is making me sad! Her memorial is due in the next few months, that will make it a year since she passed...time has really flown'

Ophelia took a moment as she was choked up at the mere mention of the loss of her best friend; she knew that she had to keep living for the sake of her family, but there just wasn't anyone she knew alive that could take Minty's place.

'I know Khadijah...I just hope that I can finally come to terms with her death in time, at least Dominic seems to have bounced back. Did you know that he's now dating my cousin Ronke?'

'Really? Well that's a turn up for the books! I would have never imagined those two together in a million years, not to mention that Ronke is a black woman! What must the toffs have to say about that?'

'Ha! I don't think that Dominic really gives a damn and from what Ronke told me when we last spoke, he is just waiting a few more months then he wants them to get married...'

'Wow Ophelia...but after what they've both been through I don't think anyone can begrudge them happiness...even if they are from completely different backgrounds. But back to me....I'll tell Hassan about taking a little vacation tonight...I'm sure that he will like the idea...'

~~~~

Efua's 18th birthday came and went; shortly after that Deji and Ophelia went off on their two week vacation in Dubai. Emmanuel was no longer a baby and had also celebrated his 3rd birthday; Angelica was already past her first year. Efua was extremely honoured that her bosses trusted her to look after both her son and Angelica by herself; Ophelia had confided in her that apart from her own mother, Efua was the only one that she could ever leave her daughter alone with. Ophelia's admission touched Efua greatly and vowed to never betray her Mistress's trust and guard Angelica's safety with her life if the need arose.

Another milestone that she had achieved that year was gaining her G.E.D; Efua couldn't believe that just three years back she could barely read but now she could understand books on advanced calculus. After much discussion with Ophelia and Deji, it was decided that Efua would study online for a degree qualification in Mathematics; it was funny to her but after all these years she'd never noticed that even when her English was poor, numbers had always made sense to her. Thankfully, the opportunity that Ophelia had given her would help her to make a good living out of that ability. Her only wish would be being able to actually attend a University, however with Emmanuel and Angelica as her main priorities, she would just have to carry out her study in what ever way she could.

Incidentally, Efua's relationship with Leon was now stronger than ever and while her bosses were away in Dubai, she allowed him to come over and stay every night.

He had been patient with her all this time regarding her aversion to actually having sex with him but one night it all came to a head Leon wanted to know what the hold up was;

'Efua honey….I don't wanna seem like I'm pressuring you or anything but I just wanna know…do you actually find me sexually attractive? I mean even when we kiss you pull away from me after a while and a dude can only take rejection for so long ya know'

Efua sighed and in her mind she knew that the time was right for him to know the whole truth;

'Leon, I can honestly say, it's not you….I do find you very attractive but my past is holding me back. Remember when I told you that Emmanuel's father ran off? Well that wasn't the whole truth….it all started when I turned 14…'

Efua then proceeded to tell Leon the whole story of Jonathan's abuse and how she came to be pregnant with Emmanuel;

'Well that's it….so now you know why I'm afraid of sex…I don't wanna go through all that again'

As the tears of shame rolled down her cheeks, Leon was boiling up inside. He wanted to snap Jonathan's neck in two.

'Efua…baby look at me, it wasn't your fault okay? I still love you and we can make love when ever you're ready. But isn't he Ophelia's daddy?'

'Yes but she has no idea that Emmanuel is her half brother'

'Honey…I don't think you'll have closure thought until you at least confront him or tell the police…it's not right for him to get away with raping a minor'

'Leon I can't, I just can't do it to Ophelia!'

'Efua…you need to do it, if not for you then for you son. He has a right to some of that man's millions and you will forever be damaged if you feel that you can't get justice'

'I don't know but let me speak to Ophelia first…I owe her that much…just let me think'

'Okay baby…take your time and I hope that you'll let me make love to you someday and help you forget that bastard…'

'Leon…I think I'm ready…tonight'

'For real? Don't go getting a brother's hopes up now! But let me see if I have some protection on me' Leon checked his wallet and found nothing 'well at least you know that I ain't been cheating on ya! Ok baby, imma bounce to the corner store and grab some aight'

With that he kissed her on her forehead and went off to buy the condoms; upon his return to the apartment, Efua was already waiting for him and she had changed into a silky robe with some slippers.

'Oh, I see that you're ready for me' said Leon

Efua giggled shyly and sat down on the side of the bed and he sat down next to her; he then kissed her tiny pink lips pulling on them a little;

'Are you sure you're ready for this…it's okay if you still wanna wait you know'

'Yes Leon…a year is long enough for you to wait and I need to feel you close to me too, please let's do it'

'Okay baby and don't worry, I'll be very gentle with you'

They kissed for a while then Leon started to lick one of her nipples slowly, and the sweetness of his hot tongue was excruciatingly tantalising; she began to feel the familiar feeling of getting wet but thankfully this time she was with somebody that she actually loved. When he finally entered her, Efua almost panicked as the memories of being violated came flooding back; she closed her eyes tightly and her body became tense; Leon sensed her discomfort and immediately stopped in his tracks

'Honey what's wrong…do you wanna stop this? It's okay, maybe it's too soon for you'

Efua looked up into the eyes of her beloved and knew that there was nothing to fear, she had to get through this and she would be dammed if she would allow Jonathan steal her happiness this time around; Efua let her body relax and kissed Leon deeply;

'No baby, I'll be okay…I just freaked out for a second, that's all. Please continue…I like what you're doing to me'

'Okay sweetie, but if you're uncomfortable just say the word aight?'

Efua nodded and Leon stared moving again slowly until she could take no more of the sweet torture;

'Faster…please go faster…' said Efua

Leon obliged her and she arched her back in response; what he was doing was making her feel beautiful; eventually she forgot her prior uneasiness completely relaxing into his seduction and by the time they had finally finished the act she actually almost reached a climax.

'Did you….'

'No I didn't come, but I nearly did…I'm sure that I will next time though. Don't worry, it's nothing to do with you, it's me and I have to try harder to let go'

'Aww Efua don't even mention it baby…considering the circumstances, you did great'

Efua slept easier that night, it was as if a weight had been lifted from her shoulders by sharing her pain with Leon. She had finally made the first step towards recovery at last.

~~~~

Khadijah felt as if *the Cotton House* was already working its magic;

from the minute that they had landed on the island she had been overcome with the most overwhelming feeling of calm. Hassan also noticed this and commented on it; it was great to finally have his wife back. The only wedge between them was the subject of Hassan's worsening gambling habit; Khadijah had found out not long before they left Dubai and decided to bring it up while they were on the vacation;

'Hassan there's no point in trying to making it sound less worse than it is….I know how bad it has become! I mean how can you think that blowing \$10 million in one night is normal? Look you know me…I will be honest with you; I'm your wife and if we can't be honest with each other then there's no point!'

'Habibi, now you sound like my mother; for God sake don't nag me like that! I know that I have a problem and I'm dealing with it …are you happy now?'

'Well not really; why do you do it when you know that gambling is even forbidden in Islam. What about your spirituality? Have you thought of that…'

'Ok then, since we're being honest…I'll tell you what this is all about. Remember that I told you that my dad really pushed me hard to succeed?'

'Yes…you said that if it wasn't for him them you wouldn't be what you are today'

'Good, but I forgot to add that he was very pushy, even more so than my mother. I was always expected to come top of my class, which I always did, but unfortunately the pressure that he put under me drove me into developing a horrible gambling habit. I know that Islam forbids gambling…but I guess I am just a man and I am weak!'

'No Hassan, you aren't weak! My husband is not a weak man…you just need to see a professional to help you deal with all of these issues. Please promise me that you'll see somebody'

Khadijah looked at her husband with desperation; couldn't he see that she was right?

'Please Hassan, you are too good for this to smear your good character…I don't think your mother being around is helping your situation either'

'Ha ha!' said Hassan laughing 'don't I know it! Once we get back to Dubai, I am going to tell her in no uncertain terms that she needs to go back to the rest of the family in Saudi. I have let her interfere in my life for too long to the extent that she stressed you out. Do you know how ashamed I was when you told me that Opheila pointed that out? Deji also noticed and mentioned the same thing to me when we were at the races with Sheikh Abdul Khan; I was just glad that Deji had the tact to say it once Abdul Khan had gone away for a few minutes'

Khadijah threw her arms around her husband in delight;

'Do you really mean it? Oh Hassan I love you! I simply love you sweetie!'

'I love you too Habibi…let me show you how much…'

By the time they landed back in Dubai, Khadijah was already pregnant with her first child; it would be confirmed in a few weeks but her female intuition told her that something inside her had changed at the Cotton House. Hassan came through on his word and five months later he had completely stopped the gambling; the prospect of being a new father filled him with a new sense of responsibility. It would seem that his beautiful wife had made him realise that there was so much more in life to live for.

Chapter 28

The end of the summer approached and Angelica was getting close to her second birthday; Deji thought that it would be a good idea to take her back home to celebrate it with her grandparents and extended family. Ophelia instantly warmed to the idea; she was six months along with their second child and the equatorial heat of Africa was all lot more desirable to her at that point than the smog filled stickiness of New York City. It had been that long since they had been back home and Ophelia also thought it a good idea for Efua and Emmanuel to tag along too; it was simply a great opportunity for everybody to catch up with their respective people.

While Efua was packing the luggage, her son kept on asking her an endless barrage of questions; she loved him to bits but she couldn't help to think that he was a lot less annoying when he couldn't talk at all. She guessed that as with all kids he was going through a phase and would hopefully grow out of it. Angelica's temperament on the other hand was exactly as her given name implied; from the way that she sat down quietly to eat to the near cherubic features on her face, anyone could tell that this little baby was sent down from heaven with magic sewn into the very fabric of her skin. Now that she was able to form a few words she had become even more enchanting; Efua's heart melted when Angelica called her 'mama' but thankfully, Ophelia wasn't at home at the time so she had the opportunity to nip that in the bud.

Incidentally, things were going great between herself and Leon and she could definitely see her future with him. Hopefully once she had completed her degree course they could start making some plans. Efua wondered what her mother would make of him; she sincerely hoped that her mom didn't have her heart set on her marrying a Nigerian man. Mummy would just have to understand that sometimes in life, things didn't always go according to plan.

~~~

A burgeoning sense of fear crept into Efua as the plane touched down in Lagos. As well as going to Africa to meet her family; she was also faced with the reality that she was back in the land of her abuser. She still hadn't told Ophelia of her shameful past with Jonathan and to be quite honest Efua didn't know when it would ever be the right time. After all that Ophelia had done for her, it seemed like a slap in the face to just bring up the subject of her molestation. Ophelia sensed Efua's discomfort and wondered what was wrong; surely she should have been looking forward to seeing her mother in the village right now, but as they reached the Emeka-Phillips compound, Efua's uneasiness seemed to be reaching a peak. Ophelia decided to find out what was wrong with her;

'Efua are you okay hun? You look quite pale…do you feel sick or something?'

'It's okay Ophelia; I'll be fine; maybe it was something that I ate on the plane'

'Are you sure?'

'Yes, I'm quite sure…thanks Ophelia'

Ophelia decided to leave it alone for now and she was sure that she would find out later; she only hoped that Leon had got that girl pregnant. Efua was destined for much better things and didn't need to be held back by another baby.

As they entered the house the maids came out to greet them and Efua saw the familiar faces of her ex colleagues light up with happiness; at that point, she was glad that she had brought them a few clothes and shoes as gifts even if they were Ophelia's old ones. Only a few years ago she herself only had some flimsy dresses to clothe her so her heart went out to all the ladies that still worked in the house.

Once they had settled down into their rooms, Ophelia and Deji went off to have a lovely dinner with her parents. Efua on the other hand, shared a simple meal with her old friends in the maid's quarters. Afterwards when she put Emmanuel to sleep in the old room that she used to share with three other maids, Efua couldn't believe the type of conditions that she had been forced to live in. The makeshift mattress bed on the floor was even more threadbare than ever and the lone mirror on the wall was misty and faded due to its age. It was almost like being in another world and in all honesty Efua didn't want Emmanuel to sleep there; the only thing was that if she did ask Ophelia to move them, the other maids would think that she had turned into a snob.

At that thought, she decided that a few weeks in there wouldn't kill her son and he probably wouldn't remember in a few years anyway. It was getting quite late at 10 o'clock, so after she had settled him into bed, Efua changed into a light dress and set about helping the other ladies with some of the house work.

Incidentally, she didn't t really need to help out as her post had already been filled by another young girl who could not have been more than thirteen, but Efua did so anyway as a sense of camaraderie with the rest of the maids. Efua wondered if Jonathan had already started bothering the young thirteen year old Charity yet and while she was ironing some of the laundry, she asked Octavia about her replacement.

'Octavia, how Charity dey find am for dis house? De *Oga* like am?' asked Efua who was feeling quite strange to be speaking broken English again;

'Humph, Efua things no dey change-o! They no dey change....*Oga*
dey like Charity too much. You go see later dis night ehn, he go call
am for mosquito net; but Efua, you see dis two eyes wey for my
face' Octavia pointed to her eyes in order to emphasise the point
'dem dey see everything wey dey happen in dis house. Charity be too
small for de *Oga* I dey pray he no go damage am one of dis
days....no be small-o'
Efua sighed audibly, so Jonathan was still up to his old tricks; why
on earth could she have imagined that any thing had changed;
Octavia's next revelation almost made her drop the pile of sheets that
she was working on;
'We no want another Emmanuel case *sha*'
'Octavia, so you know am?'
'Hum! Efua...I dey know am since day one...let me tell am for you;
every two years like dis, *Oga* dey bring a new small maid for this
house. You no be the only one, bet all de past one *Oga* make am take
abortion. The girl before dey take abortion bet she nearly don die
finish, so you be the only one wey dey born pikin for the *Oga*'
'Na true sha Octavia? Anyway, thank you, I no know all dis
information before dis night wey you dey tell me...so it no be just
me'
'Bet Emmanuel be fine boy...he go read school in America? *Shea*
Ophelia go allow am?'
'I tink say she go allow am, Ophelia no be like de father and Mr Deji
too...they be nice people *sha*'
'Okay...na good for you anyway'
They continued to chat about Efua's life overseas and how things
were in Nigeria generally and after they were done with the
housework, they both went off to bed.

Just as Octavia had said, Charity was called up to pull the mosquito
nets down and didn't come down to sleep until way past midnight;
incidentally Sandra had left for a night vigil at her church and would
not be back until the next morning. She had asked Deji and Ophelia
to come along with her but the politely declined citing the fact that
they were jetlagged as an excuse. Sandra had become increasingly

religious of late but Jonathan refused to have anything to do with the Christian fanatics that she was involving herself with, he wouldn't forbid his wife from attending Church but he would be dammed if he was going to accompany her to a stupid night vigil.

The next day while Efua was helping to prepare the evening's meal for the family, she ran across Jonathan sitting alone in the backyard; she meant to avoid him but as the head of the household there was no way that she could just walk by and ignore him. Efua quickly took whatever she needed out of the vegetable store and mumbled a quick greeting to Jonathan;
'Good afternoon sir' said Efua walking away quickly
'Hello Efua…come back here. I want to talk to you or don't you want to talk to me anymore now that you are Americanized? Don't forget if it wasn't for me you would still be a lowly maid living under the stairs of my house'
'No sir, it's not that I don't want to talk to you…I just don't want any problems and I'm trying to keep my head down that's all…I don't mean to be rude at all'
'Hmm…I see that you can actually put sentences together as well now, Ophelia has really made you feel as if you're somebody hasn't she? But anyway…listen to me Efua, the madam is going to Church again later this evening at seven so I want you to come to my office at seven fifteen do you understand…we need to catch up on lost time. Just for old time's sake'
'No Sir…I can't do that! I won't…'
Jonathan jumped up and towered over her menacingly;
'What do you mean that you won't? You won't what?'
He then grabbed her by the arm with a vice like grip; squeezing until he almost cut off her circulation;
'Seven fifteen, in my office, without fail'
Jonathan let go and began to walk off towards the house, but not before delivering his parting shot;
'And don't you dare be late…or you will regret it'
Efua had to quickly stop herself from crying; what on earth would she do! How could she escape him?

As the time approached, Efua decided to stay in the maid's room.
There was no way that he would come down there to get her and if
Octavia said he was calling for her then she could pretend she was
and refuse to leave the room. When the clock hit 7.45 pm, Efua
thought she was safe and he had forgotten about the arrangement;
suddenly she heard a loud noise at the door. To her horror it was
Jonathan and it seemed that Octavia was trying to stop him from
coming in the room.

'Octavia! I said let me in to this room right now! Efua….come out of
there!' said Jonathan loudly

Efua jumped up alarmed; she looked back at Emmanuel and he
stirred a little, it would be better for her to follow Jonathan upstairs
to his office rather than let the noise disturb her son. She steeled
herself and walked over to the door. Before she left, Efua asked
Octavia to keep an eye on her son;

'Octavia…it's okay, please I beg make you dey watch Emmanuel'

And with that, she left with Jonathan for his office; this time around
though Efua intended to fight back. He wasn't going to walk all over
her anymore.

Once in his office, Jonathan sat down on the leather couch and
spread his legs; sickeningly, he gestured for Efua to come over to
kneel on the floor between them. She shook her head firmly and
stayed by the door not moving an inch further.

'No Jonathan…no more of that; I told you that I won't do it! Can't
you see that things have changed? I have grown up now and I know
that what you did to me is wrong; I won't let you abuse me anymore!
No more!' exclaimed Efua

As a sinister twist, Jonathan started to laugh at her; *who the hell does
Efua Chikwe think she is?* he thought. It was really laughable to him
that she was trying to dictate what was going to happen; he would
just have to show her who the boss in the house was.

'What, do you think that you actually have a say in what's going on?
Efua I'm trying to make it easy for you…and you already know me, I
have my needs and if you don't give me what I want then I will take
it! And don't even think of running to Opheila because she will
definitely listen to me when I tell her that you're a little whore' spat

296

Jonathan with venom; he then lunged at Efua, grabbed her arms and
pushed her down onto the couch. His eyes were like that of a
madman and at that point she knew that he was about to rape her; as
Jonathan pressed on top of her and unzipped his pants Efua's
courage kicked into motion and she slammed her foot hard into his
groin. She didn't hear anything after that because she just kept
running; by the time she reached Ophelia and Deji's door, Efua was
crying and in a hysterical state.

Deji was giving Opheila a nice relaxing foot massage when he heard
Efua at the door, he ran over to open the door and find out what the
commotion was;
'Oh my gosh Efua, what's the matter! Calm down and tell me what it
is…'
'Please sir, please Deji I need to speak to Ophelia about it! I can't tell
you!'
'What…Efua I'm concerned about you; why can't you tell me and
anyway in Ophelia's condition, I don't want to have her worry too
much about anything'
'I'm sorry Deji, I can't explain right now, but I have to tell Ophelia
first'
Deji didn't like it, but since he trusted Efua he let her into speak to
his wife alone;
'Okay Efua, but please try not to cry ok…whatever it is, I'm sure it
can be dealt with'
'Thank you Deji, I really appreciate that' Efua replied
She then ran to Ophelia and broke down at her feet; Ophelia was
alarmed to say the least but she still tried to calm the poor girl down
'Efua, what's going on? Please don't tell me that you're pregnant…'
'No, not that Ophelia….I…I've just been attacked by your father; he
tried to rape me, only it's not the first time…'
'You said what? My father did what? Efua, you'd better run that by
me again…' said Ophelia bewildered
'There's more to it than that…to be honest Ophelia, there's so much
that I've been keeping from you'
'Well you better spill it now….'

297

Efua then proceeded to explain the ongoing saga of her abuse at the hands of Jonathan, culminated by the evening's recent event. Once Efua was done telling her story, Ophelia was open mouthed with shock and still struggling to take everything in;

'Efua, if what you're saying is true, then I'm going to need you to repeat everything that you just said in front of him! I don't know if I can believe it otherwise, I mean you're telling me that my dad is a child molester and a rapist! That is a very serious allegation so I need to see you say this to him face to face'

Ophelia stood up after that and made her way towards the door; Efua followed behind her when suddenly out of nowhere, Sandra walked into the room. She looked as if she was on a mission and immediately asked about what was going on;

'Ophelia, what's going on? I just saw your father bent over on the floor in pain; he wouldn't tell me what was wrong….Efua, do you have something to do with this?' said Sandra

At that point Efua's senses peaked; did this mean that Sandra knew something about herself and Jonathan?

'Mummy, Efua just told me something very disturbing and to be quite frank, I need to ask Daddy about it because I am just completely flabbergasted by what she's just said' said Ophelia

'Well, what did you say Efua?' asked Sandra firmly and instinctively, Efua knew that Sandra was staring her down in an attempt to intimidate her. Unfortunately for Sandra, but there was no way that Efua would back down now; even if she had to make enemies in the process, she was just tired of all the lies and deceit.

'I told Ophelia that your husband has sexually abused me since I turned 14 and that Emmanuel is her half-brother. Jonathan even tried to rape me in his office just now, but this time I managed to fight back and run away! I'm sorry that it has to come out like this but I am telling you nothing but the raw truth…'

'Truth? Efua did you say truth? Since when have you started to let such vicious lies come out of your mouth? All the men around here even talk about you letting them take turns with them; so what are you talking about being raped! Just stop lying you pathetic little whore!'

298

'I'm not lying Sandra…let's just go to your husband and see if he will lie when I bring out Emmanuel's birth certificate!'

'Don't you dare bother my husband with such rubbish! Ophelia please stay out of this okay…you don't need to deal with this at all. I will speak to you father, just get that whore out of my house!'

With that, Sandra stormed out of the room and went off to find Jonathan.

She eventually found him still in the study, but this time he was drinking a glass of Scotch; Sandra walked into the room and shut the door behind her.

'You stupid bastard! So my suspicions were true? You finally managed to impregnate one of your little whores ehn? After everything I have done to keep this family together, you couldn't keep your stupid little dick in your pants….and why the hell didn't you make her abort it!'

'Oh please Sandra…if you were doing your duty as a wife then I wouldn't need all of these girls to quench my thirst! The last one that I made have an abortion nearly died, so I just wanted to avoid getting blood on my hands that's all. You're one to talk about keeping this family together; is that what forcing our daughter into an arranged marriage was? Yes Sandra, King Olajuwon told me how you hounded him for little over a year to find out if Deji was interested in taking Ophelia as a wife. Thank God that they actually like each other…I'm sure that you would have made her marry him, even at the cost of her own happiness! Honestly Sandra, you're unbelievable coming in here judging me…'

'Don't you dare give me that rubbish you stupid man! Left to you, our only daughter would have married some uneducated black idiot with no heritage! I did what was best for her and this family; I know what is best for my daughter…Ophelia doesn't even need to think; she can just carry on living her perfect little life completely oblivious to that…she never was as decisive as Kelechi anyway so her life always needed some direction and as her mother it is my job to give it!'

Ophelia had heard enough; she'd been listening at the door because her intuition told her that Efua wasn't lying. As she opened the door and walked into the room, Jonathan looked at her blankly; had she heard what they'd said?

'Mother….father…how could you? How could you both?' said Ophelia; the devastation was absolute, her father had always been her hero throughout her life and this was the most horrible secret that she could have ever imagined him to have. Shocked and disappointed, Ophelia turned to run out of the room in tears.

'Ophelia please….I can explain' pleaded Jonathan as he ran behind her in desperation; it was almost unbearable for him to have let his precious daughter down so badly.

'Please Ophelia, I'm sorry…I didn't mean to hurt you' he protested Efua, who had also been listening, snapped at that very moment; 'You didn't mean to hurt? So you didn't mean to hurt when you took my virginity when I had barely turned 14, or was that when you forced your penis into my mouth? What do you call that, Jonathan?'

Jonathan took stock of the faces around him with shame. There was nothing he could possibly say to Efua at that point; the shit had hit the fan and his beloved daughter now knew how much of a monster he really was. Consequently, not long after Efua had spoken, the damage that had been done hit him full force and he collapsed on the floor clutching his heart; Dr Emeka-Phillips was having a major heart attack.

'Daddy, daddy please! Efua please call Deji and Kelechi! Somebody get a doctor!' screamed Ophelia

She didn't notice in the commotion that her mother calmly walked out of the room; Since Sandra's world had already collapsed, she saw no point in trying to save his pathetic little life.

When Deji and Kelechi finally turned up, they both carried an unconscious Jonathan to the waiting car and drove him to the hospital; he never did regain consciousness again and passed away peacefully in his sleep early the next morning.

The most painful thing for Ophelia was not being able to say goodbye; her father may have had some deep flaws, but she still loved him dearly. It was an eye opener for her however, to find that her mother didn't even come to the hospital to see him. It was as if she was actually praying for him to die.

~~~

Before they returned from the hospital; Efua packed Emmanuel's things as well as her own in their suitcase. She guessed that she would no longer be welcome in the house or even in Ophelia and Deji's Manhattan apartment. Hopefully sooner rather than later, she would be able to call Leon and let him know what was going on; Efua started to prepare herself for the fact that they would not be seeing each other for a very long time.

To this end, Ophelia came back to her father's house to find that Efua's bags were packed and she was just about feeding Angelica her breakfast;

'Efua, what's going on? How come you're packed already…we're not leaving yet…'

'Well, I didn't think that I'd be welcome considering what happened last night; I'm really sorry Ophelia, it was my fault that your father had a heart attack…'

'No sweetie, don't you dare blame yourself! I can't even imagine how much you've suffered all these years. I only want to apologise to you on behalf of this family for all the pain that you have endured at the hands of my late father'

'He died? Oh my gosh, I'm so sorry…'

'It's okay Efua, he died peacefully this morning. The doctors told us that if would have happened sooner or later anyway with the amount of strain that his heart was under. Apparently he had heart disease for a few years now, but I just figured that he was putting on a little weight due to his age; I never even thought to mention it at all'

'Thanks for that Ophelia, but I still feel guilty though…oh and by the way, Octavia said that you mother went to the church not long after you left for the hospital. She didn't say when she would be back…'

'Oh Efua, I don't even care to know what she's doing right now, I just can't believe that she's been playing me like a puppet all these years! My own mother you know…I feel sorry for her to be honest; she is too concerned by what society thinks rather than what's going wrong in her own family. Actually while we spent the night in the hospital, Deji and my brother suggested that we set up a family trust for Emmanuel; it's only right Efua considering what has happened. I hope that you will accept this small token for your son's sake'

'Ophelia, I don't really know what to say, I was really expecting to be thrown out by now! I just want my son to have an opportunity to have a good education, so that's all that I would ask of you. Money is not really important to me, but education is something that can never be taken away…'

'That's true Efua, you're quite right in that line of thinking…we will do anything we possibly can to help your situation and that includes setting up a fund for him…I mean he is my baby brother now!'

As a gesture of her goodwill, Ophelia hugged Efua which in turn, brought her to tears. Efua's life was about to change once again in the most unimaginable way but this time, she was fortunate enough to have someone as wonderful as Leon to share her success with.

~~~~

Dr Jonathan Ignatius Azubike Nkechi Emeka-Phillips was given a state burial; dignitaries, ambassadors, royalty and friends from around world flew in to pay their respects. Sandra, who had become a near recluse, barely spoke to anyone that had turned up to the funeral ceremony; it was left to Ophelia and Kelechi to receive them and accept their offers of condolence. The Maxwell family had actually been able to make it and it was quite surreal for Ophelia to see them again after her summer at the ranch with Sunny all those years ago. After giving up on trying to speak to Sandra, Amanda found a heavily pregnant Ophelia sitting all by herself and went to have a chat with her instead.

'Ophelia my dear, you look lovely! I know that this is a sad occasion but I must say congratulations to you…how are you coping with everything? It's just a big shame to lose such an eminent man as your late father…'

'Oh Amanda, thank you so much for that; the only thing is that I found out he had another side to him just before he passed…by the

way, Kelechi and I now have a two year old half-brother'
'Wow really? How so?'
Ophelia then explained the story to Amanda and how Emmanuel
came to be born as a result of her father's indiscretions.
'Well Ophelia, you're not the only one to have a new addition to
your family; I recently found out after my father passed, that I have
a black half-niece…but in my family's case, the story goes back a
few generations. Hopefully it won't take me all afternoon to explain
it to you'
Amanda proceeded to tell Ophelia the unbelievable tale.

Chapter 29

Amanda's father Cedric Hamilton-Jones was an amazingly rich man; he owned stock in some of the most successful corporations listed on the Dow Jones index and had an astounding personal net worth of over three billon dollars. Apart from being a wealthy individual, Cedric also had a kind heart. After going through an acrimonious divorce from his gold digging first wife Ludmilla at the end of the 1960's, he married his then pregnant girlfriend Desiree Charles.

Desiree was working as a high class prostitute in one of the many hotels that he owned a major stake in when she met Cedric and they fell in love. Soon after a few encounters as hooker and client, they eventually realised that they were somehow made for each other. Just before she met Cedric, Desiree had discovered that one of her numerous clients had gotten her pregnant accidentally. Since she wasn't the type to be deceptive, she told Cedric of her predicament almost as soon as he had pledged his undying love for her. What he did next was beyond her wildest dreams; not long before she was due to give birth, Cedric made an honest woman of Desiree and married her in a small ceremony at the local registry office.

Even though Cedric knew the baby Desiree was carrying wasn't his, he loved her so that he put his name put down as the father of the child on the birth-certificate. Using his wealth and status, he also covered up the sordid details of Desiree's past and thus their daughter Amanda Diana Marie Hamilton-Jones was born into a home of wealth, privilidge, stability and love in the spring of 1969. Amanda only knew Cedric as her father her whole life, and had no knowledge of her mother's shady past until she died of a stroke at the age of sixty-two; that was only two years before her beloved husband Cedric eventually passed.

During their twelve years of marriage, Ludmilla only bore Cedric one child, also a girl named Lucy. Despite being bank rolled by her father's billions, Lucy Hamilton-Jones was definitely her mother's daughter. She grew up to marry Blake Creighton who just happened to be the first born son of world renowned hotelier Magnus Creighton and heir to his multi-billon dollar fortune. The only children that Lucy and Blake produced were a set of non-identical twin girls who eventually became the infamous socialite duo of Chloe and Carly Hamilton-Jones-Creighton; the girls were notorious in the entertainment world for their partying, bitching publicly about other fellow celebs, going on ridiculously expensive shopping sprees using daddy's money, as well as even feuding with each other at one point. The twins re-located from their parents' New York luxury hotel to Hollywood once they hit 21 to try to break into movies; when that inevitably failed, they stayed in LA regardless just to keep up appearances. Anything was better than going back to New York City eating humble pie. Eventually, a popular entertainment network decided to give the girls a reality show about their lives in Tinseltown and it ended up being a runaway hit; Chloe and Carly finally arrived when they made the coveted cover of *Rolling Stone* magazine.

To this end and as Cedric got older, his twin grand-daughters barely visited him any more let alone his own daughter Lucy; ultimately it was clear to him that they were waiting for his appointed time on Earth to expire and get a nice windfall via his will. Cedric loved his daughter Lucy dearly, but was forever unable to build a good father daughter relationship with her due to Ludmilla's constant interfering. It was such a shame to him that she too had been influenced by her mother's passion for money and power. According to Ludmilla, no matter how much money a woman could make by herself, she was only ever as rich as her husband's worth. As a result of being fed this mantra throughout her childhood, Lucy never really loved her poor downtrodden husband Blake; she was only in love with his bank account.

Amanda also married a rich man, but in her case she fell in love at first sight with a young Gaylord Edgar Maxwell III. He was the kind stranger that saved her from being run over by a speeding truck; at the time she had been crying over being dumped by her first real boyfriend and hadn't been paying attention to the road. Gaylord jumped out and pulled her back from crossing the road with a firm grip around her tiny wait; he later revealed to her that he actually thought that he had interrupted a suicide attempt. The minute Amanda looked up at this young gentleman, who she felt at the time was actually quite forward to hold her so close, she kind of knew that he was the man she would eventually marry. After a short courtship, the couple married at the end of the 1980's and then went on to have their two children Ella-May and Troy, then lived happily ever after. Or so it would seem.

When her father died, Amanda was introduced to an unexpected new of relative; it was revealed that before he'd met her mother Desiree, Cedric had touched the life of another young prostitute woman. Ida Belle Cuthbert gave birth to his mixed-race daughter and named her Georgia Belle Cuthbert-Jones. There would have been a great scandal at the time if society ever discovered that Cedric was the father of Ida's child so he paid for her to leave her home in Harlem, New York for a comfortable apartment in the suburbs of New Jersey to raise the child. Sadly just a year or so later, Cedric had already fallen in love with Desiree and after a bitter split, Ida was left to raise little Georgia on her own. As a final act of closure, Ida moved out of the apartment that Cedric had provided and found a small place in Brooklyn to move to; she effectively cut Cedric out of their lives forever and even took up a working at the local Laundromat to put food on the table.

Georgia survived; grew up and eventually had her own little daughter named Tenetria Belle Jones. Incidentally before she passed, Ida had never let Georgia know who her biological father was, so as not to make things complicated. When Georgia herself tragically died of breast cancer at the young age of 34, Tenetria who was 16 at the time was left completely alone. Soon after her mother died Tenetria left high school and tried to get a job to make ends meet. Sadly, due to her youth and inexperience in worldly matters, she was eventually evicted by the landlord since she couldn't keep up the rent payments. Not knowing which other way to turn Tenetria travelled down south to live with some members of her extended family in Houston, Texas while she looked for a job and tried to get her life back together. It was a long way to travel to for a job, but faced with the terrifying prospect of being homeless and broke; living with family that she barely knew seemed like her only option at the time. There simply wasn't any plan B.

Tenetria ended up in the basement room of her Grandmother's sister's daughter Auntie May and her husband Uncle Bernie. Unbeknownst to Tenetria, her Uncle Bernie was a local self-accomplished pimp. Since she had tried and failed to keep a job within the first four months of being in Houston, Bernie gave his young niece an ultimatum; either join his line up of street walkers or be thrown out into the streets without a dime. In the end, Tenetria had other option but to comply; she even tried to appeal to her Auntie May, but that cry for help was met with a crushing dismissal. It turned out that Auntie May was a cold hearted and wicked woman who actually helped her husband groom young girls for prostitution.

She would eventually wean them on to hard drugs which inevitably kept them dependent on turning tricks for the drug money or in the most tragic cases, dead before their time. May let Tenetria in on a painful family secret when the poor young thing had asked her for a helping hand;

'Listen honey, don't you know it's in your blood to be a hoe? I guess you don't know that ya Grandmama Ida Belle ran off to New York to work as one do ya? My mama told me the story and she even told me not to let you live here cos your side of the family ain't nuthin but trouble. They neva saw Ida again until her damn funeral; can you imagine that? Guess she was making big money in the end….but ya mama musta lost it all or ya wouldn't be here huh?'

'Auntie May, don't you have no respect for the dead? My Grandma weren't no prostitute! She ain't never did that, you're a liar!' said Tenetria

'Look baby, whether you agree with me or not don't mean a damn thang to me…you gonna pay your way while you're under this roof and you've already had a four month free ride…nuthin lasts forever does it?'

Auntie May laughed out loud at her naïve little niece and then hit her with the conclusion of the conversation;

'Tomorrow nite you gon be riding the Caddy wit ya Uncle Bernie; time for you to earn ya keep in here shuga, ain't no use trying ta fight it' and with that May casually left Tenetria in the basement bedroom crying in the face of her abject misfortune.

To this end, Bernie had managed to get his young niece in to the game just four months after her arrival in the lonestar state. As a direct result, in the space of two years Tenetria fell pregnant twice to unknown fathers and bore two boys with just a year's separation between them. In the short time that it took for her young body to snap back to its regular small frame after the birth if her second son, Tenetria moved out of her Uncle's home and into Madame Carlina's brothel in downtown Houston. The old woman promised Tenetria a roof over her head for her and her two children, regular HIV testing and most of all an immediate abortion would be arranged for her if the unthinkable happened and she fell pregnant again for one of the clients. During her tenure at the brothel, Tenetria came into contact with most of the rich and powerful men in Texas and paradoxically Amanda's own husband. It was fate that crossed Tenetria and Gaylord's paths during her first week at Madame Carlina's and he turned out to be one of her most regular clients. For want of a better life for herself and her sons, Tenetria studied a business management degree during the daytime; she didn't want to spend the rest of her life turning tricks and besides a day would come when she would get too old for it all. Eventually, she worked hard and was able to leave the world of the sex trade altogether within three years of arriving at the brothel; thankfully, Gaylord came through on his promise to her and gave her a glowing recommendation for her character reference; to this end Tenetria found herself at the position of manager in her office within a few short years. It was only by chance that she dropped by her Uncle Bernie's house to pick up some stuff of hers that she'd left there years ago and was about to be thrown out.

Tenetria knew that fate had played her a wonderful hand. Uncle Bernie hadn't even opened the letter addressed to her from Cedric's attorney like he usually did with the rest if her mail. Had he been aware of the letter's contents, then he surely would have found a way to pay some hood chick to act as a fake 'Tenetria' just so he could claim all the inheritance money. It was almost like a dream when she eventually visited Cedric's attorney in his oak panelled office and the old man explained how her mother Georgia, was Cedric's daughter and since she was Georgia's only next of kin, she stood to inherit just over a billion dollars in cash, property, bonds and stock.
Tenetria was smiling as she walked into the will reading on that sunny spring morning; there was an audible gasp when Ludmilla and co realized that their long lost relative was very much a black woman indeed. It was then revealed that old Cedric wasn't as senile as Ludmilla had originally thought; he had switched his real will for a phoney one, so where she'd expected to inherit more than half of his money along with Lucy, he had only given them $100,000 a piece. In the final will statement Cedric had said that Lucy was more than rich

enough and didn't need his money, also that after almost 40 years of alimony payments to Ludmilla, she didn't need his money either. Finally the story of Ida and Cedric was revealed and out of regret of the way he had treated poor Ida, Cedric left a third of his wealth to his daughter Georgia, which automatically switched to Tenetria's hand since her mother had passed. Another third was left to Amanda, and the rest of the fortune was left to his nurse, house staff and a sizeable donation was spread out amongst various charities. Needless to say, the gold diggers stormed out of the attorney's office fuming; if one looked at Ludmilla closely, you could actually see the steam escaping from her ears.

~~~~

Amanda and Tenetria actually hit it off tremendously; even though she was a little mad at Cedric for having a whole other third family in secret, Amanda couldn't help but respect Tenetria for what she had achieved in her life inspite of her seemingly insurmountable circumstances. Some how along the way, Tenetria found out that Gaylord was Amanda's husband; she thanked her stars at that point for the fact that her personal rule was to never disclose the identities of her former clients. She could only imagine what it would have done to their marriage if she had just been tactless and spilled it. When Amanda eventually formally introduced Tenetria to the family, Gaylord almost choked on his glass of coke when his ex-lover walked into the room; who knew all this time that she was virtually his step-niece? He quickly composed himself and went through the formalities of handshakes and everything else without a hiccup. Thankfully, he didn't arouse Amanda's suspicions. When Gaylord eventually came to speak to Tenetria one on one, he actually felt too ashamed to look her in the eye;
'Hey…Mr Maxwell; it's good to see you again, and under the circumstances real good to see you again. How you been doin sir?' asked Tenetria; her voice seemed more relaxed and self-assured compared to the old days. It seemed that her success was agreeing with her
'Oh Tenetria…we're family now so please call me Gaylord. I just

310

feel so bad for what we did together. If I'd known who you were I would never have...'

'You would never have been my customer? Naw don't feel ashamed Mr Max...I mean Gaylord, for what we did. I guess we were in a point of our lives where that was the only way we saw out of whatever situation we found ourselves in. But I'm good now you know...honestly, in fact you really helped me a lot financially back then; only God knows why or paths crossed...and why they are crossing again'

'Sweetie, where'd you get all that wisdom from? I'm the old man around here and I'm the one supposed to be droppin' the pearls of wisdom' said Gaylord chuckling a little; Tenetria smiled back at him and shrugged;

'I dunno, I guess I been through so much that I had no choice but to pick up some common sense! Thanks for everything again though...I was actually just made Manager in my job just before I got the letter about my Grandpa Cedric so I'm good'

'But you know honey; this whole thing has made me make a decision that's been long coming. I'm gonna give up the whole brothel thing....I have a beautiful wife here that I love dearly, but I make excuses and neglect her. We used to be so in love in the beginning you know?'

'Well who says that you can't be in love again? Amanda seems like a lovely lady and every woman wants to be loved...you may be an old dog but you still got it going on in the bedroom department and you know that I can vouch for you on that!' said Tenetria laughing

'Yeah! You're right and I'm gonna show her that much tonight!'

'Hey... way to go Uncle!' said Tenetria and gave him a sharp hi-five Amanda who was coming over to them with a pitcher of lemonade wondered what was so funny;

'I see you two have hit it off already; Gaylord didn't I tell you that Tenetria is a lovely young lady?' said Amanda

'Yes you did honey...she is a nice girl' he replied standing up and putting his arm around her now not so tiny waist just like he used to back when they first met,

'But you, my dear are the only woman for me. When's the last time that I told you that…I know far too long'

Amanda was a little confused; what had gotten into her husband? She'd figured that as a result of his age, his sex drive had faltered but she was too embarrassed to bring up the subject of Viagra. To this end, Amanda frequently quenched her own sexual thirst with the help of her trusty rampant rabbit. She put her hand to his forehead mockingly as if to feel for a temperature;

'Sweetie, are you ok? No really…Tenetria he is never this affectionate. I thought you'd turned into an old man Gaylord'

'Well I guess that this whole thing with your daddy and our new family has made me realise how unexpected things can happen in life and that we need to make the most of each waking moment that we have on this small world. Amanda, I've always loved you and I never want you to forget that'

Gaylord then kissed his lady, pushing his tongue into her mouth and as she returned his gesture; Ella-May and Troy looked on repulsed;

'Eww! Oh my gosh, can you both please get a room?' said Ella-May disgusted

'Yeah…like dudes, you're not sixteen anymore! Your kids do not need to see y'all indulging in a tongue sandwich!' said a now grown up Troy

Gaylord laughed at his kids, they would have to get used to it because that's how he was gonna be from now on;

'Well in that case; we're gonna go up and get a very early night! Tenetria sweetie, it's been wonderful meeting you and don't worry our driver will take you back to your hotel. Good night and make sure you come see us again ya hear?'

Tenetria nodded; she would be sure to bring her sons next time to meet their new family.

'Sure I will and it's been a pleasure to meet you all'

'And without further ado…we bid you all good night' announced Gaylord

He then picked Amanda up off her feet into his arms and proceeded to carry her up the stairs;

'Gaylord, what are you doing! Do you wanna hurt your back!' protested Amanda

'No honey, I'm stronger than you think….I'm gonna show you honey' he replied

Ella and Troy looked at each other and said 'Eww!' in unison and looked away from the scene. Tenetria couldn't help but to laugh; Amanda was in for a long night of good loving.

'Tenetria, shall I drive you to the hotel? I don't mind and dad forgot that he gave our driver the night off' said Troy; he knew that she was family now but he couldn't help but to think she was hot. Gaylord hadn't really given the driver the night off but she was not to know that

'Oh really Troy? That would be great if you don't mind' said Tenetria

He eventually took her back to the hotel and before she left the car, Troy asked her an important question;

'Tenetria…we should really keep in touch. Here's my card, please call me if you need anything…and may I get your number?'

'Yes Troy…you may. We should keep in touch' said Tenetria scribbling her number onto a piece of paper;

As she looked into those baby blues of his, with matching chiselled jaw, Tenetria knew instinctively that it would be the beginning of a great new friendship.

~~~~

So Ophelia, that's the whole story! I would really love you to meet Tenetria sometime. I think you would really like her' said Amanda

'I'm sure that I would and the great thing is that your dear husband has found himself again!'

'Yep don't I know it! I used to complain that he didn't give me any attention before, but now I can't keep him away!'

'Are you talking about me there honey…you'll only get me going again' said Gaylord; he had creeped up to Amanda and slid his arms around her from behind giving her a little kiss on the cheek in the process.

'And Ophelia sweetie, how are you coping? You poor thing, your baby looks like it's about to drop at any moment' he said with a concerned look on his face;

'Thank you Gaylord, I'm actually doing fine. Amanda was just filling me in on your new family member and everything. It was quite a story! And you both look like a young love struck couple; you can't seem to keep your hands off each other…that is really sweet'

'Oh that's only because my Amanda makes me feel young again Ophelia, and sadly it took such shock like this for me to realise it. I guess I used to be quite a jerk didn't I Amanda?'

'Yes Gaylord, but you were my jerk….and I still loved you regardless' replied Amanda; looking up into his eyes

'Well I'd better leave you two…looks like you're having a moment here' said Opheila in stitches laughing

'Sorry honey' said Amanda 'I just got carried away for a second, this is supposed to be a funeral…damn, I feel so bad!'

'Don't you worry Amanda, there is nothing wrong with you being happy. I guess when people die we all realise how precious life is and that we should enjoy every moment with the people we love' said Opheila and then gave them both a heartfelt hug. As if right on cue, Deji came over to take his wife away, it was getting late and she needed some to get some rest.

When she eventually went to sleep that night; Ophelia dreamed of the baby kicking inside her. There wasn't long to go now and since her dear father had now been buried, it was time to look forward to the beginning of a brand new life.

Chapter 30

Ophelia looked out of the window and could instantly see the effects of the sweltering heat on the citizens of Rio de Janeiro. At that very moment, she thanked God for the miracle of a good air-conditioning system and also for the fact that Issy had installed an extremely efficient one in her home.

A lot had happened in the two years since her father Jonathan had passed; Ophelia gave birth to a son named Alexander Babatunde Akudo Olajuwon a few months after his funeral. They had chosen the name Babatunde because it signified a new son being born into one's family soon after the passing of a senior male relative and Akudo meant peaceful blessing; Deji picked Alexander for his son's first name because he loved that the name meant 'defender of men' The arrival of Alexander should have been a joyous time for the whole family; however Ophelia's mother showed little interest. Sandra had become one of the 'mothers' of the fanatical evangelical church that she was a member of and had literally shunned her family off to the side.

Another noteworthy event was Dominic breaking with tradition to marry Ronke; as everyone had expected the news was met with open arms by his very liberal parents. They were not in the least bit phased by the fact that their new daughter-in-law was a black African woman and the couple weren't married a year before Ronke fell pregnant with their first child.

In other good news, since scoring a lucrative new contract to play for the *Miami Heat*, Le Quawn and Alizé had moved down south into a huge Florida mansion. Alizé got to rub shoulders with some of the more famous basketball wives in the industry; however unlike most of them, she actually had her own career. *Transatlantic* was now a household name and was very popular with many of the players' wives on Le Quawn's team. The label had finally gone international and was being sold in stores worldwide; soon its very first fragrance was due to be launched and Adora was chosen as the face of the promotional campaign.

Incidentally, Kelechi finally married Adora in one of the most lavish wedding ceremonies ever seen on Earth; both *OK!* and *Hello* magazines held a bitter bidding war for exclusive coverage of the event, but in the end the happy couple shunned the media route and posted the pics on their *Facebook* account instead.

Not long after Kelechi and Adora's nuptials, Dominique moved back to Jamaica for good and shacked up with her beloved pool boy Devanté much to her father's dissent.

Caspian on the other hand fell way short of the fame that he was looking for and ended as his team coach's assistant, but not before he was weaned off cocaine in a twelve step rehab facility. Efua and Leon were still a couple and were making plans to eventually move in together and finally, Eduardo and Issy got hitched and moved into a beautiful colonial house in Brazil. They still kept an apartment in New York for work purposes, but once they had any free time they'd hop on to a plane headed back to South America.

~~~~

Issy had half-invited and half-dragged Ophelia into coming to Brazil
with her for a few weeks and Deji who needed a break from just
about everything, decided to tag along too. Issy had prescribed some
Polo for the guys that day and a little retail therapy for herself and
Ophelia. After they had gotten ready, the ladies left their respective
husbands and took a private jet to Sao Paulo.
Once they had landed, they were quickly driven to the most upscale
shopping district in the city and then went off to flex some serious
plastic. As they walked past a few of the stores, Ophelia felt a twinge
little of guilt; here she was shopping away and basically doing
nothing while her kids were all the way back in New York under the
ever watchful eye of Efua. She didn't even want to think of what she
would do once Efua inevitably decided to move out to start her very
own family. As if right on cue, Issy decided that they both needed
some lunch;
'Come on chica, whatever is on your mind I'm sure that you'll feel
better after you get some good food down you…let's go get some
lunch' said Issy decisively. Ophelia sighed and let her friend lead the
way;
'Okay hun, I'll tell you all about it over lunch'
The ladies went to have a light meal in a well known restaurant that
was Brazil's answer to *The Ivy* ; once they'd ordered Ophelia
decided to pour her heart out;

'Issy, I'm just so feeling guilty over being here with you just
shopping…I miss my babies and I can't help but to think that I'm not
being a good mom. It seems like with *Transatlantic* doing so well
and my busy schedule I never get to see them! And get this, when I
finally get some free time then I prance off to Brazil instead of being
at home…'
'Well Ophelia, I know I don't have kids yet, but from what I see
you're a great mom…but you're also a working mom with a career.
You always said that you didn't want to live off a rich husband, so

that means that you have to make some sacrifices with your kids. Sorry to be harsh hun but you can't have both, you can't be with your kids twenty-four seven and run a successful fashion house…it's just not possible! But real talk…I dragged you down here because you really need the rest and even Deji agreed with me, if you keep on working like this without a break then you'll just become tired and irritable, so what use would you be to the kids then huh? Just think about it girly…' said Issy while flicking a piece of lettuce to the side of her plate.

'I guess you're right…but I can't help but feel a little guilty; where are we off to next after this? I wanna get them some new clothes…I hope I can find a cute little number for Angelica…you know how she likes to dress up!'

'Yeah she's getting to be a little diva isn't she! The next department store should have some *Baby Dior* and *Petit Bateau* stuff in there'

'Oh really that's cool…hey, why have I never thought of this?'

'Of what?'

'A *Transatlantic* line for kids! It's totally the next transition for us!'

'Ophelia, that's a great idea, when we get back to the house I'll call Alizé and the team to start thinking of some good ideas for it! It's so gonna be huge…'

'Well I sure hope so…'

After a nice lunch the two carried on their shopping spree until it was quite late; upon checking her watch, Issy realised that they had missed their take off time and the plane would be grounded until the next morning. They made a quick call to Eduardo and Deji in Rio, they decided to stay the night in the Sao Paulo Hilton Hotel. After booking their separate rooms, Issy bumped into some old girl friends from Ecuador and they invited her to spend a few hours with them hitting the clubs. Issy decided to go and asked Ophelia if she would like to come too;

'Phils, I have to catch up with my girls, we've known each other from like we were knee high in Kindergarten! Wanna tag along too…I'm sure they'd love you…'

'Naw girl, you go out and have some fun…I'm gonna sit in my hotel

room, watch some *CNN* and then get an early night. We did so much walking today and I'm totally pooped!'
'Okay suit ya self…see in the morning hun'

Issy gave her a kiss on the cheek and left Ophelia in the hotel lobby then ran off with her girls; as she walked off, Ophelia felt a light tap on her shoulder
'Issy did you forget something' she said off-handedly
'Umm…last time I checked, I was a dude; do you even remember me Princess?'
Ophelia turned around struggling to place the familiar gruff voice; but the one she knew had aged somewhat;
'Oh my gosh…Sonny? It is you? What are you doing in Brazil?'
'Well hello would be nice sweetie! I saw you from across the hall and I thought to myself that I know that behind from anywhere…'
'Oh do stop Sonny! Anyway you can't really say things like that to me anymore cos I'm married now' said Ophelia flashing her ring in his face
'I know, I even thought as much; so where is the hubby?'
'Deji? He's is Rio…I was just shopping with my girl in Sao Paulo today but we got carried away and missed our flight time. The plane will have to leave in the morning'
'Oh, well I guess my luck is in! I'm actually living down here for a while, my grandparents are Brazilian and they have a farm. I come to this hotel in the evenings just to do some chauffeur work, ya know for a little extra cash…'
'Right…so that means you don't work for the Maxwells anymore…'
'No, I left there years ago; well to be honest I was thrown out of the ranch'
'Really? Why, what happened?'
'Okay, I'll give you the bite size version of it; lil Ella-May got herself sweet on me and wanted me to give her some 'extra lessons' after hours, na mean? But me, I never ever mess with any of my boss' wives or daughters. That shit just ain't right, so when I rejected her…Ella decided to tell her pops that I tried to rape her. He believed her and then asks me to leave the premises that night'

'Damn, I always thought that Ella-May was spoiled but I didn't think she'd go as far as making somebody lose their job!'

'Well my Grandpa told me to thank God I was born way after the civil rights era cos back in tha day, they would have lynched my black ass!'

Ophelia shook her head and laughed, she guessed that Sonny's old Grandpa was right.

'So, what you doin tonight, anything special?' asked Sonny

'No, just going to my room to get an early night' Ophelia replied

'What at 9 o'clock? Damn you've really gotten old!' said Sonny laughing; Opheila smacked his hand as a mock punishment

'I am not 'old' Sonny; just have to be responsible now that I'm married that's all'

'Okay, I hear that…so ain't you gonna invite me up?'

'No! I told you I'm married now so sorry, none of that'

'Well at least lemme walk you to your door; we're probably never gonna see each other again'

Opheila paused and thought about it for a second; what could it hurt? She would let him walk her up to her room and then they would say goodbye forever;

'Well okay then, since you put it that way…let's go'

They took the elevator up to her room in silence and then walked up to her room which was across the hall from Issy's. Opheila put her key in the lock then turned round to Sonny to say her goodbyes, but as she faced him she realised that he had crept up on her unexpectedly;

'Ophelia…can we please have just one more night together…for old times sake?' said Sonny in smooth and honeyed tones;

'What and cheat on my Deji? I'm sorry Sonny, what we had was a long time ago and I can't do that to him'

'Come on girl, trust me, he'll never know and you know I always keep it wrapped' he replied and showed her the condom packet that was already in his palm

'Please Sonny…I can't; I won't even be able to get Deji out of my mind…I just can't do it!'

Sonny smiled while watching her plead with him and then pulled a dirty trick; he slid his hand up to her now swollen chest and twirled one of her already hard nipples between two of his fingers. Sonny then proceeded to whisper into her ear filthily;

'Well your nipple ain't thinking of him right now from what I can feel, lemme see if the rest of your body feels the same way...'

Before she could protest, Sonny tapped into her weakness and feasted his lips on the delicate skin of her neck. Unfortunately for Deji, just as his wife struggled to re-gain her composure, the bedroom door creaked open.

THE END

A little bit about me

Hey everybody!

It's Lady Lynxx here, just wanted to tell you a little bit about me. I am a young (frustratingly) single black female that happens to live in the ethnic melting pot that is London, in the UK. I also happen to travel to New York City a lot (in case you didn't know, I am a closet shopaholic! lol!) hence the many references to that great and buzzing city. If you have never been there you should go, there is nothing like it!

I just started writing in early 2008 after being inspired by the many talented writers that I came across on the internet. I have always had stories and daydreams in my head, so one day I was bored and thought why not? What you have just read is the end result four months after that 'why not'; I hope that my humble literary efforts are an inspiration to everybody that ever wanted to write a book but never had the courage to do so, trust me if I can do it, then so can you. All you need is a little time, patience and dedication. A good thesaurus and the willingness to think outside the box wouldn't go amiss either; as a very close friend has forever indoctrinated into my brain 'you are only limited by your imagination'.

My inspirations in terms of authors are a varied bunch, they range from Alice Walker, Jackie Collins, Jeffery Archer, Danielle Steele, Josephine Cox, Marian Keys, Jilly Cooper, Toni Morrison, Chimamanda Ngozi Adichie, Tiphani Montgomery, Maya Angelou, Agatha Christie, Charles Dickens, Jane Austen, Sebastian Falkus, Roald Dahl, Cynthia Voigt, Mende Nazer, Zana Muhsen, Martina Cole, Virginia Andrews, Wendy Holden, Jane Green, Sophie Kinsella, Candace Bushnell, Chinua Achebe and many many more!

God willing, I hope to write more novels as I have so much more to give! Hopefully you enjoyed my writing and want to read more, I am currently on the lookout for a book publishing deal on the back of this so prospective literary agents or publishers can email me at the following address:

ladylynxx@hotmail.com
Readers of my novel also feel free to email me if you have any comments or questions. I will be opening MySpace/Facebook accounts for promotional purposes soon, so you will be able to hit me over there too.
Take care all of you and happy reading!

Lady Lynxx

Excerpt from my next novel, look out for it early 2009:

My Daddy's Money – the life of a Golddigger
A Lady Lynxx novel

Chapter 1

Amaya Summer had it all. The worst thing was that she knew it. Waking up in her Tribeca apartment every morning was an affirmation of that fact. Amaya switched off her cell phone alarm clock and looked at the time. Was it 6.00am already? 'Time to get up' she told her self as she rolled out of her Baker king size bed. Amaya put her slippers on and shuffled off to the bathroom.

Amaya was the hottest video model, pin up and general hip hop eye candy there ever was in recent times. Since being discovered at the age of 18 by popular DJ and magazine/club owner DJ Slay, Amaya had not looked back. As a testament to her full name, Princess Amaya Cleopatra Jade Sumner-Wilson possessed an astonishing beauty, God given to only a handful in every generation. A long time ago Amaya's name was changed to a plainer 'Amaya Summer'. When she started to become popular, she decided that the Wilson family name would not help her career neither would her mother's surname of Sumner. DJ Slay used to say that Amaya's caramel skin and long dark brown locks always made her look as if her own personal sun shined on her wherever she went. And so the name was born.

There was not a nip or tuck was on her body, nor botox or peels. That was a big part of Amaya's appeal, she was 100% natural! The fact that she was an all natural 34DD - 24 - 42 beauty set her apart from the Buffie's and Melyssa Ford's of the game. She had the perfect mix of a supermodel face, high bust, small waist and phenomenally round derrière. The curves on her body would make the most difficult F1 track look as straight as an Olympic pool. Amaya played one perpetual role of 'the hot wifey'. She looked too

refined to be prancing around in thongs and booty shaking, so she had never done either in any videos, photo shoot or magazine.
Amaya always looked sexy but classy, just like any nigga's dream wife and that was her selling point.

What no-one knew was that under the perfect shell, there was a cold, calculating and extremely determined young woman. There was only one goal for Amaya and that was to cultivate as much money as she possibly could without actually working at all. The money she earned from modelling was just 'chop change' to her and a medium used to meet all the high-rollers that she so wished. Most people could never tell that she was a ruthless golddigger, forever looking for the man with the biggest purse. That is where her 'Daddy' came into play. Not daddy in the father sense, no her father was long gone. Daddy in the 'Sugar daddy' incarnation. Amaya played them all to a fine tune and high sum before moving on. All these fools who were stupid enough to throw their money away just to stand next to her must have enough to spare anyways.
Even the apartment that she lived in was paid for in full by her ex who was desperate to keep her just before she dumped him for Byron Lord.

Byron Xavier Lord was CEO and founder of the 'GAMECity' chain of computer game supply stores and he was filthy rich. He was millionaire hundreds of times over, and a dream catch for Amaya. As self-made 52 year old millionaire to her 25 years, they were an odd couple. She didn't mind that at all though. While most of her old high school friends were shacked up with some no good bastard and at least 2 snotty kids, Amaya had the world! She had yet to consummate her relationship with Byron and he had already upgraded her *Mercedes drop-top* to the latest *Jaguar XJ8*. That was part of the game. Play the lady by not having sex with them for the first few months but keep them just about interested enough with the slickest head game in the world.
The coup de grace was the fact that she always swallowed their load. This was a huge compliment to most men. Getting the money was

too easy….just like mama had said.

While pondering on the impending photo shoot she was due to attend that morning, the phone rang. Amaya let the machine pick up,
'Hey babe, it's Byron'
What the hell could he want at this hour…?